To Peter
With very best
Joyce M

Also by Joyce Muriel:
Who is My Enemy?
Ellie's Story
Ripeness is All
The End of the Story

GOODBYE CHASTITY

GOODBYE CHASTITY

Joyce Muriel

ATHENA PRESS
LONDON

GOODBYE CHASTITY
Copyright © Joyce Muriel 2007

All Rights Reserved

No part of this book may be reproduced in any form
by photocopying or by any electronic or mechanical means,
including information storage or retrieval systems,
without permission in writing from both the copyright
owner and the publisher of this book.

ISBN 10-digit: 1 84401 981 0
ISBN 13-digit: 978 1 84401 981 6

First Published 2007 by
ATHENA PRESS
Queen's House, 2 Holly Road
Twickenham TW1 4EG
United Kingdom

Printed for Athena Press

Alex's Dream

Alex did not take part in her dream; she was the detached observer.

She was aware of being in a city, unlike any she had ever seen before. It was bathed in a golden light, like sunlight, but it was not hot; only pleasantly warm and delicately perfumed. The sky was a deep, clear blue and the buildings, all of white marble, stood out brilliantly against it.

She was aware that many people were moving quietly about but she could not see them clearly. Suddenly, one figure became very clear. He was tall and graceful, wearing a shimmering iridescent robe that changed colour as he moved. He appeared to be making his way towards a broad flight of shallow marble steps, which led to an archway supported by fluted pillars.

Above the archway were the words 'ALPHA' and 'OMEGA'. The huge letters appeared to be made of gold and were decorated with precious stones, which flashed and sparkled in the brilliant light.

Before entering the archway, the figure paused in complete stillness. For that moment his garments stopped changing colour and became pure white. After a moment, he turned his head slowly and Alex saw his face. She thought that it was the most beautiful face she had ever seen. So perfect were his features that they might have been carved out of marble by some master sculptor of past times. The forehead was broad and smooth; the nose was straight; the chin firm and strong, but the full-lipped mouth had a certain tenderness. The whole face was framed in golden curls. For a moment she felt as if his eyes dark and unreadable rested on her. *I'll never forget that look*, she thought.

The next moment, he had disappeared through the archway. She followed him into a vast hall with a domed roof, decorated with gold and jewels and supported by marble columns.

He did not linger here but moved swiftly to a large staircase at the other end. Here, another figure appeared unexpectedly before him. 'The Most Holy Lord of the Universes wishes to speak to you, Xaniel,' he announced clearly.

'I have received the message; that is why I have come,' Xaniel replied. As the other man stood aside, Xaniel went swiftly past him, up the marble stairs and through another archway into a second hall. This hall, like the first, was filled with golden light. A slight breeze moved the perfumed air and seemed to bring with it a faint sound of music, which was soothing to Alex's ear. The floor appeared to be made of glass; it was so smooth and translucent.

As Xaniel advanced slowly, Alex became aware that at the farther end of the hall was a dais, on which stood a great throne of gold, decorated with emeralds and rubies that sparkled in the golden light. The throne was surrounded by white-robed guards carrying golden swords.

Suddenly, Xaniel prostrated himself, as did all the guards around the throne, which was no longer empty. It was covered in a cloud from which a brilliant light emanated. Alex could not look at it, but she felt suddenly enveloped in warmth and love. A happiness, which she had not known since she was a small child, filled her whole being. It was like being held in her mother's arms again.

Suddenly a voice came from the centre of the cloud; a voice that was filled with incredible power, although it was at the same time both musical and gentle. 'Xaniel,' the voice said, 'you have been summoned to my throne because it has been decided that, if you are willing, you are to be sent on an important mission.'

'It is my joy to do your will in all things,' Xaniel replied.

'That is well, for your mission is difficult and may have dangers, although you will be protected. I am asking you to go to my Beloved Son's Kingdom.'

Xaniel raised his head slightly. 'Then you are sending me to the Dark Planet, my Lord? To that planet where the dark angels and their leader still maintain their futile resistance to His Power?'

'That is so. The time has not arrived yet for my son to return, but the Dark Angel is making a last desperate resistance and many of my children are suffering greatly, especially since they have been deserted by those who should guide and protect them.' There was great sadness in the voice now. 'You have to understand that you will be going into what must now be called enemy territory and great care is needed. You will find your friends in unexpected places and your enemies, too, where you might least expect them.'

'I understand, my Lord.'

'Are you willing to go in spite of these difficulties?'

'I am very willing, my Lord.'

'You are a good and loyal friend, Xaniel. Go now; my Son is expecting you. He will give you all the help he can.'

Slowly, as Xaniel stood up and turned to go, the cloud came down more thickly and the light from the throne was obscured.

In her dream, Alex struggled to follow Xaniel, but it was useless. The beautiful kingdom had vanished. She was alone in the darkness. Where was she? As she struggled to come awake, she realised that she was in her bed and that she must have been dreaming. Surely not? It all seemed so real, even now. There had been such happiness and beauty and light there. Now she was alone again and unloved. It all seemed almost too much to bear.

'You're being utterly ridiculous,' she told herself, but as she lay down again, prepared to go back to sleep, she felt afraid. The darkness of her room was no longer familiar, but menacing. Momentarily, she was convinced that something evil was waiting to seize her if she relaxed. She remembered the words spoken in her dream. This was the dark planet temporarily under the rule of the dark angels. What if her dream was true and one was lying in wait for her?

'Stop being an idiot,' she told herself severely. 'You can't let a dream influence you like this. Remember you're Alexandra Woodward, an independent young woman at the beginning of the twenty-first century, a successful executive in an international publishing firm, determined to get further promotion soon. And what is more important, my girl, you'd do well to remember that you have an important meeting tomorrow and you need your sleep.'

Nevertheless, she could not resist the temptation to press the switch of her bedside lamp. Immediately the darkness was vanquished and, with it, the fear. There was nothing to be seen but the familiar pieces of furniture, gathered together by her over the last four years in the room in the flat, which she shared with three others.

What did I expect? she asked herself. *A leering devil with cloven hoof, ready to pounce? What nonsense.* It was hard to understand, however, why she, an agnostic, should have been dreaming so vividly of heaven and angels. It must have been the influence of that stupid science fiction book she had been reading just before she fell asleep.

Satisfied, she switched off her light and lay down again, preparing to go back to sleep. Just before oblivion overtook her, she remembered vividly the beautiful angel in her dream. *I'd love to meet him*, she thought. *I'd certainly recognise him if I did!*

Chapter One

This was it: Number 48, Woodland Avenue. The young woman looked up at the three-storied terraced house. Late Georgian or Early Victorian? She had no idea, but it was definitely past its best. The four steps leading to the front door were dirty and crumbling; the paint work was peeling off. She put her heavy suitcases down and studied the array of bells with their labels. That was the one: *Flat Number 2, Woodward, Maitland, Carter and Parker*. She pressed the bell. Nothing happened. She waited; then, just as she was about to press the bell again, the door was flung open. As she retreated down the steps she became aware of a pair of somewhat grubby trainers. Her eyes travelled upwards: much-worn jeans; a loose sweatshirt with lurid design; a pale face; emphatic purple eye shadow; masses of bright red hair, arranged in spiky bunches, which, to the caller, looked as if they needed combing.

'You must be Chastity Brown. Come in.' She picked up one of Chastity's suitcases and began to run up the stairs, speaking loudly and hurriedly as she did so. 'I'm glad you've turned up now. You see, it's my day off and I want to go out. Alex told me to expect you. She can't be here. She's sorry. She's got an important meeting.' She flung open the door on the landing. 'Well here we are: home from home. I hope you'll like it.'

'I'm sorry,' said Chastity.

'Sorry for what?' asked the redhead, amazed.

'Sorry for keeping you in,' Chastity answered politely.

'Oh, don't worry about that,' said the other, easily. 'You're an important person, after all.'

'Important person?' Chastity was puzzled.

'Well, to put it bluntly, without you we can't pay the rent any more. Your letter to Alex was like an answer to prayer; that is, if any of us knew how to pray. Well, as I said, here we are. This is the living room. Quite big, as you can see.'

Chastity followed her in. It was big, rather bare, but very

untidy, with a varied assortment of clothes strewn around. She put her suitcase down.

The girl had already gone back to the door. 'The kitchen's over here, on the left.' She pointed vaguely. 'Rather small but adequate; usually looks worse than it is, because we're not all of us tidy. There's a new shower and loo.' Again, a vague gesture. 'That door there,' she pointed to a door behind Chastity, 'is the door to your bedroom.'

Chastity looked over her shoulder.

'Well, that's about it. I must fly. I'm already late. See you later. I expect Alex will be here in a couple of hours. Cheerio.' The door closed behind her. Chastity remained standing, bewildered, in the middle of the room, with her suitcases beside her. The door opened as soon as it had closed and the redhead poked around it. 'Make yourself a cup of coffee and an omelette. If you want anything else, there's a delicatessen at the end of the road. I expect you saw it as you came from the Tube.'

'Yes,' said Chastity. She advanced, curious. 'Aren't you going to change before you go out?'

'Change?' The other looked puzzled. 'I'm not going on duty; I'm going to a party,' she continued in a kindly voice, as if that explained everything. The door closed again.

Chastity walked over to the fireplace, looked into the large Victorian mirror hanging above it and raised her dark eyebrows at herself. She then turned, picked up her suitcase and walked towards the bedroom door. Her hand was just on the knob when the door to the sitting room opened again and the redhead poked around it once more.

'I was just going to unpack,' Chastity explained.

'Oh, God! What a good thing I came back! I forgot to tell you not to go into the bedroom yet.'

'Not to go into the bedroom?'

'Well, no; not yet. Louie's sleeping there, you see. She's a very light sleeper. She only got off about an hour ago. She'll be frantic if you wake her up.'

'But why should she be sleeping now?' Chastity's voice expressed her bewilderment.

'She's on nights, of course,' the other explained patiently. 'Her alarm goes off at 6.30 p.m. Then, when she gets up, you can take over. She's taken much of her stuff already, but she can't move into her new place until tomorrow morning.'

'I didn't know any of that.' Chastity sank into the armchair nearest to her, regardless of the pile of underclothes and tights on it. 'Would you like me to go away until tomorrow?'

'Good God!' The other girl came right into the room. 'Didn't Alex tell you anything?' Chastity shook her head. 'Well, it's perfectly simple. We need you to move in immediately. We can't afford to do without rent from four people. Louie has the right to stay for now because she's on night duty.'

'On night duty?' questioned Chastity.

'Yes, Louie and I are nurses. This is my day off. Alex will give you all the gen when she comes home. You'll be all right till then, won't you? I hope everything's clear now?'

Chastity nodded numbly. She could not think of an appropriate reply.

'A bit different from the vicarage, I expect,' said the other girl kindly. 'Rather more chaotic. But you'll get used to it. We all do.' She looked around the room, somewhat aimlessly. 'Make yourself a cup of coffee. You look as if you could do with it. I must fly.'

She was gone again. Chastity sat without moving and listened to the footsteps running down the stairs and the front door closing.

At last, she got up as if dazed, walked over to the mirror and looked at herself. Amazingly, she looked unchanged. Her heavy, dark hair was brushed back and loosely coiled in a knot on the top of her head, a few tendrils escaping to frame her face. Her eyes, large and serious, were also dark, with incredibly long lashes (she had always been rather vain about them). She looked down at her neat suit, unwrinkled, her black tights and her plain shoes. 'I suppose I do look rather like the vicarage,' she said aloud, addressing her reflection. 'But why not, since that was the idea?'

She sat down again, this time sweeping the tights and underclothes onto the floor. They could join the other things already there; the chair was more comfortable without them. She considered what she might do, since unpacking was out of the question. A cup of coffee? Yes. Tea would be better, but they probably would not have any. She walked to the door and considered her situation. The kitchen was on the left, over there; that was what the redhead had said. She advanced a few steps towards it, then noticed the door. A long-suppressed need of nature suddenly made itself urgently felt. Opening the door, she ran up the stairs and turned the handle of the door at the top. The door was locked. It could not be; there was no one else in. It must have stuck. She rattled it vigorously and pulled.

'I say, are you desperate?' a masculine voice called out. Apparently the shower and loo were shared. 'Hang on a minute, I'll come out and let you in.' She could hear someone moving about, then the door opened and a young man emerged, naked except for a skimpy towel around his middle. He seemed very blonde, very tall and very broad. Chastity crept past him and pulled the door to, quickly. 'Hi, there,' he called out, just as she was about to shut it. 'Be an angel and turn the hot tap on for me, so my bath doesn't get too cold; that is, if you're going to have a long sit.'

'I shan't be long,' answered Chastity hastily. This was another new experience. She turned the hot tap on, just in case. Seconds later, she emerged to find the young man striding up and down.

'A bit draughty on this landing,' he explained, then stopped and stared at her. 'You must be the new girl,' he said. 'Alex mentioned you'd be coming today.' Suddenly he began to laugh. 'She pulled my leg about you. Said you were a vicar's daughter and your name was Chastity!' He nearly dropped the towel but grabbed it just in time.

'As a matter of fact,' replied Chastity coolly, 'it is Chastity. Chastity Brown. And please don't make the obvious joke, because the answer is – I am.'

He was handsome, she noticed, even in a bath towel, and he rallied magnificently. 'Cool, eh?' he remarked. 'Well, we'll meet again, I expect. I'm Rupert. Please excuse me. My bath awaits.'

'It may soon reach you, I'm afraid,' Chastity said. 'I'm afraid I may have turned the hot tap on rather fast.'

He vanished, but not without dignity. Chastity descended the stairs and walked along the corridor to the kitchen. A cup of coffee was definitely needed.

She opened the kitchen door quietly and then stopped suddenly. It was not the state of the kitchen that caused her to stand so still. That was much as she had expected: rather small, dark and untidy, with a greasy odour compounded from onions and garlic. It was the sight of a young man with his back towards her. He was standing at the gas cooker, stirring something energetically in a saucepan. *This is ridiculous*, thought Chastity; *there seem to be strange young men everywhere. He must be an intruder.* She advanced towards the stove.

'Excuse me,' she began.

'Certainly,' he responded courteously, turning, spoon in hand. 'What do you want?'

'I would like to make myself a cup of coffee,' Chastity said firmly, and picked the kettle up off the stove. She walked towards the sink, which seemed to be full of dirty dishes, and filled the kettle from the tap. Coming back with it to the stove, she was suddenly and inconveniently aware that she did not know where to plug it in.

'Allow me,' said the young man, cleverly interpreting her blank look. With a flourish, he took the kettle and plugged it in above a nearby shelf.

'Thank you,' murmured Chastity. She walked towards the dresser and opened the glass doors of the top half. She found sugar and milk – almost sour – in a small jug, but no coffee. She stared around the kitchen.

'You'll find,' said the young man, 'that for some ridiculous reason they keep the coffee in the bottom cupboard, among the cleaning materials.' Bending down, Chastity discovered it. 'And the mugs here,' he continued, taking two down from the hooks on the wall, where they hung in a row. 'The second one is for me,' he explained, seeing her raised eyebrows. 'I like it black and very hot.'

Chastity obediently put a spoonful of coffee in each mug; then she said, very quietly, 'What are you doing here?'

'That's a good question,' he answered casually. 'And one which I might also ask.' He carefully tasted the mixture in the pan, frowned and shook in a few more herbs, tasted it again and smiled.

'I don't understand you,' Chastity replied, very quietly and precisely. 'I live here.'

He looked her up and down with a certain appreciation. 'I'm sorry I don't recognise you,' he said, 'and I'm sure I should if I'd seen you before.'

'Why?' asked Chastity.

'A manner to suit the face.' He laughed. 'Why, my dear girl, because you're quite beautiful and I appreciate beauty, particularly in women. I apologise for such an old-fashioned word as "beauty", but it is the only one that suits you.'

'And you – you are incredible,' answered Chastity, quite unmoved by compliments that were, she thought, obviously insincere. She looked him in the face: red-brown hair, cut fairly short; mocking, strangely-coloured eyes – she could only call them tawny – and an attractive but sensual mouth. Dressed in a casual jacket and trousers, he was slightly built and only a few inches taller than she was.

'Do share my risotto,' he begged, holding out his saucepan towards her. 'You look hungry.' She was, and it smelt delicious. 'Make the coffee while I dish up, there's a good girl. We can talk much better over food. I'm starving. This is my first meal since breakfast.'

Chastity obediently poured the boiling water onto the coffee, while he spooned the risotto into two bowls. He then drew up a chair to the table with a flourish and pulled out another for himself. He waved her to the chair. 'Talking after eating,' he suggested. 'Don't you agree?'

Chastity was very hungry. The situation was unexpected and inexplicable, but explanations could wait. She sat down and took the spoon he offered her. She tasted the first mouthful, while he watched her. 'Like it?' he asked.

'Very good, thank you,' she replied politely. They both began to eat with enjoyment but in silence. The young man finished first and, without speaking, helped himself to a second cup of coffee and a cigarette. At last, Chastity put down her spoon. Still without speaking, he offered her a cigarette. She shook her head. The time had come to resume their interrupted conversation.

'I enjoyed the risotto,' she said. 'Now, perhaps, you'll tell me what you're doing here?'

Chastity was never one to waste time in idle conversation or to circle around a point for reasons of delicacy. She believed that two of her principal objects in life should be the pursuits of clarity and truth. The presence of this strange young man who appeared to be so much at home needed explanation, and she was not to be deterred by charm or even by risotto.

He regarded her for a moment with slightly-raised eyebrows and a strange little smile. She thought that he was probably trying to think of a convincing explanation for his impudent intrusion. She would have been surprised to know that he was actually thinking that he really had been right in his first impression. She was beautiful and definitely interesting; worth a little effort, perhaps.

'Well?' asked Chastity, somewhat impatiently. 'You surely don't live here? As far as I understand it, this flat is certainly overpopulated without you.'

He took a sip of coffee. 'You could say,' he replied, 'that I eat here.'

'Eat here!' exclaimed Chastity. 'Are you broke or something?' Stories of dropouts and down-and-outs passed rapidly through her mind, although he certainly did not look like either. His shirt and trousers were, in fact, surprisingly elegant.

'No, no,' he protested. 'I always bring my own food, or,' – with a hasty look at the coffee – 'I always pay back what I borrow. It's just a convenience.'

'Convenience?' Chastity was amazed. 'I shouldn't think it can be very convenient for Dorothy, Louise and Alex.'

'Oh, I assure you,' he replied easily, 'I'm very careful not to clash with them; except when they invite me, of course. And I'm quite useful for mending things, particularly electrical gadgets.'

'I see,' said Chastity in the tone of one who obviously did not. There was a moment's pause, then, still relentlessly determined to pursue the truth, she continued, 'But I still don't see why it should be convenient for you to eat here if you have a place of your own. You do have a place of your own, I suppose?' she asked, with raised eyebrows.

'Naturally,' he replied casually. 'I have a very small flat in a slightly more expensive area.' He stopped, as if he considered this sufficient explanation.

Chastity was relentless, however. 'Well?' she questioned once more.

To her surprise, he turned and looked straight at her. 'I've explained my presence,' he said, 'but what about yours? What are you doing here?'

'I have just come to live here,' replied Chastity, in the manner of one who could not possibly see what business it was of his. 'I replied to Alex's advertisement for a fourth person to share the flat. We agreed on terms, so here I am.'

'Oh, no.' He looked at her with something like dismay. Dismay, she noted, definitely mixed with amusement. 'Don't tell me you're Chastity Brown, fresh from the vicarage, pure by name and pure by nature.' He laughed.

'Chaste in name and nature,' corrected Chastity. She had become accustomed to jokes about her name.

'Well,' he said, struggling with obvious amusement, 'if you'll take my advice, Miss Chastity Brown, you'll go straight back where you came from. This is no place for you. Surely your father must have a nice young curate you could marry? The romantic novels can't be all wrong?'

'As a matter of fact, he doesn't, and I wouldn't want to if he had,' Chastity replied succinctly.

'Really?' queried the young man. 'You begin to interest me even more, Miss Brown. Perhaps you would give me further details?'

'Certainly not,' said Chastity firmly. 'I've told you who I am and why I am here, but I still don't understand your position in the slightest.'

'It's quite simple, really,' he said, 'though I'm not sure you'll approve. Do have some more coffee.' Chastity refused impatiently. 'Well, some months ago, I was indiscreet enough to ask a friend to share a flat with me. It seemed quite a delightful idea at the time.' He paused. 'Now it just seems boring and I stay away as much as possible. I cook my meals here and sleep out whenever I can.'

'But that's ridiculous,' said Chastity, looking at him with something almost like compassion. 'Surely your friend can understand you don't want him any more. After all, it is your flat. You should simply ask him to go and be quite firm about it.'

The young man regarded her steadily for a moment. 'I suppose you might be right,' he said judicially, 'but the situation isn't quite as you imagine it. The friend is "she" and not a "he", and she insists on going all feminine and helpless on me when I suggest she departs. It's strange,' he continued thoughtfully, 'how clinging the so-called "liberated" woman can become when one no longer wants her. But perhaps you are a supporter of Women's Rights or whatever they call it these days?'

'No,' said Chastity, blankly, 'I don't think I can exactly say that I am. I really don't know.'

'Oh, dear,' he said, with apparent concern. 'I'm afraid I've upset you. I shouldn't have exposed you to the realities of life so suddenly. But then I did warn you.' His tone was quite tender. He put his hand gently on hers and looked deeply into her eyes.

Unmoved, Chastity removed her hand. 'Perhaps you'd better wait until you have a vacancy,' she said, somewhat enigmatically.

He looked at her with amazement and amusement. 'By God!' he exclaimed. 'I believe you are different.'

Chastity was impatient. 'Everyone is different,' she said. And then, even more impatiently, 'I wish you'd tell me your name. I believe that people are usually introduced to one another.'

'Of course,' he replied formally. 'Strangely enough, my parents seem to have had a sense of humour as bad as if not worse than yours.' Before Chastity could protest, he stood up, bowed formally and said, 'Unicorn Jones at your service, ma'am.'

'Unicorn!' exclaimed Chastity. 'I can't see any sense in that.'

'Neither can I,' agreed Unicorn cheerfully. 'I understand it was my mother's choice, but, since she died when I was quite young, I was never able to ask her. My father has always expressed complete ignorance on the subject – rather untruthfully, I'm inclined to think.'

'One would certainly imagine that he would have some idea.'

'Of course,' Unicorn continued sadly, 'people make the

obvious sexual jokes about it – purity and the phallic symbol and all that, you know.'

Chastity nodded, although she was not quite sure that she did know. Caution, however, counselled her to refrain from further questioning.

'I suppose you might say that it is responsible for my rather hectic sex life,' Unicorn continued mournfully. 'What else can a man do when saddled with a name like that? You know,' he continued, eagerly, 'it's rather odd that you and I should meet, isn't it? Fate, you might say.'

'*You* might say that,' corrected Chastity, 'but I'm not sure that I would.' She stopped as she suddenly became aware that Unicorn was no longer looking at her but was staring over her shoulder at the window behind her.

'Prepare yourself for a shock,' he said. 'I think we have an unexpected guest.'

Chastity turned to look at the window. The head and shoulders of a slim, pale, dark-haired young man were framed in it. With one hand he was precariously clinging to the top of the ladder and with the other he was making frantic gestures to be let in. Chastity also became aware that it had started to rain rather heavily and the pale young man was looking somewhat damp.

'Don't worry,' said Unicorn reassuringly. 'It's only Paul. I expect Rupert has locked him out again.'

For once, Chastity found herself at a loss for words. The afternoon was definitely becoming rather bizarre.

Unicorn walked across the room without undue haste, slipped the catch and lifted up the window. 'Come in,' he said, somewhat irritably, 'before you get soaked. Though why the hell you can't go in by your own window, as you usually do, I don't know.'

Paul climbed in with difficulty. 'Thank you, my dear Unicorn. It's that bloody Rupert,' he explained as he shook some of the water off, onto the kitchen floor. 'I'm sorry, darling,' he said, suddenly seeing Chastity. 'One really shouldn't use such words in front of a lady, and one can certainly see that you are a lady. But then, Rupert really is, too – I mean, not a lady,' he added hastily. 'You've no idea,' he said, turning towards Unicorn, 'how that creature treats me. Why I put up with it, I don't know.'

'Don't you?' asked Unicorn, rather sardonically. 'For heaven's sake, sit down, have a coffee and let us hear it all in comfort, since you obviously intend to tell us.'

Chastity, realising what was required of her, mechanically refilled the kettle and put it on the stove. Equally mechanically, she plugged the kettle in where Unicorn had previously shown her. Paul had, meanwhile, taken off his wet jacket and hung it carefully over the back of the chair.

His dark hair was long and wavy, and he was quite good-looking in a soft, effeminate way. He was wearing a pale mauve shirt with a tasteful deep purple tie. His nails, Chastity noticed, now almost without surprise, were painted a deep purple to match.

'I shall catch my death of cold,' Paul was saying fussily, 'and that'll teach him a lesson.'

'You, too, perhaps,' commented Unicorn.

Paul looked as if he might burst into tears, but instead he sat down in Chastity's chair and accepted the cigarette that Unicorn offered him.

'Well,' said Paul at last, turning to Chastity for sympathy, 'you'll hardly believe it, angels...'

'Try us,' replied Unicorn, putting coffee into three mugs.

'Well, I was sitting quietly in the living room, doing my embroidery. I'm making a set of chair backs,' he explained, 'and it's very intricate work – takes a lot of concentration. Well, I was just doing a most difficult stitch, when Rupert burst in. He was in a bad mood. I could see that from the first moment. His bath had been interrupted by some wretched girl who wanted to use the loo. He'd plunged straight in as soon as she taken herself away and had nearly scalded himself to death – the silly girl had left the hot tap running, you see.'

Chastity felt a guilty twinge.

'He was nearly skinned alive, or so he said. He should have tested it, of course, but poor, dear Rupert is very careless about details like that. Well, to cut a long story short, he was so upset that he pulled the plug out and lost all the hot water and there wasn't any more. You know what the water system's like. So, naturally, he wasn't in a very good temper. Rupert loves his bath.'

He paused. Chastity hastily walked to the stove, unplugged the boiling kettle and made the coffee. Paul sipped his appreciatively, shivering dramatically as he did so.

'It's all very clear, so far,' Unicorn prompted him. 'I can understand how and why Rupert was in a bad temper, but I'm still no nearer understanding how you came to be on a ladder in the rain.'

'I'm coming to that,' replied Paul, taking another sip of coffee. 'You see, darling, I was preoccupied with my embroidery at that moment. It was a difficult stitch and I do like it to be absolutely perfect.' He paused again.

'For heaven's sake, get to the point, man,' Unicorn said impatiently.

'Well, I suppose I wasn't as sympathetic as I might have been, but, then, Rupert has absolutely no understanding of the feelings of an artist. He's rather lacking in the finer feelings, you know.' He took another sip of his coffee. 'I'm positive I shall catch my death,' he murmured, 'but thank you, angel, for this simply divine coffee.' He smiled sadly at Chastity.

'Do go on,' said Unicorn. 'I can't stand the suspense.'

'Well,' continued Paul, 'he was simply furious. Said I didn't care what happened to him; never had cared, in fact. He added a few adjectives, but I don't care to repeat them.'

'I'll imagine them,' said Unicorn.

'He said I cared more for my f— embroidery. I told him not to be silly. He literally rushed towards me.' Paul shuddered at the very memory. 'Said he was fed up with living with a crazy old woman like me. I was terrified, my dears; Rupert can be quite violent at times, you know. So I dropped my embroidery, rushed to the door and fled.'

'And, of course,' commented Unicorn, 'he locked you out, as usual.'

'Of course. So I got the ladder. I always keep it ready in the garden,' he explained to Chastity. 'But you'll never believe what the bastard has done this time.' His voice rose almost to a shriek. The other two waited silently for the climax. 'He locked the window,' he whispered dramatically, 'and stood there, laughing at me, while the rain poured down on me. And he didn't care.

I'm beginning to think he's really depraved.' His shoulders shook. He buried his head in his hands. 'Oh, it was terrible.' His shoulders shook even more. He lifted his head. 'So I had to come to you, and you, being the angels you are, gave me refuge.' He drank down the rest of his coffee. 'I do hope he hasn't ruined my embroidery,' he added wistfully.

Before either Unicorn or Chastity could answer, there was the sound of heavy footsteps coming down the stairs.

'I think you'll soon have your answer,' murmured Unicorn. 'That sounds remarkably like Rupert on the warpath.'

The kitchen door was thrown open and the large, fair young man burst in. He was furious but, at least, fully dressed this time. Chastity had been prepared for anything.

He ignored the other two and advanced on the shrinking Paul. 'What the fucking hell are you doing here?' he demanded. 'Telling lies about me, I suppose.'

'Now, Rupert, dear,' begged Paul, 'please don't make a scene. You know how I hate scenes; they upset me so.'

'Oh, my God!' groaned Rupert. 'Can't you…'

Chastity felt herself being gently pushed through the door by Unicorn.

'This is where we make a tactful exit,' he explained, closing the door firmly behind them. 'Lovers' quarrels should be private; don't you agree?'

'Oh, certainly,' replied Chastity, feeling rather dazed.

'They'll make it up and go back in a few minutes,' continued Unicorn. 'Then we can wash up. In the meantime, we may as well sit quietly in the living room and have a cosy chat.'

Chastity settled herself in the armchair she had previously cleared. Unicorn, after adding a few objects to the heaps already on the floor, stretched himself on the settee. 'Now,' he said, 'we can talk, or perhaps you would prefer to be quiet for a bit.'

'I think I would,' Chastity replied, closing her eyes. The events of the afternoon had certainly not improved her headache.

'What the devil are you doing here?' a female voice exclaimed crossly. 'Can't a girl ever have any peace?'

Chastity opened her eyes to see Louie (it could only be Louie, surely?) standing accusingly over Unicorn, wearing only a bra and pants. 'Really, Unicorn,' she continued, 'you might have the decency to take your girlfriends to your own flat, particularly when you know I want to get some sleep. It's not my fault that you're overcrowded.'

Chastity jumped up to protest, but Unicorn was before her.

'You're quite right, Louie,' he said smoothly, taking Chastity's hand. 'It's very thoughtless and indiscreet of me. Come along, my sweet.' He turned towards Chastity with an adoring smile.

'I should think so,' muttered Louie, 'and don't come back until I'm gone, if you must come back.'

'I won't,' promised Unicorn, shutting the door behind them.

I'm a weak-minded idiot, thought Chastity, allowing herself to be led; where, she knew not. 'I need to go somewhere,' she said, 'where I can think. I need to think.'

'Ridiculous,' answered Unicorn. 'You need a drink, not a think.'

'I don't drink,' replied Chastity, firmly.

'Well, you can sit and watch me,' said Unicorn with equal firmness. 'I do.'

Chapter Two

'Well, I feel better now,' said Chastity, finishing off her second brandy and putting down the glass.

'I'm not surprised,' remarked Unicorn; 'two neat double brandies ought to achieve some effect.' He looked at her critically as she sat opposite him in the dark, crowded and noisy lounge of the nearest local, apparently quite unmoved. Not a hair was ruffled, not a crease was showing; her glance was as clear and direct as ever. People pushed past her to the bar, but she appeared to be quite unaware of them.

'I thought you said you didn't drink,' he remarked with some irony.

'I don't usually,' replied Chastity, 'but I've been well trained, you might say, in the ways of this world. One doesn't forget one's early training so easily, you know.'

'No, I suppose not,' Unicorn murmured, hiding his surprise. This girl was tantalising and demanded further investigation. 'Would you like another one – a treble this time, perhaps?'

Chastity considered the matter seriously for a moment. 'No, I think not,' she said, decidedly. 'I've had just enough to give things a slightly rosy glow. More would be a waste of money. But do have another yourself, if you feel the need. I'm quite happy to sit here. After all, there doesn't seem to be anywhere else for me to sit, at the moment.'

'That's true,' agreed Unicorn cheerfully. 'I won't be long.'

It took him a few moments to get served in the crowded bar, and when he came back he found her apparently absorbed in thought. 'You look very serious. Is anything wrong?' he asked lightly.

'No,' she said, 'nothing's exactly wrong. I was just wondering what my father would think about this.'

'Your father? Surely you're a bit too old to be worrying about that?' He sounded surprised and almost disappointed.

'What age would that be?' was all she replied.

He studied her critically. 'It's difficult to say, but I should guess somewhere between twenty and thirty. Am I right?'

'Absolutely.'

'You're not very informative, are you?'

'I don't intend to be.'

'So I can see. Perhaps you can at least tell me whether you think your father would approve?'

'I imagine so, since he sent me here.'

He raised an eyebrow. 'Sent you?'

'In a manner of speaking, yes.' She paused. 'Well, perhaps that's not completely true.' She was silent for a moment, and then she suddenly asked, looking directly at Unicorn: 'There's not much point in talking at all, is there, if one doesn't at least try to be truthful?'

Unicorn was a little taken by surprise, but he rallied quickly. 'I don't think most people would agree with you,' he said, 'since most of us use words to screen rather than to reveal ourselves.'

Chastity looked at him somewhat impatiently. 'You're doing it yourself,' she said, 'just wanting to sound clever. I don't want to know what you think most people do; I want to know what you really think.'

'Then,' answered Unicorn, 'the nearest I can get to it is to say that the truth is very difficult to know and often very dangerous to speak. Remember that, if you've come looking for it.'

They regarded each other seriously for a moment.

'But I ought to warn you,' he added lightly, 'that words are my business. I am a freelance journalist.'

'Isn't that a rather precarious life?' asked Chastity.

'It might be, but I make it my business to know lots of the right people. I also have a small private income and a wealthy father, so it's not a bad life.'

She was silent.

'You disapprove, I suppose?' he asked. 'My frivolous attitude to life annoys your Christian conscience, I expect.'

'Why should I disapprove? Surely what is important is what you think about it?'

Looking sympathetically at her, Unicorn decided to avoid

answering that. 'I think you must still be feeling a little shocked. Perhaps another brandy would be a good idea after all?' Not even this girl, he thought, could be immune to three brandies. He half rose.

'Absolutely not. Why do you think I should be feeling shocked, anyway?'

'Well, I don't imagine your reception was exactly as you had expected, much more casual, I should think. Am I right?' As she merely nodded, he continued. 'Then, when you seek refuge in the kitchen for a comforting cup of coffee, you find an intruder who is apparently quite at home and, in your eyes, somewhat outrageous, I should imagine. People don't behave like that in the vicarage, do they?'

'Not usually. I was surprised to meet you, I admit, but it was really very fortunate, since you told me where the coffee was and lit the gas and even fed me! I decided you were really very kind.'

Unicorn was almost speechless. 'To the pure, all things are pure,' he murmured at last. 'I don't think I ever believed that before now. But surely the eruption of Rupert and Paul shocked you a little? Or was it Louie?' He leaned towards her sympathetically, thinking at the same time how delightful it would be to bed her, beautiful and untouched as she was. Putting one hand gently on hers he avoided looking directly at her. This was the time for sympathy, not for revealing his inner lustful thoughts.

To his amazement, she laughed suddenly. 'Louie at least was truthful and she gave you a great opportunity, of which you took full advantage.' Startled, he looked up. She was genuinely smiling. 'A woman in her underclothes isn't likely to disturb me, is she?'

Although somewhat disconcerted, he rallied. 'Surely, you found Rupert and Paul a little disturbing? You don't meet couples like that in the vicarage, do you? Or is your father very left wing? Does he, perhaps, support homosexual priests?'

'My father sees people as they are and he doesn't judge rashly. I try to do the same. I think Rupert is very handsome and Paul is rather loving. What do you think?'

'I think I'm somewhat amazed, but I must admire your Christian charity.'

'Don't you mean my naivety?' she challenged him.

'Perhaps, but I need to know more about you to be sure. Why, for example, have you come to London?'

'To work.'

He sighed. 'Can't you possibly be a tiny bit more explicit? Or is a deadly secret? Are you, perhaps, a foreign agent?'

'Much duller, I'm afraid. I have come to work for a charitable organisation. They have a small office in this area and I start work there next Monday.'

'Ah, at last your guilty secret is revealed! You are one of the world's "do-gooders".' He looked mockingly at her. 'I should have guessed. I can see the headline already: *Vicar's daughter comes to save souls in Sin City*! It makes quite a good headline, but, I'm afraid, I would need something lurid to follow it, if I am to keep the reader' s interest.'

Chastity was unmoved. 'I'm afraid I haven't anything to offer.'

'Perhaps I can help you?'

'Help me? How?' She had been glancing down into her empty glass, but suddenly she looked straight at him with her beautiful dark eyes.

For a strange moment, he couldn't continue; it felt as if she were looking into the depths of his sordid soul. With an effort, he rallied. 'I can introduce you to some of the entertainments of London.'

'I don't imagine that the entertainments are very attractive in "Sin City" as you just called it.'

'How do you know, if you've never tried them? We can have a good time together, if you'll let me show you round. I'll pick you up tomorrow evening. We'll have a meal in a cosy little restaurant I'm specially attached to and then go on to a club.'

'Aren't clubs for teenagers?'

'Some, of course, but not the ones I'll take you to. A beautiful girl like you deserves to have some fun. What do you say? You might even save my soul at the same time.'

'Does it need saving?' She looked down again. 'You're tempting. I'll think about it.' She paused, then added, suddenly, 'I think you ought to know that the organisation I belong to is for saving bodies; souls are incidental, as you might say.'

'I'm not sure I understand you.'

'It's quite simple. The charity I am working for is a medical one. You shouldn't make assumptions about vicars' daughters.'

'It's obvious then, isn't it, that you must educate me? It's your Christian duty, surely?'

Smiling, she looked at her watch. 'Perhaps, but I think my Christian duty at the moment is to return to the flat and remove my suitcases from the living room, if I can.'

'Perhaps you're right,' agreed Unicorn. 'Although I rather suppose,' he continued, 'the events of this afternoon have made you feel like rushing straight back to the peace and sanity of Priors Hamlet?'

'No; that would, I think, be rather too precipitate,' she answered. 'Although, I must admit, my welcome was not quite as I had imagined it.' She glanced at her watch. 'Louie really ought to be dressed by now and there's even a chance that Alex might be back. I certainly ought to go back and unpack.'

She half rose from her seat, but Unicorn gently pushed her down again. 'No,' he said. 'I shan't agree to take you back until you've had one more drink and arranged when we can meet again.'

'Since I don't know my way back, I shall have to agree to your taking me,' she answered. He noticed with amusement that she did not seem at all impressed by his suggestion that they should meet again. She was remarkably cool, in fact. Very intriguing. 'But I definitely don't want another drink, and we can arrange our next meeting some other time.'

There was almost a promise there, he thought, but he decided not to press it. 'Not even one small drink?' he pleaded.

'Definitely not.' She rose to her feet.

Reluctantly, he stood up, too. 'I expect you're right.' Gently, he put his arm around her waist to steer her through the crowds and was encouraged when she didn't object.

When they re-entered the flat with the assistance of Unicorn's key, it was immediately obvious that Alex had returned some time before, for the sitting room was now completely tidy and looked far more inviting. Alex, who had apparently been in the kitchen, came hurrying to meet them. Ignoring Unicorn, who stood by the door, she welcomed Chastity, apologising profusely for being unavoidably absent when she arrived, in spite of her earlier promise to be there. 'I explained everything to Dot this morning, and I hope that she met you and helped you to feel at home?'

This proved difficult to answer, but Chastity decided on tact. 'She did meet me, but I'm afraid she hadn't much time. She was going to a party.'

Stepping forward, Unicorn added cheerfully, 'And so, like a true knight, I rushed in and offered my assistance to the damsel in distress; first by offering her some sustenance and then by taking her to a place of refuge; namely, the local hostelry.'

'How kind of you and how typical!' It seemed to Chastity that Alex was unnecessarily hostile to Unicorn. 'I'm quite sure that you'd make the most of any such opportunity, even if it wasn't really necessary.'

'Oh, it was necessary, I assure you, darling. For one thing, you've forgotten Louie, who was still in possession.'

'Oh, my God, yes!' Alex was at a loss for words.

'But that wasn't all.' Unicorn was obviously enjoying himself. 'It seemed that everyone, and I don't exclude myself at first, was determined to frighten the poor girl away. After that, the poor girl badly needed a drink and a place in which to be at peace.'

'I'm afraid I've treated you badly.' Alex turned towards Chastity. 'I can only hope that Unicorn is exaggerating, as he often does.'

'Not entirely.' Chastity smiled. 'I was, in fact, pleased to have his help.'

'I'm not sure I understand.' Alex looked bewildered.

'Allow me to enlighten you.' With a flourish, Unicorn settled himself comfortably in one of the armchairs. 'Sit down, both of you, and prepare to listen to Sir Unicorn's true account of the sad story of Lady Chastity's welcome.' Quickly and humorously, he told Chastity's story to an angry and finally, in spite of herself, amused Alex.

Chastity remained aloof during much of this, studying Alex as if she were a specimen previously unknown to her. Tall and slender, Alex seemed to be the epitome of the successful, young professional woman. Wearing a pale grey business suit with long jacket and short skirt, she displayed a considerable amount of elegant, nylon-clad leg as she relaxed in her armchair. Her short, blonde hair was a smooth, gleaming cap surrounding her rather round face, which had been cleverly made up to enhance her good points and disguise her less attractive ones.

'Oh, God!' she exclaimed, as Unicorn's story came to a dramatic end with Louie's outburst. 'I'm so very sorry,' she murmured, turning towards Chastity. 'I should have been here, as I promised. What must you think of me?'

With some amusement, Unicorn noticed that Chastity chose not to answer this directly. 'Fortunately, I didn't have time to think, and it was really quite amusing, but I am grateful for Unicorn's help.'

'At last, someone has recognised my true worth.'

'It's not the first thing one usually notices about you,' Alex retorted.

At this moment, Chastity decided to stand up. 'Do you think you could show me to my room now? I would like to unpack, or at least remove my cases from your living room.'

'Of course.' Alex jumped to her feet. 'Louie went about an hour ago and the room is completely ready for you.' She hurried across the room and opened the door through which Louie had emerged. 'This is your room. I'm afraid it leads directly off the living room, but it's a good size and I think you'll find it comfortable.'

Following her, Chastity looked around quickly. The room was indeed larger and brighter than she had expected, although it was barely furnished, with little more than the mere necessities. 'I'm sure I shall be comfortable here.' She walked over to the window, from which, she was pleased to find, there was a comparatively pleasant view of neighbouring gardens with several attractive trees.

'I'm afraid it's a bit bare,' Alex apologised, 'but that gives you more of a chance to put your own stuff around and make it more personal. The bed's comfortable and there's plenty of drawer and cupboard space.'

'It'll suit me very well. I haven't many possessions, but I travel light and I'm not used to luxury.' As she moved towards the door, Unicorn appeared, carrying her two cases, which he placed on the bed. After thanking him, she made it quite clear that she now wished to be alone to investigate her new home.

'She certainly travels light,' Unicorn remarked to Alex as the door shut behind Chastity. 'Cases quite light; no laptop; no TV; no radio, apparently. Perhaps they don't have a surplus of such frivolities in the vicarage.'

'Probably not.' Alex remained standing, obviously waiting for him to go, but he seemed reluctant.

'I don't believe she's thought about food,' he remarked unexpectedly. 'I offered to take her out for a meal, but she refused.'

'Wise girl. But, in case you're really worrying, which I admit seems highly unlikely, I intend to feed her this evening. It'll give us a chance to discuss various arrangements, rent, et cetera. No one else will be around. It'll be much safer for her too.'

'Do you always have to impute the worst motives to me?' He sounded unusually irritated.

'Can you blame me? I do know you pretty well. Remember?'

'For Christ's sake, can't you ever forget that we were once lovers? It wasn't any more important to you than it was to me. You simply like to pretend that it was. In any case, I thought we were now supposed to be friends. Or was that just another ruse?'

'I suppose we are, as far as ex-lovers ever can be.' She chose to disregard his final thrust.

Turning away from her impatiently, he walked towards the window, where he stood looking out into the street for a few minutes. Still obviously irritated, he turned around again. 'Why the hell are you so protective of this particular tenant? It's rather out of character, isn't it? No one can accuse you of being the motherly type. Is she a long-lost relative or something?'

'She's different. Maybe I'm getting sentimental in my old age, but I simply don't want to see you ruin her; that's all. And I know you see any new woman as your natural prey, but I suggest that you leave this one alone. There are plenty other, more suitable women around. I don't usually care, but this time I do, so be warned, Unicorn!'

He laughed. 'We're getting a bit melodramatic, aren't we? Nevertheless, I have to agree that for once you're right. She is different and that's why she interests me.'

'Forget it. I told you.'

'I don't believe that Chastity is as naïve as you seem to think. What do you know about her, anyway? How did she come to be your new tenant?'

'I'm not really sure. It was all a bit unusual. I put an advertisement in the London evenings, and two days later I had her letter.'

'What's unusual about that?'

'Nothing, except that she wrote from this small place in North Yorkshire. It seemed very unusual that she should see the advertisement.'

'Obviously she's very well organised. Is that why you chose her?'

'Partly. But the real reason was that she asked in her letter whether I was the Alex Woodward who was at St Ethelburga's Public School for Girls and who might remember her cousin, Caroline Brown.'

'And that clinched it?'

'I do remember Caroline. We were in the same year and the same House, so we were pretty close friends. We'd been rivals occasionally, however, but without any ill will. Caroline was far too pleasant and intelligent for anything like that to occur. I'd sometimes wondered what had happened to her, so I rang straight back.'

'And so you chose her because she was old Caroline's cousin and therefore the right sort of person? A suitably respectable girl with the right middle-class background? A bit different from your Dots and Louies and even our blonde bombshell, Eva.'

'I don't see why you should make fun of me. You're just the same sort of snob at heart.'

'Absolutely.' Unicorn smiled cheerfully. 'You've made a very good choice, and I shall certainly enjoy getting to know her better. I can assure you that it's been a very enjoyable experience so far. Virgin territory. Very unusual these days, don't you think?'

'You're being pretty foul, aren't you? Why can't you leave her alone?' Alex was surprised at how furious she felt. 'She's had a quiet life and she's come here to do a serious job.'

'With a medical missionary society, I believe. Very noble, but the poor girl clearly needs to learn how to enjoy life and I'm sure I'm the right one to help her. If you had wanted so much to keep her away from me, don't you think that you should have made sure that you were here when she arrived?'

'I only wish I had been!'

'But we both know why you weren't, don't we?' Shrugging his shoulders, he moved away from the window. 'Be your age, Alex. You can't control my life. We aren't lovers any more.' He moved towards the hall door. 'I'd better go now; a deadline calls.'

'Why don't you go then?'

For a moment he hesitated. He wanted to speak to Chastity, but it didn't seem worth his while to battle any more with Alex. There were easier ways, he decided.

Then, as if on cue, Chastity came through the other door. 'I'm sorry to interrupt you but I've left my handbag in here and my keys are in it.' After looking around, she hurried towards the armchair where she had left it.

Intercepting her, Unicorn retrieved it and handed it to her with a flourish, then kissed her hand. 'I'm afraid a deadline calls and I must go, but you haven't forgotten, I hope, that you agreed to have a meal with me tomorrow. I'll pick you up at seven thirty.'

Her dark eyes looked into his and once again he had the strange sensation that she was reading into the depths of his soul. For a moment she did not reply, then she said firmly, 'I didn't agree, but I do now. Only for a meal; nothing else.'

'I accept.' He smiled his most charming smile. 'You've made me a happy man.' He went towards the door and opened it. 'See you tomorrow.' With a final wave to Alex, he was gone.

Chapter Three

'I rather wish that you hadn't agreed to see him again,' Alex found herself exclaiming as the door closed behind Unicorn. *Whatever made me say that?* she wondered immediately afterwards. *I must be mad.* 'I'm sorry,' she added quickly. 'It's absolutely no concern of mine. I have no right.'

Apparently unmoved, Chastity looked at her seriously, then merely asked, 'Why?' Without saying any more, she waited.

Realising that this was a question she could not now avoid answering, Alex fumbled for the right words, 'Because he's very charming and extremely unreliable,' was all she could find to say.

'You think he might break my heart?'

'If he did, yours wouldn't be the first. He always seems to care, but he doesn't.'

'And so you thought you should warn an innocent stranger?'

'Sorry. I know I shouldn't have said anything.'

'Why ever not? You obviously mean to be kind.' Chastity moved as if to return to her room.

'Do you really mean that?' Alex felt suspicious of such apparent simplicity.

'Of course.' Chastity suddenly turned towards Alex and frowned a little. 'You did mean to be kind, didn't you?'

'Yes. Some people might see it differently. They might think I was jealous.' *Christ, what's the matter with me?* Alex asked herself. *I never talk like this.*

'And are you jealous?'

Now was the opportunity to retrieve the situation with a light laugh and a casual retort, but instead Alex again found herself speaking the truth. 'Yes, I suppose I am, a bit. It's stupid, I know, but you see…' She stopped abruptly. Surely she wasn't going to tell this stranger something she had never admitted to anyone?

'He broke your heart.' It wasn't a question, but a statement.

'Yes; it was years ago, however, and we're friends now.'

'I'm very sorry.' Chastity was obviously sincere. 'Thank you for warning me. I'll be extra careful. But I don't think I'm really his type, do you?'

'Perhaps not, but that might make it all the more challenging to him, don't you see?'

After considering this for a moment, Chastity agreed, sadly. 'I think you may be right. But you really don't need to worry, Alex. I'm not as naïve or as foolish as Unicorn may think. I'm here to do a serious job, and that's my only concern. But thank you for caring about me.'

As she moved to return to her room, Alex said quickly, 'I was hoping that you would have supper with me. No one else will be in tonight, so we'll have a chance to get to know one another a bit better. I've bought a pizza and some salad, so it won't take long to prepare. What do you say? I can get it ready while you unpack.'

'Thank you. It's a very kind suggestion, especially as, I must admit, I haven't actually given any thought to such mundane matters.' She smiled at Alex. 'I haven't much to unpack, as you've probably noticed, so I can be ready when you are.'

'Good. I'll call you when the meal's on the table.' Alex suddenly felt unusually cheerful. Was it the thought, she wondered, of talking to someone who had connections with her schooldays? She had certainly enjoyed those days before her ambition had brought her to London. Since then, her life had been challenging, exciting but very rarely happy.

Half an hour later, as they ate their supper together, Alex outlined the way life was managed in the flat. 'You can be as private and as communal as you wish. Very often, those of us who are at home eat together, but, if you want to entertain in your own room, that's all right. Your own room is your private domain. Of course, we try to be as considerate as possible. That's where Louie failed, I'm afraid. The chief difficulty is occasionally having to share a bathroom with Rupert and Paul, but it usually works quite well, better than it did for you this morning, as the door to the stairs is usually locked.

'In any case, Dot should have told you that we have a small cloakroom, with a shower that opens off the hall. One day, when I can afford it, I intend to have a bathroom made out of one of the bedrooms. But that would mean having one less tenant and, of course, less rent, so, until that day we continue the arrangement with Rupert and Paul.'

'This is your flat, then? I hadn't realised that.'

'Yes; it was a struggle to get it and to keep it, but I've managed for the last eighteen months.'

'You've been very successful. What do you do?'

'I work as an editor in a publishing firm. I'm hoping to get a promotion soon, and, when I do, I'll be able to start making changes.'

'Is your aim, then, to have the flat to yourself one day? Is that what you want?'

'Absolutely. Ever since I came to London, seven years ago, I've been scheming to get the job I hope to get in the next month or two and to have my own home. I like this part of London, so I think I've been pretty fortunate.'

Feeling, as she did at that moment, that she had been very successful, it was rather deflating when Chastity quietly asked, 'And then what?'

She managed to shrug, however, and reply casually, 'An even better job, I hope, and a house. Or I may take a job in New York, as my firm is based there. Do you disapprove?'

'Not really. I was only wondering if you had any plans to marry and have a family.'

'Not at present. There has to be a suitable candidate available, doesn't there? In fact, at present, there's no one in my life I would want to marry and, to be perfectly honest, I don't think there's anyone who would want to marry me.' Again she wondered why on earth she was telling this strange woman all about herself. To hide her embarrassment, she laughed lightly. 'Marriage and babies have never figured much in my dreams. I've always been ambitious. I like to have a man around, but I don't see the need for marriage.' She looked directly at Chastity, deciding that it was her turn now. 'Neither do you, apparently. But then, perhaps you're younger than Caroline and me. You look younger, but I imagined that you were about the same age as her. Am I wrong?'

'No, Caroline and I are close in age.'

'Do you know her well?'

'In some ways very well; as you know, we didn't go to the same school, but we met often in the holidays.'

'I've quite often wondered how she was getting on. She was so brilliant at school that I've always expected to hear great news of her.'

'I'm afraid there'll be no news of Caroline, great or otherwise,' Chastity replied slowly.

'What do you mean? Why not?'

'She died nearly seven years ago.'

Momentarily, Alex felt too shocked to speak. 'How terrible!' she managed to say at last. 'Whatever happened? Was it an accident?'

'You couldn't exactly call it an accident. After a brilliant start her life simply fell apart. After taking her degree, she married a diplomat some fifteen years older than she was and went with him to Africa. They adored each other and were very happy. Caroline also loved Africa and the Africans. She set about getting to know African women and trying to help them. She seemed to have found her vocation.'

'What happened? What went wrong?'

'First of all, she had a baby girl who died when she was about three weeks old. Her husband tried to console her, but then he was killed in a terrorist explosion. Soon after that, Caroline herself died of an obscure fever she had caught in some African village. Her father told me that he thought she had lost the will to live.'

'Oh, my God! How terrible!' Alex could not find words that were adequate. 'Poor Caroline!' Her eyes filled with tears. 'Her father must have been heartbroken. They were always so close.'

'He still is. That's why, when I came home recently, I went to stay with him, but there is little that one can do.' She made it quite clear that she had no wish to say more.

'You haven't been living in England, then?

'Not for some years.'

'Oh, of course; I remember now. Unicorn mentioned that you worked for a medical missionary society.'

'Alas, poor Unicorn!' Chastity smiled, unexpectedly. 'He thought he had me placed as the vicar's daughter who had naïvely come to London to save souls. I had to tell him that I was a healer and not a preacher. Bodies, not souls, are our primary concern. He seemed to be disappointed. But I'm sure he'll soon invent some new romantic fantasy for me!'

Surprised, Alex stared at her. 'Surely, you don't consider Unicorn to be a romantic? That is the last thing I would ever say of him!'

'Perhaps we mean different things by the word "romantic"? I'm really trying to say that he prefers to take refuge in fiction, rather than to seek the truth. It's one of his ways of avoiding responsibility.'

'I would certainly agree that he does like to avoid responsibility.' Although she tried to speak lightly, Alex could not entirely hide her bitterness. 'But, even though one knows he's unreliable, it's still possible to be attracted by him, you know.'

'So you're still telling me to beware?'

'Absolutely. Remember: pride comes before a fall.'

'I'll do my best to remember it tomorrow evening.'

'What will you wear? Have you anything suitable? I don't want to be rude, but you did say that you'd brought very few things with you.'

'That's right, and, although you're too polite to say it, I'm sure that you're thinking that, if they're all as fashionable as this suit, they won't be much good.'

Chastity sounded amused, rather than offended, and, although Alex would have preferred to be evasive, it seemed impossible to lie with Chastity's strangely luminous dark eyes fixed on her. 'Well, I have to admit it's not exactly the latest fashion.'

Chastity laughed. 'Obviously not. I realised that I soon as I saw you. Yours has a short skirt and a long jacket, while mine has a longish skirt and a short jacket.'

'It wouldn't be so bad if the skirt was really long.'

'But, as it is, it's dowdy, would you say?'

'I'm afraid so.'

'That's a pity, but it will have to do. I'm not paid much. There's no spare money for clothes; certainly not useless glamorous ones. But that's a good thing, don't you think?'

'I'm not sure what you mean.'

'It seems to me that if I look a dowdy frump I'm much less

likely to attract the unwanted attentions of Unicorn, and, since I don't want to attract him, why should that worry me?'

'Have you considered that your looking different might be the very thing that attracts him?'

'Well, in that case, I must simply take my chance.'

'But it's not just Unicorn. Surely every woman wants to look her best when she goes out to a fashionable restaurant?' Alex looked and sounded worried.

'I do have a plain black dress, which is suitable for most such occasions. I won't let our sex down. Don't look so shocked, Alex!'

Suddenly they were both laughing. *She does remind me of Caroline*, Alex thought. *I suppose that's why it's so easy to be friendly with her.* She decided, however, not to mention Caroline, as she already felt that Chastity did not wish to speak any more about her cousin. 'I won't worry you any more,' she said aloud. 'You seem to be perfectly in charge of the situation.' They smiled at one another as she stacked the dishes on a tray. 'I'll dispose of these and brew some coffee. Make yourself comfortable in the meantime.' She went out quickly, closing the door behind her.

Left to herself, Chastity wandered round the room, which, she now realised, was bigger than it had first seemed. The table at which they had been eating was placed in front of a large window, overlooking the street. Apart from this, there was space for two armchairs, a comfortable divan strewn with bright cushions, several sets of shelves and cupboards, three occasional tables and a wide-screen television on a stand. There were scarcely any ornaments and only one picture, of a sunny Mediterranean scene. It was an unexpectedly impersonal room.

Having finished her survey, Chastity settled down in an armchair with a magazine she had discovered. She had hardly begun to turn the pages when she heard the sound of the front door being opened, followed by quick footsteps coming along the hall. She scarcely had time to be surprised when the door to the living room was flung open and a brilliant apparition appeared, exclaiming loudly, 'God, am I glad to get home! British Airways is a bloody disgrace!'

Startled, Chastity jumped up to face a tall, slender young woman with shining golden hair flowing down to her shoulders.

She was wearing a long, purple woollen coat, which, as she moved, swung open to reveal a purple mini skirt worn with a vivid cerise top, which exactly matched the colour of her full mouth and long nails. She was wearing high-heeled gold and purple sandals, which made her slim bronzed legs look even longer.

Stopping abruptly just inside the doorway, she stared back at Chastity. 'Who the hell are you?' she demanded. 'And what on earth are you doing here?'

'I'm Chastity Brown,' Chastity replied quietly. 'I'm Alex's new tenant. I only arrived today.' Receiving no reply, she persevered bravely. 'I imagine you must be Eva?'

'Right.' For a moment Eva seemed to be overcome by shock. Still staring at Chastity, she murmured, 'Good God!' Then, with an obvious effort, she seemed to recover. 'Where's Alex?' she demanded. 'Don't tell me she's out?'

Sitting down again, Chastity hurried to reassure her that Alex was only in the kitchen making coffee. Without deigning to answer, Eva flung her coat onto the floor and sank into the other armchair. Chastity's fascinated eyes observed that the cerise top, which, like the mini skirt, was scarcely sufficient to cover her voluptuous curves.

'God, do I need a drink!' Eva exclaimed. 'I don't suppose you have anything to offer?'

Fortunately, at that moment Alex reappeared, carrying the coffee tray. She was obviously not expecting to see Eva, for, as she put down the tray, she exclaimed, 'What's happened? I didn't expect to see you before the end of the week. Has Max lost his charm? Or has the Caribbean suddenly become boring?'

'Neither. We came back early because Max was urgently summoned to New York by his firm. He had only a few hours' notice, so he dumped me in a taxi at Heathrow and here I am, tired and disillusioned. The plane was delayed; the airport was in its usual state of chaos. I am so fed up that I can't even face bringing my bag up. I must have a drink first. Any offers?'

'Coffee?' Alex suggested brightly as she poured out two cups for herself and Chastity.

'That's positively an obscene suggestion to make to anyone in my fragile state. But don't worry; I'll go to my room in a minute.'

'Don't move,' Alex ordered. 'Never let it be said that I refused to supply a desperate friend with a reviving vodka.' As she spoke, she moved towards the drinks cabinet.

'Be a real darling and make it a double,' Eva suggested. After taking a sip of her large drink, she turned towards Chastity. 'I think I ought to apologise for giving you such a rude greeting. I'm afraid you were just one more shock after thirty-six hours of shock. The brain simply refused to cope, but I really am sorry.'

Chastity smiled back at her. 'There's no need to apologise. I do understand. I've had a few shocks myself today.' She didn't elaborate further, being content to sit quietly while Eva described to Alex in vivid language the horrors of her return journey. As she listened, however, she became aware of a tension in the atmosphere; not simply tension, but tension mixed with hostility on Eva's part. Either Eva had taken an instant dislike to her or, more likely, simply wanted her to go so that she could talk freely to Alex.

Whatever the reason, it was obviously more sensible for her to remove herself as quickly as possible. After gulping down her coffee, therefore, she stood up, thanked Alex for her hospitality and begged them both to excuse her, as she was very tired.

'I don't blame you,' Alex replied. 'You've certainly had a hectic first day, partly because of me, I'm sorry to say. If you do need anything, please let me know.' Although she could not say it, she was reluctant to be left alone with Eva. Chastity, however, hesitated no longer. With a quick goodnight to both of them she was gone, seeking sanctuary at last in the quiet of her own room.

'Where ever did you get hold of her?' Eva asked, as soon as the door closed behind Chastity. 'The ark, perhaps? I couldn't believe my eyes when I saw her sitting there! She's such a proper little miss – not our sort at all! Is she paying double or something?'

'I don't know why you have to be so rude about her,' Alex retorted sharply. 'She's the cousin of an old school friend of mine. And, if her clothes are a bit unfashionable, I don't see why it should worry you.'

'Sorry! Sorry!' Eva laughed 'It's not just the clothes, it's everything. I simply don't like her. She makes my flesh creep. I can't imagine what she does for a living.'

'She works with a medical mission and has been overseas for some years, I believe.'

'Ah, that's it!' Eva took another sip of her drink. 'She's one of those pious do-gooders. She won't approve of you when she gets to know all about you. But I suppose you haven't told her?'

'It's really no business of yours. Why are you being so unpleasant? What's wrong?'

'Everything!' Eva finished her drink. 'You won't believe it; I really though I'd come back engaged, but instead Max and I are finished.'

'Why do you say that? Because he had to go back to New York? Aren't you being a bit silly? You know his work often takes him off at short notice. You can't have luxury without paying for it.'

'It wasn't just that. I realised it wasn't working after about ten days. I was waiting for him to say something and, sure enough, he did. He says he'll be in touch, but I know he won't. What's wrong with me, Alex? Every relationship I ever have just falls apart.'

'You don't love him, do you?'

Eva opened her blue eyes wide. 'I thought we were fun together, but apparently Max no longer does. Love was never exactly part of the bargain. Frankly, Alex, I'm feeling pretty desperate. I'm not getting any younger. What am I going to do?'

'Have another drink.' Alex suggested, 'and then go to bed. There's nothing like a few vodkas for getting rid of the blues. You'll feel better tomorrow.'

Eva held out her glass. 'Have one with me. You don't have to pretend, now that Miss Prim's gone to bed.'

Although she wanted to refuse, Alex found herself saying, 'I think I will after all.'

Chapter Four

'I'd like to propose a toast to the most beautiful woman in the room!' Raising his glass, Unicorn glanced across at Chastity as she sat opposite him at a quiet corner table in one of London's more exclusive restaurants. He admitted to himself that she had once again surprised him.

Without making any concessions to fashion or to the opinions of others, she had contrived to appear even more beautiful. When he had first seen her wearing a simple straight black dress, without any adornment except for an unusual jade necklace, he had been unable to comment, so unexpectedly striking was the effect. The only change she had made had been to loosen her heavy, dark hair and allow it to fall smoothly to her shoulders. He felt she had passed a test, but what test, he wasn't sure.

Now, however, his smile was still slightly ironic and there was a sardonic glint in his tawny eyes. How would she react to this approach, he wondered. 'To my beautiful Chastity!' Taking a sip from his glass, he smiled at her.

After glancing around the restaurant, Chastity smiled slightly. 'I think you may be right, but there isn't much competition, is there?'

Putting down his glass, he laughed. 'Perfect! How do you do it?'

'Do what?'

'Remain apparently impervious to all my flattery and admiration?'

'Well, it's all rather irrelevant, isn't it? I'd much rather talk about something more interesting. Surely you would too?'

For a moment he sidestepped the challenge, finding himself unprepared. 'Hadn't we better choose our food first?' he suggested, handing her a copy of the menu. She made her choices with surprising speed, choosing the simplest dishes available, it seemed to him. When he remarked on this, she merely replied that, in the last few years, she had lost her taste for rich and expensive food. She didn't refuse wine but left the choice to him.

'Where have you been to lose your taste for rich food?' He was curious, for there didn't seem to be anything self-righteous about her attitude and she certainly had no need to diet. She spoke as if she were simply indifferent.

'I've been in some of the poorest parts of the world, most recently in East Africa. Being in such places gives one a distaste for luxury and helps one to learn what is important.'

He smiled mockingly. 'Of course, I should have remembered that I'm dining with a humble missionary. A kind of second St Teresa of Calcutta, I suppose.'

'Don't be ridiculous, Unicorn!' For a moment her dark eyes flashed at him, but her voice remained calm. 'I'm not a missionary, humble or otherwise; I'm simply a healer, a doctor.'

'A very dedicated one, it seems.'

'Perhaps.'

'But since you make no claims to be a saint you can, perhaps, relax tonight and enjoy yourself?' He re-filled her glass; she didn't object.

'I hope to enjoy myself; after all, you do have a reputation.'

'Do I, indeed?'

'You most certainly do; at least, so I have already been told.'

'You shouldn't believe everything you are told. Who has talked about me?'

'Alex and Paul.'

'Paul! I'm surprised! When did you talk to him?

'This morning. I went shopping and bumped into him in the supermarket. I found the place confusing and he was helpful.'

Unicorn smiled. 'I can imagine it. He's the perfect little housewife, isn't he? He's found his rightful place in life, at last, as Rupert's wife.'

Chastity didn't laugh, but instead regarded him seriously with her unfathomable dark eyes. 'I know his behaviour does seem laughable at times, but I admire him for having the courage to be himself.'

'Maybe, but that doesn't stop him from being spiteful. You have to remember that he doesn't like me. He never has.'

'Have you known him for a long time?'

'Yes, we go back to Oxford; the same college in fact. We both read English and we were both involved in drama. He hadn't come out then, so I thought that he was simply a stupid and affected prig pretending to be what he wasn't.'

'And so you were unpleasant to him?'

'Whenever I could get the chance, which was quite often. It wasn't kind of me, but then, I'm not particularly kind. He spread some malicious gossip about me and I challenged him. Naturally, he ran away. I'm surprised to know that he's still doing it.'

'I doubt if he said anything more than the truth.'

'Which is?'

'That you enjoy attracting women but you're never faithful to them. He only wanted to warn me, as Alex did. Is it so wrong?'

There was a strange glint in the tawny eyes that looked fiercely at her. 'Not entirely,' he replied at last. He spoke quietly, but she could tell he was angry. 'But another way of presenting the truth might be to say that I've never met a woman who was worth my fidelity. Nor have I ever met a woman who would want me to be faithful to her.'

'Not even Alex?'

'You hardly know Alex. She might not be the same as your cousin remembered her. You shouldn't condemn on unreliable and insufficient evidence.'

She smiled at him, unexpectedly. 'I have no wish to do so.'

'Then don't be afraid to get to know me. I promise I won't rape you, although I might be tempted, since you're such a sexy woman, as they say. I don't imagine that you realise how tempting you are.' As he looked closely at her, he frowned. 'But perhaps the truth is that you do, but you don't care. I can't decide, in fact, whether you're an angel or a devil.'

'You use strange words,' she began.

'You're a strange person. I'm determined to get to know you, I warn you.'

'But you said that I should get to know you and not listen to malicious gossip. So far, however, I've learned very little, except that you're an investigative journalist. What does that mean? What do you actually do?'

'I investigate scams, frauds, et cetera. I reveal the unpleasant and often hidden truth to the gullible public.'

'And do the public want this? Do they like it?'

He shrugged. 'They seem to; at least, they pay a lot for it. At the moment, I'm doing a series of investigations for a television company.'

'And what is that concerned with?'

'Mostly with many of the dubious activities of the sex business. I don't suppose that you're aware that many young girls are smuggled into this country with the promise of jobs and then find themselves forced into prostitution. They become sex slaves, with little or no hope of getting out of it. There are some very unpleasant people involved.'

'Surely they must object to your looking into their activities?'

'If they realised what I was doing, they most certainly would, but obviously I do try to keep my investigations secret, although I have had one or two sticky moments.'

'You risk your life, then?'

'I doubt if they would actually kill me.'

'But you can't be sure.'

'No, I suppose not.'

'I see.' Looking steadily at him, she said no more for a moment. Her lack of reaction puzzled him. Suddenly, she asked quietly, 'Why do you do this work?'

'It's my job.'

'You weren't forced into it, were you? You must have chosen it, therefore. So, why did you?'

For a second, he felt baffled. 'Why, indeed?' he asked himself. 'I'm not sure that I did actually choose it. I was offered the chance to do an investigation. It sounded a bit more exciting than the political commentary I was doing and the pay was good, so I took it. As I was successful, I continued with it. What other reason could there be?'

'I thought you might want to help people and to discover truth. Don't you?'

At that moment, to Unicorn's relief, the waiter arrived to deliver their main dishes. This gave him time to consider a suitable answer. But what answer would be suitable for this unusual young woman? As the waiter moved away, he became aware that she had not been diverted, but was still waiting for an answer. He laughed. 'Truth? And what is that?'

She smiled. 'Hardly an original answer, I'm afraid; as you may remember, Pontius Pilate made it first.'

'Now you're going to preach at me. I thought it would come out at some point.'

'Not at all. I'm only trying to get some information. Do you really care about the truth? Are you seriously looking for it when you investigate?'

'Truth in a limited sense, perhaps. But, even then, it's very difficult to be sure.'

'But surely you care about the people, like these unfortunate girls you were talking about. Don't you want to help them?'

'I leave that missionary work to others. They're often too stupid to help; in any case, I'd probably make things worse.'

'Do the people, your public, want to have these revelations?'

'They seem to. My articles and my programmes are pretty popular.'

'But does anything good result from your revelations?'

He shrugged. 'Rarely, I imagine. People enjoy having their sympathetic emotions roused. They agree how dreadful it all is. They feel better, then, without having to do anything about it: "how shocking", I expect they say. You can hardly believe that there are people who behave like that, can you? Then, with the comforting belief that they would never do things like that, they twiddle the knob and look for fictional sex and violence, which is much more exciting.'

'You sound very cynical.'

'Perhaps. But that is what I believe is mostly the truth. And you did say that you were interested in the truth. Or would you rather that I pretended to be a noble crusader with the most altruistic motives?' His smile was mocking.

'Why should I? We would never get to know one another that way.' She met his sardonic look without flinching.

'You might not like what you discover. Doesn't that worry you?'

'Why should it? There is probably an equal chance that I shall discover things that I like.'

'I suppose,' he mocked her, 'that you are, after all, one of those naïve people who believe that there is good in everyone, just waiting to be discovered.'

'Sometimes I think that one finds what one is looking for.'

'Precisely, and it is, therefore, very likely that one will be deceived.'

'But it is also possible that I'm not deceiving myself. There may be good where you would deny the possibility.' Smiling, she looked directly at him.

'Well, then, let me put your doubts at rest.' He took a long drink from his glass of wine and then turned to look at her. 'I'm selfish and faithless. I enjoy the good things of life: good food, good wines, travel, personal comforts and, above all, the solace of attractive women. I'm willing to work hard for short periods, provided that the work is interesting and well rewarded. I've never felt myself committed to anyone and I don't want to be. I can be kind if it is in my interest to be so, but I feel no obligation if it isn't. As far as I know, that is the truth, so you have been warned. What do you say?'

For a few moments she seemed to consider what he had said, then she replied with a smile, 'I should think that you are fairly accurate. At least your estimate of yourself is less malicious than Paul's and less sentimental than Alex's. But I'm not really in a position to judge. I've only known you for a couple of days.'

'Are you willing to risk knowing me longer?'

'Why not?'

'Aren't you afraid that I might break your heart? Isn't that what they're all telling you?'

'They're assuming, aren't they, that I have a heart that is willing to be broken?'

It was his turn to ponder over her words and to consider her carefully. 'I'm not sure that you have,' he said finally. 'But I'm damned sure that you're one of the most attractive and tantalising women I've ever known. As I said earlier, I think you're either very good or very bad. I wonder which it is?'

'Are you willing to risk finding out? I ought, perhaps, to warn you that, although I have a heart, I'm a woman with a vocation but—'

'That sounds a bit more encouraging,' he interrupted her.

'Don't be too romantic!'

'That's the first time any woman has ever said that to me. I like it.'

'I'm afraid, interesting though this is, we'll have to get back to more mundane matters,' she suggested. 'The waiter is hovering with the menu.'

To his surprise, she chose a solid English pudding with custard sauce. 'I've a longing for some stodgy English food,' she explained.

The rest of the meal passed quite quickly, without any further soul searching. Unicorn was determined to be his most entertaining and Chastity seemed content to be an attentive listener. Soon after ten o'clock, however, she suggested that they should leave.

As they came out of the restaurant, they discovered that it was raining heavily. Leaving Chastity sheltering in the doorway, Unicorn hurried off to find a cab. His search only took two or three minutes but, as he approached the doorway again, he was startled to find Chastity talking to a tall, fair man wearing a dark overcoat. As soon as she saw Unicorn, she said something to the man, who, with a quick goodbye, disappeared into the crowd.

As he led her to the waiting taxi, Unicorn exclaimed, 'You didn't waste much time!'

'What do you mean?'

'Simply that in less than five minutes you seem to have found another admirer.'

'Oh, no; that was someone I work with.'

'I thought you'd only just arrived in England?' He couldn't understand why he should feel so suspicious, but he did.

'I've worked with him before. When he saw me standing in the doorway, he was pleased to know that I had come to England and we would be working together again.'

'He went off quickly.'

'He was in a hurry. He has an important appointment.'

'Is he a doctor, too?'

'He is a great healer, but our organisation has sent him here on another, even more important, mission.'

It was quite clear that she didn't want to say any more, so

Unicorn felt unable to ask her any further questions. *Why should I care?* he asked himself. A disturbing thought came into his mind. *Surely I can't possibly be jealous?* There seemed to be no straightforward answer to that.

As soon as the taxi came to a stop, Chastity leapt out quickly, so quickly that Unicorn thought she might be intending to vanish without more than a quick goodbye. To his surprise, she didn't, but waited until he had paid the taxi driver, then invited him to come up for a coffee. Was it possible, he wondered, that she was not as invulnerable as she appeared?

'Where? Are you inviting me to the kitchen?' he asked as they hurried up the steps and through the front door. It had stopped raining but the air was still very damp.

'No, in my room. I equipped myself this morning, with Paul's help, so I want to display my new possessions.'

'Fine!' He waited while she found her key and opened the front door of the flat.

As they were walking along the corridor towards the living room, she stopped suddenly. 'Please understand that I'm only inviting you to a cup of coffee; no more.'

'Understood.' He smiled.

As she walked into the living room, she stopped abruptly. A man, strange – at least to Chastity – was stretched out comfortably in the armchair opposite to the door. He was dressed in a dark, formal suit with a white shirt and tie, although the tie had been loosened. As he stood up to greet her, she saw that he was taller and broader than Unicorn and that his smooth, dark hair was tinged with grey. He wore a ready, practised smile as he moved to meet her. Before Chastity could answer him, Unicorn spoke over her shoulder.

'Hello, James. Sorry to disturb you.' As Chastity moved aside, Unicorn greeted James with a somewhat mocking smile. 'We've just been out for a meal. Came home a bit earlier than usual.'

At that moment, Alex came hurrying in, carrying a tray with a *cafetière* and mugs on it. In contrast to her visitor she was informally dressed in a black velvet housecoat and slippers. As she saw Chastity and Unicorn, she stopped abruptly. 'I didn't think you would be back so soon.' As neither Chastity nor Unicorn made any reply to this, she continued quickly. 'I'd better introduce you. This is James Macmillan, my boss and good friend. James, this is Chastity Brown, my new tenant and a cousin of an old school friend of mine. And, of course, you and Unicorn already know each other.'

Stepping forward, James, still smiling, gripped Chastity's hand firmly and announced that he was delighted to meet her. It was clear to Chastity, however, that Alex was far from being at ease.

'Why don't you join us for coffee?' Alex asked brightly. 'There's enough for all of us.'

'Thanks, but no thanks,' Unicorn said firmly, before Chastity could answer. 'Chastity has promised me a coffee, chiefly because she wants to display her new acquisitions, so I'm keeping her to her promise.'

Undecided, Alex turned towards Chastity. 'Unicorn's right,' Chastity added swiftly. 'I do want to show off my new belongings.'

'Well, we'll say goodnight then,' James said. 'I hope to get to know you better, Chastity, some other time.'

Unicorn leaned against the closed door of Chastity's room and looked around curiously. It was large, simply furnished and very austere. Everything had been stowed away and the surfaces were bare except for two finely-carved animals on a shelf and a crystal ball, which shimmered with many colours as the light was reflected from it. Then he saw the most striking ornament – a magnificent woollen divan cover, woven in a most intricate pattern from many vivid colours. 'This is beautiful!' he exclaimed, as he walked nearer to examine it more closely. 'How did you get it?'

'An African lady made it for me. She wanted to show her gratitude because I had saved the life of her small grandson, or so she said.'

'Hadn't you saved him?'

'Yes, I suppose so, but at almost the same time I failed to save another woman's baby daughter, so I couldn't feel triumphant.'

'You can hardly be blamed for that.' Sensing her sorrow, he would have liked to comfort her, but he didn't know how to do it.

It was not something he was accustomed to doing, and Chastity gave no sign of wanting him to do so. Nevertheless, their eyes met and, for a brief moment, he felt closer to her than he had done all evening.

'It is a terrible experience to hold a dying baby in your arms and to know that you are helpless.' Her voice was quiet and unemotional but he could feel her pain, reluctant though he was to do so.

'I've never had such an experience, but I'm sure it must be painful.' *Nor have I ever had an experience like this*, he thought.

Without answering him, Chastity turned away and walked over to the table in front of the window. 'I'm very proud of my purchases. Come and look.' She spoke in her normal voice, pointing to a new coffee machine and elegant china displayed on a brass tray.

'Very impressive.' He had to smile at her obvious, almost childish pleasure. 'A change from the wilds of Africa, I imagine.'

She returned his smile. 'It's all prepared. I only have to switch it on and in minutes the coffee will be ready.' Having pressed the switch, she drew the curtains and sat down on a chair beside the table. 'Make yourself comfortable in the armchair.'

While they waited, he studied her again. Yes, she was very beautiful and extremely desirable. She seemed friendly, but his instinct warned him to hold back from his normal reaction to a situation such as this.

Suddenly, she broke the silence, 'I was surprised to find Alex's boss here at this hour. They must be very good friends. You have met him before, haven't you?'

'Often.' He smiled mockingly. 'I'm afraid, my dear Chastity, that you're still too innocent. They're not friends, but lovers, and have been so for two or three years. I expect he'll spend the night here, or part of it. He often does.'

'Why don't they marry?' The coffee was ready and she began to pour it out.

'Because he's already married.' Unicorn took the proffered mug. 'He's been married about twenty years and has a couple of children.'

'Does his wife know?'

'Probably. I suspect it's one of those secrets that everyone knows.'

'Alex seems to be wasting her life.'

'Don't waste any sympathy on her. She's schemed for this. He's been a great help to her in her career, and her next big promotion will be almost entirely due to him. Of course, she may drop him soon after that. Who knows?' He sipped his coffee appreciatively. 'This is very good. I hope you're not shocked to know the truth about Alex?'

'Not shocked, just sorry. I wish she hadn't thought it necessary to give me the wrong impression. Nevertheless, she is unhappy, you know.'

'She may be, but it's not because of me. Whatever went wrong went wrong before she met me. Do you believe me?'

After a moment's silence, she replied slowly, 'I think I do.'

'Thank you, but you mustn't forget I'm a villain. Remember, as Hamlet says, "one may smile and smile and be a villain".'

She surprised him by laughing. 'I think that might apply even more to James Macmillan. He certainly smiles a lot.'

'Be careful. Don't let Alex hear you.' For a few minutes they sat in friendly silence, enjoying their coffee, when abruptly his dismissal came.

'I'm afraid you must go soon. I have work to do tonight.'

'Very well; I'll go without protest as long as you promise to meet me again.' Standing up, he walked towards her and put his mug on the tray. He was tempted to kiss her, but he knew it was not the right time. Instead, he took her hand and put it to his lips. 'Goodnight, my angel. Do you promise to meet me again?'

'Yes, if you're sure that is what you want.'

'I'll ring and arrange something for the weekend.' With a wave he was gone, sure that this was his best exit.

Alex's Second Dream

That night, Alex had another memorable dream. Once again, she was an observer and not a participant.

She was walking in a beautiful garden on a warm spring day. The sun was shining in a cloudless sky of deep blue. A slight breeze, delicately perfumed with the scent of blossom, gently stirred her hair. The soft, green grass was starred with daisies. Blue forget-me-nots clustered around the trees. Crimson tulips and golden daffodils vied with one another. Although she could not see it, she could hear the soft, soothing sound of water falling in a fountain. Purple pansies and yellow primulas snuggled together in little hollows. Many of the trees were covered with softly-scented pink blossoms, some of whose petals were gently drifting towards the ground.

Noticing a bench under one of the trees, she sat down on it, content for a moment to enjoy the peace and beauty of her surroundings. It was then that she became aware of something completely unexpected. The garden, which stretched as far as her eyes could see, seemed to be peopled with small children and babies. There were several little groups of toddlers happily playing, and close to her bench there was a cradle in which a baby was lying peacefully asleep. Nearby, there were other cradles sheltered under the trees.

At first she thought that the babies and toddlers were unattended, but then she became aware of shadowy white figures that seemed almost to float about the garden, obviously caring for the children and the babies.

Intrigued, she stood up and walked on. As she approached another cradle, she stopped to watch the baby. This was a chubby baby with pink cheeks and curly fair hair. He was smiling happily and crowing cheerfully as he kicked his feet and waved his hands, apparently delighting in his new-found powers. She, who had never had any interest in babies before, was entranced by this one.

After a while, she reluctantly tore herself away from the baby and wandered on towards a small hillock, which seemed to be the centre of the garden. At the top of the hillock there was a weeping cherry tree, heavy with deep pink blossom. Under the tree there was another bench, on which a woman was sitting. The woman was wearing a cloak of deep blue material, bluer even than the sky, which fell in graceful folds around her, parting at the front to reveal a gown of deep rose pink. The woman was gazing down at a cradle placed near her feet and her bright, golden hair fell in loose curls to her shoulders.

As Alex came nearer, the woman suddenly raised her head to reveal a pale, delicate face of haunting beauty. More impressive than her beauty, however, was her air of tranquillity and the loving welcome of her smile. For a brief moment, Alex happily imagined that the smile was for her, but she almost immediately realised that the smile was not for her but for someone else who was approaching.

There was something familiar to Alex about the figure who was approaching in his robe of delicately changing colours. As he came nearer, she saw clearly for the first time his beautiful face, surrounded by golden curls. It was the angel, Xaniel, whom she had seen in her earlier dream.

He was carrying something carefully in his arms and, as he came nearer to the woman in blue, Alex saw that it was a tiny baby wrapped in a shawl. This baby did not look happy, as had the other babies she had seen. On the contrary, it was pale, emaciated and apparently lifeless.

Her heart stabbed with pity, Alex watched as Xaniel knelt before the woman and offered the baby to her. 'Mary, Mother of God,' he said softly, 'here is another rejected baby needing your love. Before it could be born, its mother had it removed. Now only your love can restore its life.'

Suddenly it was clear to Alex that the woman must be the Virgin Mary. She watched as Mary gently took the baby, wrapped the thin shawl more closely around it and then held it tenderly to her breast. While she did this, her tears dropped gently onto the baby's tiny face. The baby opened its eyes briefly, then seemed to relax into the arms that were holding him so closely and compassionately.

Alex felt her own eyes fill with unaccustomed tears. She, too, longed to hold the baby to her breast and comfort it.

Having handed over the baby, Xaniel stood up and, just as he did, Alex glimpsed another figure moving swiftly away. It was a woman carrying a baby. She, however, was not wearing a robe, but an ordinary summer dress and there was something familiar about her. Just as she moved away, Alex recognised her. Although there were subtle differences, she was convinced that the woman was Chastity Brown. Before she could call to her, however, the woman had vanished and Xaniel was making his farewells.

'I must leave you, dear Mother,' he said. 'I have been sent on a mission to Earth and I must not delay any longer.'

As he spoke, he vanished. The beautiful garden vanished, too, and Alex woke up with her eyes still full of tears, tears which she was amazed to find were real. 'Why ever should I have such a dream?' she asked herself. 'I don't know any babies and I've certainly never thought about a heaven for babies, or for anyone else for that matter! And why do I feel so unhappy? It's ridiculous!'

As she sat up, she remembered her vision of Chastity. Why on earth had she dreamed of Chastity in heaven with a baby? Suddenly, the answer occurred to her. It was, of course, not Chastity but Caroline, her cousin, who had figured in her dream. Chastity's account of what had happened to Caroline must have been the origin of her strange dream. That tragic story had upset her more than she had admitted even to herself. She felt ashamed to admit that, years ago, she had envied the beautiful and attractive Caroline, who had seemed destined for success. The story of her terrible end had swept away all feelings except pity and, strangely enough, anger at the thought of such a waste of potential. If such things could happen to a good and talented person, what point could there be in life? Obviously, her brain had tried to supply her with a compensating theory. Unfortunately, however, her waking mind could only dismiss it as a fantasy. It would be better, she decided, not to dwell on such thoughts.

Chapter Five

'Hi, there! Mind if I join you?'

Startled, Chastity looked up from the bowl of cereal she had just poured out for herself in the kitchen. She had been expecting to have a solitary breakfast. Dot – it had to be Dot with that violently red spiky hair – was standing in the doorway, wearing a dark blue satin kimono splashed with vivid birds and flowers. Her scarlet lips were parted in a friendly smile that was almost as striking as her kimono.

'Of course not!' Chastity smiled back at her.

'I rather believe I owe you a bit of an apology,' Dot remarked cheerfully as she advanced into the kitchen.

'Do you?'

'Yes. I didn't give you proper instructions about the loo, et cetera. Alex was pretty furious with me, I can tell you. Apparently, I "exposed a well-brought-up young lady to unnecessary embarrassment." So I'm sorry.'

Chastity laughed. 'No need to worry! At least as a result I met Rupert in all his glory, with only a towel to protect him. Perhaps I should thank you.'

'Lucky you!' Dot set out a bowl for herself. 'Not many have seen our Greek god at such close quarters! Forbidden territory, alas! What a waste, don't you think? Still, you do have the ever-fascinating Unicorn to console you, or so I've been told.' Pouring out some cereal for herself, she settled down opposite Chastity. 'Where is he, by the way?'

'Where is who?'

'Unicorn, of course!'

'Why should I know?

'Oh, God, I've put my foot in it again! I'm always doing that. Sorry.'

'I'm not sure that I understand you.'

'Well, I saw Alex earlier this morning and she told me that you had brought Unicorn back with you last night. And she sort of implied...' She paused as if uncertain and looked nervously at Chastity. 'Sorry again; it's none of my business.'

'I see.' Chastity, she was relieved to hear, didn't sound annoyed. 'Your information was correct, but what Alex inferred from it was not. Unicorn did come back with me. He had coffee in my room and he left just after eleven.'

'By which time, I imagine,' Dot remarked, standing up to put some bread in the toaster, 'Alex had already retired with James. Obviously she imagined that you would behave in the same way.'

'It seems so, but she was wrong.'

'It must have been a somewhat unique experience for Unicorn. How did he take it?'

'He went quietly after I had promised to meet him again.'

Dot looked admiringly at her. 'You must be a miracle worker! I think I'd better ask you for a few tips. In the meantime, shall I put a slice in the toaster for you?'

'Please. I'll make some coffee, if you're agreeable.'

'That sounds fine. We'll have a nice, friendly chat. You can be my agony aunt. I certainly need one.'

'I'll try, but I doubt if I'm qualified for that. By the way,' she asked as she began to make the coffee, 'where's Eva? If she's in, do you think that she would like a cup of coffee?'

'Eva? She's on holiday until tomorrow, isn't she? With Max, I thought.'

'She was supposed to be, I believe, but she came back on Wednesday night. The holiday had apparently been cut short, as Max had to go to New York unexpectedly. They'd travelled home earlier. He'd left her at Heathrow and she came back to the flat alone. I felt she wanted to talk to Alex, so I left them. I haven't seen Eva since.' She stopped speaking as she realised that her words had had a considerable effect on Dot, who was standing as if transfixed, holding a piece of toast in her hand.

'Christ! What a tragedy!'

'A tragedy? Hardly that, surely?'

'Of course, you don't know Eva. She'd pinned all her hopes on this holiday with Max. She's been the top model for his magazines for two or three years now. That was a slippery slope, hard to keep her footing on, but for the last few months they've been an item and, when he invited her on this holiday, she really thought she'd made it. I do believe that she actually thought she'd come back with a ring on her finger. It didn't really seem likely, but one never knows. Now she's going to be devastated.' After offering Chastity a piece of toast, she sat down to butter her own vigorously.

'I'm not sure that I understand.'

'Well, she's reached the big "3-0" you see. Between ourselves, I think she's probably past it. It's always been a struggle for her to keep her figure and her looks. She took to drugs at one time, I've been told, but now I think vodka's her favourite consolation. If Max has chucked her, it'll be all downhill for her from now. She's probably been drinking steadily since Wednesday night.'

'So it wouldn't be a good idea to offer her a coffee?'

'Definitely not!' Dot buttered her toast. 'She's probably sleeping it off. There'll be hell to pay if we disturb her.'

'It all sounds very sad.'

'Life is sad, don't you think? When we're young we think we've got lots of chances and lots of time, and suddenly we get to our thirties and realise that time's running out and we seemed to have missed our chances or put them off for too long. We keep going by trying not to think about it. But you can't always do that, can you?' Suddenly, Dot didn't sound cheerful any more.

Chastity looked quickly at her. 'Has something upset you?'

'Nothing's changed. I'm just feeling a bit morbid, that's all. I've haven't lost my job. I haven't broken up with Richard, my long-standing boyfriend. But last night I suddenly woke up in those dreadful small hours and this frightening thought came out of the blue: what the hell am I playing at? What future is there for me? What do I want, anyway?' She shrugged her shoulders hopelessly and began to spread marmalade thickly on her toast. 'Silly, wasn't it? I suppose most people feel like that sometimes. Don't you think?'

She looked up and found herself looking into Chastity's beautiful, dark eyes. She felt that although this strange, calm young woman might not share her feelings, she understood and sympathised. It seemed easy to talk to her. Without waiting for

Chastity's answer, she continued, 'To be perfectly honest, I'm getting unpleasantly near to the big "3-0" myself and I think it's time I tried to sort a few things out, if it isn't already too late.' She paused, wondering if she had already said too much.

'I'm not sure it's ever too late, unless we think it is, so what is worrying you most?' There was genuine concern expressed in Chastity's quiet tones.

'Lots, really. But I suppose that the most important question is "what on earth should I do next?" God may know, but I certainly don't.' Dot ran her fingers through her spiky hair, with the result that it became even spikier. 'You see, Richard and I have drifted along for ages. I suppose I just assumed that we'd get married one day or make some permanent arrangement. It didn't seem possible while Richard was still studying, so I didn't worry. We were enjoying ourselves and there was plenty of time, so what the hell?' She stopped to take a bite of toast.

'So what has changed?'

'Suddenly, there isn't any time. Richard has just been offered a registrar's post in a big hospital up north near where his parents live. It's a splendid opportunity, so he didn't hesitate. He didn't consult with me. He'll be gone in about a month.'

'Leaving you behind. Is that what you mean?'

'That's for me to decide, apparently. He says that I can easily get a job in the same hospital, or at least in another one nearby, and he'd like me to. It seems that he wants us to carry on as before.'

'But you don't want to?'

Dot didn't answer immediately. Chastity waited patiently until, finally, Dot spoke. 'I thought I did at first, even persuaded myself it would be good to have a change, but now I'm not so sure. Would you be willing? What do you think?' Before Chastity could answer, Dot continued quickly, 'Sorry, I had no right to involve you, especially as we've only just met. I'm simply desperate to talk to someone, especially someone who might be objective.'

'I'm quite willing to try.' Chastity smiled reassuringly at Dot. 'Doesn't it really depend on what you want for yourself in life?'

'That's just it. I'm not sure. In the middle of the night, I realised that I wasn't even really sure what sort of a person I am. I thought, "I've lost myself." That sounds crazy, I know, but that's what I thought. Perhaps I should forget all about such silly thoughts?'

'I certainly don't think so. You can't simply pretend that you haven't asked yourself that question. It demands to be answered, and it is dangerous to ignore it. I believe that each one of us is unique and has a unique destiny. True happiness lies in discovering that and then living it out.'

'I imagine you've probably done just that. But I've been pretending for so long that I don't know whether I can stop it, or even if I want to. But I won't waste any more of your time with this rubbish. I'm sure that you've lots more important things to do.' After quickly finishing her coffee, she seemed about to stand up.

Putting out a hand to restrain her, Chastity said, quickly, 'Don't run away now. This is important. What are you really trying to say?'

'Well, you've asked for it,' Dot replied after a moment's hesitation. 'It all goes back years. I was very ambitious when I came to London to train years ago. Everyone had expected me to train in the local hospital in the town where I lived. But that didn't satisfy me. I was sure I could do better, and I proved it. I was thrilled when I got here.'

'What went wrong?'

'My bubble burst. I quickly realised that I was no longer the personality I had been at home, but just an insignificant, mousy little girl from the provinces who had managed to scrape into this prestigious hospital. I couldn't stand it, so I gave myself a makeover. Result: the Dot you now see – loud, cheerful, lots of make-up, bright red hair, clothes to match. Quiet, mousy Dorothy has been completely buried.'

'And which one loves Richard?'

Dot shrugged her shoulders. 'I haven't a clue.'

'Perhaps it's more important to ask, "which one does Richard love?" '

'Dot, I suppose, since he's scarcely met Dorothy, or not very much, anyway.'

'And so you're afraid to give up your job and go north with him. Perhaps even afraid that, if you do that, you'll lose Dorothy for ever.'

Dot stood up. 'You're right! I've never admitted it before, even to myself. I'm afraid that I'll be giving up everything I have here for nothing much.'

'Does that mean' – Chastity also stood – 'that you're afraid, too, that Richard doesn't love you? Is that it?'

After pausing for a moment, Dot answered, slowly. 'Yes, I suppose that's it. You're right.' It seemed like a revelation to her. 'If he loved me, now would be the time for him to offer me a permanent relationship, preferably marriage. Is that what you think?' Without waiting for an answer, she continued, 'I have a secure job where I am and good prospects of promotion. Why should I give all that up for nothing? I've been an idiot far too long. Thanks for listening; you've helped me to see things more clearly. I'm afraid I'll have to rush now – I'm late already – but thanks.'

Placing her hand on Dot's arm for a moment, Chastity gently restrained her. 'Don't be too hasty. Please give Richard a chance before you condemn him; perhaps you should let him see more of Dorothy.'

'You mean I've been too successful at being a good-time girl?'

'It may be. You still have some time. Make use of it.'

'You're an angel!' Dot exclaimed. 'I'm glad I talked to you. You've helped me to see things more clearly. See you again soon. Bye for now.'

Left to herself, Chastity returned to her interrupted breakfast. She had little to do until four o'clock, when she had rather rashly agreed to have tea with Paul in his flat. When he had explained to her that Rupert had to go north on a business trip and would not be back until late, she had sensed that he was lonely and so had accepted his invitation.

Promptly at four o'clock Chastity knocked at the door of Paul's flat, sure that he would appreciate punctuality. The door was opened immediately by Paul, elegantly dressed in a pink shirt with a Regency style frilled cravat and purple trousers. He was delighted to see her. 'Come in, darling,' he said, in his precise, high-pitched tones. 'It's good to have company, especially when Rupert's away until some ghastly late hour.'

He led her proudly into their living room, where the table was laid for afternoon tea in front of the fire. It was covered with a dainty lace-edged cloth, and the elegant china had fluted gold edges and a pattern of roses. There was a matching plate of wafer-thin sandwiches and another of little iced cakes.

For a moment, waves of nostalgia swept over Chastity. 'That looks lovely!' she exclaimed. 'I haven't seen a tea like that since I left home. It's very kind of you to invite me!'

Pleased, he stood, smiling with his hands clasped in front of him. 'I thought you would be the right person to appreciate it, although, unfortunately, not many people do these days. I do think, however, that we should try to maintain standards, don't you?' Before she could reply, he gave a little wave of his hand and motioned her to a seat in the armchair. 'I won't be a minute, darling. I'm just going to brew the tea. I think it should be absolutely fresh, don't you?' He bustled off into the kitchen.

Chastity leaned back in the chair, which was very comfortable and decorated with a chair back embroidered by Paul. She had already discovered that embroidery was his chief hobby. It was all a little bizarre and unexpected but strangely restful.

He came in, carefully carrying a teapot that matched the cups. Putting the pot down, he prepared to pour out the tea. 'Milk and sugar, darling? Help yourself. Don't be shy. I thought you might be feeling a little homesick. This isn't home, of course, but we do our best.'

'You certainly do.' Chastity helped herself to a delicious sandwich and a fragrant cup of tea. Paul sounded rather like a fussy maiden aunt, and she hardly knew whether to laugh or cry. It was, perhaps, a strange parody of home, but it was comforting and she smiled gratefully at him.

Placing two lumps of sugar in his cup, Paul stirred his tea carefully and then took a delicate sip. 'I always buy the best-quality tea. I think it's worth the extra, don't you?' He tasted a sandwich with obvious satisfaction.

Chastity agreed, although she had never thought much about the matter, at least not for a long time. 'I don't know what filling you have in these sandwiches,' she remarked, 'but they are truly delicious.'

'It's my own recipe. I'll let you have it before you go. I like experimenting in the kitchen. Rupert thinks I'm a bit fussy, but he enjoys his meals. He actually prefers it when I'm "resting" between shows because then I can really concentrate on our comfort. We are really very well suited,' he added, offering her another sandwich, 'although you might not think so.'

'I'm sure you are,' Chastity said decidedly.

'I expect it all seems a bit strange to you.' He leaned forward, putting his elbows on the table and resting his chin on his hands. 'I mean, with your church background. But I have very strict standards, you know, and so has Rupert. We don't in the least approve of some of the things your flatmates get up to. Not, of course, that I think that you are one of that sort, darling. Have a cake,' he said suddenly, offering her the plate of very attractive cakes. 'I made them myself this afternoon. I always think it's a good idea for one to keep busy, don't you?'

Chastity, hardly knowing how to reply to this stream of talk, accepted a cake and pronounced it good, proving her point by eating two more, much to Paul's satisfaction.

As soon as they had finished eating, Paul stood up. 'I'll clear away now,' he said, 'and then we can have a nice, cosy chat; that is, if you can spare the time?' Realising that he was really longing for that, Chastity assured him that she could easily spare the time. Refusing all offers of help, he swiftly cleared the table, reappearing finally to settle down in the armchair opposite her.

The question she had been expecting came quickly. 'I hope you had a good evening with Unicorn?'

Resisting the temptation to be too provocative, she replied, demurely, 'The food was good, the wine was good and the conversation pretty good too.'

'And how about Unicorn? Was he good?'

Was he malicious or merely concerned? she asked herself. Did it, in fact, matter? 'He was good, too. I took him back to my room for a coffee and he left just after eleven, without even trying to kiss me.'

'A reformed character, then?'

'I would doubt that. Perhaps it was simply my lack of charm.'

'I would doubt that. I imagine that now you think I was exaggerating and being malicious?' She noticed that his voice and attitude had changed. There was no affectation now.

'Oh, no. I don't doubt the truth of what you said. Unicorn himself boasted about his vices. He even boasted about his malicious behaviour at Oxford towards you. I'm quite sure that he was speaking the truth, and I can understand how you must feel about him.'

'He injured a very dear friend of mine, a woman, but that's all in the past now. I suppose, now you know the truth about him, you won't be seeing him again?'

'I have already agreed to see him again. He was very anxious that I should.'

'Was that wise?'

'I have a passion for truth, and I don't think that Unicorn has supplied much of that yet. I suppose I want to see behind the mask.'

'I thought you said that he had boasted of his vices?'

'But that was just the usual façade. He never revealed the frightened, wounded person who, I suspect, lies behind that.'

'Be careful, Chastity, darling! I think you're tending to romanticise our friend. He's not Mr Rochester.'

'And I'm not Jane Eyre.' Chastity smiled reassuringly at Paul. 'My job has trained me to study people physically and psychologically.'

'Ah, that's why you call yourself a healer? That's a bit upsetting for an odd person like me.'

'I don't believe you. I think you're comfortable with yourself. Of course, you still enjoy exaggerating a bit.'

'That's the actor in me.' He smiled mischievously. 'I can't give that up.'

'But you have found the right way of life for you with Rupert, haven't you? You love him and you're happy to be with him. And he quite enjoys your eccentricities.'

'If you're referring to my cookery and my embroidery, I don't see why anyone should object to them. I wouldn't object if you liked plumbing and carpentry. In fact, you'd be very useful.' He straightened his cravat with his slim, fine fingers, on one of which he wore a large Cornelian ring. 'We are having a delightful chat, aren't we?' The familiar Paul peeped out for a moment.

'And Rupert?' she asked suddenly.

'Ah, Rupert!' A shadow seemed to pass across his face. 'He loves me, but he gets irritated sometimes, as you have observed. It's hard for him, but it doesn't last.' He sighed. 'We all have our cross to bear. Rupert has his, and his is mine, too. Perhaps you understand?'

'I'm not sure that I do.' She didn't press him, however, being convinced that he didn't intend to say any more. Already he was putting on his mask again. She looked at her watch. 'I'm afraid I must go. I'm expecting a visit from a colleague soon. Thank you for a delicious tea.' She stood up, preparing to go.

He, too, stood up. 'Thank you for the cosy chat. I feel pretty sure now that I don't need to worry about you, darling. I know that I'm quite safe with you, but I'm not sure that Unicorn is. I must tell Rupert. He'll be amused.'

'Will you also tell him,' she asked bluntly, 'that you stopped acting with me and that I met the soul of Paul?'

Their eyes met. For an instance there was a complete silence, as if time had stopped, while Paul considered.

'You have told only a little about yourself,' he said at last, 'but our souls have met. I've trusted you. Please trust me.'

'I do.' Chastity kissed him gently on the cheek.

'Remember,' he warned her, as she was about to leave, 'that, although Unicorn may be wounded, as you think, he may still be capable of evil.'

'I know.'

'Good. Now hurry away, darling. You have your appointment and I have a special meal to prepare.'

Chapter Six

After her recent experiences, it was no surprise to Chastity to find yet another strange man in the living room of the flat. As she entered the room, he seemed about to knock on Eva's door.

'I don't think you should do that,' she warned him.

Startled, he spun round. 'Why the heck not? I've just flown back from the States and I've brought her presents, candy, perfume and a bunch of roses.' With a wave of his hand he indicated his expensively-wrapped offerings, which were lying on the table.

It was then that she realised that he must be Max. With interest, she looked at him. He was a broad-shouldered, slim-waisted man, casually but very expensively dressed. Vivid blue eyes stared back at her from a deeply bronzed, rugged face, which unexpectedly creased into an attractive, friendly smile. His short-cropped, crisply curling hair was white, so he was at least middle aged. His voice was deep and he had what she imagined might be called a transatlantic accent.

'Who the hell are you, anyway?' he asked, advancing a little towards her. 'Have we already met?' He looked at her with growing interest. 'No, I don't think so. If we had, I'm sure I would have remembered you.'

'We haven't met. I'm the new tenant. I took over Louie's room a couple of days ago.'

'I guessed we couldn't have done. You know Eva well?'

'Not really. I've only met her once, but I was told that it would be wiser to leave her alone at the moment.'

'I guess I know her better than you. I'm grateful for your advice, but I don't think I'll take it.' Walking towards Eva's door, he hammered firmly on it. 'Let me in, honey. It's Max. I've just gotten back from New York.'

'Go away.' Eva did not sound encouraging.

Undeterred, he rattled the door handle. 'Don't be like that, honey! I've come straight here from Heathrow.' Still no response. 'I've brought you some presents. Don't you want to see them?' He tried to turn the handle. 'Come out, honey. Don't stay there sulking. You'll like what I've got. Honest, you will. I've brought your favourite candy, your favourite perfume and some gorgeous flowers; don't you want to see them?' Once again, he tried to turn the door handle.

After a moment's reflection, Eva spoke again. 'Don't come in. I'll be out in a few minutes.'

'What did I tell you?' Max turned triumphantly towards Chastity, who had waited to see the outcome. 'She never could resist a present. She just wants to doll herself up. She doesn't like to be seen unprepared.' He settled himself comfortably in an armchair.

Deciding that it was time for her to go, Chastity began to walk towards her door.

'Stop!' Max said suddenly as he jumped to his feet. Startled, Chastity obeyed him, turning towards him. For a long moment, he surveyed her from top to toe. 'Why the heck,' he asked unexpectedly, 'do you fasten your hair back in that hideous knot? It looks as if it could be beautiful.'

Without waiting for her permission, he walked up to her and quickly removed a few pins, so that her hair fell, dark and shining, to her shoulders. She was too surprised to protest. 'Sorry, honey. I simply couldn't resist it. I photograph women, you see,' he said, as if that explained everything. He looked at her admiringly. 'It's perfect, just as I thought. Deeply dark, but not quite black, and with those exciting red and gold tints. I've never seen anything quite like it. Who gave you that hairdo?'

'God.' She looked directly at him, smiling slightly.

'God?' For a moment he was nonplussed. 'That's a new one to me.' Then he laughed. 'I see. You're joking, honey. You mean it's natural?'

'I'm afraid so.'

'And those eyes? Are they natural, too? Not cleverly tinted lenses?'

'No lenses. They, too, are just as God made them.'

'Well, I must say He did a good job.' He looked at her with

growing admiration. 'Complexion natural, too? No artificial boobs?' A little horrified, she shook her head. 'The natural woman! Christ, this is a miracle!'

'Every human being is a miracle,' she retorted.

'Sure.' He dismissed that. 'But you're an extra-special miracle. You're the answer to my prayer. The woman I've been looking for.'

At this moment, Eva's door was flung open and she emerged. With her golden hair piled up elaborately, her face most exquisitely made up, her perfectly-rounded breasts seeming to be about to emerge from her short, tight-fitting top, she was a miracle not of nature, but of art. 'I actually thought you had come to see me, Max, but I was obviously mistaken.' She spat out the words, clearly controlling her anger with difficulty.

Thinking it might be wiser to disappear, Chastity began to walk away, but, with an imperious gesture, Eva stopped her. 'Don't go, Chastity darling; Max might not like it. After all, you are the answer to his prayer; the woman he's been looking for.'

'Don't be silly, honey,' Max said quickly. 'That was business. This is pleasure. I've come straight from Heathrow just to see you and to bring you your presents – some candy and perfume from New York and red roses from the florist.' He pointed to the packages still lying on the table. 'I chose the finest roses they had just for you, honey.' He held out the roses to her. For a moment, Eva hesitated, and then she snatched the bouquet from him, tore off the wrappings and flung the flowers across the room.

'Keep your fucking roses,' she screamed, 'and your fucking candy and perfume. I don't want them. They mean nothing. Why don't you give them to her?' She pointed at Chastity. 'She'll probably appreciate them.'

For a moment, there was silence. Chastity, feeling herself drawn into something she could not understand, could not think of an appropriate reply. Even Max seemed temporarily at a loss for words.

'Well, why not?' Eva asked him. 'She's the answer to your prayer, isn't she?'

Trying to placate Eva, Max moved towards her. 'Honey, you're making a big mistake. You're not understanding.'

Ignoring him, however, Eva turned her attention towards Chastity. 'You bloody bitch!' Her voice was full of venom. 'You can't leave any man alone, can you? Isn't Unicorn enough for you? I told Alex she shouldn't have accepted you. You make me shudder. You're one of those bloodless, high-class tarts. I know your sort. You can stick the knife in and still remain a lady.'

Chastity remained silent, still unable to think of an appropriate reply.

Max protested. 'You're getting it all wrong, Eva. You're not seeing things straight. Try listening.' Turning towards Chastity, he apologised. 'I'm sorry. Eva's a bit over the top. Perhaps if you went away…?'

Chastity was only too ready to agree, but, before she could move, Eva advanced towards her. 'Don't you dare to try to wriggle out of everything. At least have the guts to admit the truth.'

'There is no truth to admit.' Chastity looked straight at her. 'I've scarcely spoken to Max.'

'Liar!' Eva screamed. She lunged towards Chastity as if she would attack her, but, catching hold of her arm, Max forcibly restrained her. 'Let me go!' she yelled, trying to pull herself away from him, but, putting his other arm around her, he restrained her even more firmly.

'It's time to stop, before you do something you'll regret.' His voice was steely.

'What is going on?' Alex's voice startled them all. Standing in the doorway, calm and immaculate as always, she was staring with amazement at the scattered roses and at Eva struggling furiously in Max's arms.

'Eva's having one of her outbursts,' Max explained. 'She discovered me having a friendly talk with Chastity and she seemed to think that was a sufficient excuse for scratching the poor girl's eyes out.'

'Why don't you tell the truth, you fucking liar? She was making up to you and you were loving it.' Eva's golden hair had fallen down in a mass of tangles. Tears mingled with mascara were running down her cheeks. 'You seem to think that I'm a complete fool.'

'Fine. If it's the truth you want, then you can have it. I've humoured you far too long.' Max's blue eyes were steely now and his voice had an angry rasp.

'Don't!' Suddenly afraid of what he might be about to say, Chastity moved forward.

'Keep out of this, honey. This is between Eva and me,' Max warned her. 'She's had it coming for a long time.'

Chastity turned towards Alex, seeking some support, but Alex, settling herself comfortably in an armchair, legs crossed, seemed prepared to enjoy the scene.

'Well, don't say I haven't warned you, honey. Since it's the truth you want, you can have it.' As he spoke, he released Eva, who didn't move but stared piteously at him. 'I did actually say that Chastity was the answer to my prayer, but it wasn't meant in the way you seemed to think. Although, of course, if we get better acquainted, she might just be that, too.' He spoke slowly, obviously enjoying himself, and it wasn't pleasant to hear. 'What occurred to me when I looked at Chastity was that she is exactly the girl I need for my next big promotion. It's amazing!'

'What about me? Shouldn't you use me? I'm your chief model.' Eva's voice was little more than a whisper.

'Only till the end of the year. Remember? Your contract has to be renewed then.'

'Do you mean that you won't renew it?' Eva could hardly speak; her voice was choked with sobs.

'Not on the same terms, I'm afraid, honey.'

Suddenly, anger overpowered Eva again. 'You bastard! You've been making use of me all the time.'

Max only smiled. 'It's the way of the world, darling. Fashions come and fashions go. The latest idea, in New York and in the States generally, is for a complete change. One of the biggest dress firms has been doing some research and has come forward with the idea that many women now want something different.'

'Do you have to go into this now?' Alex asked, coldly. 'This is hardly the time or the place.'

'I'm sorry,' he apologised, 'but Eva obviously needs to know, and this is as good a time as any, in my opinion.' Turning towards Eva again, he continued, 'It appears that women in the US want to be natural and feminine again. They are demanding that their clothes should be attractive and modest. It's taking on in a big way over there, and I want to be the first to introduce it here.' He smiled at her as if this explained everything.

'I don't understand. What has that got to do with your double-crossing me?'

'I'll spell it out for you. Big boobs, especially artificial ones, are out. Belly buttons are out. False eyelashes, obviously dyed and tinted hair, et cetera, et cetera. They're all out, honey, as from next spring.'

'I could change,' Eva offered. 'I have before.'

'The trouble is that it's a bit late now, honey. Not so easy to change. And the public will want someone new.'

'Like Chastity?'

'Like Chastity,' he agreed maliciously.

'I knew it would be bad having that bitch here.' She turned towards Alex, screaming again. 'Why the fucking hell did you let her come here? She's not one of us.' Without waiting for an answer, she rushed into her room, slamming the door behind her. Her screams and sobs could still be heard.

Standing up, Alex faced Max. 'Did you have to do it in that brutal way?'

He only shrugged. 'Why not? She's been asking for it for months; years, if the truth be told. I thought that, if I took her on holiday, it might do her good. But she was so bloody paranoid, every time I even looked at another woman, that I was glad to have an excuse to get away.'

'Then why did you come here? Why didn't you at least leave her alone?'

'Because, whether you believe it or not, I've always had a soft spot for her.'

'You mean while she was still profitable, don't you?'

He laughed. 'Put it that way, if you like, but the fact is that I came straight here from Heathrow, bearing gifts and an invitation to dinner. I thought that might cheer her up. But I only had to have a quick word with Chastity here and you saw how she reacted. Crazy! How can a guy cope with that? Why should I?'

Without bothering to reply to him, Alex turned to Chastity.

'I'm very afraid she may take an overdose, as she has done before. Do you think it's possible?'

'Perhaps I should go and see what I can do.'

As Chastity moved forward, Max intervened. 'I wouldn't do that if I were you, honey. You're not exactly the flavour of the month, are you?'

'I'm not sure if that would be a good idea, after all.' Alex sounded even more worried.

'My advice is to leave her to get over it. The more you react, the more fuss she'll make.' Max picked up his jacket, clearly intending to leave. 'In the meantime, I'll go and find myself a solitary dinner, unless, of course, either of you would care to join me. No? Perhaps not. I guess it might be risky.' As he came up to Chastity, he stopped. 'The offer's still open. What do you think? It could be very profitable for both of us.'

'The answer is "thank you, but no".'

'OK, honey, the choice is yours. But here's my card. If you change your mind, just give me a bell.' He smiled at them both, cheerfully. 'I'll leave the presents for you both.'

Just as he was moving to the door, the front doorbell rang loudly, startling them all. 'I'd better go and see who it is,' Alex said quickly, only too glad, it seemed, to get away from the problem of Eva.

As she opened the front door, she found herself confronting a stranger. In the dim light, she could only see that he was tall and fair-haired and wearing a long, dark overcoat. 'Chastity is expecting me,' he explained. His deep, musical voice had a strange effect on her. She felt it was familiar, but she knew that she had never met him before. Nevertheless, it seemed to stir strange, undefined memories.

Feeling embarrassed, she turned away quickly. 'She's in the living room,' she told him. As they walked along the hall to the living room door, Eva's sobs became audible. 'I'm afraid we're in the middle of a rather distressing crisis,' Alex said, feeling that some explanation was necessary.

When they finally entered the living room, Max was discovered alone, gathering up the despised roses. Chastity was no longer there, but a sudden scream from Eva made it clear where she must be. 'Don't you dare come near me, you bitch. I hate you.'

'I'm afraid that Eva's in a very hysterical state about various things that have gone wrong in her life recently,' Alex began trying to explain.

'She's also bloody hung over, drugged out of her mind and quite paranoid,' Max interrupted coldly.

'And you haven't helped,' Alex retorted angrily.

'No reason to, honey.' He was quite unperturbed. 'When I tried she threw my gifts into my face, so I told her the brutal truth, as I should have done months ago; she's simply passed her sell-by date.'

'Perhaps I can help?' the stranger suggested quietly. Without waiting for their response, he entered Eva's room, closing the door firmly behind him.

Max stared at Alex. 'Who the hell's that guy? Why should he think he can help?'

'I haven't a clue, but since he's Chastity's colleague, I imagine he's a doctor. They belong to some missionary society and have just come from Africa, I believe.'

'Christ! You don't mean to tell me she's a doctor?'

'Yes. Not quite the sort of person to be your new model!' Alex obviously enjoyed giving him the information.

Max only grinned. 'Why not? Why shouldn't she want to earn some extra money and have a good time, just like any other girl?'

'And end up like Eva, I suppose?'

'Why should she? Eva had plenty of fun and plenty of money. She just acted like the good times would never end, and then she tried to escape the truth with drink and drugs and useless men. It's not my fault she's ended up here with scarcely any money and less of a future.'

'Why did you take her away?'

'I suppose I thought to cheer her up a bit.'

'Well, it didn't. The poor fool actually thought you cared about her and that the holiday might lead to something more permanent.'

'Never marriage.' Having finished picking up the roses, Max laid them on the table. 'I don't do marriage any more. Twice is enough. Eva knew that. But, if she hadn't been so fucking paranoid, something might have come of it. But she was and it didn't.' He looked ruefully at the roses. 'These are going to die.'

'I'll get a vase. At least we can save the roses.' On her way to the kitchen, Alex stopped. 'Listen!'

'To what?' For the first time, they both noticed the silence. Eva's hysterical sobs and screams had completely stopped.

'Well, thank God for that!' Relieved, Max sat down. 'I didn't want another suicide attempt just now.'

Returning with the roses in a vase, Alex found him still sitting there. 'How about a drink?' she asked.

'I could certainly use one.' As they sipped their drinks, they waited in silence for some news of Eva. It was some twenty minutes later, however, before Chastity came out, followed by the stranger.

'How is she?' Standing up, Alex faced Chastity. 'Will she be all right?'

It was the stranger who answered, in that voice that seemed so mysteriously familiar. 'She's asleep now and will probably sleep till morning, when Chastity will be able to give her further help if she needs it.' As he spoke, he turned to go and Alex could not see his face.

Max stopped him with a quick gesture. 'You can't go before we've thanked you. You're not just a doctor; you're a fucking miracle worker.' He turned towards Alex.

'I agree,' she responded swiftly. 'Won't you both at least stay and have a drink with us?'

'Thank you, but I'm afraid we can't. Chastity and I have an important appointment.' As he spoke, he went through the door into the hall, followed by Max, who was announcing that he would have to go. Picking up her jacket, Chastity hurried after them.

When Alex reached the front door, Max had already disappeared. The stranger was waiting for Chastity. Turning, he helped her with her coat. 'Thank you, Jan,' she murmured.

It was at this moment that Alex saw him clearly for the first time. Never before, it seemed to her, had she seen any man so beautiful; that was the word that sprang to her mind. It was not only the perfection of his physical features, but it was the sense of a rare spiritual and intellectual power that overwhelmed her. As he looked at her she felt that he was reading into her soul and she shrank away with the painful feeling that all the shoddy lies and evasions of her life were known to him.

It was only for a few brief seconds, for almost immediately he turned towards Chastity and, taking her by the arm, he propelled her gently through the door. With a quick wave, they were gone.

As she returned to the now deserted and silent sitting room, Alex was haunted by that face and those eyes. They couldn't possibly be familiar to her, and yet they were. Why? As she sat alone in the quiet room, she suddenly seemed to hear herself saying, 'I'll know that face if ever I see it again.' She knew then, without doubt, that Jan's face was the face of the angel she had seen in her two vivid dreams which had haunted her ever since. But how could this possibly be? It was unsettling to dream so vividly of someone she had never met, but it was frightening to meet that person.

What did it mean? She told herself she was being silly and superstitious to think that it could mean anything; it had to be coincidence. Nevertheless, she could not help speculating. Who was this unusual man? What was his connection with Chastity? It was not surprising that Unicorn had so little success when he had a rival like Jan! It would be fun to tell him, she thought.

The unexpected ringing of the telephone interrupted her thoughts. It was Unicorn, wanting to speak to Chastity. 'Sorry to bother you,' he apologised, 'but I don't think she has a mobile.'

'I doubt it, but in any case she's just gone out. With a colleague of hers called Jan.' It pleased her to tell him this.

'Is he a tall, fair-haired bloke?' he asked after a brief pause. 'If so, she met him last night when we were coming out of the restaurant.'

'It seems to be the same man. By the way, when did you leave last night?'

'Straight after coffee, but you had already retired with James. Chastity was, I think, a little shocked by your behaviour.'

'I hardly think so. Do you want to leave a message?'
'No need; I'll ring tomorrow.'

The flat was silent again and she was alone with her disturbing thoughts.

Chapter Seven

When she opened her door in response to a gentle knock, Chastity was surprised to find Unicorn standing outside. 'I thought you were going to telephone me?'

'I did, last night, but Alex told me that you had just gone out with your colleague. She was somewhat maliciously delighted, I suspect, to be able to tell me how handsome he was. I hope you had a pleasant evening?'

'I did, thank you.'

'I imagined that you had, since Dot, whom I met when I first arrived here this morning, told me that you hadn't returned until the small hours. Is that true?'

'Yes.' She said no more, but turned the gaze of her luminous dark eyes on him.

He made an effort to continue as lightly as he could. 'So now you understand why I, like a grieving knight, have come looking for my faithless lady?'

She smiled slightly. 'That's very poetic but hardly the truth, is it?'

'If we're going to discuss truth again, may I come in so that we can do it more comfortably?'

'Why not?' She opened the door more widely, inviting him in. The room was unchanged, being as bare and unadorned as when he had last seen it, except for a portfolio lying on the table. Chastity was looking very beautiful in a long, loose robe, deep violet in colour. She had that remote air which had so challenged him when he had first met her. 'I've just made some coffee,' she surprised him by saying. 'Would you like a cup?' He watched her as she brought out two cups from her cupboard and filled them. 'I suppose Alex told you about Eva?'

'Yes.' Settling himself in an armchair, he took a cup from her.

'Then she probably also told you that it was my colleague,

Jan, who is a very skilled doctor, who quietened her down and eventually got her to sleep.' She sat down opposite him.

'Alex didn't tell me much. It was actually Dot who told me more about it when I talked to her about an hour ago.'

'Haven't you seen Alex, then?'

'Alex isn't here. Apparently, as soon as Dot came back from work, Alex handed the care of Eva over to her and went off for a weekend with James. Dot was rather relieved when you came back.'

'What if Dot hadn't conveniently come back?'

'Alex would have gone just the same. She usually gets her priorities right, as you know.'

'That's one of the things I've noticed since I came to London. People seem to be unwilling to take responsibility for others or to help others.'

He shrugged carelessly. 'Too many people living too close together, probably. It's a form of self-protection.'

'I suppose that may be the reason.'

Suddenly, he found her distant air, which seemed to imply criticism, very irritating. 'A sense of responsibility didn't stop you and Jan from going out for your evening's entertainment, did it? It didn't even make you hurry back. You apparently decided to trust Alex's sense of responsibility.' As soon as he had spoken he was furious with himself for revealing the unreasonable jealousy he felt.

Chastity, however, answered him seriously. 'In the first place, I had no doubt that Jan's remedy would work and that Eva would sleep for several hours. Secondly, we were not going out for an evening's entertainment but to work. We had a serious commitment to many people, some of them in greater need than Eva.'

'Are you telling me that you and he had serious work to do as doctors?'

'Yes. We are both doctors. Surely you realised that?'

'And Jan is your superior, as it were?'

'Yes; that is why I was sure that he could deal successfully with Eva.'

There were many questions he wanted to ask, but he put them on one side for a moment. 'Well, you were right. Jan did deal with

Eva. She apparently slept all night and she seems pretty sane this morning. But then you know that because you took her some breakfast, I believe.'

'How do you know?'

'After I talked to Dot, I went in to see Eva and had a chat with her.'

'I didn't know that you knew her.'

'Oh, I've known her for years. I was responsible for getting a room here for her when she was very down about a couple of years ago.'

'You seem to have been kind to her.'

'Don't sound surprised and don't take too rosy a view. I merely talked to her. There's nothing I can do for her. She ignored my warning two years ago and has succeeded since then in throwing away most of her assets – even Max, who has been amazingly faithful. She's been a bloody fool and she knows it.' He finished drinking his coffee and put down his cup firmly. 'What can anyone do for her? She's being trying to self-destruct for years. Now she's pretty much succeeded. So, what's left?'

'Her friends could try to show her that they still care about her.'

'You mean "love your neighbour" and all that crap?' He laughed. 'It doesn't work, Chastity darling. Believe me, I know.'

Although his anger and bitterness were only too evident, Chastity made no comment but deliberately changed the subject. 'I don't believe you came to me to talk about Eva,' she said, as she took his cup and put it on the tray. 'What did you have in mind?'

'You're absolutely right, of course.' His good humour was apparently restored. 'I've come to ask you if you are willing to keep your promise to see me again?'

'Of course I am. Have you anything in mind?'

'I was hoping you would have a meal with me tonight?'

'I'd be pleased to,' she began, then broke off and started again. 'The only trouble is that tonight is rather difficult, as I have to work with Jan again and for several more nights.'

'What hours are you working?'

'It won't be as long as last night. We won't be starting before ten, but I have to be punctual.'

'That might make a restaurant meal a bit tricky.' He considered. 'Why don't I cook a meal for both of us in my flat? We can arrange the time to fit in with your commitments. What do you think?'

She looked steadily at him. 'For obvious reasons, I'm not sure whether it would be wise for me to agree to that.'

He smiled. 'You don't want to believe all that other women tell you. In any case, I promise to be on my best behaviour. You see, I really want to get to know you. I'd like to have a chance to get to know you better. Surely you can't object to that?'

She looked steadily at him. Wisely, he made no more appeals. 'How can I refuse such an invitation?' she asked finally.

He stood up. 'Then you will come?'

'I will. What time do you suggest?'

'About seven thirty. I'm afraid I can't be ready before then. Shall I come and pick you up?'

'No, just give me your address and I'll get a taxi.'

After scribbling down the address on the pad she offered him, he went quickly, convinced that he would be foolish to linger.

Almost half an hour later, Chastity's solitude was again disturbed. This time it was Eva who wanted to speak to her. It was a very different Eva, however, from the one she had previously met. Wearing an all-enveloping black wrap, her face entirely devoid of make-up and her blonde hair hanging lankly, she looked exhausted and much older. It was hard to believe that a few hours could have made such a difference. Without waiting for an invitation she came straight into the room, shutting the door behind her.

'I've come to apologise.' Her voice was clear but strangely lifeless. 'I said some disgusting things to you, even when you were trying to help me. You might have thought that even I, stupid though I am, would have realised that Max was up to his usual tricks. But I didn't, and I'm sorry for accusing you. I also want to thank you and your friend for helping me. He's a wonderful doctor.' She paused, as if exhausted.

'There's nothing to forgive,' Chastity said quickly. 'You were ill and needed help.'

'A self-inflicted illness, I'm afraid.' Eva didn't seem to know what to do next. As if unsteady, she clutched the back of the armchair. 'Do you think I could have a cup of coffee?' She sat down suddenly in the armchair. While Chastity hurried to reheat the coffee remaining in the percolator, Eva sat silently with her eyes closed.

'I'm afraid you're still not feeling well,' Chastity remarked as she finally handed Eva a cup of coffee. Remembering that Alex had said that Eva had already tried twice to end her life, she was deeply concerned.

'I'm not going to do anything rash,' Eva answered, as if reading Chastity's thoughts. 'I've been that way before.' She took a sip of coffee slowly; then, lifting her head, she looked straight at Chastity. 'Did Unicorn come to see you after he'd been talking to me?'

'Yes, but he didn't really come to talk about you.'

'Of course not. I'm not important enough for that.'

'He said you were old friends. I'm sure he wants to help you, as any friend would.'

Eva smiled slightly. 'I'm not sure that he does, but perhaps he is trying in his peculiar way.'

'What do you mean?'

'Well, he did his best to convince me, as if I needed convincing, of my utter unimportance in the general scheme of things. Then he said it didn't really matter, as everything is futile anyway. His final suggestion was that, if I was broke, I should try to sell my story to a Sunday paper. When I said it probably wasn't interesting enough, he agreed, then offered, for a share of the profits, to tart it up for me and make it acceptable.'

'How could he be so cruel?' Horrified, Chastity sat down opposite Eva.

'I'm afraid that Unicorn doesn't find it too difficult to be cruel, although he can sometimes be kind when it suits him. It's funny, isn't it, but I really think I came to tell you this as much as to apologise. I don't know why I'm bothered, except that you and your doctor friend were the only people who tried to help me. Please, don't let Unicorn deceive you.'

'It's kind of you to worry about me.'

'I'm not sure that I am really being kind. It may be that I only want to hurt Unicorn back. But when I remember that dishy doctor friend of yours it hardly seems necessary to bother. It's obvious that Unicorn hasn't got a hope in hell, and I'm glad that he hasn't.'

'Jan is my colleague; my superior, in fact,' Chastity explained; 'not my lover.'

'That doesn't mean he can't be, surely? It would certainly teach Unicorn a badly-needed lesson.'

'That will never be,' Chastity replied firmly. 'We are close only because of our work.'

'Your work matters a lot to you, doesn't it? It's not simply a means of making money?'

'That's true.'

'If I'd had something like that, I might have been different. But then I'm probably too selfish and too vain, as Unicorn says.'

'If Unicorn says things like that, I don't think you should pay much attention to him. I know that life can be changed, that people can change.'

'You sound very sure.' Eva suddenly looked interested. 'Are you speaking from experience? Has your life been changed?'

'Yes, very much so, several years ago.'

'And you believe that I could change mine? That I'm not completely hopeless.'

'No one is. Everyone has their part in the plan of the universe. Sometimes we only find it through failure and loss. You must search, but you also have to be humble.'

Eva was looking deeply into Chastity's dark, luminous eyes, as if she saw her answer there. 'Thank you. I shall think very seriously about what you've said. About time, too, some would say. Already, I've made one decision. It was half made when I came to see you, but talking to you has helped me to make it completely.'

'What is that?'

Eva stood up. 'I've decided to live, although I'm not sure how. But I do feel sure that it's better to be a living failure than a dead one. There's still hope if you're alive. Thank you for the coffee.' She moved towards the door.

'Come again, whenever you want to,' Chastity replied warmly.

'I will. In the meantime, I think I can trust you with Unicorn, although I'm not sure how much I can trust him with you. He may have a hard time.' The door closed behind her and Chastity was left to ponder over what she had learned that day.

It was Dot who, over a shared sandwich lunch, provided some of the missing pieces. After a couple of hours spent in a nearby beauty salon, Dot had been somewhat miraculously transformed into a natural brunette, whose short, silky hair framed a delicately made-up face. A far more attractive version of Dot – or was it Dorothy? Although she was not sure which, Chastity expressed her approval of the result.

Dot was pleased. 'It's much easier to live up to at least.'

'What does Richard think?'

'He hasn't seen it yet, but he will do this evening, when we have a date. He probably won't notice.'

Chastity laughed. 'Only if he's blind.'

'The really important thing is,' Dot said earnestly, 'that I've begun to change or perhaps just to revert to type. I've been thinking a lot since we talked together.' She hesitated, obviously wondering if Chastity would still be interested.

'I would love to know your conclusions, if you want to tell me.'

'I'm bursting to tell you. I don't know anyone else who would understand.'

'So what are your conclusions?'

'If Richard won't make a decision, I must.'

'Have you decided to go north with him then?'

'No. I love my job here and I have a pretty responsible position. It would be quite wrong to walk out simply because Richard calls. I really ought to give a good notice of my intentions, so I'm going to tell him that if he still wants me after about six months I'll be prepared to join him, but only if he makes a definite offer of marriage. After six months apart we should both be sure how we feel. If we don't, then we never will. What do you think of that?'

'It sounds sensible to me. I think you're being very brave.'

'Half of me is dead scared, but it's the only thing I can do. I'm quite certain that I really want a husband and a couple of children.

Probably most girls would agree, if they had the guts. But I can't afford to wait much longer, and if Richard still doesn't want to commit himself I must find someone else who is. I suppose that's not very romantic. Does it sound too calculating to you?'

'It sounds not only sensible but also possible. Don't let him scare you.'

'I certainly won't. Tell me, though, haven't you ever thought you might want that?' There was a silence, which seemed to Dot much longer than the few seconds it lasted. 'I'm sorry,' she apologised. 'I had no right to ask.'

'It is not an option for me,' Chastity said slowly and firmly.

'Does that apply to Unicorn?' Dot ventured to ask.

'Of course. I was interested to meet him; that was all. And now I'm very intrigued to know more about him.'

'What do you mean?'

'Why is he so involved with everyone here? Why does he come and go as he chooses with his own key?'

'I'm not really the right person to tell you. I've only lived here for eighteen months and I've never been in the centre of things. Louie, your predecessor, was, but she left suddenly after a flaming row with Alex. I knew her, she found me my room here, but I was never in her confidence. I've always spent most of my spare time with Richard, so their goings-on never bothered me. Unicorn has never been interested in me, so nobody was jealous, as they seem to be about you.'

'Do you think that Alex is jealous? Why, when she has James?'

Dot shrugged. 'He's a career move, that's all.'

'That's rather unpleasant, isn't it? Do you think she might still want to be involved with Unicorn?'

'I honestly don't know, but there does seem to be something that still holds them together, although it must be about four years since they separated. I sometimes wonder if it's money. Perhaps Unicorn has a share in this flat.'

Chastity frowned. 'It seems that the truth is hard to discover. What about Eva? Do you know anything about her?'

'Not a lot, except what is obvious. But I do believe that Alex and Unicorn have manipulated her even more than Max... Why are you so interested?'

'I've had a strange feeling, ever since I came here, that something is very wrong. I want to understand what it is. That's why I've accepted Unicorn's invitation for me to have supper with him in his flat tonight.'

'Have you actually agreed?'

'Yes, but with certain conditions.'

'You'd be wise to make sure that they're kept. Remember the old rhyme!'

'What's that?'

'"*Will you come into my parlour,*" said the spider to the fly. "*It's the prettiest little parlour that ever you did spy.*"'

'Fortunately, I'm not a simple fly.'

'No, somehow I don't think that you are. How are you going to get there? Is he going to pick you up?'

'I told him I would get a taxi, since I don't know the way.'

'That's fine, but what's more important is how are you going to get away?'

'I have to leave at ten o'clock because I'm working with Jan again.'

'That's perfect. Jan can collect you and make sure you get away, otherwise you might find it pretty difficult.'

'Unfortunately, Jan's not available.'

'But, surely, if you let him know…'

'That's not possible. I shall have to find another way. But don't worry, I will.'

It was not until later in the afternoon that a possible solution occurred to her. She would ask Paul, who had promised help if ever she needed it. Unfortunately, it was Rupert who answered the door. He looked handsome but not very encouraging; nevertheless, when she asked to speak to Paul, he led her quickly to their sitting room, calling Paul as he did so. Paul, hurrying in from the kitchen, greeted her warmly.

'I'm hoping you can offer me some sensible advice,' she said.

'We certainly will, if we can.' He looked towards Rupert, who nodded encouragingly. 'I'm just taken some scones out of the oven and made a pot of tea,' he continued, 'so why don't you join us? It'll be much more pleasant to discuss problems over tea, don't you think?'

'I simply can't say no.' Chastity smiled at both of them. 'I used to love home-made scones and it's years since I had one.'

'Good. It won't take a minute.'

Chastity was urged to sit down in an armchair while Rupert laid the table. In a few minutes, Paul came in with scones and the tea. After helping herself to butter and home-made jam, Chastity took her first bite. 'They're delicious! I'm afraid I'm going to be very greedy.'

'Now, tell us the problem,' Paul asked after a few minutes. 'Is it something to do with Unicorn?'

'How did you guess? With the hope of getting more information about him, I think I've agreed to something a little risky and I need some support.' Without giving them an opportunity to ask why she needed more information, she quickly outlined the situation.

'You're right. It could be tricky,' Paul agreed.

'The solution's simple,' Rupert exclaimed before Paul could say any more. 'I'll take you there and call for you at ten o'clock.'

'There's only one snag,' Paul added quickly. 'You'll have to ride pillion on Rupert's motorbike.'

'I don't think that will worry someone like Chastity. I promise not to take any risks. What do you say?'

'I've never done it before, but I think it should be fun. But don't I need a helmet?'

'That shouldn't be difficult.' Rupert stood up. 'I'm sure I can find you one. I'll go and look now.'

'I'm afraid I'm being a bit of a nuisance,' Chastity remarked to Paul, as she accepted yet another scone.

'Don't be silly, darling; you've made Rupert's day giving him such a chance to show off his newest bike, which, even to my jaundiced eyes, is quite magnificent. He's always been mad about bikes. One thing we disagree about. You've probably saved me from having to agree to a spin. I can't thank you enough, darling. I'll lend you my padded jacket to show how grateful I am.'

Chastity was soon satisfactorily equipped in a well-fitting helmet and Paul's jacket. 'I'm getting quite excited,' she said, looking at herself in a mirror.

'Perhaps it's only fair to warn you, darling,' Paul told her, 'that

Rupert used to race bikes before he became a highly-qualified and respectable engineer.'

'And before you stopped me,' Rupert retorted. 'But, don't worry,' he said, turning to Chastity. 'I promise to be really steady tonight.'

'I'm sure I can trust you,' Chastity said firmly, as she parted from them.

'Expect me at a quarter past seven,' Rupert called out as she went down the stairs.

'I was doubtful about your new friendship,' Rupert remarked as he and Paul went back into their flat, 'but I've changed my mind.'

'I thought you might when you met her.'

Chapter Eight

The living room of Unicorn's flat was surprisingly large and well furnished. As she looked around it, glass in hand, Chastity realised that it was a room with several functions. One corner, with desk, computer and all accessories, was obviously his office; another corner served as dining room; and the area in which she was sitting might be called the 'relaxation room' with its comfortable armchairs, bookshelves, television and DVD cabinet.

Unicorn, after greeting her with obvious but restrained pleasure, had led her to this chair, thrust a glass into her hand and had gone almost immediately to the kitchen to dish up the food. Having left her helmet and jacket with Rupert, she had arrived immaculate in her simple black dress and matching jacket, so Unicorn had naturally assumed that she had travelled by taxi.

What could one learn about him from this room? she wondered, as she looked around her. The furniture, the carpet and the soft furnishings were all simple but in good taste and obviously expensive. Money, it seemed, was no problem for him, either because he was so successful in his work or because he came from a wealthy background. She had the feeling that, if she wandered around and examined closely the few pictures and ornaments, she would discover that they, too, were valuable.

Perhaps Dot was right: money was the secret of his relationship with Alex. She was aware that all her new acquaintances were puzzled by her desire to know him more, especially when they had made so clear their unfavourable opinion of him. She had been warned and yet she persisted. Obviously, therefore, they were suspicious of her assertion that she was not sexually attracted to him. It was probably only the appearance of the undeniably handsome Jan that had made them sure of that, at least.

She had just begun to examine the books on the shelf nearest to her when Unicorn returned, carrying a large dish of food that smelt temptingly delicious. 'It's an Italian veal dish,' he informed her; 'tasty but not too over-sophisticated for you.' It was accompanied by salad and garlic bread. He placed the dish on the table, where two places were already laid with fine silver and crystal glasses, one of which he was already filling with more wine as she came to take her place.

'You're right,' she exclaimed. 'This is very good. I didn't expect you to be such a clever cook, although the risotto you gave me when we first met was good, so I should have been prepared.'

He laughed. 'It's a false impression I labour to create. I only know a few recipes, but I make a point of being very good at them. The only problem is that one must be careful not to invite the same people too often.'

'You didn't have to admit that.' She smiled at him. 'You should have left me in my ignorance.'

'The trouble is that you have this strange effect on me. You make me want to speak the truth. That can't be bad, can it?' He raised his glass. 'Let's drink to our continuing relationship and to truth.' She raised her glass to his, but without making any response. 'Does your silence mean, as I suspect it does, that you are doubtful? Doubtful of our relationship or of my ability to be truthful? Which is it?' His tawny eyes flashed a challenge to her.

'Without truth, there can be no lasting relationship.' Her dark eyes met his steadily.

'I intend to speak the truth about myself. That is why I was pleased that we should meet here, where no one can interrupt us. But, if I'm prepared to speak the truth, you also must be truthful. Is that agreed?'

'Of course, but it's for you to start, I think.'

'Agreed. But perhaps we should have a truce while we enjoy this food, which is best eaten hot.'

'And which certainly deserves to have our full attention,' she replied as she took another mouthful.

It was not until he had served coffee and brandy and they were comfortably seated in the armchairs that he began to talk seriously again. 'I wonder why you chose to come into the lion's den?' he asked her suddenly. 'I'm sure that you must have had many warnings, so isn't it rather foolhardy of you? Or are you simply so sure of yourself?'

To his surprise, she laughed. 'You're right: I have been warned. One person put the same idea to me, but not quite so dramatically. She suggested that I might be a foolish fly being tempted into the spider's parlour.'

'And what did you say?'

'That I didn't see myself exactly as a foolish fly.'

'And I'm not a spider. I'm too impatient to qualify as one.'

'You would much rather be regarded as a lion?'

'Definitely. And it might be wiser for you to consider me in that light.' He spoke casually, with a smile, but his eyes flashed and she was unsure whether his smile was truly friendly. 'Many people will tell you, I'm sure, that I prey on people, especially women. You have been warned.'

'Oh, dear! It sounds threatening. I promise to be very careful.'

'Don't forget that you have your name to live up to. If, in fact, that is your real name. Is it?'

'My name is Chastity. You won't find anyone who knows me by any other name. Chastity Brown, although we don't normally use surnames in the organisation for which I work. But Alex has told you that.'

'Alex only knows what your letter told her: that you are the cousin of her school friend, Caroline, who is dead and so cannot be referred to. There is no other confirmation, is there?'

'That is true. Caroline cannot vouch for me.'

'Then I must take your word for it that your name really is Chastity.'

'How suspicious you are! I have accepted that Unicorn really is your name, although that sounds even more unlikely.'

'There are many to vouch for it. But you are right. It is unlikely. That is one of the truths I'm prepared to tell you. Unicorn Jones is an entirely assumed name.'

'It always seemed too strange to be true, but everyone seems to accept it. Why?'

'It must be the power of the media.'

'Why did you assume it?'

'For several reasons. The first one, perhaps, to break away completely from my family. Any name would have done for that. But I also decided to take a name that would not easily be forgotten. That is a great asset for a budding journalist.'

'But why did you want to break away so completely from your family?'

'Do you really want to know these things, Chastity? Is it important for you to have the truth about me?' He leaned towards her, putting his hand on her thigh. His voice and manner had changed. 'Or wouldn't you much prefer it that I made love to you? I'm very good at that. It could be a great experience. I'm sure that I've never met anyone as desirable as you. And I believe that you find me attractive, even though you don't want to admit it. We have at least an hour before you need to go, if, indeed, you are still determined to go.' He leaned closer and gently brushed her lips with his, while his hand massaged her thigh.

Chastity remained strangely still and silent for a moment, then she firmly removed his hand, drawing back from him at the same time. 'I would rather hear about your family and why you changed your name; that is, if you're willing to tell me.'

For a moment he remained close to her, then, smiling slightly, he moved away and leaned back comfortably in his own chair. 'I believe you actually mean that, so I have no alternative but to try to satisfy the curiosity which was apparently the real reason for your coming to visit me. It was curiosity, wasn't it?'

'I suppose you might call it that, but I would rather say that I don't find myself willing to accept other people's views of you. They might easily be biased.'

'Thank you. That is at least slightly more flattering.' He took a slow sip of his brandy but seemed disinclined to say any more.

'When did you change your name?' she prompted him.

'Years ago, when I decided, in spite of my family's opposition, to become a journalist. My father is both very wealthy and very influential and has always had decided views as to how I should live my life, especially as I am his only son and heir. I think I was born rebellious – wicked, my grandmother would say – but, when I was young, I was forced to accept the right prep school and the right public school. I hated them both and was frequently in trouble but clever enough to escape being expelled. Tell me, you went to a public school, I believe. Did you like it?'

'Not much, but I took refuge in working because I already knew that I wanted to be a doctor.'

'Strangely enough, I finally decided that it might be more profitable to work hard. I did and gained an Open Scholarship to Oxford.'

'Surely that pleased your father?'

'Yes, but unfortunately it strengthened his belief that I should be best placed in the Diplomatic Service, as he had always intended. He didn't know, of course, how much I had already been corrupted.' He stopped speaking abruptly and took another sip of his brandy.

'Corrupted? Whatever do you mean?' Chastity turned to look at him.

He didn't answer her at first but finally replied, with a slight touch of mockery, 'It's a sordid story, Chastity darling, not really suitable for a pure soul like yours. I wouldn't want to spoil your girlish illusions.'

'How strange! When we first met, your aim seemed to be just the opposite. You wanted to tempt me into sampling the pleasures of London, to teach me how to enjoy life and to free me from my innocence! Don't you want to any more?' Again, she turned to look directly at him. Their eyes met.

'How the hell do you do it?' he asked with unexpected violence.

'Do what?'

'Don't pretend that you don't really know!' Turning towards her, he seized both her hands so fiercely that he hurt her. She did not, however, flinch, nor did she turn away from his gaze when he looked into her eyes as if he were trying to read into the depths of her soul. 'You have made me want to be honest with you as I've never wanted to be honest with any woman before. It's very mystifying.' Releasing her hands, he turned away. 'Admit it. You're really just the same as all the others. It's just that you're not only more beautiful, but you're also more successful at leading men on with your unbelievable indifference. You're a bit of a devil, I think.'

'I can't imagine why you are saying that.'

'It's obvious. Why else would you have come here tonight?'

When she didn't reply, he added impatiently, 'For God's sake, admit it. I've found you out. There's no point in pretending any more. You might as well tell the truth.'

'I came partly because I was curious, but, more importantly, because I am convinced that you have been hurt and wounded and need help before it's too late.'

Utterly amazed, he stared at her. 'Surely you don't expect me to believe that nonsense? You may be a missionary, but I'm not in need of your charity!'

'But you do believe it in your heart. You want to talk to me.'

She waited while he considered his reply. Finally, after draining his glass, he spoke without looking at her. 'All right, you can hear my sordid story. I'll have to leave you to decide for yourself whether or not it's true. You'd do well to remember that I am, by profession, a purveyor of lies and half-truths. Are you still willing to take a chance? Remember, you're in the spider's parlour. You may be more of a silly fly than you think.'

'I'm willing to take the risk.'

'Very well. In a way, it's a boringly familiar story these days. My corruption began when I was just fourteen and at boarding school. Contrary to what you might have expected, it wasn't brought about by a paedophile master, but by my housemaster's attractive wife. I was a virgin and a solitary rebel, more innocent than most of my contemporaries, I imagine. She was a perpetually unsatisfied whore. I believe that I was the first pupil she targeted. Before then, it had been her husband's colleagues who had more defences. She was very skilled and experienced and her appetite seemed to be insatiable. If I flagged, she had many interesting ways of arousing me. Our meetings became almost daily occurrences. Sometimes I hated it, but there seemed to be no way to escape her. I became obsessed, I think, kept in thrall in spite of myself. A stupid story, isn't it?' After offering her more brandy, which she declined, he poured himself another generous measure. He didn't seem to want to say any more.

'How did it end? Was there a scandal?' It was difficult to tell from her quiet voice how the story had affected her.

'No, that was somehow avoided. At the beginning of my Lower Sixth Form year, her husband suddenly moved to another school. I imagine that my headmaster must have become aware of the situation, but nothing was said to me. In addition to his normal desire to avoid any scandal, there would have been his dread of having to face the anger of my influential father.'

'What about you? How did you feel?'

'I was frustrated and furious but, at the same time, unexpectedly relieved, so I decide to work hard and to avoid any such entanglements in the future.'

'Then you went to Oxford?'

'Yes, to Magdalen College. I enjoyed my studies and threw myself into several university activities. And achieved a certain kind of popularity, I think.' Chastity remembered Paul's comments about him but said nothing. 'I behaved as many students and took what sexual satisfaction I needed without any commitment, however slight. I was determined to avoid another disastrous affair.'

'And did it work?'

'Yes, until my third year, when I had a big twenty-first birthday party, which pleased my vanity. One of the guests was a junior English lecturer. She was twelve years older than I was. She was obviously attracted by me, and I succumbed. She became the second important woman in my life. Although I was seven years older, I seemed to be as easily seduced and enthralled as I had been before.'

He turned towards her with a mocking smile. 'Poor Chastity! How can you possibly decide whether I am an outrageous liar or a pathetic victim? Am I simply appealing for your sympathy, a well-known way to a woman's heart, or telling the truth?'

'Perhaps neither is true, or perhaps both are?'

'Clever. I should have expected that.'

'Did you love this woman?'

'Love? It's not a word I use much. I'm not sure that I know what it means. Do you?'

'I could explain what I mean by "love" but we're not discussing that, are we? Tell me, was it you who ended the affair?'

'I suppose one might say that I did. She suddenly wanted a commitment which I'd never promised and certainly couldn't give. My father also became very pressing at the same time. I decided that the time had come for me to free myself. As soon as I had taken my degree, I left Oxford, changed my name and began the difficult start to my journalistic career. I was determined to cut myself off completely from my past life. My choice of name was meant as an added insult to my illustrious family. I don't suppose you can understand that, nor the feeling of freedom that it gives one.'

'I think I can a little. My life changed completely several years ago.'

'When you became a missionary, do you mean? Whatever prompted you to do anything like that? But then, I know you were brought up in a good Christian family. Your father, the vicar, would expect his daughter to accept a life of service to others. It seems delightfully old-fashioned but hardly real.'

'Things like that still do happen, even in the twenty-first century, among people who are very different from the ones you're accustomed to.'

'But then I'm only assuming that your father was a vicar. It was Caroline who was the vicar's daughter, wasn't it?'

'My change in my life had nothing to do with my father. I was compelled to realise that this was my vocation. And that accepting that was the only way to give purpose and meaning to my life.'

'And you actually think that life can have meaning and purpose?'

'Without that our lives are empty and unhappy. We are in danger of cutting ourselves off, not only from God but from other humans, and we are very alone.' She looked steadily at him with her dark, beautiful eyes.

'As I am; is that what you mean?' His attempt to sound sardonic failed even to himself. 'Aren't you being naïve to say that to me? Don't you even now understand that I'm a heartless seducer? Surely Alex, at least, has hinted to you how I have ruined her life?'

'Yes, but I don't necessarily believe her. I know you can be cruel, however, as you were to Eva this morning.'

'I offered the only hope I could think of: a chance to earn money, which she has always coveted. I even promised to help her.'

'Sometimes money isn't enough.'

'For you, Chastity, it obviously isn't, but Eva is greedy. Like most of us, she's devoted to Mammon, as you might say. I should know; I've served him myself for many years, with great success as you can see.'

'I can only see that you're very unhappy, and I pity you.' As she said this, she stood up. 'I'm afraid it's almost time for me to go.'

Standing up swiftly, Unicorn faced her. 'You can't go. I won't let you!'

'Surely you won't try to force me to stay?'

'No. I'll beg you, because I need you. I've talked to you as I've never talked to anyone else.' Putting his hands on her shoulders, he drew her close to him, looking deeply into the dark eyes raised to his. 'I believe that you can teach me something about love.' He kissed her with a tenderness that was both unexpected and unnerving. Gazing into his eyes, Chastity seemed unable to move away.

Suddenly, the doorbell rang loudly. 'Damnation!' Unicorn exclaimed. 'Who the hell can that be coming at this moment? A devil from hell, perhaps?'

'I'm afraid it's not so dramatic. It's my escort.' She moved away. 'He's come to collect me so that I don't fail to keep my appointment.'

'You witch! You've been deceiving me. You haven't trusted me at all! Is that the right behaviour for a Christian?'

'When Jesus sent out his disciples, he told them to be "as gentle as doves and as wily as serpents." I've only been trying to follow this advice. I've tried to listen to you without prejudice, but I've not suspended the use of my reason. Surely, you can't object to that?' Before he could answer, the doorbell rang again. 'You'd better answer it or he may think he has to knock the door down.'

'Very well.' He picked up her jacket before moving towards the door.

'Shall we meet again?' She sounded concerned.

'Certainly not for some time; perhaps never. I'm flying to Eastern Europe tomorrow evening and perhaps to Russia in search of some villains and their secrets.'

'That sounds dangerous. Please, take care of yourself.'

'Haven't you heard that the Devil takes care of his own? You're the one who needs protection, I think. Where are you going to find it?'

She smiled serenely. 'God looks after his own, too.'

As the bell rang impatiently again, Unicorn opened the door to find Rupert, resplendent in his leathers. 'What the devil are you doing here?' he asked furiously.

'Rupert kindly offered to take me to the place where I'm working with Jan,' Chastity explained quickly.

'Sorry to be so insistent,' Rupert apologised pleasantly, 'but Chastity insisted that she mustn't be late.'

'I see.' Unicorn turned towards Chastity, his tawny eyes flashing savagely. 'Don't let me keep you from your good work. You've had your entertainment. You fooled me cleverly. I'm sure that Paul will enjoy the story.' With ironical politeness, he helped her into her jacket. 'Goodbye,' he called out to her as she hastily followed Rupert down the stairs.

Chapter Nine

As soon as Rupert, still in his dressing gown, came into the living room for a late Sunday morning breakfast, he was aware of the tension in the atmosphere. The elegantly-laid breakfast table, the two perfectly-boiled eggs, the fresh toast, the aromatic coffee that Paul, immaculate in elegant shirt and cravat, was pouring into his cup all served to emphasise it.

Rupert recognised the signs only too well. A quick explanation was needed if one of Paul's emotional outbursts was to be avoided. He began carefully, while buttering his toast. 'I appreciated the coffee and the sandwiches which you left ready for me last night.'

'It was the best I could do. I'm afraid it became too late for me to wait up for you. I finally went to bed just before one. I appreciate that you gave me a quick phone call to inform me that you would be late, but I hardly expected it to be later than midnight.' Paul's voice was becoming shriller and higher – another bad sign. 'I do think that you might show some consideration, especially as I have an important audition today.' He took off the top of his egg with a fierce cut.

'I'm sorry there wasn't time for more than a very brief phone call.'

'Am I to suppose that Chastity's charms overcame you? Having rescued her from Unicorn, were you tempted to enjoy her company yourself, especially as silly old me was safely at home, studying his part? You never could resist a pretty girl, could you?' Picking up his knife, Paul seemed ready to stab Rupert with it.

'Shut up, for God's sake!' Rupert shouted, suddenly exploding. 'And stop letting your insane jealousy get the better of you. Just listen to the truth for once.'

'I will,' Paul replied with an attempt at chilly dignity, 'when you give me some truth to listen to.'

'OK. Here it is. I scarcely saw Chastity, except when I took her there and brought her back.'

'And where, pray, was "there"?'

'It was a grim-looking convent in the East End. Some nuns, with the help of volunteers, do a nightly soup and sandwich run for the homeless, some of them in the West End. Since two people had gone on holiday, Chastity and her doctor colleague, Jan, have volunteered to help them out. I thought it was pretty good of them.' He stopped to take a mouthful of egg and toast.

'I can't disagree with you, but I still don't see why you were away so long.' Paul was quieter, though still suspicious.

Rupert smiled at the memory. 'It was all completely overwhelming. As soon as I delivered Chastity, a boss nun – Mother Mark, they called her – came rushing up with arms outstretched. "Thanks be to God," she said. "My prayers have been answered. You've brought me another man." Chastity was as bewildered as I was until Mother Mark explained that the driver of the second van had just rung up to say that he had injured his right arm and couldn't drive that night. I was God's answer to her prayers! What could I say? If I didn't agree to drive the second van, a lot of miserable people would go without their soup and sandwiches that night. Surely you wouldn't have wanted me to turn it down?'

'Of course not, but couldn't you have spent a little more time on the phone and explained it all?'

'You'd better tell Mother Mark that. We were late already. She scarcely allowed me thirty seconds. God's work was all that mattered. And I think, perhaps, it is God's work, Paul. Believe me. I'm ashamed to think that I've been too selfish before to consider how many homeless and hungry people there are in this wealthy country of ours. I'm sorry I upset you, but I'm not sorry that I stayed and helped.' Looking at his partner, he hoped for an understanding response, but little seemed to be forthcoming.

Paul put down his egg spoon carefully on its plate and placed the butter knife neatly back in its dish. After that, he straightened his cravat and smoothed his cuffs, while Rupert waited. 'It seems that you had little alternative,' he said at last, 'but I would have been happier if you could have withstood this importunate nun long enough to give me a fuller explanation. Naturally, I was worried.' Before Rupert could reply he continued smoothly, 'I presume you brought Chastity safely home, or did her friend do that?'

'I brought her back. That was why I was even later, because she and Jan were much longer away than expected. When they did return, Chastity was very upset and Jan spent several minutes comforting her, after which he talked to Mother Mark, who later told me what had happened. It was very sad.' He paused to take several sips of coffee.

'What had happened?' Paul was impatient again. Rupert was often so slow in telling a story.

'Apparently, they had been taken to a girl, a child in fact, of about fifteen, who was giving birth in a doorway. Someone rang immediately for an ambulance, but the birth was going badly, so Jan and Chastity took over. The baby was born before the ambulance could arrive and while Jan attended to the mother, Chastity tried to revive the baby. Unfortunately, it died in her arms, which upset her very much.

'Mother Mark took Chastity into the chapel for a few minutes and also into the convent to clean up. In the meantime, Jan explained to me that although they had experienced much in the Third World, it horrified them to see so much suffering here, in one of the world's wealthiest cities. They had seen many children in Africa orphaned because of Aids but they had not expected to see so many "orphaned" in London because of the apparent indifference or even hostility of their parents. He spoke very calmly, but his words had a great effect on me. I seemed to see the world and myself quite differently.' He sat still, his breakfast apparently forgotten.

'Good God, Rupert, you're not going to tell me you've seen the light, are you?' Paul's voice was shrill and artificial again. He was obviously upset. 'Since you can't go to Damascus, perhaps you ought to go to church!'

'Of course not! It's got nothing to do with church.' Rupert resumed his breakfast. He didn't want to talk any more about it, since he felt quite unable to describe what he had experienced, especially as Paul, unexpectedly, seemed to find it amusing. 'I was only trying to explain why I was late.'

For a few minutes they continued their breakfast in silence, until Paul enquired, petulantly, 'What about Unicorn? You haven't said anything about him.'

'What about him?'

'Did your arrival upset him as I hoped it would?'

The malice in his tone annoyed Rupert. 'I can't understand why you just don't forget about him. Why can't you?'

'Because I think it's time he suffered a little as he's made others suffer.'

'Well, he definitely wasn't pleased to see me, but I had the feeling that it was Chastity who had upset him more. He was furious, but mostly with her, I felt.'

'Oh, dear, we'd better to continue to keep a friendly eye on her then.'

'She should be all right for the next week or two, as he's apparently going on a trip to Eastern Europe.'

'Perhaps, if we're lucky, one of the villains he is so fond of will assassinate him.'

'I wish you wouldn't always be so vindictive about him. I don't like it.'

'I'm sorry. You're right, of course. But some things are hard to forgive. And he still provokes me, whenever he can. You must have noticed that.'

'Of course I have. I'd have punched him on the nose before now, if you weren't always so strong against that sort of thing.'

Paul laughed. 'I might change my mind, especially if he tries to harm Chastity. I think she's an unusual young woman.'

'So do I, but I don't think that Unicorn has the ability to harm her. She certainly seemed to be in charge of the situation last night.'

'I'm glad to hear it.' Paul stood up. 'If you've finished, I'd like to clear away.'

'Leave it all. I'll deal with it all, just as you want it to be done.' Rupert grinned cheerfully at his partner. Reluctant though he was to relinquish his duties, Paul was finally persuaded.

'Are you all prepared?' Rupert asked. 'You're looking extremely smart.'

'I think so, but one can't be too particular, you know. One has one's reputation to maintain.' He straightened his cuffs carefully. 'I shall have to leave earlier than I intended, as Terry O'Dowd has invited me to lunch. He can be very helpful, but I'm afraid it means that you will have to have lunch by yourself.'

'No need to worry. I'll go for a spin on my bike and get a pub lunch in the country. It'll do me good. When do you think you'll be back?' he asked as Paul was leaving the room.

'I'm not sure, I'm afraid. It depends how things go. I'm sorry.'

'Don't worry. Good luck, anyway.'

'As you know, one doesn't believe in luck. If the part is right, it will be offered to one. If not, one is better without it.'

As Paul left the room, Rupert returned to his breakfast and to a leisurely read of the Sunday paper that Paul had discarded. It was over half an hour later when Paul returned, even more elegantly attired and finally ready to go.

'You're a bit early, aren't you?'

'I don't think so. I don't want to arrive hurried and dishevelled.'

'Let me know the outcome when you can,' Rupert said as they kissed goodbye.

'Of course I will.' Paul paused in the doorway. 'If you have a bit of time to spare, do you think you might make a quick call on Helen? Just to please me,' he added when he saw Rupert's frown.

'I'll do it to please you, but I can't think of any other reason. I hardly know her. She belongs to your past, not mine.'

'I appreciate how you feel, Rupert, dear, but she rang me last night and was very depressed. Stephen's in trouble again at school. I had to tell her I simply couldn't visit her today, but, if you just popped in, it might cheer her up.'

'I can't think why. Why the hell do you keep on bothering about her? It beats me.'

'Because,' Paul replied with considerable dignity, 'she was very kind to me when I had no other friends. Now that she needs a friend, surely you don't think it would be right for one to forget one's obligations, do you?'

'Of course not. Sorry. I'll go, if only to please you. Now get off quickly before you make yourself late. No need to worry,' he added, as he saw Paul look meaningfully at the still-littered table. 'I'm just about to start. I won't let you down.'

'I know that. You never have yet.'

'But if you hang about any longer I might be tempted to throw you out.'

With a quick wave, Paul vanished. 'One doesn't want to risk that,' he muttered, shuddering.

It was about an hour later that Rupert, now fully dressed and ready to go out, looked through the window and saw Chastity coming slowly along the street. She had given her arm to an old lady whom he recognised as Mrs Allen, who lived alone, he believed, in the semi-basement flat. They stopped for a moment to chat at Mrs Allen's door, then, as the old lady disappeared, Chastity moved towards the steps leading up to the main front door.

Leaning out of the window, Rupert called to her. 'Are you busy? I'd like to have a word.'

'Not particularly.'

'Good, then I'll come straight down.'

'Please come by the stairs. No ladders.' She smiled cheerfully up at him.

'Don't worry. I leave ladders to Paul in his dramatic moments.'

In what seemed an incredibly short space of time, he came running down the steps towards her. 'I wanted to make sure that you're all right,' he said, coming abruptly to a halt in front of her. 'I realised that what happened last night upset you a lot. I was very sorry but I didn't know what to do, except to bring you back as quickly as possible. I'm afraid I'm emotionally inadequate, as Paul often tells me.'

'You couldn't have done anything I would have appreciated more.' She smiled at him.

'I hope you're feeling better now?'

'Much. Jan told me this morning that he'd been to the hospital and the girl is recovering. The Sisters have offered to look after her when she comes out of hospital.'

'That's good news.' Rupert hesitated for a moment, then continued quickly, 'I wonder if you'd care to join me this morning? Paul's gone off for an audition, so I was thinking of taking a spin in the country, to a quiet pub where I know you can get a good home-cooked meal. What do you think? Would you be willing to join me?'

To his relief, she didn't hesitate. 'It sounds lovely, but you'll have to lend me the jacket and helmet again.'

'That goes without saying. Come up now and I'll kit you out. How have you come to know Mrs Allen?' he asked as they walked up the stairs. 'I've only spoken to her twice in two years. You've only been here five days and you're chatting like old friends. How do you do it?'

'I met her coming out of church. I offered her my arm, as I saw she found walking difficult. It wasn't until we were almost here that I discovered where she lives. I've promised to call on her tomorrow after work. She's rather lonely, I think.'

'I expect you're right. You might not have realised it, but last night opened my eyes to quite a lot of things. I wasn't very pleased to see how thoughtless I'd been for years. It was quite a shock. I tried to explain to Paul, but I don't think he understood.'

'He hasn't seen what you saw,' Chastity reassured him. 'If he had, he'd understand.'

'I expect you're right.' Rupert handed the jacket and helmet to her. 'I must say that they look better with trousers than with your party dress. However did you manage on that bike?'

'Not easily.' She laughed. 'That dress has had to accommodate itself to many situations.'

'Even to being covered with blood.' Immediately, he wished he hadn't mentioned that, but Chastity took it calmly.

'That's nothing. The stains have washed out.'

'Do you think that they'd mind me turning up again tonight?' he asked as they walked down the stairs.

'I'm sure that Mother Mark has already taken it for granted that you will. She would never believe that anyone would want to miss such a chance.'

'That's all right then.'

Less than an hour later, they were comfortably settled at a table for two in a quiet, old-fashioned country pub. Rupert had a pint of beer in front of him, Chastity a half-pint, and two home-made steak and mushroom pies had been ordered. After taking a long pull at his beer, Rupert put down his glass and leaned back comfortably. 'This is very pleasant, I think. I hope you aren't disappointed.'

'Definitely not. It's years since I've been in an English pub. Thank you for suggesting it.'

Rupert looked around. There were several other couples and, in the opposite corner, a family of four: mother, father and two children. 'I feel ordinary here with you,' he said, then stopped, embarrassed. *Oh, God, why did I say such a stupid thing?* he asked himself. But, as Chastity looked sympathetically at him with her dark, beautiful eyes, he felt reassured.

'It's being gay, you see,' he explained. 'I'm not trying to deny it and I'm happy with Paul, but it's not what I ever wanted or dreamed about when I was younger. I grew up in an ordinary happy family with two brothers and a sister, and I always imagined I would be like them. But I wasn't, although it took me some time to understand it. I hope you don't think I'm talking rubbish?'

'No, because I, too, suffer from being different, although not in that way. It's very hard, but one simply has to accept it.'

'I always planned to be like that family over there. You know, with a house, a wife and two or three children. I was never short of girlfriends, but I was never tempted to go very far with any of them. I told myself that I hadn't yet met the right girl. Then, one day, I fell in love for the first time, but it wasn't with a girl: it was with a guy. I broke it off after a few months. I was shattered. I went through a wretched time. It was Paul who rescued me. He made me admit the truth about myself and told me that I would only be happy if I had the courage to admit what I was. In the end, I agreed. We're happy, but sometimes the old dreams come back.'

'Is that why you quarrel sometimes?'

'Yes; I get irritated and angry, especially when Paul gets jealous. If a girl flirts with me, he thinks I'll leave him or something. I won't, but sometimes I can't stop wanting a family too. I suppose I'm just too bloody selfish.'

'That's not the whole truth. It's very natural to want children, but if, for some reason, you can't have them, then you have to find another way of satisfying your feelings.'

'You know what you're talking about, don't you? You're not a lesbian, are you?'

'No. There are other reasons for not having children. You have to accept that if you can't have your own there are many children who can be helped by your loving care.'

'I began to see that last night.'

'Good. Then come again and perhaps you'll get your answer. Perhaps the life you live with Paul, although good, is a bit narrow?'

The arrival of their pies prevented further serious conversation for some time, but, as he finally put down his knife and fork, Rupert returned to it. 'Paul gave me some damn good advice, but he ought to give himself some. He, too, still lives too much in the past.'

'What do you mean?'

'Well, you must have noticed already that he positively hates Unicorn?'

'I don't think I would use such a strong word as "hate".'

'You might if you heard him sometimes. It all goes back to his time at Oxford, which was pretty miserable, chiefly because of Unicorn, who found him a good subject for mockery. The one person who helped him and showed him how to believe in his talents was, surprisingly, a woman: a lecturer called Helen Wallace. He has a somewhat excessive attachment to her, still, and he still hates the man who made her pregnant and then left her. As a result, he continues trying to help her and her child.

'She had to give up her career and now earns a precarious living as a teacher of English to foreigners. The boy has turned out to be very difficult – autistic or something – so I suppose she needs help, but I don't think that Paul's the right person. Oh, hell,' he broke off suddenly, 'I can't imagine why I'm telling you all this. I don't usually confide in people, especially about Paul.'

'Don't worry.' Chastity smiled at him. 'People often confide in me, perhaps because I'm a doctor. But why are you so upset about this now?'

'Because, like a fool, I promised Paul I'd go to visit Helen this afternoon. She apparently rang him last night and he's worried because she's very depressed but he can't go today because of his audition. He seems to believe that a visit from me might help!' He finished his beer and looked dolefully at Chastity.

She laughed. 'Don't be so sorry for yourself. It isn't really much to ask, is it?'

'Perhaps it's not much, but I doubt if it'll be a success. I scarcely know the woman, I don't like her much anyway and I haven't a clue what to do with a difficult boy of about eleven.'

'Has Paul?'

'I very much doubt it, but he knows and likes Helen and anyway, he's much better at acting than I am.'

'Rot. You'll do fine. Don't think about it any more.' Chastity looked at her watch. 'I think we'd better go back now, or you won't have time to prepare yourself.' Standing up, she made ready to go. 'Are you determined to come again tonight?' she asked as they walked towards the bike.

'I most certainly am! You shouldn't even ask me. It's your job to keep me up to the mark – to the Mother Mark, perhaps I should say. You have an important job to do here.'

'I shall write it down in my diary: new project, "The Regeneration of Rupert". Don't worry, you are now in my capable hands. I am a practised soul saver!'

'I'm not sure what to make of you. What is the truth?'

She laughed as she seated herself behind him. 'That's your new project: "The Unravelling of the Mystery of Chastity"!'

Chapter Ten

The early Sunday evening calm in the flat was shattered by the unexpected return of Alex. Chastity and Dot were sharing a quiet supper in the kitchen when they heard Alex's key in the lock, followed by hasty footsteps along the hall and the quick opening of the sitting room door.

The listeners shared a sense of unease as they looked at one another. This was increased as Alex uncharacteristically slammed the sitting room door behind her, throwing down her travel bag immediately afterwards. 'Is anyone at home?' she called out irritably.

'Chastity and I are in the kitchen,' Dot answered. 'Would you like a cup of coffee?'

'I don't know,' was the surprising reply. Silence. Then, suddenly, she made up her mind. 'I think I would like one after all.' She appeared in the kitchen doorway. At first glance she appeared to be the usual self-assured, elegant Alex, but something in the flash of her eyes and in the irritable tone of her voice told them that she was, in fact, both angry and disturbed. Dot stood up to get another cup.

'Would you mind bringing it into the sitting room?' Alex moved away. 'Why don't you both join me there? It's more comfortable.'

Dot and Chastity exchanged a quick glance, deciding silently to humour her. 'OK,' Dot replied quickly. 'We won't be long. Would you like something to eat?'

'No, thanks.' She disappeared.

When they both came into the sitting room with the coffee Alex was standing, staring out of the window. 'We didn't expect you back so early,' Dot said, putting the tray on the table.

'I changed my plans.' Alex moved quickly from the window and sat down as the other two did. After taking several quick sips of her coffee, she suddenly put her mug back down on the tray.

'Does anyone know where Eva is?' she asked, looking around.

'I've only just got back, so I haven't seen her since yesterday morning.' Dot looked towards Chastity.

'I spoke briefly to her this morning before I went to church,' Chastity responded.

'How was she?' Alex took another hasty sip of her coffee. 'Or didn't you bother to find out?'

Dot seemed about to make a hasty reply to this implied insult, but, after checking her with a little gesture, Chastity replied quietly, 'She was still rather depressed but otherwise quite well. She didn't seem at all likely to do anything foolish. She said she was going out and that she had left a note for you. I think that must be it on the shelf over the television.' She pointed to an envelope propped up against a vase.

Alex leapt to her feet. 'Why didn't you tell me?' Hurrying across the room, she snatched up the letter and tore it open. Dot and Chastity watched with some trepidation while she read the note with obvious irritation. 'My God! She wasn't just going out! She's gone away to "sort out her life", or so she says. What's more, she doesn't say where she's going or when she'll be back! Nor does she enclose her next month's rent, which is due tomorrow. Not a word about it, in fact!' Crumpling up the letter, she flung herself back into the armchair. 'The perfect end to the perfect weekend!'

'I expect she'll be back in a day or two.' Dot tried to be consoling.

'And what if she isn't? It may not seem much to you, but one month's rent means quite a bit to my budget at the moment.' She picked up her mug and emptied it thirstily. 'Everything seems to be going wrong!'

After giving Chastity a puzzled look, Dot tried once more to be soothing. 'She's been with you a long time. Surely you know you can trust her, Alex?'

Alex laughed scornfully. 'And twice during that time she's been on rehab, and at least once she's tried to top herself. Hardly the sign of a trustworthy character, would you say?'

Thinking that might be the clue to some of Alex's agitation, Chastity interposed. 'I'm quite sure that you don't need to worry about that now. We had a long talk on Saturday morning and, by the time she left me, I felt sure that she'd rejected that idea.'

'Indeed? How come she talked to you so much? You hardly know her.'

'She wanted to thank me and, especially, Jan for helping her on Friday night.'

'I see. And I suppose she also told you how much I had let her down?'

'I don't think that was uppermost in her mind.'

'But you did, didn't you?' Dot asked bluntly. 'You simply went off for your weekend with James without a thought for her, assuming that we would cope.'

'Yes, I did, didn't I?' Alex jumped up and began to pace furiously about the room. 'Which just goes to show what a selfish, stupid egotist I am, doesn't it? Which probably makes it all the more likely that she'll let me down. She's spiteful enough.' She turned towards Chastity. 'Even you can't deny that. She attacked you for no reason at all. You must have understood what she's really like. She's devious and manipulative. She's wasted everything she's ever had and she hates me for being more successful.'

'All that I clearly understood was that she's desperately unhappy.'

'Why don't you ring Max?' Dot suggested. 'He might know something.'

'I doubt it, but it might be worth a try.' As Alex took up the phone, Dot and Chastity retreated to the kitchen with the tray, hoping to escape.

'Whatever's the matter with her, do you think?' Dot asked. 'I don't think I've ever seen her like that. She's usually pretty cool.'

'I don't imagine that it's just Eva, do you?'

'Probably not.'

As they were still tidying up the kitchen, Alex appeared in the doorway. 'Max hasn't a clue. He's heard nothing from her, in fact, but he's promised to let me have her rent tomorrow. So that's one relief. He sounded rather upset.'

'So he should be,' Dot muttered.

Ignoring Dot's comment, Alex turned away. 'I suppose I'd better unpack and prepare for tomorrow.'

As she was on the way to her room, the front doorbell rang.

'I'll go,' Dot said quickly. 'It's probably Richard. He said he might drop in.' A few moments later, she came back to the kitchen, disappointed. 'It's James,' she explained. 'He wants to see Alex. I've told her and left him in the sitting room. He seems a bit agitated too.'

As Dot was shutting the kitchen door, they heard Alex say loudly and angrily, 'Why the hell have you had the nerve to come here? I told you I didn't want to see you, and I haven't changed my mind. Why should I?'

James's reply was muffled as Dot quickly shut the door.

'It seems there's trouble in paradise. And, what's worse, unless she takes him into her room, we're stuck here. Or have you a better idea?'

Chastity laughed. 'I think we should finish tidying up the remains of our supper and then come out boldly. They probably won't notice us.'

For about ten minutes they were aware of loud voices coming from the sitting room, although they couldn't distinguish the words. Suddenly, the doors were slammed again and there was silence. After waiting a minute, they ventured to come out. They discovered Alex alone. Curled up in an armchair, she didn't look happy.

'Is something wrong?' Dot felt obliged to ask.

When Alex looked up, it was obvious that she had been crying. 'Nothing much. James and I have split up, that's all. If he does come again, I don't want to see him. I'm not in. Is that clear?'

'Perfectly. I'm sorry, though.'

'No need to be. He's a bastard. Not worth worrying about. I'm only sorry that I've wasted so much time on him.'

'Didn't he help you to get the promotion as he promised? Surely he didn't let you down on that?'

'No, I was given that on Friday. We went away to celebrate, or so I thought. But then... It's not easy to explain, Dot. Things just went wrong. That's all. I'd never realised before how totally self-centred he is.'

'I see.' Dot obviously didn't see, but, equally obviously, she didn't want to spend any more time on the discussion. 'I'd better go to my room now. I need to sort out some things for tomorrow. Let me know if there is anything I can do to help.' She left without waiting for any reply.

Chastity hesitated. It was clear that something James had done had greatly upset Alex, but was there anything she could usefully say at this moment? While she was hesitating, the telephone rang again.

'Do you mind answering it?' Alex asked. 'It might be James.'

It was Max, however. Even so, Alex took the phone with reluctance. 'I'm sorry, Max,' she replied to his opening remark. 'I really can't tell you any more about Eva. I've been away all weekend. Perhaps Chastity can. They did have a chat. I'll put her on to you.' She passed the phone to Chastity.

Max sounded extremely worried. 'I'm afraid,' he admitted, 'that Eva's finally gone off to end it all. And I have to admit that I was pretty bloody brutal to her. I thought it might be the best way to bring her to her senses, but now I'm not at all sure. I'm scared, honey.'

'I do understand. But I don't think you need to be. She and I had a long talk, and at the end she seemed to have decided quite definitively for living.'

'But it's so unlike her to be quiet. In the past, we've always had a great drama. Don't you think that this silence is worrying?'

'Not necessarily. It might, in fact, be a good sign. I think she genuinely wants to sort her life out.'

'I only wish I could tell her that I do actually care about her. That's why I took her away, but she wouldn't let herself believe it. Every time I looked at another woman, she went paranoid. She couldn't believe that they were just merchandise to me. We've known each other a long time and she's always been different as far as I'm concerned, but she's never allowed herself to believe it. I suppose you don't believe it either?'

'I think I do. But why, then, were you so brutal to her? Even before that last time you saw her, you'd cut your holiday short, and that upset her.'

'That was business. Couldn't be helped. But I was damned glad of the excuse. She was becoming impossible. Utterly paranoid.'

'Why ever did you come round then, and make it worse?'

'You'll laugh. Because I was sorry. I brought her presents to prove it and she threw them back at me. You saw how she reacted to you. What was a guy to do? But now, I admit, I'm scared. Fucking scared.'

'I think that Jan might be a better person to help you. He has more experience.'

'Can you give me his number?'

'No, I can't do that without his agreement. But I am expecting him to come round here soon. When he does, I'll explain it all to him and ask him to contact you.'

'Is that a promise?'

'Yes, a promise.'

'Then I'll wait, but do tell him I'm pretty desperate.'

'I will.'

As she put the phone down, Alex exclaimed, 'Did you say that Jan is coming here. Why? No one's ill!'

'He's coming to see me about some work we have to do tomorrow.' She had scarcely finished speaking when the front doorbell rang. 'That should be him now, I hope.'

As Chastity hurried to open the front door, Alex sat up quickly, smoothing her hair and her skirt. There was a short delay before Chastity returned with Jan. She had obviously explained some of the situation for, as he came in, he was saying, 'I'll get in touch with Max as you suggest. Do you have his phone number?'

'If Chastity hasn't, I have,' Alex intervened quickly. 'It's a terribly worrying business. I'm very upset. It will be wonderful if you can help. She must be so unhappy.'

Turning suddenly, Jan gazed at her with his deep, violet-blue eyes. He was dressed in his usual dark clothes, which accentuated the pallor of his beautifully chiselled features and the golden halo of his hair.

As he looked at her, Alex felt afraid and ashamed. She was convinced that her anger, her bitterness and her guilt were all clear to him. No false words could hide the truth from those piercing eyes. She felt herself shrinking away from what he might say. Still he continued to regard her. They were alone now. Chastity had gone to her room.

At last, he spoke in his deep but amazingly gentle voice. 'Eva may be unhappy. But you are unhappy too. Very unhappy.'

'Don't you really mean that I'm just a selfish bitch who wants to look good by pretending to care?'

His regard didn't waver. 'No. You are a wounded person who hides her true self because she is afraid of being wounded again.'

Alex tried to laugh. 'That's very flattering, but I can't believe that anyone else sees me like that. I certainly don't.'

'That is because you are afraid to accept your true self. I believe that it was you who first wounded yourself and, perhaps, someone very dear to you, and, as a result, you are unable to believe that you have any value.' Jan turned away. 'I must leave you now. I have matters to discuss with Chastity about our work tomorrow. But remember, if ever you are ready to talk to me, I will be ready to listen. In the meantime, you could find a good friend in Chastity.'

He was gone before she could reply. Her mind, however, was in such a turmoil that she didn't think she could have replied. She was still sitting there when he and Chastity came back into the sitting room some time later.

'Everything seems to be pretty clear,' he said to Chastity as he moved towards the door, turning as he did so to give a courteous farewell to Alex, to which she mechanically replied. As they went through the door, she heard Jan say, 'Will your friend Rupert be coming again tonight to help?'

'Oh, yes. He's very keen on the idea and he'll give me a lift on his bike again. I think that Mother Mark's made another conquest.' They were laughing as they made their way to the front door.

Suddenly, Alex was angry again, violently angry, and, as Chastity came back into the sitting room, she burst out: 'You're an amazing person, don't you think?'

'I don't know why you should say that.'

'Well, it was just about ten days ago, wasn't it, that you came among us, seemingly shy, out of touch and friendless? It was a good act, I must admit. I congratulate you on your success.'

'Why do you say that?' Chastity was puzzled by the anger in Alex's voice.

'Well, look at you now! You have a most attractive friend and protector. He was always there, of course, only we weren't aware of him. Since then, however, you've captivated Unicorn, of all people, and now, it seems, you fancy having a go at Rupert. I know he, too, might be considered very attractive, but surely you realise what he is? Or don't you care? Will any man do?'

'Of course I know about Rupert. Paul is my friend, too.'

Alex laughed mockingly. 'Oh, do stop it. Surely you can't expect me to believe any longer that you're so sweet and naïve?'

'I don't understand you.'

'If you know Paul, then you must know how jealous he can be, particularly as women always find Rupert attractive. Do you find it amusing to rock the boat? I suppose it might be quite fun for someone pretty selfish, like me, say? But not what one would expect from "do-gooder" Chastity, the little saint you pretend to be. Give it up, please.'

Although Alex's look and tone were both deliberately provoking, Chastity remained calm. 'I'm afraid you've mistaken the situation, Alex. Rupert has volunteered to help out with some work which Jan and I do. With Paul's agreement, incidentally, he took me last night on his bike to the convent where we are giving temporary help with the nightly soup run. That's all it was.'

'If so, why is he going again?'

'Because, to his surprise, he enjoyed helping. Another driver had just reported sick, and Mother Mark seized on Rupert as a gift from God. Now she expects him to be there as long as he is needed and he simply can't resist. I doubt if you could. But what is wrong, Alex? Why are you so angry? It isn't because of Rupert, surely?'

Alex suddenly collapsed. 'No, of course it isn't. I'm simply making it an excuse.'

'It's James, isn't it?'

'Yes, can you believe it? It's bloody James. I shouldn't really care, but I do. I feel so used.'

'But I thought you said that he didn't let you down. You got the promotion, didn't you? Or am I wrong?'

'No, you're not wrong. We went away this weekend to celebrate. It was fine until this afternoon. We came back to the hotel for tea after an exhilarating walk. As we were sitting by the fire, happily relaxing, he dropped his bombshell.' She stopped, clasping her hands tightly together.

'I don't think I understand.' Chastity moved closer to her.

'Why should you? I'm a bloody fool for caring. I don't know why I do. It's my vanity, I suppose. All the same, it hurts.'

'I'm sure it does, and I'm very sorry.'

Alex laughed bitterly. 'You won't be when you know what it is. You'll think it's just what I deserve. It may be, but it doesn't make it easier to bear.' She moved away from the comforting hand Chastity had placed on her arm. 'In your eyes, I'm a sinful woman, so why shouldn't I be punished? I never wanted you to know about James, and you wouldn't have known if fucking Unicorn hadn't made it his business to tell you. Damn him!'

'Why don't you just tell me what James said?' Chastity spoke with an unexpected authority.

After staring at her for a moment, Alex answered her as if she were obeying an order. 'He told me that we'd have to be more careful about our meetings during the next few months; no more weekends away. When I asked why, he told me—' She broke off for a moment, then continued. 'Oh, God, it's so humiliating. He told me that his wife was pregnant and he didn't want to risk upsetting her during that time! He was so smug about it! He had no idea why I should be upset. Of course he said he didn't love her, but she was his wife and she very much wanted another baby. And surely I could understand that as his wife, Hilary, was the sister of the managing director, any talk of divorce would be a disaster. We'd both understood that from the beginning, hadn't we?' She stopped, staring at Chastity with tearless eyes. 'It was like seeing yourself in the mirror for the first time and realising how ugly you really are.' She remained silent for a time, but she didn't move away when Chastity sat on the arm of her chair and put her arm around her.

'I told him that I thought it would best if we didn't see one another, except when we had to. I packed and left straight away. And then he dared to come here! I didn't feel rational! I wanted to kill him! It was frightening. I'm sure I frightened James. He's not very brave. He crept away, hoping that I would see things differently tomorrow. I was glad, because I felt that at least I'd humiliated him a little, too. The trouble is that I'll probably accept it all in a day or two. Even now, part of me can see that it's quite funny really. I thought I was using him so cleverly, while all the time he was using me to satisfy his lust and pretending to give me help that I probably didn't need.'

She closed her eyes and leaned against Chastity's comforting arm. 'You mustn't have any illusions about me. My ego is hurt, but I'm not sorry for any of it. I'm not the stuff that Christians like you are made of. I shall simply carry on. I don't believe in guilt and all that nonsense. Thank you for being kind, but it won't work. Sorry to disappoint you, but there it is.'

Without replying directly, Chastity suddenly stood up and moved away. 'Have you eaten recently?' she asked.

Surprised, Alex stared at her. 'Not since breakfast. I skipped lunch. But why on earth are you asking me that?'

'Because I think you need to. You look pale and exhausted. Strong emotions use up a lot of energy, don't you think?'

Alex laughed. 'And there was I expecting a sermon!'

'I think that what you need at the moment is a shower, followed by a tasty omelette and fresh coffee. After you've had the shower, get into bed and I'll bring the meal to you. That's my practical sermon, if you like! Don't argue; just get started!'

As she stood up, Alex exclaimed, 'When you talk like that, you do remind me of Caroline when she was Head of School! I suppose that's natural, since you are cousins.'

'I suppose so.' Chastity was already on her way to the kitchen. There was no time to waste.

Some twenty minutes later, Alex, sitting up in bed, was presented with a delicious-looking supper. As she took the first tasty bite, she realised that she was in fact hungry. Smiling at Chastity, she thanked her. 'I haven't felt like this since I was a kid at school. I suppose we all like being mothered. Do you know, I actually think I shall sleep.'

'Good, then I'll leave you. I must change before Rupert calls.' Bending down, Chastity gave Alex a light kiss on the cheek.

'Don't be deceived by me,' Alex warned her suddenly. 'I'm

still a sinner, you know. "A woman taken in adultery." I believe that's how they put it in the Bible, isn't it?'

'You must also remember, then, that Jesus simply told her to go home and sin no more.'

'That's the difficult bit, I'm afraid.'

'You might change your mind.'

'I might, but I doubt it. Sin is attractive, you know.'

Chastity made no reply except to smile as she picked up the tray. On her way to the door, she stopped suddenly to look at an unusual ornament on a shelf. 'You still have your bronze elephant with the wicked green eyes,' she exclaimed.

'Why do you say "still"?' Alex asked. 'You can't have seen it before. You haven't been in this room.'

Gazing at the little elephant, Chastity murmured, 'I don't know.' She seemed bewildered.

'Caroline must have told you about it. I had it in my sixth form study. She often looked at it. She once said she thought there was something evil about it. Perhaps that's what interested you. Perhaps she talked about it.'

'That must have been it.' Chastity turned away. 'I'll leave you now to sleep. I hope you will.'

'Don't you think I should repent first? Surely you should give me some good advice?' She had a childish desire to provoke Chastity.

Chastity, however, remained unperturbed. 'Only you can decide that.' She was gone, shutting the door quietly behind her.

Alex's Third Dream

Alex found herself facing a door. It was a huge, studded, metal door that looked impregnable, but when she turned the key, it opened with surprising ease. For a moment she hesitated, feeling strangely afraid that going through the door might be a momentous, life-changing action. 'Nonsense,' she told herself. 'I can just take a peep and come back if I don't like what I see.'

She was hesitant for a moment then curiosity overcame her. What would it be like on the other side? Tantalising visions of a life of ease and pleasure urged her on. It would be stupid to miss this opportunity because she was too timid even to try it. Pushing the door until it opened enough for her to pass through, she moved forward into this other world. Suddenly, to her horror, as she moved, the door began to close behind her with a frightening final clang. Turning, she tried to stop it but she was too late. Frantically she searched for a handle, but there was none – only smooth, unyielding steel. There was no alternative, it seemed, but to go forward.

As she did so, she realised that she was now in a world of deep twilight. It was dark, but there was enough light for her to perceive that a vast, empty plain stretched around and in front of her. As she continued to move forward, slowly, she noticed a few stunted trees and, in the distance, shapes that might be mountains, several of which seemed to be alight with lurid flames.

Shivering, she also became aware simultaneously of the chill wind, which swept ceaselessly across the plain with a moaning cry. It was the kind of wind which aroused a primitive desire for a warm, safe shelter among friends. There was no sign, however, of any shelter, so, pulling her coat more closely around her, she moved on.

It was then that she first realised that she was not alone. She became aware, for the first time, of shadowy shapes all around her. As if driven by the wind, they were all moving, as she found herself being forced to do, towards the mountains. With a sudden panic, she clutched at one of the stunted trees, hoping to keep still. For a moment her onward flight was halted, but it was, however, obvious that the remorseless pressure of the wind could not be resisted for long.

'Where am I being forced to go?' she asked herself. 'Where are all these people going, if, indeed, they are people?' She called out, still clinging desperately to the tree: 'Where are you going? Please tell me. I'm lost.' But no one paused or answered. She tried to clutch hold of one of the shapes, but it slipped through her fingers as if it had no substance.

Suddenly, she noticed that none of the shapes was speaking. Although they moved together, they appeared to be completely unaware of one another. There was no sound, except for the ceaseless moaning of the wind. She noticed one of the shadows fall to the ground, but, without pausing, all the others swept on, over and around it. And no one made any sound. She was in a twilight world without colour, sound or contact. However much she cried out to them, none of these shadows would heed her, so intent were they on following their own way. They would have no compassion on her, however lost and frightened she might be.

'Where am I? How have I got here?' she called out, again. The shadows remained oblivious; not one answered, but, as they drifted past, she caught a brief glimpse of a face, or of what might once have been a face – a terrifying mask, now, with wide, empty eyes devoid of expression and a mouth set in a meaningless smile that conveyed neither comfort nor friendliness. 'How have I come here? How has this happened?' she called out again.

Unexpectedly, a voice answered her; a calm, musical voice that reminded her of Jan. 'You have been making your way here for many years,' he said.

'I don't understand.' She stared around, but she couldn't see where the voice came from.

'You have already passed through many doors. You scarcely noticed them but simply went on. Tonight, you have been brought to the last door for you. As you came through it, you entered the world of empty souls completely without love, compassion or hope.'

Terrified, Alex asked, 'Do you mean I have to stay here for ever?'

'No, that depends on your response. This is a warning, perhaps your final warning. You are very fortunate. Not many get such a warning.'

'Why have I been allowed one? What have I done to deserve it?'

'It isn't because of anything you have done. The Lord of the Universe has granted it to you at the request of a loving, compassionate soul, who still remembers a kindness you once showed.'

'Who can that be?'

'Look back on your life and it may occur to you.'

Alex carefully considered the last few years of her life but no one occurred to her – unless…? Her heart beat faster at the thought. 'It isn't Martin, is it?'

'No, it isn't Martin.'

'So, he hasn't forgiven me? But why should he?'

'I know nothing about Martin. You have to go further back.'

'I can't think of anyone.'

'Do you remember a schoolgirl of thirteen, a new girl in your dormitory? Coming amongst those who had already been together for at least two years, she was naturally vulnerable. She was, however, especially vulnerable because her mother had just died and she had never been away from home before. You were the dormitory prefect, and you knew that at least one girl in your dormitory would delight in tormenting this girl and that, if she did, others would follow. You therefore protected her, talked to her, helped to unpack and made it clear that the popular Alex Woodward would not allow any unpleasantness.'

'You must mean Caroline Brown.'

'Yes. That was her name.'

Alex was tempted to lie, but her instinct told her that lying would be useless. 'I didn't do much. The truth is that I didn't really care about Caroline; I only wanted to prove what a good dormitory prefect I was. I wanted our House Mistress to like me. But the real joke is that, in the end, Caroline did much better than I did. She was more intelligent and even became more popular, in a funny sort of way. She became Head of

House and then Head of School, while I was always the Deputy.'

'Nevertheless, she still remembers and is still grateful.'

'But Caroline is dead, or so her cousin told me recently.'

'No souls die. They simply pass through a door into another world, an appropriate world. Some are like this, but others are beautiful and happy.'

Alex shuddered as she became conscious again of the chill, ceaselessly blowing wind. 'And, once one has passed through a door, is there no way out?'

'I can say nothing about that. That is in the power of the Son, whose mercy is infinite but whose justice must also be satisfied. For you, however, this vision is only a warning. For you, this time, there is a way out. You must go against the crowds, back to the gate.'

Alex tried, but, as soon as she let go of the tree, the wind forced her on. 'I can't. I haven't the strength on my own.'

'I will help you.' Suddenly, she found herself lifted up and moved towards the door against the power of the wind and against the pressure of the shadowy crowds. At last, she saw the door again. As it began to open, she noticed that the shadowy crowds coming through were, like refugees, clutching their most treasured possessions. But, as they came through the door, the wind tore these from them, in spite of their piteous cries.

'Now!' the voice said. Suddenly, Alex found herself thrust through the door, which closed firmly behind her. It was still dark – much darker, in fact – but at least she was safe. Or was she?

As she sat still, shivering and frightened, she heard the sound of a door being gently closed and of soft footsteps. A thread of light appeared on the floor. What was happening? Suddenly, she realised that her dream was over. She was sitting on her own bed in her bedroom. Her fingers found a familiar switch by her bedside and her room was revealed. She was cold because her duvet had fallen to the floor.

Quickly, she slipped off her bed. Hurrying towards the door, she opened it a crack. She needed reassurance. 'Who's there?' she called out.

'It's me, Chastity. I've just come back from the soup run. I'm sorry if I've disturbed you.'

'I'm glad you have. You woke me up from a horrid dream.' Opening the door a little wider, she saw Chastity standing in the middle of the living room.

'Would you like a hot drink?' Chastity asked.

'No, thanks. I'll be all right now. It's comforting to know that you're back.' As she snuggled into the duvet and began to feel warm and sleepy, an unexpected thought struck her. How strange it was that Caroline's cousin, Chastity, had suddenly appeared to rent a room in her flat. Was that also Caroline's doing? *What utter rubbish*, she told herself. However vivid her experience had been, it had only been a dream.

Chapter Eleven

It was just past five o'clock on the following Monday evening and already growing dark when Chastity walked down the steps to the semi-basement flat of Number 48. After ringing the bell, she waited patiently. A few moments later, she heard Mrs Allen coming along the hall to the door with slow, painful steps.

The door was cautiously opened on the chain, 'Who's there?' Mrs Allen asked nervously.

It would have been shocking to Chastity that an old lady should feel so nervous if she had not already discovered that this brilliant metropolis had its dark and frightening aspects. 'It's only me, Chastity Brown.' She tried to sound reassuring. 'Have you forgotten that you invited me to tea? If it's inconvenient, I can come some other time.'

'Of course not. You're a little earlier than I expected. Do come in.' The chain was slipped off and the door was opened wide. Mrs Allen smiled happily at her guest. 'I'm sorry I sounded so "off-putting" but I get nervous on these dark evenings, especially since my husband died two years ago. You hear of such dreadful things happening, don't you?'

'I'm afraid I have to agree, although I have only been in London for a fortnight.' Chastity followed Mrs Allen down the dimly-lit hall into the brightly-lit living room of the flat. It was cosy and welcoming on that chilly, windy November evening. The gas fire was burning, several lights were lit and heavy curtains were drawn over the big window, which, Chastity guessed, must lead to the little garden.

As she took off her jacket, Chastity surveyed her hostess with some surprise. The half-formed image of the frail, old lady whom she had helped home from church disappeared. Although she was probably in her late seventies, Mrs Allen was unexpectedly smartly dressed in a green and heather tweed skirt, a toning green blouse and a heather-coloured cardigan. Her silvery-gold hair was cut short to frame a somewhat long face, remarkably free from wrinkles. Her eyes were still a surprisingly bright blue, with a look of keen intelligence. Although she was small and slightly built and moved painfully with the aid of a stick, Mrs Allen was clearly no little old lady looking for someone to lean on but a resolute being who took care of herself.

'I hope you have a good appetite,' she remarked as she moved towards the table, which was already laid for a meal.

'I certainly have. I didn't have time for more than a coffee and a bun for lunch.' Chastity sat down readily in the chair that was offered to her.

'You've had a busy day, then?'

'Very.'

'In which case you probably won't object to a cooked meal; a chicken and ham pie, in fact?'

'It sounds heavenly. To be honest, I wasn't looking forward to cooking myself a meal, especially as I have to go out again later.'

'That's good.' Mrs Allen spoke briskly. 'I often have my main meal about this time, so I took a chance that you might want to share it. If not, I can manage scones and a cake. I must admit that it's a pleasure to have someone to share a meal with me.'

'If it doesn't sound too greedy, I can eat all that you want to put in front of me.' They smiled at each other like old friends.

When Mrs Allen went to the kitchen to attend to the meal, Chastity looked around her living room with some curiosity. Although it was large, it was full of furniture, mostly old and a little shabby but nevertheless tasteful and comfortable. The most noticeable feature were the bookshelves, which covered the whole of one wall. They were packed full of books of all kinds, large, small, paper-backed and hard-backed. Some were obviously old, others very new. Chastity decided she would study these if she got the opportunity. This meeting was intriguing and completely different from what she had expected.

During the course of the meal, she discovered that her hostess, Elizabeth Allen, was a seventy-four-year-old widow who had once been a history teacher. 'My husband died,' she explained to Chastity, 'two years ago, and since then I've been on my own. Of course, my two children visit me, although they both live some way out of London. My daughter very much wants me to make my home with her or near her. But I'm not sure that I'm ready for that yet.'

'You want to keep your independence?'

'Very much so. I like this flat and the garden which goes with it. We moved into this about ten years ago when we sold our house a few streets away. But, I'm afraid, I may have to face the inevitable soon. My arthritis has become much worse during the last year, so I haven't been able to get out much, and, in any case, I have very few friends here now; several have moved away and others have died. My daughter, Susan, worries about me, so I have more or less agreed to move after Christmas.' She spoke firmly and without a trace of self-pity. 'The trouble is,' she continued, smiling, 'there are too many of us old people around today, we've lost our rarity value. In any case, change is part of life. Whenever you think you're settled, that's the dangerous moment. The earthquake is about to come. But perhaps you're too young to have noticed that?'

'Not really. I have already experienced several big changes in my life. The latest was when I was sent here recently from East Africa.'

'That certainly sounds a big upheaval. I'm very curious to know what it is that you do. But, before you start to tell me, may I offer you a glass of wine? I've had this bottle for a couple of months, but drinking alone never seems very tempting.'

'You can certainly tempt me!' Chastity smiled happily as her hostess filled a glass and offered it to her.

Soon the delicious chicken pie had been served and Mrs Allen was free to resume her questions. 'Now, please, do tell me a bit about yourself.'

As simply as possible, Chastity explained that she was a doctor who worked for a world-wide society with the aim of caring for the poor and rejected, regardless of colour, race or creed.

'That is splendid work. Are you connected with the Catholic Church, or with some other church, perhaps?'

'We are mostly Christians, but we're not connected with any church. We would find that too restrictive. We feel that we are called to care for all who love and need us.'

'And does it work?' Elizabeth asked, with, perhaps, a trace of scepticism.

'It does, because we are so well directed and, perhaps, because we are only a comparatively small organisation. Of course, I can understand that you may find that hard to believe.' She looked earnestly at Elizabeth with her beautiful, dark eyes.

'After talking to you, I don't think I do. But tell me, why have you come to London? Surely, Africa needs you more?'

'Others are working in Africa. We have a special mission here. There is much poverty and suffering in London, you know.'

'Of course, that's perfectly true. Far more than we realise or want to realise. I got a good idea of that when I was teaching in one of the poorer parts of London. I had special responsibility for those who were disadvantaged by family circumstances or disability. Often, unfortunately, there was not much I could do except listen.'

'That's very important. So few people now seem to have time even to listen.'

'Yes. I felt so strongly about it that I decided to do some part-time teaching, even after I had retired. Jack, my husband, was very supportive, even when I brought some of these unhappy children home. Then we moved here and it was hard to make fresh contacts, but we tried until Jack became ill. Since he died it has become difficult for me, especially because of the arthritis, and I have begun to feel very isolated. All the same, I still think there might be something I could do.'

'There is, I'm sure. If you have that feeling then it means that God has something for you to do. Jan, who is my superior, might be able to give you some help. I'll speak to him tonight.'

'That's very kind of you, but I'm pretty useless, I'm afraid.'

'No one is useless. But you mustn't be afraid. Fear prevents action.'

Their meal had just ended and Mrs Allen, who was pouring out the coffee, stopped suddenly and put down the pot. 'I'm sure you're right. I've begun to feel that fear is the cause of much evil today. I believe it's because they're afraid that so many people drink, take drugs, have sex, as they now call it, and even spend lots of money on useless goods because they're afraid of facing their fears or, perhaps more accurately, their chief fear, which underlines all the others.'

'And what do you think that is?'

'I believe it's the fear of death, which, in the end, makes everything seem pointless. The less faith in God that people have, the more they will fear this unavoidable end and the more they will try to hide this fear even from themselves. Perhaps you haven't been long enough in this country to know that you can now talk about anything except death, unless, of course, you make a joke about it. That is, I think, one of the worst burdens put upon the old.'

She spoke with such feeling that Chastity was startled. 'But surely that can't be true of you, Elizabeth? You have faith, don't you? Surely, you told me that you are a Catholic?'

'That's true, but I'm afraid it doesn't mean as much as it ought. The Church is no longer the ark it once appeared to be. During the last few years certain shocking revelations have made us realise that it's not only a secretly male-dominated organisation but also very much a hypocritical one with very little time for people such as me. Since Jack's death, I've often felt alone and afraid. At first I pretended to myself that I was naturally afraid of losing my independence and of having to rely on others. But recently I've had to admit to myself that I don't fear that half as much as I fear death. Like many others, I suspect, I would cling to life on almost any terms.

'Neither Church nor science give one any help. People seem to have little time for compassion or understanding. The old and the sick are expected to be full of vitality, enjoying their retirement and always planning their next holiday. Oh, dear!' She broke off suddenly. 'I don't know what came over me! I just intended us to have a pleasant chat together. I'm so sorry!'

'Don't be! I can understand, but you shouldn't be afraid of death, you know. Of course, we all have a natural fear of the unknown, but our fear of death has been unnaturally increased, firstly by the churches threatening dire punishments if we don't obey their arbitrary rules and, more recently, by the scientists' assurance of annihilation, whatever we do. Neither can prove what they say. I've seen many people die and the truth seems to me to be that at the appointed time our soul simply goes through a door into another world.'

'Do we all go into the same world?' Although doubtful, Mrs Allen clearly wanted to believe.

'No, I think we choose which door will face us by the way we live our lives, by the choices we make in this world.'

'Then I might not meet Jack again?'

'Of course you will meet Jack. Can you believe that the loving and compassionate Lord of the Universe would want to separate you? Consider the all-embracing love of Christ, who is, as St Paul says, "The invisible God made visible." Bring Him truly into your life and you will no longer be afraid. I know this from my own experience.'

'Thank you. You're a very comforting person to talk to. I hope we shall meet again.'

'We certainly will. And I'm sure that Dr Jan will find some way in which you can help and that will also help you.' Smiling, Chastity stood up. 'I'm afraid I have to go soon, as Jan and I help the nuns with their nightly soup run, but I'm not going before I've helped you to clear up.'

'I can manage that in my own time. I'd far rather that you talked to me. That will do me more good.'

After a brief hesitation, Chastity sat down again.

'You know,' Elizabeth continued, 'there's only one other person who has ever talked to me in the way you have. I haven't seen him for some months and I've missed him.'

'Who was he? Did he live in one of the other flats?'

'I don't think he actually lived there, but he had a lot to do with the people who live in the flat above. He may have stayed there for a short time. He usually seemed to be with that red-haired young man who visits them often. I think he's a journalist.'

'You must mean Unicorn? Unicorn Jones?'

'Yes, that's right! I've seen him once or twice on television. I think he's intelligent but not, perhaps, very pleasant. That's why I was surprised that Emmanuel was apparently so friendly with him.'

'Emmanuel! That's an unusual name!'

'I know, but that's the name of the young man I'm talking about. Have you met him since you've been here?'

'I don't think so. What does he look like?'

'He's the sort of person you would remember. He's tall and thin, with very dark hair and a pale face. He's not particularly good-looking, but there's something attractive about him, especially his smile, which is very friendly. He looks foreign, but he speaks perfect English.'

'What does he do, do you know?'

'I don't know. I imagine he might be a journalist, like Unicorn, but we only had a few brief chats, usually when we met in the street. He was always kind and helpful, then he disappeared.'

'Disappeared? What do you mean?'

'Well, it's a silly word to use, I suppose. I'm just being stupid, making a drama out of nothing, but, all the same, it did seem rather sudden.'

'Why do you say that?'

'Well, the last time I saw him, he invited me to have a cup of coffee with him in the little café near the shops. I was quite flattered that an attractive young man should bother to ask me to have a coffee with him. As we talked, however, I thought he seemed even paler than usual and upset.'

'Did he say if he was?'

'No, and I didn't like to ask him, although now I wish I had. We talked about the news – about terrorism. He agreed with me that Iraq shouldn't have been invaded. He seemed to think that the politicians were spreading a fear of terror for their own ends. It might reach a point, he said, that any stranger, however innocent, might not be safe.

'I said that it reminded me of the time, years ago, when all kinds of people were accused of being secret Communists. He was too young to remember, but he was interested to hear about it. We talked for a few more minutes, then he said that he was sorry but he had to leave. As he left, he gave me a friendly kiss and said that he would see me again soon. But he never did. I often thought I should have encouraged him to talk, but I've always been too reserved; selfish, really, I suppose.'

'You would naturally think that, but he might have thought it wiser not to talk.'

'Perhaps.' Mrs Allen sounded doubtful. 'It sounds stupid, I suppose, but do you think he might have been arrested? He might have been worrying about that. He could have been an Arab. What do you think?'

'I'm a stranger here,' Chastity reminded her, 'so I really don't know, but I will see if I can find out anything from the others in the flat. There's probably a straightforward explanation.'

'I'd be glad if you would. It would put my mind at rest.'

'I'm afraid I really must go now, but don't worry, I'll certainly ask them.' After putting on her coat, she kissed Elizabeth Allen on the cheek. 'Thank you for your wonderful hospitality. I will see you again. I promise.'

'And you won't disappear?'

'On my honour, no. Stay where you are; I can see myself out.'

'Thank you for coming. It's been the happiest evening I've had for a long time. You will ask you doctor friend if there is any little thing I can do, won't you?'

'I certainly will. I'll call on you on Wednesday, about five, to tell you the results of my inquiries.'

When she arrived back at the flat, Chastity found Dot alone in the sitting room. She had been listening to the seven o'clock news but switched it off as Chastity came in. 'You're late back, aren't you? I hope you're paid overtime. Though I suppose we who are dedicated to the service of the sick and suffering shouldn't have such mercenary thoughts. I have to confess that I do, but I'm not a saint like you.' She grinned cheerfully at Chastity.

Chastity laughed. 'Forget the saint, please! You know that doesn't apply. In this case, it certainly doesn't apply at all. I don't even deserve any overtime. I've been having a very good meal with Mrs Allen, who lives in the ground floor flat.'

'However did you manage that? I've hardly spoken to her.'

'I gave her a helping hand coming home from church and we talked.'

'You know,' Dot said, looking at her with mock horror, 'it's time you learned the unwritten law of London life.'

'And what is that?'

'You must not be friendly with your neighbour. In fact, your neighbours don't exist. You have sinned dreadfully – first Paul, then Rupert, now Mrs Allen, to say nothing of Unicorn.'

'*Mea culpa, mea maxima culpa!*' Chastity smiled cheerfully at her.

'And don't think, my girl, that you can take refuge in that stuff about loving your neighbour. It simply won't wash any more. If you don't believe me, look at the news from Iraq. Oh, God, it's awful.' She was suddenly serious. 'On second thought, don't look at it.'

'Oh, there you are, Chastity!' Alex suddenly came out from her room. Her tone was cool and rather frosty. It was clear to Chastity that Alex now regretted the confidences she had made the night before, as people so often do. 'You've had a long day, haven't you?'

'Don't sympathise with her,' Dot said, cheerfully; 'she's been fraternising with Mrs Allen in the ground floor flat. I didn't know you were in,' she continued. 'I hope your day hasn't been too bad.'

'Much the same as usual.' Sitting down, Alex picked up a magazine and began to flick through the pages.

'James wasn't too difficult, then?'

'No; I managed to avoid him most of the time, then I came home early and worked in my room.'

'You didn't see Max?'

'No; should I have done?'

'He came with a letter for you. I would have called you, but I didn't realise you were already at home.'

'It's probably Eva's rent.'

'I think so. He seemed pretty worried about her.'

Alex shrugged. 'He should be used to her. Have you got the letter?'

'I put it in the kitchen. I'll get it and put the kettle on. I've got something for you, too, Chastity,' she said, halting Chastity who was about to go to her own room. 'Yours is more exciting.'

'Lucky you!' Alex murmured.

In a few moments, Dot returned to the sitting room carrying

an envelope in one hand and a magnificent bouquet of red roses in the other. After giving the envelope to Alex, she handed the bouquet to Chastity. 'There's a card to say who sent them. I've been dying to know.'

Slowly, Chastity opened the card. The message was simple. *'Just be true to your name until I return. Apologies. All my love, Unicorn.'*

'Do tell us,' Dot said eagerly. 'Who sent them?'

'Which of your many admirers?' Even Alex seemed interested. 'Paul, Rupert, Jan?'

'Unicorn.'

'Of course, we should have guessed that.' Alex sounded quite amused. 'It's a typical Unicorn gesture. The only mystery is why he hasn't come hot on its heels, demanding his reward.'

'He went off to Eastern Europe or some such place yesterday.'

'That makes sense.' Suddenly, Alex seemed to be friendlier.

'Shall I put them in a vase for you?' Dot asked. 'I love arranging flowers.'

'Please, but I'm afraid I haven't a vase.'

'Why don't you use the one on the shelf?' Alex offered.

'That would be just right.' Dot was already taking it down.

'In that case,' Chastity said quickly, 'the roses must stay in here so that everyone can enjoy them.'

'That's generous of you,' Alex said, smiling at her, 'but I'm not sure that Unicorn would be pleased.'

The atmosphere was unusually comfortable and pleasant. Dot was snipping off the ends of the roses and Alex seemed relaxed, when Chastity suddenly remembered the question she had promised Mrs Allen that she would ask. 'Do either of you remember a young man called Emmanuel?'

Alex sat upright but said nothing.

'I'm not sure,' Dot replied casually. 'I do seem to remember someone of that name popping in and out occasionally. You must remember him, Alex, because he was a friend of Unicorn's, wasn't he?'

'Unicorn has had many so-called friends. I can't possibly recall them all.' Alex sounded tense and angry.

'But you must remember this one,' Dot protested, 'because, now I come to think about it, he stayed here for several days at one time, didn't he?'

'He may have done, but that was only to oblige Unicorn. I knew nothing about him and didn't want to.' She turned towards Chastity. 'Why are you asking about him, anyway? You didn't know him, did you?'

'I had tea with Mrs Allen and she mentioned him. Apparently they talked occasionally, and she was wondering why she hadn't seen him for some time. She seemed to think that he'd disappeared suddenly, that something might have happened to him.'

'Is that all? Good God, people come and go in London all the time. He just went off somewhere else, I suppose. Why should it worry her?'

'I think she thought that, because he looked foreign, he might have been arrested as a terrorist.'

Alex laughed. 'What utter crap! She's just a silly old woman wanting a bit of drama in her dull life. Surely you can see that, Chastity? Why should you worry about it?'

'I think it was the unusual name that interested me.'

'Is that all? I'm afraid I can't help you, and I can't understand why you should expect me to waste my time bothering about it.' There was no doubt that Alex was ruffled, although she was trying hard to conceal the fact.

'You can always ask Unicorn,' Dot suggested. 'After all, he was his friend.'

'I don't think I shall bother.' Chastity smiled. 'It hardly seems worth worrying about. I'll go and make some coffee instead, if you all approve.'

'What an excellent idea.' Alex was smiling. All was harmonious again, but, as she went into the kitchen, Chastity wondered why Alex had been so agitated at the mention of Emmanuel.

Much later that night, when she and Jan were free to talk for a few minutes, she told him about Mrs Allen and all she had learned about Emmanuel. 'You told me,' she reminded him, 'that this mission had an extra purpose: to find someone who was missing. Am I right in thinking that the person is Emmanuel?' Without looking at her, he nodded. 'Then do you want me to find out more about him? Is that why I was sent to that particular house?'

He turned his pale, sculptured face towards her, looking into her soul with his dark, blue eyes. 'Don't force anything, Chastity. Be very careful. I suspect that there is evil behind this, very powerful evil. Your faith is great, but you are human and, therefore, no match for the Dark Angel and his followers. I have been sent as your protector. You must keep close to me. Remember that at all times.'

For a moment, she felt his hand rest lightly on her head as he blessed her. She seemed to feel the warmth of Christ's love flowing through Jan into her and driving away her sudden fear.

There was no time for more, as Mother Mark was quickly approaching them, but Chastity felt that her real mission had at last begun.

Chapter Twelve

The rest of the week passed uneventfully until the Thursday evening, when Max rang and asked to speak to Chastity. Obviously very curious, Dot summoned her to the phone. Max was brief, merely asking, without any preliminaries, if she would meet him at her local pub in about half an hour. When she hesitated, he urged her, 'Honey, I desperately want to talk to you about Eva. You haven't heard anything, have you?'

'No, nothing. I'm sorry.'

'Then I guess I'm pretty worried. We might put our heads together; what do you say?'

She agreed without further discussion. It was obvious that he cared a lot and was very worried. Somewhat surprised, she told Dot.

'They've known one another a long time,' Dot told her. 'I think he's helped her through one or two bad times before. He's a pretty straightforward guy, really.'

Max was already waiting when Chastity arrived at the pub. Only a few people were there on this cold, November weekday night, and he had already found a table and two seats in an isolated corner. She quickly spotted him, with his obstinately curly, short-cropped grey hair, and went swiftly towards him. On seeing her, he stood up, waved and welcomed her with his irresistible, friendly smile that lit up his whole face, even his eyes. He was so friendly that it was impossible to stay aloof. As she sat down, he greeted her enthusiastically. 'Good to see you, hon, looking as beautiful as ever. I was worried you might change your mind.' And then, somewhat in contradiction, he added, 'I've ordered us a couple of lagers. I hope that's OK with you.'

'Thanks, that's fine.' Chastity nodded. He had a wonderful gift for making a woman feel important to him. She began to understand why Eva had been so distressed at the thought of losing him.

'I'm sorry,' she began quickly, 'but I really haven't anything new to tell you. Eva hasn't communicated with anyone; not even Alex, who is, perhaps, her closest friend.'

At the mention of Alex, he interrupted her, with a slight grimace. 'Alex! That doesn't bother me. She's better not communicating with her!' His geniality had suddenly vanished and his eyes had become watchful. 'If Alex is an old buddy of yours, I'm sorry, but all the same, I'll tell you my belief. Alex is no friend to anyone but herself! If you don't like it – tough! But that's what I think.'

'Alex and I are not friends. We simply have a connection in the rather distant past.' As she remembered Alex's attitude to Eva and, even more recently, to James, she thought she could understand him. 'I think I know what you mean.'

'Good.' He relaxed. 'I guess I didn't present myself in the best light when we first met.'

'No, I don't think you did. You certainly said some harsh things,' she accused him.

'Sure, I know I did, but I was actually trying to help Eva. She'd been working me up for days, but I still wanted to help her. It all went wrong, however.'

'She wasn't likely to be conciliated by your telling her that she's past her sell-by date! Surely that wasn't helpful? Or do you think it was?'

'It wasn't, but I had to make her understand that her days as a top model were over. I'd tried being kind about it, but she just wouldn't listen. So I tried being brutal. You saw the result of that!'

'She simply wasn't fit to cope with it.'

'You're damned right – she wasn't! I was a bloody fool – not for the first time! But I don't want to go into that now. Eva and I go back a long way – over ten years – and we've been through some tough spots. She's helped me and I've helped her. We're buddies. But this is different. She's never cut herself off from me before. It's like she's vanished, and I'm real worried. Can you understand?' There was no denying the concern shown both in the expression of his mobile face and in his voice.

She hastened to reassure him. 'I do understand.'

'Then tell me honestly and don't hold anything back. You

talked with her last. Do you think she was suicidal?' He finished his drink rapidly while he waited for her reply.

'No,' she said, finally and firmly. 'I'm sure she wasn't. When she left me, she had made up her mind that, however difficult it might be, life was worth living. She wanted time to sort her life out, but no more. That is why she went away: to think.'

'That's good to hear. But then, where is she now? How's she living?' He ran his fingers through his hair. 'She hasn't got much money, you know. She should have had plenty, but she wasted it and not all on expensive living, drugs and drink. A lot of it, I believe, went to her so-called friends. Alex, chiefly. At least, that's what I think.'

'I don't know anything about that.'

'Of course you don't, honey. Anyone can see that you're a good girl.' Grinning unexpectedly, he looked at her appraisingly. 'You really would make a brilliant model, you know, for the "New Woman" of the twenty-first century. I'm not kidding. A big fashion house in the States is talking of launching such a campaign. I'd like to beat them. What'd you say? There is plenty in it for you and your good causes.' Before she could reply, he broke off. 'Oh, shit, I didn't mean to say any of that. It seems I can't help myself.' He looked at her like a naughty boy caught out.

Chastity smiled at him. 'I'm afraid there's still no deal, but I will help with Eva if I can. She's had breakdowns before, hasn't she?'

'Sure, but this is different. It's been coming on for some time. She pretended it was about me and all that shit, but that wasn't the whole truth. Something else was worrying her. She tried to hide, but there were times when I thought she was frightened.'

'Frightened?' Chastity stared at him. 'What about?'

'I don't know. That's the truth. But I'm pretty damn sure that she was. It all started about a year ago, when she told me that a young guy, a friend of Unicorn's, apparently, who often visited them, seemed to have disappeared.'

Chastity's heart missed a beat. 'Was he called Emmanuel?'

'Sure, honey. That's the guy. You've heard of him, then?'

'Only a few days ago, and not much then.'

'Well, Eva had known him for some time and she kinda liked

him and trusted him. She said there wasn't anything sexy about him and that was a relief to her. He was just a good guy, she said.'

'Did you meet him?'

'No; I wish I had.'

'Have you any idea about what happened?'

'Not really. Eva would never tell me. She tried to make a joke about it, but she was upset. I could tell that something bad had happened or she thought it had. Although she tried to hide it, I'm pretty sure she was scared.'

'Why do you think that she wouldn't say anything, even to you?'

'Because she didn't want Alex and Unicorn to know.'

'Know what?'

Max shrugged his shoulders and put his hands flat on the table, as if to declare that he had nothing hidden. 'That's all I know, hon, and a lot of that is guesswork. But I'm damned sure that it's good guesswork. And that's why I'm scared now. I want to tackle those two, but my hands are tied. I don't know enough. I guess Eva means a lot more to me than I've ever admitted.' He was looking at her as if asking for her help.

Chastity suddenly felt chilled. As she looked around the pub, with its smoke-laden atmosphere and its few pathetic fairy lights trying to give it an air of spurious gaiety, she was unexpectedly filled with suspicion. The scattered, mostly male customers sipping their drinks and smoking all seemed normal. But were they? Were some of them not what they seemed?

Max was staring at her as if puzzled.

At that moment, she felt a firm hand pressing gently on her shoulder and a voice, reassuringly calm and familiar, spoke friendly words. 'Hello, Chastity! I'm glad I've found you!' Turning her head quickly, she found herself looking into Jan's familiar eyes. His pale, beautiful face with its halo of golden curls seemed to shine out in the twilight world of the pub.

'Oh, Jan, it's you! You startled me! How do you come to be here?'

'I came looking for you. I needed to talk to you, so I went to your flat. You were out, but Dot told me you might be here, so I came to see if I could find you. I'm sorry if I'm interrupting you.' He looked towards Max.

Max stood up to greet him. 'That's fine, Dr Jan. I remember you well. You're the doctor who was so good with Eva. I'm sure pleased to have a chance of meeting you again. I have to go soon, but will you have a drink with me first?'

'Thank you.' Jan sat down between Max and Chastity. 'Just a glass of red wine, please.'

'Nothing for me, please,' Chastity said as Max looked at her.

'You're sure?'

She nodded.

'OK, then I'll go get me a refill and order the doc's wine.' He went off briskly to the bar.

'Why did Max want to see you?' Jan asked.

'He wanted to talk about Eva. I told him that when she left me she was definitely not in a suicidal mood. I think he cares much more for her than he usually admits.'

'Did he say anything else?' Jan asked.

'Yes, but it was very odd. Strangely enough, it was about Emmanuel. Eva knew him and liked him and was very upset when he disappeared. She used the same word as Mrs Allen, oddly enough. Eva, however, was also frightened.'

'Hush,' Jan interposed quickly. 'Don't say anything more now. It's wiser to be careful,' he explained, as she looked at him, startled. While Chastity was considering this, Max returned to the table with the drinks.

'Thank you,' Jan said as he accepted the glass of wine. Without hesitation, he continued, much to Chastity's surprise. 'Chastity has been telling me that you are worried about Eva and about what has happened to her.'

'I sure am. Can you help, Dr Jan?'

'I can definitely assure you that she is safe.' He smiled slightly as both Chastity and Max stared at him. 'Even Chastity has not known this until now,' he explained to Max.

'But how do you know?' Chastity asked, trying to hide the hurt she felt.

His smile and the gentle touch of his hand on hers told her that he understood her feelings and would explain but not now. 'I was concerned about her,' he continued, turning directly towards Max, 'and came to call on that Sunday morning. As I approached,

I saw her leave the flat. Naturally, I spoke to her. It was quite clear that she wasn't really in a fit state to go off on her own. Nor did she have any clear idea of where to go, so I offered her a refuge with a trusted friend of mine in a clinic that we have. She's being looked after well and is improving. I'm sure she'll soon feel ready to get in touch with you. At this moment, she is trying to sort herself out and finds the peace and tranquillity of her present surroundings very helpful. But I don't think that she is ready to talk to anyone yet; not even you, Max, her oldest friend.'

For a moment, Max sipped his drink as he considered what Jan had told him. 'Thanks,' he said finally. 'You're a great guy, Jan. Just tell her, will you, that I care a lot about her and when she wants to see me, I'll be there.'

'I will, indeed.' Jan smiled reassuringly at him.

Max looked at his watch, drained his drink and then stood up. 'I'm sure grateful to both of you. And, if there's anything I can do, just let me know. I'll be in touch.' With a friendly smile and a cheerful wave he was gone.

Without speaking, Chastity waited for Jan's explanation.

'I imagine,' he said calmly, 'that you're wondering why I haven't told you any of this before?'

'I'm sure that you have good reasons.' She knew that the very human hurt she felt was not appropriate.

'Chiefly, I wanted to protect you from Alex and Unicorn. It would have been hard for you to resist pressure from them if you knew. As it has turned out, there was surprisingly little pressure.'

'Yes; if they had any feelings at all about her disappearance, it seemed to be relief that she had gone. Alex's strongest worry, apparently, was about the rent.'

'They were more callous than you had expected?'

'So much so that I began to wonder if they had ever been Eva's friends.'

'Oh, they certainly had been, but she had become a liability.'

'Did you know about Emmanuel? Has she told you about him?'

'Oddly enough, she never mentioned him. It was from you that I first learned about him.' He sipped his glass of wine thoughtfully.

143

'But you knew that we had to find someone, didn't you?'

'Yes, that was among my instructions. But they were not as clear as you might have expected.'

'Max has just told me that she began to be depressed and frightened about the time Emmanuel disappeared, but she wouldn't give him any reason.' She quickly told Jan all that Max had said, then continued, 'It was foolish, perhaps, but I began to feel afraid and I was very relieved when you arrived.'

'It wasn't foolish. I knew that you needed me. I have been sent here not only to help you but also to protect you. We'll say no more about Eva at present. She is safe for the moment in our refuge, though she cannot stay there forever. But now it is time for you to have a little relaxation. I have arranged a happy evening for us.'

'But surely we have to go on the soup run soon?'

'No; that's what I came to tell you. We're no longer needed except in a medical emergency. The sick volunteers have recovered.'

'What about Rupert? He'll be expecting to pick me up.'

'No, that's been dealt with as well. As I left your flat, I met Paul and asked him if he would give Mother Mark's message to Rupert; she wants to keep him on her list, but she won't need him for a week or two.'

'I imagine Paul was quite pleased.' Chastity smiled mischievously.

'I think he was, although he tried to conceal it. But he also gave me a message for you.'

'For me? What on earth was that?'

'He wanted to know if you had any free time this week. I told him that you were free tomorrow as we are working on Saturday. He then said he would like to talk to you and wanted to know if he could invite you to lunch tomorrow. I suggested that he ring you later tonight when you would be in. I hope that doesn't upset you?'

'Of course not. I have a weak spot for Paul.'

'Then there is nothing to stop us from having a refreshing three hours' break, which I think you need.'

'What are you suggesting?'

'First we'll eat, then we'll go to a concert, for which I have tickets.' He smiled suddenly. 'I was going to say "to a concert of heavenly music", but perhaps it would be truer to say "the nearest to heavenly which Earth can offer." What do you say?'

'It sounds wonderful.' Suddenly, Chastity realised how much she needed to escape for a few hours from the people at Number 48, Woodland Avenue. 'You really are an angel!' They were both laughing as they left the pub with its still oppressive atmosphere.

Chapter Thirteen

It was precisely 12.30 p.m. when Chastity rang the bell of Paul's flat. His phone call of the previous evening had not revealed much. He had simply told her that he had discovered a fascinating recipe in one of the old recipe books he collected, which he was longing to try out on someone. When she had protested that Rupert would be the right person, he had laughed. 'Don't be silly, darling! Food is just fuel to Rupert, like petrol for his bike. I need someone with a discriminating taste. Do say yes! I can promise you a rare gastronomic delight.'

It was only after she had accepted that he had told her that another friend had been invited. 'Not for lunch; I want that to be special, just for the two of us, but for coffee afterwards. I especially want you two to meet. I'm sure it will be a pleasure for both of you.'

That was all she had learned, and now, as she stood waiting for Paul to open the door, she was feeling very curious. Who was the mysterious friend he so much wanted her to meet?

Paul was dressed even more elegantly and flamboyantly than usual. His patterned silk cravat was carefully knotted and the maroon in the pattern perfectly matched the maroon of his velvet jacket. His dark hair was smoothly brushed back, with just the hint of a wave. His one earring reflected the gold of his cravat pin. His well-manicured nails were lightly varnished.

Chastity was pleased that she had decided to wear her only black dress, with a casually-draped, emerald-green scarf. Her punctuality pleased Paul, too, as she had known it would.

With a welcoming smile and a flourish, he conducted her to her seat at a beautifully-laid table. There was no awkward waiting time as everything was ready. Disliking the contemporary taste for exotic and foreign dishes, Paul concentrated on what he called the 'glorious traditions of truly British foods', delving into his collection of old cookery books to find new and delectable dishes.

This day's choice of a Cumbrian sausage dish was as good as he had promised.

It was not until they reached the dessert that Chastity ventured to ask about the other visitor, who would soon be arriving. It was, as she had half expected, Helen, Paul's one-time Oxford tutor, whom Rupert had been bullied into visiting on the Sunday of Paul's audition. She remembered that Rupert had told her that Helen had been a woman with a brilliant academic future who had given everything up to care for her illegitimate, autistic son, who was now ten years old.

Without saying much, Rupert had made it clear that he had no great liking for Helen, but Paul was most enthusiastic in praising her. She had been an inspired lecturer and a most stimulating tutor, he declared. It was she who had been Paul's defender, giving him not only the courage to defy those who mocked him but also to be true to himself and to discover his acting talents. Her abilities were considerable, Paul stated. She had obviously been set for a splendid career. *What could have happened?* Chastity wondered.

'An unspeakable lout, with no morals and no care for anyone but himself, seduced her. Worst of all, when the affair became public, he blamed her, declaring that she, an experienced woman, had seduced him, a young and inexperienced student. He was believed and she felt that she had no alternative but to resign. When she told her lover that she was pregnant, he denied that he was the father but, "out of kindness", offered her the money for an abortion.'

Paul stopped suddenly. His anger and distaste were obvious. 'What do you think?' he finally demanded of Chastity. 'What would you call a man who behaved like that?'

Knowing Paul's inflammatory disposition and seeing his obvious partisanship, Chastity was aware that she must express herself carefully. For a moment she studied the delicious lemon tart Paul had placed in front of her, then, suddenly, she lifted her head and looked directly at him. 'It seems a cruel way in which to behave. Were there no extenuating circumstances?'

'None, whatsoever. What do you imagine there could be? Helen lost her career, her promising future and most of her so-called friends. She now lives in a tiny flat and struggles to keep her autistic son and herself by teaching English to foreigners part-time. What could be worse for a highly intelligent and sensitive woman?' It was clear that Paul cared greatly and was deeply involved; he was not playing a part. 'Surely, Chastity, you of all people cannot be suggesting that there can be any excuse for behaviour such as his? I am amazed.'

'It was a wicked way to behave, but he was young and might have repented. I would hope that he has. Does he know that he has a son?'

'No, he doesn't. Nor would Helen want him to know. She wouldn't want her afflicted son exposed to the mockery of that monster.'

'I can understand that, but—'

He interrupted her before she could finish her sentence. 'I know you're a Christian and so you're bound to talk about repentance and forgiveness and all that. But talking about it is one thing; doing it is another. It's quite different, then, isn't it when you're actually involved? You must be realistic. Don't you understand that, Chastity dear?'

Chastity gazed directly at him with her dark, luminous eyes. She spoke in a voice he had not heard her use before. 'I do have more experience that you seem to think, Paul. Forgiveness is realistic. It frees one from slavery to bitterness and anger. I know that from personal experience. Many years ago, I had to forgive a great wrong done to me. My life was disrupted, my future changed. I do know what it's like.'

'I'm sorry,' Paul put out a friendly hand towards her. 'I had no idea.'

'Why should you have? You assumed, quite naturally, that I had always been a medical missionary. That is quite natural, since I have never wished to talk about my past. Nor do I wish to say more now. It's hardly relevant.'

'Please, don't be angry with silly old me,' he pleaded with her. 'It seems even clearer to me now that you're just the right person to talk to Helen. The help I can give her is so limited. I know that.'

Without answering him directly, she questioned him. 'Surely,

Rupert went to visit her when you were busy auditioning? He told me you had asked him to. Didn't that help?'

Paul smiled. 'He tried to, bless him, but he isn't quite the right person to advise a lonely mother, now is he? Apart from that – I'm sure I'm safe speaking the truth to you, Chastity darling – Rupert is just a tiny bit jealous. Utterly ridiculous, of course, but he's apt to get silly ideas at times.'

Smiling back at him, Chastity privately wondered whether that was the true reason why Rupert had said that he didn't like Helen. Or could there be another reason? Aloud, she said in her normal voice, 'Well, you have no reason to worry about my being jealous. I'll be pleased to meet Helen and to talk to her.'

'Good. I was pretty certain you would be, once you'd heard her story. I'll make sure that you have some time to talk together.' Normal relations were resumed. Although he felt curious about what Chastity had said about herself, Paul felt it would be wiser to respect her reserve and not to ask further questions.

As soon as lunch was finished, Paul cleared the table and hurried into the kitchen to make the coffee. While he was still in the kitchen, the front doorbell rang. 'Don't worry! I'll go,' Chastity called out as she hurried to the front door.

When she opened the door, she found herself confronting a pale, slim woman in a shabby overcoat. Smiling nervously, the woman said, 'You must be Chastity. I'm Helen.'

'Do come in.' Chastity welcomed her. 'I'm afraid Paul's busy with the coffee.' As she spoke she helped Helen out of her coat and, after hanging it up in the small hall, she led her into the sitting room just as Paul came in from the kitchen. After greeting Helen effusively, Paul insisted on making somewhat unnecessary introductions, so it was some minutes before they were able to sit down and sip the coffee that he had poured out.

As Helen and Paul exchanged remarks about Rupert and about Helen's son, Stevie, Chastity was free to sit back and study the other woman with considerable interest. The initial impact was surprisingly neutral. At first glance, Helen seemed to be almost colourless, with mid-brown hair, pale skin and eyes of no definite shade. Her plain beige woollen dress, worn without any ornament or make-up, only strengthened the effect. It was difficult, Chastity decided, to imagine Helen being involved in a passionate affair with a student at least ten years her junior.

She was brought back to reality by Paul's offer of a second cup of coffee.

'I'm afraid we've been neglecting you, Chastity darling. Helen and I have scarcely met recently, and I'm afraid Rupert's visit wasn't much help.'

'He was very kind,' Helen protested gently, 'but I'm afraid I was not in an encouraging mood, and Stevie was also being difficult.' She turned and looked directly at Chastity. 'My ten-year-old son is autistic,' she explained. 'I don't know if you know anything about that and its difficulties?'

'Chastity is a doctor,' Paul reminded her.

'Of course; how silly of me. You did tell me.' Opening her heavy-lidded eyes, she looked straight at Paul, while her lips curved into a surprisingly seductive smile. Noticing this, Chastity began to understand why Rupert might not like her. Helen was, perhaps, not what, at first sight, she seemed to be. Paul responded by smiling back and patting her hand gently.

Helen then turned to Chastity. 'You probably know more about the condition than I do, then?'

'I'm afraid I'm not a specialist in such conditions,' Chastity spoke quietly, determined to hide the slight irritation she felt; she reminded herself that Helen's life must be hard and lonely. 'I've spent much of my time as a doctor to poor Africans in sub-Saharan Africa, where such illnesses are unknown, but I did have some experience when I was training. I can appreciate that you must have many difficulties, especially as you are on your own. I presume that Stevie has been diagnosed as suffering from Asperger's syndrome?'

'Yes. He is quite severely affected, though there are others much worse I know.'

'Naturally it is harder for dear Helen,' Paul insisted on adding, 'because she is quite alone and has no partner.'

'I hope you've been able to find a suitable school?' Chastity asked sympathetically.

'I have been lucky there, but, of course, there are days when he refuses to go and that can be very difficult, especially if it clashes with my part-time job as a teacher of English as a second language. There are times when I feel quite desperate and don't know what is best to do.' Helen spoke with a weary air of resignation.

'I have told Chastity,' Paul interrupted angrily, 'how you have had to give up a really promising career because of the disgusting behaviour of the man you loved and who said he loved you until he was required to prove it!'

'But there are compensations, aren't there?' Chastity looked directly at Helen as she spoke. 'At least you have your child. Not all mothers have that.'

Before Helen could reply, Paul broke in vehemently. 'Of course Helen will agree that there are compensations, but nothing can excuse the way she was treated. And not even a child can compensate fully for the loss of a brilliant career.'

'Please, Paul,' – Helen spoke with an unexpected firmness – 'you should not presume to tell Chastity what I feel; you can't know.'

For a moment there was an embarrassing silence until Paul, with an obvious effort, managed to reply calmly. 'You're right, Helen, of course I shouldn't. The trouble is, one allows oneself to get too involved. One apologises humbly.'

'You're readily forgiven.' Helen smiled at him again.

'In that case,' Paul said, standing up, 'I shall retire to the kitchen to sort out the dishes, leaving you two to get to know one another. There is more coffee if you want it.' Ignoring their protests, he departed to the kitchen with an elegant flourish.

'I'm afraid I've hurt Paul's feelings.' Helen sounded a little regretful.

'Nevertheless, you were quite right. He was presuming. But I'm afraid that I, too, was presuming, when I suggested that you might not sufficiently appreciate the consolation of your son.'

'No, you justly reminded me of the great asset which I seemed to be undervaluing. My son, afflicted though he is, is the great joy of my life. The trouble is, when, at times, I get weary and depressed, I begin to feel that I can't cope any more. Then, I'm tempted to feel sorry for myself and to regret what I did.'

'And Paul encourages you to think like that sometimes, I imagine. Am I right?'

'Unfortunately yes. His hatred for Gervase, my one-time lover, is greater, it seems, than any other feeling, and he tends to give the impression that I must feel the same.'

'You must excuse him. He can't possibly know the great joy a child can give its mother.' Suddenly there was an unexpected note of great sadness in Chastity's voice.

Opening wide her heavily-lidded eyes, Helen looked closely at Chastity. 'You speak from experience, I feel; you are a mother aren't you?' When Chastity didn't immediately answer, she continued, 'Perhaps I should say that you have been a mother, haven't you?'

Faced with a direct question, Chastity could only answer with the truth. 'I have had a child. You are right.'

'Where is that child now? It isn't with you, is it?'

'She is dead. She died when she was very young.'

'What about her father?'

'He died soon afterwards.'

Without saying anything, Helen leaned forward and took Chastity's hand in hers. For a few moments they were both silent, until Helen said softly, 'You have really suffered. My complaints must seem so petty to you. How did you manage to go on living? You obviously have done so most successfully.'

'I was rescued by love and shown how much love I could give to others in return. God offered me a vocation and a new way of life, which meant putting aside my former life and all regrets.' Quickly, she resumed her normal calm demeanour and gently removed her hand from Helen's. 'None of my new friends in London know about my past. I would prefer you not to mention it to anyone, not even to Paul.'

'Of course I won't. I realise that you were honest with me because I directly asked you. I certainly won't take advantage of that. I feel very humble,' Helen continued. 'I have no right to claim your sympathy.'

'And why not? True, I have lost both my child and my husband but you have been cruelly betrayed by the man you loved and trusted and because of that your career has been destroyed. Paul may exaggerate – he does tend to do that, I know – but what he says is still true and is still hard to bear, I'm sure.'

'There are many strands in the truth,' Helen replied slowly.

'Do you mean that Paul doesn't know the whole truth?'

'How could anyone? No, what I'm saying is more serious even than that. Paul never wanted to know the truth. He had his own, very strong reasons for disliking Gervase, and so he was pleased to find further reasons for hating him and for feeling justified in doing so.'

'You mean that you allowed him to believe something that was wrong? That you didn't try to put him right?'

'I'm afraid that must shock you, but it's mostly true. I desperately needed Paul's support. I'd lost not only my career but also many people I'd imagined were my friends. And, even if I'd tried to tell Paul, he wouldn't have wanted to know.'

Chastity considered this statement carefully. 'I can imagine that being true of Paul,' she replied finally. 'There are also times, I think, when he doesn't want to forgive.'

'You're right, and that has made it difficult to talk to him. But, since you have been so honest with me, I would like to try to tell you the truth.'

'If you're sure.'

'I am. I'm convinced that I can trust you. Gervase and Paul were both my students, both outstanding in different ways. Gervase made Paul the butt of his somewhat cruel mockery, while I tried to protect him and to restore his confidence in his own considerable but unusual talents.'

'Didn't that annoy Gervase?'

'No, he found it amusing or said he did. It was then, however, that I began to suspect his weakness.'

'His weakness? What do you mean?'

'He was greatly attracted by an older woman with some sexual experience, like me, and almost seemed to avoid women of his own age. He struggled hard against it, but he desperately needed something more erotic than a young and inexperienced girl could possibly offer him. He was extremely attractive and I saw no reason to resist the temptation. To be truthful, I made myself as desirable as possible. You may not think it now, but I did have a certain attraction.'

As she once again opened her heavily-lidded eyes and curved

her lips into a voluptuous smile, it seemed to Chastity for a brief moment that the rather neutral woman she had been talking to vanished and an enchanting siren took her place. Then the smile vanished, the eyelids were lowered and Helen was back again. 'You see what I mean?'

'So, Paul is wrong? You did seduce your student?'

'Yes, but I was punished. The true irony was that I became even more enslaved than he was. And so I brought about my own downfall.'

'What do you mean?'

'Two things. I couldn't bear to think of losing him. And I also had a desperate longing for a child. I knew he would never agree, but I thought, wrongly as it turned out, that if I became pregnant he would stay with me.'

'Are you telling me that you actually cheated him?'

'Yes. I suppose it sounds horrible to you, but I have to admit that it's true. I had agreed that I would take the Pill, but, without consulting Gervase, I stopped taking it. When I told him that I was pregnant, that I must have made a mistake, he was furious. He refused at first to believe me.'

'Surely he had to believe that you were pregnant?'

'Eventually I convinced him, but then he said that I had either planned it deliberately or it was the child of some other man. When I suggested a test, he refused.'

'Are you saying that he refused to discuss the matter with you, even after the first shock, which must have been great?'

'Yes. He was very cruel. I had destroyed the romance. We had been studying fourteenth- and fifteenth-century literature – Sir Gawain, King Arthur and his Knights, the Quest for the Holy Grail. Somehow, he had made our love affair part of all this and suddenly I had shattered it with a stroke of reality. Babies have no part in courtly love. It sounds crazy, perhaps, but I think that there is some truth in it.'

As Chastity seemed to have no comment she wanted to give, Helen proceeded. 'Our love affair somehow became public. He accused me. I had to resign. Suddenly, it seemed I had no friend except Paul. Having flung Gervase's money back at him, I desperately needed Paul's help. I didn't dare to tell him the truth.

I didn't think he would understand that although I might be thought to have acted badly, I only did it because of my love.'

'I think he might, perhaps, have found it difficult to understand.' Chastity gave no further judgment but returned to practical matters. 'Does Gervase know about Stevie?'

'No, we have never spoken to each other or seen each other since. He started life afresh and so did I.'

'But surely he would help you. Whatever he may have said in his first anger, Stevie is his biological son.'

'I don't want him to. I couldn't trust him and, in any case, I'm sure he would be quite indifferent. He might even laugh at me. I couldn't bear that!'

'Of course you couldn't, but surely no man would act like that!'

'You're think I'm exaggerating? I can understand that, but I'm not. When I last spoke to him, he frightened me. I felt that he had become almost evil. Perhaps he had dabbled too much in the magic which seemed to fascinate him.' She shuddered. 'I don't want to see him again, and I wouldn't want poor Stevie to be exposed to him.'

'If those are your true feelings, then you're better without him. But that has cut you off from people, which isn't good for you and Stevie, is it?'

'No, and that was why I was so pleased when Paul suggested that I should meet you. I don't suppose you realise that you're the first person I've ever told this story to? I feel happier for telling it. It must be true, as people often say, that confession is good for the soul.'

Several thoughts occurred to Chastity, the most important being that a good confession, to be salutary, should be complete and honest and should imply repentance, but she decided that the time was not right, so she merely asked, 'Why me? You scarcely know me.'

'I suppose Paul's glowing recommendation pre-disposed me to think well of you, but when I met you I had this feeling that you are good and understanding. And when you were so honest with me, I felt I had to respond. You will come and visit Stevie and me, won't you?'

'Of course I will. We must find a time which will be convenient for both of us.' They were still discussing this possibility when Paul came back into the room. Helen had to leave soon afterwards, but not before they had made an agreement.

When he returned from seeing Helen off, Paul expressed his satisfaction. 'You're an angel, Chastity darling. It's a long time since I saw Helen looking so cheerful. Thank you.' He kissed her enthusiastically on both cheeks. 'It will be so good for her to have an intelligent and understanding woman friend. She told me you've promised to visit her and Stevie soon.'

'Yes, quite soon.'

'I expect she was very interested to hear about your work?'

'We didn't talk much about me. Helen told me more about what had happened to her.' She stood up. 'I really must go now.'

'Nonsense, darling! You have time to have a sherry with me.' Rather reluctantly, she accepted the sherry, but, to her surprise, Paul made no move to get it. Instead, he leaned forward to talk confidentially to her. 'She told you, then, about the rotter who ruined her life and how much she suffered?'

'Yes. She seemed anxious to tell me the full story.'

'I'm sure she was. I'm sure that she confirmed all I had told you and more. But did she tell you his name?'

'She called him Gervase. Why do you ask?'

'He was Gervase, but he changed his name. You have met him.'

'I have met him?' Chastity was bewildered.

Paul raised his eyebrows. 'Think, darling. Who would fit the description? I should have thought it was obvious.'

'I'm afraid it isn't to me.'

'Surely, Chastity, even you can't be so naïve? His new name is Unicorn. Don't tell me you didn't have any suspicion?'

For a long moment, there was a complete silence as Chastity looked steadily at him. 'I understand,' she said finally. 'Thank you for telling me, Paul. It makes many things clearer.' She stood up again. 'Now I really must go. Give my love to Rupert, won't you?'

Paul followed her as she went into the hall. He helped her

fussily into her jacket, protesting as he did so. 'I didn't mean to upset you, Chastity, darling. Please forgive me if I have. I just thought you would prefer to know the truth.'

'You haven't upset me, and I do prefer to know the truth, although it isn't always easy to be sure of it. Thank you for the lunch.' With a swift smile, she was gone.

Chapter Fourteen

She was awake, but the fear was still with her. As she lay shivering, trying to recall her dream, all she could recall was darkness and a feeling of horror as she struggled against an evil being that was trying to gain possession of her. Somehow, she had forced herself to wake up. That had worked in the past, but not now.

She was awake, but she was still terrified. Why? Still she felt the presence of something evil and shapeless in the darkness of her bedroom. Something that was still trying to drag her away. She wanted to cry out, but her throat was paralysed, as it had been in her dream. Suddenly, she remembered what she had been taught as a child. The Devil always shrank away from the cross. Forcing herself to sit up, she made the sign of the cross, slowly and deliberately, saying aloud, in a firm voice, 'In the name of the Father, the Son and the Holy Spirit – go from me!'

Immediately, she felt a sense of release. With fingers that still trembled, however, she switched on her bedside lamp. The darkness was banished and it was clear in the light that the room was empty and completely normal. Elizabeth Allen told herself how foolish it was for a seventy-year-old woman to behave as she had done. At the same time, she knew that she did not feel safe and that she would not dare to sleep again before daylight.

For the next two hours she sat upright, with her lamp switched on until she saw the first chinks of light showing through the small gaps between her curtains. Slowly she got up and, after putting on her warm dressing gown and cosy slippers, went to the kitchen to prepare breakfast for herself. She did not, however, feel safe from fear and anxiety until she had switched on all the lights and the radio.

As she thought over her dreams and terrors of the last few nights, particularly of the last night, the worst of all, she realised that she must talk to someone. But who could she talk to? Her daughter was far away and, in any case, was unlikely to be sympathetic. She no longer had any close friends. It would have been different if Jim had still been with her. She realised more than ever how isolated she had become.

Suddenly, she remembered the new friend she had acquired, Chastity, with whom she had spent such a pleasant evening and who had promised to help her. Luckily, it was Sunday. She was fairly sure to see Chastity at church if she went to the early Mass. It was not, however, until she was walking home that she saw Chastity. She had almost given up hope of seeing her until she noticed Chastity coming out of church a little way behind her.

It was only when Chastity was close to her that Elizabeth realised with dismay that she was not alone but was walking with a tall fair man in a dark overcoat, who was talking earnestly to her. Deciding that she could not interfere, Elizabeth made as if to go on, but she was too late. Chastity saw her and immediately called out to her.

To Elizabeth's relief, Chastity was pleased to see her and introduced her to the man who was accompanying her. 'This is Jan, my fellow doctor and mentor. You remember my mentioning him to you? Jan, this is the Mrs Allen I was telling you about.'

As Jan turned with a smile to look at her, Elizabeth suddenly felt completely reassured and at peace. 'He is a really good man,' she thought as she looked into his deep blue eyes. Without any feeling of awkwardness, she found herself inviting them both to coffee. To her pleasure, they both accepted immediately.

As soon as they were in Elizabeth's living room, Chastity insisted on making the coffee, leaving Elizabeth and Jan together. She was amazed by how easy she found it to talk to him. In an incredibly short time she was freely answering his questions, telling him something of her life as a teacher, her interest in children with special needs and, finally, about her forty-five-year happy marriage, which had ended with Jim's death two years earlier. Even Chastity's return with the coffee did not stop the flow.

'You must miss your husband very much,' Jan said gently. Somehow, as he looked at her and spoke to her, Elizabeth had an amazing sense of release. She wanted so much someone to talk to, and Jan was that person, even more than Chastity. She felt that he was both wise and kind and that she could trust him.

'I do,' she whispered, and for the first time she allowed her tears to fall in public. That was a relief.

She became aware that Jan was holding her hand and that Chastity had put an arm around her. She felt enfolded in love and her dark fears were banished.

'You know that you will follow him through the doorway and meet him again.' Jan was not asking a question but making a statement that allowed for no doubts.

'Yes, Chastity reminded me of that and I have no doubt now. But…' She paused.

'You have to live alone in the meantime,' Chastity said, finishing her sentence. Elizabeth nodded.

'But now that we have found you, you will no longer be alone,' Jan added. Releasing her hand, he smiled at her as he leaned back and sipped his coffee.

Chastity removed her arm; Elizabeth wiped her eyes and gratefully took the coffee that Chastity offered her. 'I'm so glad I met you both this morning,' she said, after she had taken a drink of her coffee. While she was still wondering if she could tell them the story of the last few days and especially of the last night, which had been so terrible, Jan asked an unexpected question.

'You have had some recent trouble, I think, which you haven't mentioned. Am I right?' She nodded, too surprised to answer. 'In that case, why don't you tell us and let us help you?'

'It all sounds a bit crazy,' she managed to say at last. 'I think I'm simply getting morbid and thinking too much about myself.'

'Why not tell us? Then we can be the best judge of that,' Jan urged her, while Chastity smiled encouragingly.

'I've been having some horrible dreams – nightmares, I suppose I should call them. They've been coming every night, so I'm almost afraid to go to sleep.'

'What happens in them?' Chastity asked as Elizabeth paused, wondering how to continue.

'Nothing much. That's the strange thing. It's just that I'm trying to escape from something evil, which is threatening me. Before it can reach me, I wake up. But last night was worse.' She shivered, reluctant to continue.

After a moment's pause, Jan said, gently but firmly, 'Tell us about that in all the detail you can remember.' With his remarkable blue eyes fixed on her, she was unable to refuse. At first she faltered, but, as Jan encouraged her with his kindly look, she became fluent and didn't miss any incident or feeling.

'You did well,' Jan praised her warmly; 'you remembered the good teaching of your youth, and the dark forces were banished by the cross and by your faith in it, as they always will be.'

'Then you don't think it was something I just imagined?'

'Of course not. The dark angel who had visited you in your dreams grew bolder, refusing to go away when you woke up, but you vanquished him.'

'I never really thought of it like that; at least, not since I was a child.'

'It must be shocking to you, but, for some reason, you have been made aware of the true nature of the world which all humans inhabit. Many of them never realise it.'

'Do you mean a world outside the material world?'

'Yes; although you are mostly unaware of it, you live in a world in which spiritual powers are engaged in a gigantic struggle.'

'The fight between good and evil; is that what you mean?'

'Yes, that is so. But what intrigues me is the reason why you have been made aware of this at this moment. Has something happened? When did your dreams begin?'

'The answer to that is easy. The first dream came a few nights ago. It was the night Chastity had supper with me. It was Monday, I think. I'm right, aren't I?' She looked towards Chastity, who nodded in confirmation. 'I decided, when I thought about it, that it must have been because I had told Chastity about Emmanuel. It upset me when he seemed to disappear, and I know that I was thinking about it again when I went to bed. All kinds of frightening and gruesome ideas were flitting through my mind just before I went to sleep, and so I decided afterwards that they had caused my dreams. I tried to forget about Emmanuel until I heard from Chastity again, but I couldn't. And last night was so bad that I decided that I must talk to you. I was looking out for you, I'm afraid.' She looked apologetically to Chastity.

'I'm very glad you did. I should have spoken to you sooner.'

'That doesn't matter. Did you find anything out about him?'

'Nothing conclusive. As soon as I went back, I spoke to my two remaining flatmates. Alex was very uncomfortable and tried to lie by pretending that she didn't remember him, but Dot, who is very honest, wouldn't allow that. But all I really learned was that Alex was determined to avoid the subject. She did say that Unicorn would know more, but that doesn't help because at this time he is travelling somewhere in Eastern Europe.'

'That's a pity! But what about your other flatmate? There is a third one, isn't there?'

'You're right. There's Eva, who is a model. She's ill and isn't here at present.'

'I'm sorry about that.' Elizabeth felt that the truth she was seeking was eluding her more and more. 'She's the blonde glamorous one, isn't she?'

Chastity nodded. 'She became ill soon after I arrived and went away to recuperate.'

'That's strange. I remember now that she was the one I often saw talking to Emmanuel. She might have been able to tell us something, don't you think?'

Instead of answering her, Chastity turned to look at Jan, who had not spoken for some moments. Elizabeth was struck by his strangely remote look. He seemed almost as if he were in a different world. Perhaps he was uninterested in this seemingly pointless conversation, she thought. After all, he was a dedicated and extremely skilful doctor who had many needier patients to worry about. Even as she thought this, however, he turned towards her and smiled, as if divining her thoughts. 'I think you should tell Elizabeth,' he said to Chastity, 'about our conversation with Max.'

'I was wondering if perhaps I should.' As briefly as she could, Chastity told Elizabeth all that Max had revealed about Eva and Emmanuel. 'I'm afraid it doesn't answer any questions, but it confirms that you had reason to be worried about him, don't you agree?'

'Yes, that seems clear. The poor girl seems to have become quite mentally unbalanced. I hope she has someone kind to look after her?'

'She's being cared for in one of our houses,' Jan assured her, 'but she isn't well enough to be questioned about anything like that.'

'Of course not! Poor child! The life she has led must have been a strain for years. I wonder why girls do it? They think they're so knowledgeable, but really they're very innocent and vulnerable. I suppose we're all a bit like that,' she added suddenly, 'but some of us are luckier. I know I was.'

They were all silent for a few moments, then Chastity spoke. 'I'm afraid we must leave soon. Jan and I have a busy afternoon and evening with some difficult cases, people who need help badly but even in this country don't know where to get it.'

'Of course you must go. I'm sorry I've delayed you.' She was amazed to find that it was almost midday. 'But do please allow me to give you some lunch before you go.' When they seemed to hesitate, she pleaded with them. 'It won't take long. I'll heat up some soup and make sandwiches. You must have a meal before starting a long day's work.'

It was Jan who answered. 'If you'll eat with us, then we accept gratefully.'

Standing up, Chastity added, 'You must allow me to help you. It will do Jan good to have a quiet rest. The principal work is his; I only assist.'

'A very able assistant.' Jan smiled at her.

It was when they were working together in the kitchen that Elizabeth suddenly made her confession. 'I'm so glad that you and Jan agreed to stay for lunch. But I'm afraid that my invitation is as much for my own benefit as for yours.'

'What do you mean?'

'It's so nice to have pleasant company that I'm dreading your going.'

'Last night's experience upset you a lot, didn't it?'

'Much more than it should have done, I'm afraid. I expect you'll think I'm a bit of a baby.'

'Of course I don't. It's quite understandable. When I return this evening, I'll come back, if you'll allow me, and spend the night in your spare room.'

'That's too much to expect! I couldn't think of letting you do that.'

'All the same I will. I won't be any trouble to you because I'm used to having to move about and I'll bring my own sleeping bag.'

Elizabeth's eyes filled with tears. 'Thank you. You're so very kind.'

'That's settled, then.' Chastity smiled at her. 'Of course, it isn't a solution to your problem, but, at least, it's a start. We can ask Jan if he has any better idea over lunch.'

Oddly enough, it was Jan himself who brought up the subject, soon after they had started their lunch. 'It has occurred to me, Elizabeth,' he said, speaking quite casually, 'that you have recently begun to feel lonely and, after your recent experiences, vulnerable. Am I right?'

He looked steadily at her, smiling slightly. As she looked back at him, somewhat surprised, she realised that he was older and much more mature than she had thought when she first met him. Deceived by his handsome features and unusual golden hair, she had supposed him to be about the same age as Chastity, but now she felt that he had the wisdom and understanding of a far older man. She understood why Chastity worked with him devotedly and called him her 'mentor'. *He is a man I can trust completely*, Elizabeth thought.

Becoming aware that he was awaiting her reply, she said quickly. 'I'm afraid you're right. I'm probably a silly old woman, but I do feel like that. I feel safer at the moment, however, because Chastity has kindly promised to spend the night with me. I'll probably be over the worst by tomorrow.'

'You're being brave, and I'm sure that Chastity will be a great comfort to you, but that's only a temporary solution; you need something more permanent.' He paused, looking steadily at her for a moment, then continued, 'You're an intelligent woman who is used to being active, particularly in caring for other people: your pupils, especially the less gifted ones; your own children and, in his last years, your husband. I imagine that, when he died, you were tired and almost glad to have a rest for a time.'

'You're quite right,' she agreed. 'I was, for a time, but now I feel useless. I want to do something helpful, but I can't imagine what that can possibly be.'

'Chastity mentioned that to me and I think I may have an answer. You can help me to solve a problem.'

'How can I possibly do that?'

Jan smiled as he helped himself to another sandwich. 'I need someone to help a young man whom I recently met in a hostel when I was called in there to deal with someone who had been injured in a fight. Sean – that's his name – had not been involved in the fight, but he'd been very helpful in separating the two men, or so the warden told me. It was Sean who forced the aggressor to give up his knife. A brave action, don't you think?'

'Very brave! But how can someone like me possibly help him?'

'Life has dealt him some very bad blows recently. He has lost pretty well everything, but he's determined to start afresh. He has a steady job now, but he desperately needs a home. The hostel is no place for him. I am hoping that you might be willing to rent your spare room to him. What do you think?'

'Do you trust him?'

'Yes. He has many good qualities, but he needs a home and a little stability.'

'If you trust him, then I'll take him on a month's trial.' Almost horrified at her boldness, she looked at Chastity, who smiled reassuringly at her. 'How soon would he want to come?' Already, Elizabeth admitted to herself, she was hoping for a delay, some excuse to hold back a bit. But Jan didn't work like that.

'I'll speak to him. I imagine that he'll be prepared to come tomorrow evening. You do have a room ready, don't you?'

It was impossible to deny that. 'But I don't know if it will suit him. It's not very well furnished. Apart from the bed, there's not much more than a small wardrobe and a chest of drawers.'

'I'm sure that it'll be more than adequate. Sean has very few belongings. It's not simply because he's had difficulties, but I believe that he travels light, as Chastity and I do.'

'I see.' There was no further objection she could now make. 'Will he want me to provide food for him?'

'You can arrange that between yourselves,' Jan suggested.

Unexpectedly, Chastity intervened. 'I think he needs a bit of mothering. I also think that he'll be grateful for it and that you'll enjoy it.'

'Have you met him, then?' Elizabeth was relieved to know this.

'Yes, once. I liked him, although he's not an easy person. He has difficulties in expressing his feelings, but I would say he's genuine.'

Jan laughed. 'He's not an ogre, Elizabeth! On the contrary. He may be a bit wild at times, but he's been brought up well. He knows how to defend himself in the jungle, but he'll be well mannered with you. He was brought up as a Catholic. His full name is Sean O'Reilly. His father was an Irish Republican, I believe, who married an English Protestant. Unfortunately, it didn't work out. The father disappeared, perhaps killed. The mother resented the son she'd been left with and eventually remarried an Englishman who wasn't too keen on an Irish stepson. I can't tell you much more. I'm sure you'll discover the rest yourself.'

'It sounds an unhappy start. How old is he?'

'In his early thirties, I think.' Finishing his coffee, Jan stood up.

'My son would have been twenty-eight,' Elizabeth said.

'Your son?' Chastity was surprised.

'Yes. He was killed in an accident many years ago. I still miss him.'

'Then you will be all the more ready to welcome Sean. I was sure you would.' To her surprise, Jan bent and kissed her on the cheek. 'Chastity and I must go now. I hope to bring Sean tomorrow.' Chastity also kissed her as she promised to return that evening. They were gone, but Elizabeth Allen's world had been completely changed.

Chapter Fifteen

'Hi, there! Is anyone at home?' Sean O'Reilly called out cheerfully as he closed the front door of the flat behind him.

'I'm in the kitchen,' Elizabeth answered. 'The meal's almost ready to serve. You've just got time to freshen up if you hurry.'

'OK! Will do.' Sean's face appeared briefly around the kitchen door. 'It smells good.' He gave her a friendly but rather shy grin, as he had done when they had first met only four days before. 'See you.' He disappeared.

It was amazing, Elizabeth thought as she laid the table, how quickly he had settled in and how easy it had all been, in spite of her fears. Dr Jan had been right. As she put the final touches to the meal, she remembered clearly the previous Monday evening, when Jan had first brought Sean to see her. She had been nervous, expecting to meet some neurotic young man with all the signs of an unhappy past. The reality had been so different.

She had found herself being introduced to a slim but muscular young man of around thirty, wearing shabby but spotless jeans, a checked shirt and a well-preserved leather jacket. His dark hair, although cut deliberately short, insisted on falling into rebellious waves. With his regular, clear-cut features, he was good-looking, even beside Jan. But what she noticed most were his dark brown eyes, which looked straight at her, fearlessly yet appealingly, and next his warm, friendly grin as he shook her hand firmly with his own work-calloused hand.

He certainly travelled light, as Jan had said, his only luggage being one travel bag and, strangely enough, a document case. He had caused hardly any extra trouble for her. After the first morning, he had insisted that she should stay in bed and let him get his own breakfast. After his cheery farewell the first time, she had got up quickly, suspicious as to what disorder she might find. To her surprise, he had left everything amazingly neat and tidy.

He had told her that he would be back about six thirty, and he had kept his word. She had kept hers by producing a hot, tasty meal. She found it stimulating to have someone to cook for. He was easy to talk to and the time spent over the evening meal passed quickly. After that, he helped with the clearing away. Once or twice, he had watched a television programme with her. Most of the time, however, he spent in his own room, listening to the radio.

He always said 'goodnight' to her before going to bed, which he usually did quite early. She found it comforting to know that he was there, and her bad dreams had, so far, not returned.

Her thoughts were interrupted at this point as he came bounding into the living room, very ready for the hot meal she placed in front of him. 'It's a cold, frosty night,' he remarked. 'This hotpot's just the job. You're a good cook. I reckon I've struck lucky.'

'So have I.' They smiled at each other. So far, she hadn't asked him any questions and he had volunteered little information, except to tell her that although he was a qualified HGV driver, he had had to accept an inferior job driving a light van. He intended to improve on this, however, as soon as he could.

'This is the best meal I've had,' he continued, as she offered him a second helping, 'since the stew I used to buy at a small bistro in France. Of course, they gave it some fancy French name, but to me it was just a delicious stew, and it was what I needed after a hard day's driving. That and a glass or two of wine, much better than any I've ever been able to afford in England.'

'Have you been to France often?'

'Yes; at one time I went nearly every week. I drove my truck from the north to Dover, went across on the ferry and then drove across France to Strasbourg, then back again. I made several drops on the way, of course, so it took several days.'

'Where did you spend the night?' She had never known anyone who had lived like this.

'Mostly in the bunk in my truck.'

'It must have been a hard life – all that driving and the responsibility.'

'I suppose some people might think it was, but I loved it. Once I got in my truck, I felt free.' He paused to open the tin of

Coke he had brought in with him. Elizabeth wondered why he had given up the job if he liked it so much, but she felt that she had no right to ask.

There was no need, however, for her to ask, as Sean, for the first time, was in an expansive mood. 'Of course, they were a cowboy lot I worked for. And they didn't care how I did the job as long as it was done. That suited me down to the ground. It meant I could take it easy when I felt like it and then make a dash to catch up. It was a bit hairy at times, but it worked. That's what I liked. I don't work regularly. You don't get that sort of freedom with the big companies, but you get job security and better pay.' He continued to eat silently.

'Why did you give up the job?' she finally plucked up courage to ask him.

'Because I was a fool.' His bitterness was obvious. 'I fell for the security bait and better pay. Well, not so much me as Sharon.'

'Sharon?'

'Yes, she was my partner. She nagged at me until I gave in. She wanted a bigger house and all those things most women always seem to want. And, of course, after Terry was born it was all the more important.'

'I didn't know you have a partner and a son.' Elizabeth was surprised.

'Did have, you mean. When things went wrong she left with another guy she'd been seeing for some time, although I didn't know. What's more, she took Terry with her. I haven't seen either of them since. I don't even know where they are.'

'What a terrible thing for her to do!'

Sean shrugged. 'I can't really blame her. She was only looking after herself and the kid, as she saw it. After a time, you see, I couldn't hack the new job. It was too regulated, like being in the army or something. The bosses wanted to know where I was and what I was doing for every single minute of the day. I just couldn't take it. In the end, I had to chuck it or go mad. Sharon didn't understand that. All she understood was no pay cheque. It's natural.' He paused to take a swig of his Coke.

'After they went, I lost it completely. Practically became an "alco". I ended up jobless, penniless and finally homeless.' He grinned at her. 'Pretty effing stupid wasn't it?'

'Didn't anyone care?'

'There wasn't anyone to care. There never had been before Sharon and now there wasn't again. I'd reached the bottom.'

'How ever did you get out of it?'

'Sheer luck. I went back to the village where I'd lived for several years when I was a kid and actually met an old mate of mine. He gave me a right bollocking and then found me this job through a cousin of his who lives in London. It isn't much, but it's a start, and at least I'd had the sense to keep my driving licence clean, so I got the job and managed to scrounge a room in the hostel. That seemed a great break after a few nights' dossing on the streets.'

'Have you been there long?'

'A few months. It wasn't much good. Most of the guys there were no-hopers. I didn't want to become like that again.'

'It was very lucky that Dr Jan found you, wasn't it?'

'The best bit of luck I've had in years. He's an amazing guy, don't you think? Everyone respects him, even in that godforsaken dump. There wasn't any reason for him to bother with me, but he did. And he understood just what I needed.'

Elizabeth smiled. 'He understood what I needed too. An amazing guy, as you say.'

'Do you know anything about him?'

'Nothing, really. I met him for the first time on Sunday, when he was with his colleague Dr Chastity. I'd only met her twice before, but she'd been very friendly. I invited them to coffee because I wanted to talk to Chastity, but I found myself talking to Jan instead. He realised that I was lonely straightaway and suggested you as a lodger. Much to my surprise, I agreed. I was shocked after I'd said it.'

Sean laughed. 'That was just how I felt! He's such an amazing guy that you hardly have to tell him anything. He just knows. And what's more amazing, he's right. At least, I think so. I hope you do, too. You don't regret taking me in, do you?'

'Of course not! I feel ten years younger!'

For a few minutes more they lingered over their meal, till Elizabeth asked, 'Are you going out tonight?'

'No. Do you want me to? If I'm in the way, I can always go into my room.'

'You don't have to do that. I just thought that, since it's Friday night, you might be planning to go out. Most young people do these days, I understand.'

'You mean I might want to have a good time getting pissed and picking up a bird? No, thanks. I've done that far too often in my pre-Sharon days and afterwards, like a bloody fool. Birds and booze have lost their appeal, for now at least. I want to make something of my life before it's too late. You approve of that, don't you?' He looked almost aggressively at her.

'Of course I do,' she answered him quickly. 'There's a good detective film on television later. Why don't you watch it with me? You did say that you liked detective stories, didn't you?'

'Suits me fine. Tell you what: you make yourself comfortable in your armchair. I'll clear away and make coffee for us. You don't have to worry. I promise to leave the kitchen just as you like it.' Before she could protest, he had her settled in her chair and was already stacking the dishes quickly and deftly.

Leaning back and closing her eyes, she relaxed happily, listening to his movements in the kitchen. It was amazing how her life had changed in a few days. Becoming aware that Sean had returned to the room, she opened her eyes. He had just come into the room, carrying a tray with mugs and the coffee pot.

'I was wondering if you'd fallen asleep?'

'I think I did doze off for a minute, but I'm ready for the coffee.'

'Good. It just needs a few minutes to settle. I used the proper stuff; no instant for you. Tell me,' he asked, casually and unexpectedly, 'did you ever meet a guy called Emmanuel? I believe he hung out around here at one time?'

'Emmanuel?' She sat up, shocked, staring at him.

'I thought you'd remember if you'd met him. It's an unusual name, but I don't suppose it's very likely.'

Making a big effort to speak calmly, she replied, 'I did, in fact, meet someone with that name a few times.'

'Was he a slim, dark guy who spoke English well but with a bit of an accent – a friendly sort of bloke?'

'That sounds like the man I met. What made you think that I might know him?'

'He mentioned these parts when I talked to him.'

'You talked to him? When was it? Was it recently?'

'No. It was months ago. I'd practically forgotten all about him until Dr Jan asked me if I'd ever met him.'

'Dr Jan? Did he know Emmanuel, then?'

'I'm not sure. I rather think that a friend of his wants to find this guy, Emmanuel, and he's asked Dr Jan to look out for him. He seems to have disappeared and his mates are worried about him. When I told Dr Jan about my meeting with Emmanuel, he seemed to have the idea that I might have been the last person to see him.'

In spite of herself, Elizabeth was curious. She wanted to shrink away from the subject because of her irrational fear that something evil had happened to Emmanuel, but she still felt that she ought to confront it. 'Where did you last see him?'

'It was in a quiet, back-street pub one night, near the hostel.' Sean sat down, obviously forgetting the coffee for the moment. 'It was raining heavily and I went in for shelter, not for beer. I was also desperate for a bit of human companionship. I saw this guy sitting at a table by himself, drinking a Coke. He had a kind of lonely air, so I joined him with my drink. He seemed pleased and ready to talk.

'He didn't tell me much about himself except his name and that he had been spending some time in this part of London – he even mentioned this road. When I tried to ask him more, he changed the subject and began to talk about me. I don't usually talk about myself; not truthfully, at any rate. I don't believe people are interested, so I usually put on this act. I'm this macho guy who likes a good time and doesn't care a fuck. You know what I mean?'

'You didn't try that on with me, did you?'

'I knew that you were genuine, otherwise Dr Jan wouldn't have brought me here.'

She smiled. 'And you didn't try it on with Emmanuel?'

'I was just about to when he suddenly lifted his head and looked straight at me. Do you remember his big, dark brown eyes? He reminded me at that moment of the bitch I had when I was a kid. She followed me everywhere, and when I got mad and kicked and swore at her she'd just come back and sit looking at me. She cared, and so did Emmanuel; too much for his own good, I reckon.'

'I, too, felt that about him,' Elizabeth interrupted him. 'He'd been hurt, but it didn't stop him caring. Nothing ever would. I thought that Christ might have looked like that at times.'

'I don't know about that, but I do know that I had to tell him some of the truth about myself. He listened carefully. He didn't say much, but he made me feel better somehow. I felt it might be worth carrying on.'

'What happened?'

'Nothing. It was late and we left the pub. He said he hoped we'd meet again and I agreed. He turned left; I turned right. I looked back, but I couldn't see him. He seemed to have disappeared. When I told Dr Jan about it, he seemed to think that I might have been the last person to see Emmanuel. It's weird.'

They were both still silent when, unexpectedly, the front door bell rang sharply. 'Who on earth can that be?' Elizabeth wondered. If Sean had not been there, she would have been afraid.

'No need for you to move. I'll go and see.' He went off quickly, and upon flinging the front door open, he found himself, to his surprise, confronting Chastity. She looked much the same as she had when he had last seen her. Her hair was strained back into its unflattering bun; she was wearing her dreary, unfashionable suit, but, much to his surprise, she was carrying an elegant bouquet of deep red rosebuds.

They stared at each other until Chastity spoke. 'I've come to bring these roses for Elizabeth. It's not a bad time, is it?'

'No, we've just finished our meal. She'll be pleased to see you.' Standing aside, he followed her down the hall, wondering, as he had done the first time he met her, how anyone could wear such hideous clothes and still look beautiful.

'Who is it?' Elizabeth called out.

'It's me,' Chastity answered, as she came into the living room.

'I was wondering if you would like these roses. They have been sent to me and I have nowhere to put them, especially as I had a similar bunch last week and they're still perfect.'

'They're beautiful! But surely they must have come from some admirer. Won't he be hurt when he discovers that you've given them to me?'

'Unicorn sent them. He's away until next week, so he won't know. I don't see why he should care if he did. I would like you to have them. Please accept them.'

'Thank you so much!' Elizabeth kissed Chastity impulsively as she took the roses.

'I'll get a vase,' Sean suggested. 'I've seen one in the kitchen.'

As he vanished, Elizabeth begged Chastity to sit down and stay a little while.

'I'm afraid I can't stay long as I have a report to write.'

'At least stay for some coffee. Sean's just made some.'

'Thank you. That would be very pleasant.' After sitting down, she asked quietly, 'Are you comfortable with Sean?'

'Very. He's no trouble. On the contrary, he's very helpful.'

'I'll tell Jan tomorrow. He'll be very pleased, but I expect he'll come to see you himself soon.'

Elizabeth had just begun to pour out the coffee when Sean returned. He'd found a suitable vase, he explained, but had left the flowers soaking in a bowl of water. 'But you'll never guess what I found in one of the kitchen drawers!' Putting down the extra mug he'd also brought, he produced in his left hand a box of Scrabble. 'This is one of the few games I enjoyed playing when I was a kid.'

'Jim and I played quite a lot when he was ill,' Elizabeth explained. 'I put it away when he died and forgot about it.'

'I'm sorry I didn't know. Would you rather that I put it away again?'

'Of course not.' She opened the box. 'It's all here. It might be fun to have a game again.'

'Why not?' Sean turned towards Chastity. 'Would you care to join us? It'd be more fun with three people.'

'Chastity is very busy,' Elizabeth said quickly.

'But not too busy,' Chastity cut her short. 'I used to enjoy playing at school. I'm sure I've got time for one game, at least.'

It was a lively and fiercely competitive game, at least as far as Sean and Chastity were concerned. Elizabeth was surprised and pleased to see how young and carefree the two of them suddenly looked and how much they both delighted in the competition, which finally left Sean a cheerful and rather exuberant winner.

'You shouldn't be so cocky,' Elizabeth admonished him.

'Why not?' he challenged her. 'After all, I'm only a semi-literate trucker and I've just beaten a school teacher and a doctor.' Turning towards Chastity, he grinned at her cheerfully. 'It's done you good to have a break, doc! Why don't you go the whole way and let your hair down literally? I bet it's beautiful.'

It was a deliberate challenge. Elizabeth held her breath. But, after looking straight into his eyes, Chastity said coolly. 'Why not?' With deft fingers she released the masses of her hair, which fell dark and shining almost to her waist. Her unusual beauty suddenly seemed to shine out.

For a moment Sean was silent, then, at last, he said, 'I see why you hide it. If you didn't, you'd have all the men lusting after you.'

'It would make little difference,' Chastity replied coolly, 'since I have no desire to reciprocate their feelings.' Her dark, luminous eyes now challenged him.

'OK,' Sean said quickly. 'I believe you. I'm a friend and no more. You must believe me.'

'I do.' For a moment they smiled at each other, then, turning towards Elizabeth, Chastity said, 'I've had a lovely break, but I'm afraid I must go now.'

'Come again soon,' Elizabeth invited her.

'I'll see you out,' Sean offered. As he came back, he said fervently. 'I don't believe I've seen anyone so beautiful before.'

'It's not just the face; it's the soul, too. I can't think of any man who would be equal to her except Dr Jan himself.'

'I know I'm not,' Sean replied.

'Do you think that she and Dr Jan are really...' she hesitated and then went on, '...very close?'

'Close, but not in the sexy way you're hinting. I'm surprised at you. They're both dedicated to the work they do and I guess that's all. Sex isn't everything, you know.

Elizabeth laughed, 'That should have been my line, not yours.'

'Ah, well, my years of booze and birds have taught me something about life!' He began to collect together the Scrabble pieces. 'I don't know why, but I've just remembered something Emmanuel said when I last met him.'

'What was that?'

'He said, "I'm afraid that the end of my time here is coming soon. I can't avoid it." '

'Didn't you ask him what he meant?' Elizabeth felt a cold shiver pass over her.

'No. I was too sorry for myself. I imagined that he was just feeling suicidal, as I was. But now I realise he wasn't. He was speaking the truth and I was too fucking selfish to notice. He was afraid, I think, but he was brave because he went off to face it alone. I might have helped him! Christ, what a selfish bastard I am!'

'You can't honestly blame yourself.'

'Guys like me never do anything useful. We're too selfish.'

'That's rubbish and you know it. At least you can tell Dr Jan. It might help him. I'm sure that he wants to find out the truth.'

'You're right. That's one thing I can do. It might not be too late. But, how can I get hold of him? I've missed my opportunity again.'

'I'm sure he'll come here soon, but, if he doesn't, you can tell Chastity. She'll know what to do.'

'You're right. I'll do just that.' He was relaxed again. 'Now, you sit down and make yourself comfortable. I'll switch the TV on. Our programme's just about to start.' Sitting opposite him, Elizabeth relaxed happily. Life seemed comfortable and secure again.

Several hours later, alone in his bed, Sean remembered clearly Emmanuel's face. For the first time he understood. He saw again the pain and fear in those remarkable brown eyes and the courage of the smile with which Emmanuel had walked away, apparently to his death. He was a good man, Sean realised, and whatever threatened him was evil.

'Good' and 'evil' were words he had never much thought about before. Now he knew that they described powerful forces that existed. He saw in his mind's eye the face of Jan, who had spoken to him so wisely and so firmly and, above all, with such understanding that it had scarcely seemed necessary to tell him anything. He was good, and his goodness was more powerful than even Emmanuel's. That was clear to him now.

As he was about to fall asleep, a vision passed before his eyes of Chastity with her shining, dark hair, her unfathomable dark eyes and her brilliant, joyous smile. He had exclaimed to Elizabeth about her beauty and Elizabeth had said it was not simply a beauty of her face but also of her soul. Soul! He had never thought much about souls, but now he was sure they existed. It seemed to him that he already loved Chastity. It was a feeling, however, very different from any he had ever felt before. Certainly, it was in another world from those grubby, brief sexual episodes, which he had tried to glorify by calling them 'love'. Remembering his frequent crude taunts about this so-called love and about women, he blushed for himself. What an ignorant fool he had been! He had never before seen more than the surface of things, but now his eyes had been opened with a glimpse of the abiding reality.

Chapter Sixteen

On arriving back at the flat, Chastity found Dot busily ironing to the accompaniment of loud pop music. As soon as she became aware of Chastity's presence, she switched off the radio. 'Sorry! I wasn't sure you were coming back. If I'm in your way, I'll move to the kitchen. I've just got to iron these clothes before tomorrow. I've been putting it off all week.'

'Do carry on.' Chastity sat down. 'Don't let me interrupt such a worthwhile task. I must go and work myself soon.' For the moment, however, it seemed more fun to watch Dot. 'Is Alex in?' she asked idly.

'Yes. She came in just after you left. She's preparing herself for an exciting evening with Les Girls.'

Chastity frowned. 'What does that mean?'

'A night of drinking, I suspect. A night when the girls go out drinking, trying to pretend that they don't mind that there's no men in their lives, although they're hoping they might meet one, quite desperately in fact.'

'I can't imagine Alex behaving like that. At least, I've never seen her doing it.'

Dot carefully selected another garment from the heap. 'Perhaps not, but this is the "post-James" era,' she explained as she firmly smoothed out a cotton shirt. 'When she had him, Alex could feel superior, but without him she's just another of the post-thirties, feeling desperate. You probably think I'm being a bitch, and maybe I am, but it's still true. In their thirties, lots of women become obsessed with their empty wombs. It's more about wanting to be a woman than needing a man. A frightening thought! Times have changed since you were last in the "civilised" world, I imagine.'

'They obviously have! But, at least you're safe. You have Richard.'

'Yes, I have Richard, and so I can cheerfully spend Friday evening ironing because there is Richard tomorrow.'

'I suppose you must include me among the desperate women?'

'Not really.' Dot considered the question. 'You're different. You have that old-fashioned thing, a vocation, and you could obviously have Unicorn, too, if you wanted him. Although she tried to laugh it off, I guess Alex was pretty livid when I told her about the second bouquet.'

'It might have been better not to have told her.'

'Don't be an idiot! Why ever not? She needs bringing down a peg. Where are they, by the way? What have you done with them?'

'I took them to Mrs Allen, who lives downstairs. She was delighted, and I certainly don't need two bouquets. The others are still alive, as you can see.'

Putting down her iron, Dot began to laugh. 'Poor Unicorn! How have the mighty fallen!'

'You seem to have found something to laugh at! Can I share the joke?' It was Alex's voice. Turning around rather guiltily, they saw her standing in the doorway to her room. Chastity had never seen her dressed like that before. The elegant, professional woman had vanished. She was wearing a black mini that clung to every curve; long, sparkling earrings, which almost reached her shoulders; and a matching pendant, which nestled provocatively between her much-exposed breasts. Her hair was loose and fluffy, her lips deep red and pouting, her eyes darkly made-up.

'I don't see why you shouldn't,' Dot answered, before Chastity could prevent her. 'You'll never guess what Chastity has done with Unicorn's latest floral tribute!'

'I'm sure I can't. Do tell me.'

'She's given them to that old Mrs Allen who lives on the ground floor. And what do you think? The old dear was delighted with them.'

For a moment there was silence, then Alex laughed. Startled, Chastity looked at her and realised that the laughter was, amazingly, genuine. 'Poor Unicorn!' Alex sat on the arm of a chair. 'I don't think that anyone has treated one of his romantic gestures so dismissively before. He won't like it, you know. He'll be very angry, I should guess, if you tell him. Will you tell him?'

'Certainly, if he asks me and maybe even if he doesn't ask me.'

Dot, too, was laughing. 'I'd like to be a fly on the wall when you tell him. Wouldn't you, Alex?'

Suddenly, Alex was serious. 'You must be careful, Chastity. He's not what he seems. There have been times when I've hated him. Or perhaps it was myself I hated.' She looked sadly at Chastity.

Without stopping to think, or so it seemed, Chastity asked, 'Do you have to go out tonight? Why don't you stay in with Dot and me?'

'Why don't you?' Dot urged.

Alex regarded them with a slightly ironical smile. 'How sweet of you, or is it really that you want help with the chores? Sorry, but I never was the domesticated stay-at-home type. Furthermore, my friends are expecting me.' She stood up. 'If I don't go now, I shall be late.'

'At least don't go dressed like that,' Chastity said, calmly. Dot caught her breath, horrified.

'Whatever do you mean? Have you gone completely mad, Chastity? I don't tell you what to wear, although your clothes are revoltingly dowdy and dreary. Why, then, do you insult me? I'm not one of your pathetic, poverty-stricken clients. I suppose it's all right for you to patronise them, but don't try it with me.' Alex was furious.

Nevertheless, Chastity stood her ground. 'I'm sorry I've annoyed you. I certainly didn't mean to patronise you or anyone. It's just that I think that your clothes give the wrong impression of yourself.'

'What the fuck are you talking about? You scarcely know me, anyway.'

'But I know how you used to be.' Chastity looked at Alex without flinching.

'And what is that supposed to mean?'

'When you were at school. When you were in the sixth form, people respected you and you always helped to keep the weaker ones out of trouble when they were tempted to drink too much and misbehave with the boys at those horrible parties we had sometimes.'

'Oh, my God! Grow up, Chastity!' Alex gave a mocking laugh. 'You're talking about thirteen years ago or more! You're talking about another world, another age. You can't be a pious prat of a schoolgirl forever, you know! Even if *you* want to, I don't. There's no future in that.'

'Is there any future in what you're doing? What has changed you, Alex? What are you afraid of?'

For one moment it seemed that Alex was going to hit Chastity as she glared at her. She half-raised her arm, but, as Chastity stood unmoved, she slowly dropped it again. 'You're just a fool, Chastity! I haven't really changed. I was simply acting a part then: the perfect schoolgirl, admired in the whole school and much loved in the House. I succeeded to a point, but there was always your precious cousin who always did better, apparently without any effort. There were times when I think I hated her. But how can you possibly know any of these things? You weren't there!'

When Chastity did not reply, Alex continued, 'I suppose dear Caroline told you? Why the hell should she, and when did she? Did you spend all your time together after school, devoted little cousins, until she married some wretched curate and you became a holy missionary? Of course, I remember now that you told me she'd died. I'm sorry about that, but that doesn't explain you.' She looked suspiciously at Chastity. 'I don't remember Caroline mentioning a cousin Chastity. Who the hell are you? Why ever did you come here?'

'I explained that in my letter and you had my references.'

'Don't you think you're getting a bit paranoid, Alex?' Dot tried to intervene. 'Chastity doesn't mean to upset you. We both thought that you might be overreacting to James, that's all.'

'And what if I am? Is it any business of either of you? I intend to have a good time. OK, I'll probably drink too much, but I'll have fun with people who know what life's about. Will you please give up and get out of my way? Now!'

Without another word, Dot returned to her ironing and Chastity moved aside. Alex went quickly out of the room and, a few minutes later, they heard the front door slam behind her. 'Phew! I'm amazed we've survived.' Dot let out her breath. 'Whatever did you do that for?'

'I don't really know. I just thought I had to. She's so unhappy.'

'Aren't we all? That's life, isn't it?' Dot unplugged her iron.

Chastity sat down again. 'I thought things were going well for you now? You certainly look good these days. Surely Richard approves of the new you? Of Dorothy, I mean?'

Dot shrugged. 'Who knows? He's still around, that's true. But he's giving his farewell party in two weeks' time, and little Dot-Dorothy is required to be very busy helping him to arrange it.'

'I didn't realise it was so soon.'

'Time, as always, rushes past, or so it seems. A few days after the party he goes up north, and a couple of days after that he starts his new job.'

'And what about you? You did tell him what you thought, didn't you?'

'I certainly did. I thought about what you'd said to me and it made sense.'

'And what did he say?'

'That's the trouble. When I look back, I realise that he didn't actually say anything definite. Oh, he talked things over with me, appreciated my point of view. He was terribly amenable, in fact, but...'

'But what?'

'He avoided giving a real answer. It all needed thinking about it, he said. Of course, he agreed in principle. But was this the right moment? Wouldn't it be better to move north first before we finally decided? And so on.'

'And what did you say?'

'There wasn't much more for me to say, was there? I reminded him about my chance of promotion and that I didn't want to miss it for nothing. When I pushed him, he did say he didn't like us being apart for six months. When I didn't give in, he said he'd like to think it all over and we'd talk about it again. I'm still waiting and time's running out. If you ask me, he's terrified of committing himself.'

'He wants you, but he also wants his freedom. Is that what you mean?'

'That's about it. He's being terribly sweet and loving and waiting for me to give in, to "trust him", as he puts it. And my trouble is that I'm feeling very weak, especially when I look at Alex and Eva.'

'I don't think you need to give in, certainly not yet. I'm sure that he doesn't want to lose you.'

'I'm not exactly giving in. In fact, I'm pretty sure that I've made up my mind. I'd rather like to talk to you, if you've got a few minutes.'

'Of course I have. I'd like to hear.'

'Well, I'm beginning to feel that I've given Richard his chance. There's really nothing more to say. If he can't decide in a fortnight's time, I must.' She paused for a moment and then continued, 'If he doesn't want to make a decision, then I shall. I've decided that I shall accept the promotion and, as soon as I can, I shall move into a flat with a radiologist I'm friendly with at the hospital. I don't want to stay here, especially when you leave, as I expect you will. I want a more permanent home. What do you think?'

'You do enjoy your work, don't you?'

'Yes, and with more responsibility I'm sure that I shall enjoy it even more. If it doesn't work out, I shall make a complete break and go overseas, perhaps with an aid agency.'

'You sound pretty confident.'

'I am.'

'Have you thought that you might now be sorry if Richard decides in favour of marriage?' Chastity's smile was definitely mischievous.

'Do you specialise in asking awkward questions? Frankly, I'm not sure. I'll have to see how I feel if he does. Will that satisfy you?'

Chastity laughed. 'You have my blessing.'

'I should think so, since you're largely responsible for my rethink. It was you, after all, who convinced me that it wasn't just my right but my duty to be true to myself. I'd never realised, until I started thinking seriously about it, how dependent I'd become on Richard. When he suddenly announced that he was leaving, I was ready to give up everything so long as I didn't lose him, and he seemed to expect that I would. I was well on the way to becoming a battered wife or, what's worse, a battered girlfriend. What is it that makes women so ready to be subservient?'

'I suppose it's because they long to love and be loved. They're also afraid to lose their chance, and men exploit this. Don't forget, however, there are also some women who do the same towards men.'

'I believe you, but I haven't met any. But the fact is that Dot was ready to grovel and Dorothy isn't. Richard's attitude should be made clear in a fortnight.' After folding up the last garment she had ironed, she took the iron and the ironing board into the kitchen and returned smiling. 'Thank God that's done! What a relief! By the way, you're invited to this ridiculous party. Dr Jan, too, if he can bear it. Can you manage it?'

'I should think so, but I can't answer for Jan.'

'Well, I hope he can, but no need to worry; Unicorn will be back and I'm sure he'll be willing to come with you, although it's not exactly his scene.'

'I don't know about Unicorn, but would it be in order if I invited Mrs Allen's new lodger, Sean O'Reilly? He might enjoy it.'

'Ah, now I see why it took you so long to deliver the roses! You're really quite a wicked young woman, aren't you?' The idea seemed to be greatly amusing to Dot.

'Rubbish!' Chastity smiled back at her. 'I was asked to join in a game of Scrabble, which was fun. I felt like a schoolgirl again.' She sighed. 'That doesn't happen often. Is everyone in this house invited?'

'Sure, even Paul and Rupert. Paul is a bit disdainful, but Rupert seems quite keen. I think he might be quite human if Paul would let him off the leash a bit. What do you think?'

'I really have no idea. I imagine their relationship is rather a complex one. I hope they'll enjoy the party. It's going to be rather large and rather mixed, isn't it?'

'You can say that again. I can't think why Richard wants to waste his money on it. He seems to have gone a bit mad; madder than usual, I mean. I think it's supposed to be his last fling before he settles down to respectability.'

'Why are you so worried about it?'

'I just have a feeling that it might go wrong. It's to be one of these way-out, liberated parties; a don't-be-afraid-to-be-yourself party, however unpleasant you may be. In fact, the more obnoxious by my old-fashioned standards the better. Chavs particularly welcome.'

'Chavs? Who or what are they?'

'Now you're asking! I asked several people for a definition, but they always seem to come up with something different. I think, basically, a "chav" is loud, aggressive, self-made and pretty rich. Although I can't imagine that Richard knows any millionaires.'

'Perhaps I'll fit in after all,' Chastity replied unexpectedly. 'I'm rich, and, according to Alex, I'm aggressively unfashionable and very much myself.'

'You, rich!' Dot was amazed. 'But I thought that you lived a life of poverty or something like it. Was I wrong?'

'That is my choice. But some years ago I inherited a large fortune, mostly in property and land. It's all tied up and has to be maintained. Any surplus income I give to the society I work for. I would consider it wrong to sell any of the estate; it should be passed on.'

'That sounds positively saintly.'

'Certainly not. I don't need the money or want it.'

'Do you think Unicorn knows?'

'What possible concern could it be to him? Oh, I see. You think that is why he is courting me. Oh, dear, how unflattering!' She laughed.

Dot was embarrassed. 'Oh, curses, I've put my foot in it, as usual. Sorry! Your money might be an added charm, but it's obvious it's you yourself he wants. He's not short of money, anyway.'

'So I don't need to worry. That's good.'

Dot yawned suddenly. 'I'm sorry, I seem to be very tired. I think I'd better go to bed before I say anything else stupid. I've got a big party-planning day tomorrow. How about you?'

'I still have some more reports to write for Jan before tomorrow. I must start now or I'll never finish them.'

It was late when Chastity finally settled down in bed, and, at first, sleep would not come easily. Her thoughts were occupied with many of the problems she had encountered recently. What was the truth about Emmanuel? she wondered. Why was Alex so desperate and so unwilling to be helped? What had changed her so much? And then there was Unicorn's surprising persistence. How should she receive him when he returned, especially now that she knew the truth about Helen?

Slowly, she sank into peaceful oblivion – then, suddenly, she became aware of brightness and warmth. Opening her eyes, she discovered that she was resting on a comfortable wooden bench under the shade of a widely-spreading willow tree, the delicate fronds of which were floating caressingly in the gentle, refreshing breeze. Behind her, she could hear the sound of water falling. Turning her head, she was able to see a pond, into which a stream trickled gently over a waterfall of grey rocks with a soothing sound. Before her stretched a green lawn, broken up occasionally by groups of brightly-coloured flowers under trees, some of which were covered with fragrant blossom.

Standing up, she began to wander slowly across the lawn, stopping occasionally to enjoy the perfume of the blossom. Where was she? Why had she come here? Then, as she saw a man coming towards her, she remembered. She had been brought here to meet Tim. It was so long since she had last seen him.

'Tim,' she called out as she ran towards him. Turning towards her, he hurried to her with arms outstretched. 'Darling,' she said as he drew her close to him. Their lips met. For a few blissful moments they stayed together. As he released her, they walked back together to the bench with their arms entwined.

Now they were sitting together on the bench. He was holding her close and she was resting her head on his shoulder. Looking up through the delicate tracery of the willow branches, she could see the small white cloud drifting lazily across the azure sky.

She could not see his face, but she had no need to. The clear lines of that face, with its broad forehead, straight nose, firm chin and the unexpectedly tender curves of his lips, were always in her mind. Looking up for a moment, she saw his dark hazel eyes underneath straight, bushy, dark eyebrows. His look was one of tender concern as he kissed her again.

She was ecstatically happy. She felt secure and protected, as she had always done with Tim. Nothing could harm her. Suddenly, she moved away a little. This hadn't always been true. 'Where is Rosie?' she asked. 'Isn't she with you?'

'No, not this time. This is an extra meeting. I've been sent to comfort and warn you, my darling. It's not good for Rosie to be here.'

'Warn me? What do you mean?'

'You are in a more dangerous situation now than you have ever been.'

'Are you saying that London is more dangerous than the wilds of Africa?'

'Much more, because the danger isn't obvious. You must be very careful. People are not what they seem. Some are serpents. You must beware of being deceived.'

'But surely Jan will protect me?'

'He will when he can. The Lord himself will protect you, but there are times, as you know, when even this must seem to fail. Be brave, my darling, as you have always been. Rosie and I are waiting for you.' He bent to kiss her again, but she pulled herself away.

'I don't want this. I don't want it any more. I want to stay with you.' Her eyes were full of tears. Even as she spoke, however, the garden began to dissolve into mist. At last she was once more in the darkness of her bedroom and the tears were now rolling down her cheeks. The dream, the vision had gone. For the first time in all the years, she felt afraid, rebellious and alone. Why was that? Nothing had changed, except that Jan had, unusually, gone away for a couple of days. *He will be back later today*, she comforted herself, *and I can ask him*. In the meantime, she had to be careful. But who was it who threatened her? she wondered.

Chapter Seventeen

It was several days later when Chastity, returning to the flat early one evening, found Unicorn already in possession. He was sitting comfortably in one of the armchairs, reading the early edition of the evening paper and sipping a whiskey. It was far too early for anyone else to be at home.

'However did you get in?' she asked him.

Putting down his glass, he smiled and stood up. 'I still have my own key. Remember?'

'I didn't think you were due back until Sunday.'

'I wasn't, but I made an extra effort to get back a couple of days sooner. After reporting to my editor, I came straight here and waited. That way, I thought, I was sure to see you as soon as possible.' Before he could kiss her, as he intended, she put out a hand to stop him. 'Are you still angry with me?' He was obviously disappointed.

'Angry? No; I understood how you felt when we parted. You told yourself that I had deceived you. But it wasn't true, was it?' Her sombre, dark eyes looked steadily into his tawny ones. She saw a flicker of anger that almost immediately vanished.

He laughed softly. 'Are you saying that you merely circumvented my bigger intention to deceive by arranging for Rupert to be your rescuer, even though I was honest with you and told you things about myself that I'd never told to any other woman?'

'You were honest, but not completely honest, and your honesty had an underlying ignoble aim.'

There was definitely a flickering fire in those eyes now, although his voice was calm. 'And what was that?'

'My seduction, if I may use such an old-fashioned term. I don't intend to be seduced by you or any man, nor do I intend to put myself in any compromising situation.'

'I see, but I don't think you are as immune as you pretend to be.' His eyes seemed to blaze. He was a tiger who leapt towards her, seizing her fiercely in his arms, kissing her violently many times. 'You're beautiful and I want you. I've been thinking about you every day. No woman has ever had this effect on me.'

His fire met her ice, but the ice didn't melt. She managed to move her face away. 'If you intend to rape me, you should choose a less public place, don't you think?'

Her words were like a whiplash. Instantly, he released her. 'I thought you would understand that I love you. My roses were meant to tell you that. You did receive them, didn't you?' Looking around, he saw the few remaining ones of the first bouquet in their vase. 'I see you did, but surely that's not all of them?'

'No. I gave the second bouquet away to Mrs Allen, a lonely old lady who lives in the ground floor flat.'

Releasing her completely, he moved away. 'I don't understand. Why did you do that? Do you want to torment me? Are you a devil or an angel?'

'Neither. Just a woman who isn't sure what you are.' Before she could say more, there was the sound of someone's key in the front door.

'Will you trust me enough to allow me to come into your room for a short time so that we can talk?'

'Certainly.' She didn't hesitate. 'Talking might be a good idea.'

He followed her as she led the way into her austere room. Shutting the door behind him, he leaned against it, while Chastity, after switching on a lamp and taking off her coat, sat down, obviously waiting for him to speak.

Moving further into the room, he sat down opposite her. She clearly did not intend to begin. For a few seconds they gazed at each other, then Unicorn leaned back, smiling. 'My romantic gestures didn't please you?'

'Did you think that they would?'

'They were in the nature of an experiment, I suppose. Your honesty actually pleases me. Even more pleasing is the thought that you didn't throw them away in a grand gesture but made good use of them.'

'You seemed to be angry.'

'Only for a moment, until I realised how true to yourself you have been. It may be annoying, to you as well as to me, that you have only succeeded in making me love you more. Or perhaps that was your aim?' He was still smiling.

'Sorry, but I have no such clever plan. I simply did what seemed right to me. I didn't want to destroy such beautiful flowers. I didn't want them for myself. Furthermore, I distrusted your motives.'

'You were right. Such an extravagant gesture is suspicious and I'm not a man to be trusted.'

Smiling mischievously, she said, 'That I do believe, Unicorn, and I like you the better for admitting it.'

For the first time, he felt that there was a bond between them. 'Then you must also believe, however incredible it may seem, that when I say I love you, that is true. Irritating, perhaps for both of us, but also true.' Without waiting for her to reply, he stood up. 'I'm afraid I must go. I have to meet the big boss, Old Lord Harry himself. I have been summoned to the presence. May I, however, collect you for a late supper, as soon as I'm free? We will have time then to continue this conversation.'

For a moment, she hesitated. 'I'll wait here,' she said finally.

'Good. That's all I ask for.' After kissing her lightly on the cheek, he was gone.

It was nearly two hours later when the phone rang. 'Sorry. It took longer than I expected,' he apologised. 'If I take a taxi, I can be with you in about twenty minutes. Can you be ready?' That was easy, she assured him. 'I thought we might go,' he continued, 'to a quiet Italian restaurant, where the food is simple but excellent and we can talk in a quiet corner for as long as we like. Will that suit you?'

Once she had joined him in the taxi, he made no attempt to embrace her, as she had half expected, but merely took her hand and held it firmly. He had an air of suppressed excitement, she thought. Or was it something else? Certainly, he was more disturbed than he had been earlier.

It was a cold, damp, misty night towards the end of November. The moon was almost obscured by shivering clouds. The mist seemed to cling to everything; even the streetlights were dimmed. Chastity had a sense of unreality. 'I hope your interview with your boss wasn't unpleasant?' she asked, convinced that something had disturbed him deeply.

'No, on the contrary. He congratulated me on my recent work. What he mainly had to say was of a personal nature. It came as quite a shock; not unpleasant, rather exciting.'

'Oh!' For some reason, she did not want to know what had been said. To divert him, she asked quickly, 'Who is your boss?'

He laughed. 'You really don't know, do you? He's pretty famous, or rather I should say, more correctly, notorious – Lord Harry Fairword, the billionaire chairman of the *Daily News* Newspapers Ltd. He dominates the media, press and television, here and in most of the Western world, particularly in Canada, where, I think, he originated, although no one is sure about that. It was his money, I imagine, that bought him a barony and considerable political influence. We usually call him Old Harry and we tend to think he invented the name "Fairword". Rather too good to be true, don't you think?'

'Perhaps you simply suspect him because you, too, invented your name. What do you think?'

'Be careful, Chastity; I might come to doubt you.'

Before she could think of a suitable retort, the taxi had stopped. They had reached the Italian restaurant, which, to her surprise, proved to be an unpretentious, homely place in a quiet back street. 'Don't be deceived by appearances,' Unicorn hastened to say. 'I know the proprietor well and the food is excellent.'

As soon as they came through the door, the proprietor hurried to meet them. He was younger and slimmer than she had expected; black-haired, with long-lashed, dark brown eyes and a most appealing smile. His manner was courteous and welcoming, without being servile. 'We have reserved a quiet table in the corner, *Signor*,' he said, leading them to it. 'Your favourite wine is awaiting you at just the right temperature, and Francesco' – he indicated the waiter standing nearby – 'is waiting to look after you.'

'Thanks, Roberto.' Motioning the waiter aside, Unicorn himself pulled out Chastity's chair. She was content to let him order the meal while she sipped the delicious red wine. *Truly a beaker full of the warm South*, she thought, remembering Keats.

The dining room was larger than might have been expected

from the undistinguished exterior. Most of the tables were full, as far as she could tell. It was difficult to be sure, however, as the lighting was discreetly dimmed. Nevertheless, it had a pleasingly quiet and restful air and, from the first few mouthfuls, she realised that the food, without being extravagant, was likely to be extremely good. Unicorn had shown his usual flair.

'I hope you like it here?' he asked.

'Very much so.'

'Good. I particularly want this meal together to be special without being ostentatious.'

'Well, you have achieved that, I think.' Cautiously, she refused to ask why he wanted it to be special. She admitted to herself that she was ridiculously nervous as to what he might say. To avoid that, she asked quickly, 'Can you now tell me something about your trip? Was it successful?'

'Of course.' From the mockery of his smile, she realised that he was aware of her subterfuge. He talked freely and wittily, nevertheless, during the next half hour, of the many places he had visited and of some of the odd and often sinister characters he had met. He had visited a surprising number of places in the Balkans and Eastern Europe, apparently posing as a tourist collecting picturesque places and interesting characters for a book.

'But you weren't really a tourist, were you?' she asked, wondering for a moment if she had misunderstood the nature of his work.

'No, I'm an investigative journalist, remember? I was actually investigating drug trafficking and the trade in women, two trades Lord Harry is particularly interested in. Many of our readers, too, seem to be greedy for a diet of dark and deadly deeds, so long as they are served up with a rich sauce of sex and violence. In this way they can satisfy their lower instincts and still feel good because they are condemning these things and sympathising at a safe distance with the victims.'

'I hope you're not as horribly cynical as you sound.'

'Probably more. But I've never hidden my feelings from you, have I?'

She could not deny that. 'But it must be dangerous for you,' she persisted; 'isn't it?'

'Dangerous, at times, but always profitable.' His tawny eyes were strangely opaque. Whatever his feelings might be, he was determined to hide them. 'I did what I was paid to do and that's all there is to say. But I don't want to waste my time talking to you about that. I came to see you immediately on my return to make sure that I wasn't rejected and to tell you, although it shocks me almost as much as it does you, that I thought about you every day and have decided that I must actually love you. Can you believe that?'

His tone was flippant and he was smiling, but, as she looked searchingly into his eyes, she was forced to believe that he was in earnest. 'I do believe that you mean what you say, *now*.' Her emphasis was firmly on the final word.

'Do you doubt whether my feelings are permanent? Or is it that you question whether such a man as I am can have any idea of what you mean by "love"?' Releasing the hand he had just taken in his, he leaned back and took a sip of his wine. He seemed to be savouring both the wine and the situation.

Was now the right moment, she wondered, to reveal what she had further learned about him from Paul and Helen? One day, if she was to continue to know him, it had to be told. Even as she hesitated, however, the hovering waiter wanting to know their choice of dessert made it impossible for her to say anything like that.

As the waiter disappeared, Unicorn leaned forward again and shared the last of their wine with her. 'If you have so little faith in my love, then you'll probably be shocked to know that someone else has a considerable amount.'

'Someone else? I can't imagine whom you mean, unless it is some silly idea of Alex's.'

He laughed. 'Quite wrong. It's someone far more important than Alex is. None other, in fact, than Lord Harry himself.' He leaned back again, enjoying her surprise.

'Lord Harry? Surely, you don't mean whom I think you mean?'

'I most certainly do. Lord Harry Fairword himself, my boss, and no other.'

'But how? Why? I don't understand.' She stared at him. It

seemed impossible to believe that Unicorn could have confided in Lord Harry. 'Surely you haven't confided in him?'

'Certainly not.'

'Then what has happened? Why are you telling me that he believes in your love for me?'

'Simply because that is what he told me,' They waited for a moment until the waiter had come and gone.

'Please explain.'

'I can only tell you the facts. I can't give you an explanation. You remember, don't you, that, when I left you earlier, I told you I had been summoned to his presence?'

She nodded. 'I wondered if you had perhaps done something to upset him, in spite of your editor being pleased.'

'I had a similar thought, but we were both wrong. When I arrived there, I went straight by the express lift to the tenth floor, where he holds court. Without hesitating, Margaret, his secretary, took me straight into his presence. His office is huge, with large windows taking up the entire wall behind his desk. He had his back to me, as he usually has towards visitors, because he enjoys the magnificent views of London. Probably pleases his god complex. The room is barely furnished, and it always seems a long walk to that desk and to that unwelcoming back.

'Tonight, however, he swivelled his chair around as soon as I came in, stood up and came to meet me! He's a big, heavy man, you know, but he can move very quickly, as he did tonight. Almost before I knew what was happening, he was shaking my hand and congratulating me on a very successful trip. The right sort of material, he said, not only for TV but also for a series in the newspaper. The next moment, I was sitting in a chair opposite and he was offering me a cigar, which I refused, incidentally. He also produced his most jovial smile. Quite terrifying, some people say, but tonight it seemed genuine.'

'But what has this got to do with us?'

'Be patient. I'm just about to tell you. When he had finished his congratulations, he said, with what I suppose should be called a leer, that he would have seen me earlier if he had not been told that I had rushed off to see you, my new lady love. Of course he understood, he hastened to add, that I would naturally be anxious to see you after a couple of weeks' absence.

"'If I had known that you had wanted to see me, I would have postponed that," I told him, anxious, as always, to appear the eager slave. His reply amazed me. "Nonsense, Unicorn, my boy," he said; "such an exceptionally beautiful and talented young woman should never be kept waiting."

'For the first time in my life I was at a loss for words. I just managed to stammer, "Do you know who the lady is, Lord Harry?"

"'Naturally." He was very pleased with himself, rubbing his hands and grinning at me. "I've always made it my business to know about the private lives of my chief employees. A necessary precaution in this business. Surely you know that Unicorn, after all these years?"

"'I've been told that you do," I replied, "but I wasn't sure that it was true."

"'It is true; does that upset you?" The smiles and the joviality had vanished as if his face had been wiped clean. I have noticed that happen before but never so obviously.

"'Why should it?" I asked him. "I have no guilty secrets, as far as I'm aware; none, at least, that you don't know about."'

Obviously, Lord Harry must know about Unicorn's change of name, Chastity thought, but she said nothing.

'Then he said, "If you need any more convincing, I'll tell you that your lady's name is Dr Chastity Brown. She is well known in certain circles for her work among the sick and poor in several parts of Africa. She has a somewhat eccentric partner, who prefers to be known as Dr Jan. Am I right?"

'I agreed that he was. He then went on to say that I had met you when you first arrived in London and that I had shown my usual good judgment by recognising your exceptional attractions straight away. He further said that it appeared that I was just as devoted after our separation. I agreed that this was so; out-of-character, as it might seem. Whereupon he grinned again, "Don't worry," he said; "it's only to be expected, if you believe in the old legends."

'When I said that I didn't understand, he laughed. "Do you

mean to tell me you don't know the story about the unicorn, the most chivalrous and gentlest of beasts, who can only be lured out of the forest by a truly chaste maiden?" I said I'd never heard that yarn; he replied, "Well, it's obviously true, isn't it?" He was enjoying it all so much that I felt like wringing his neck, but, instead, I asked if that meant he didn't disapprove. "Of course not." He was almost fatherly. "You have my blessing and you can tell the lady that." '

'What would you have said if he had disapproved?'

'I'd have told him to go to hell, where he belongs.' He answered with unexpected savagery. 'Do you believe me? Or do you think that I'm just another servile lackey of his?'

'Oh, I believe you, but,' she added mischievously, 'he's not as infallible as he seems to think.'

'How not?' He was smiling now.

'I'm not a chaste maiden, I'm afraid.'

'Don't tell me you haven't lived up to your name! I don't believe you! I can't be so wrong!'

'The "chaste" is right,' she reassured him, 'but not the "maiden". I should rightly be called a chaste widow, I'm afraid.' She waited for his reaction, wondering if she had been too trusting.

When his reaction came, it was surprising. 'That's a relief.' He was smiling.

'Whatever do you mean?'

'Someone suggested – I think it was Alex – that you were probably some kind of nun.'

'And that worried you?'

'A little. I'm capable, I think, of taking on most rivals, but I felt that God might be a little too much for me.'

'Then you no longer have any need to worry.'

He waited for her to say more, but, since she appeared to assume that all that was necessary had been said, he finally asked, 'Aren't you going to tell me any more about your marriage?'

'No, it isn't necessary at present. My marriage was very happy, but it ended suddenly when my husband was killed. My whole life changed and I don't look back.'

'You returned to your maiden name, I presume?'

'Didn't your brilliant Lord Harry tell you that?'

'I'm afraid not. He knows nothing about you from before you became known as a doctor.'

'Good. My name is Chastity Brown and that's all anyone needs to know.'

'Even me?'

'Especially you.' After looking at her watch, she said, 'It's time I went. I have an early start tomorrow.'

Putting out his hand to restrain her as she was about to stand up, he said, 'I'm afraid I have another message for you from Lord Harry. He wants to meet you.'

For a moment she neither moved nor spoke, then she said, very decisively, 'Certainly not. I have no wish to meet Lord Harry Fairword. Please tell him so. It would be a waste of time for both of us.'

'That's a tricky message for me to deliver. He's an extremely powerful man. Perhaps you don't quite realise how powerful. He can build up a man and then destroy him.'

'I do know that. And I dislike it.' She turned the gaze of her unfathomable eyes on him. 'Perhaps that doesn't worry you?'

Ignoring her question, he persisted, 'You don't seem to realise how flattering it is for him to ask to meet you. Prime ministers, presidents, celebrities of all kinds have begged for such a favour.'

'And afterwards he has destroyed them, if he felt like it. With the help of people like you, of course.'

'We're only doing our job.' He looked at her with a mocking smile. 'They destroy themselves, of course, because they care so much for money or power or both. People like me are just his humble instruments, doing what we are told to do,'

'After the Second World War,' she reminded him, 'soldiers were told that doing what you were ordered to do was not a sufficient excuse for doing wrong. They were told they had a higher duty. If you love me, as you say you do, why are you so willing to betray me?'

'I'm not. I just don't think that you should run away from the challenge. I believe that you're much more than a match for him. I don't know what your reasons are, but I believe you should face him. In any case, it will only be a short meeting, because he's invited us both to a reception he's holding tomorrow. It can only be a matter of drinking a glass of wine, eating a few snacks and talking to Lord Harry for five minutes at the most, with other people around. What do you say?'

Without looking at him, she stared straight ahead and considered the matter.

'Please,' he urged her, 'have some faith in me. I would betray others, quite probably, but not you. Don't you understand?'

Unexpectedly, she smiled, but her eyes were sombre when she looked at him. 'I'll speak to Jan and, if he agrees, I will come.'

He was tempted to protest, but he knew it would be useless. 'Very well. I'll present myself to you at 9 p.m. tomorrow. If you've decided not to come, at least talk to me.'

Chapter Eighteen

On the following morning, Chastity was able to have a long talk with Jan. For some days she had been longing for a chance to talk fully with him, but, until this moment, it had not been possible. She had almost begun to feel that he had been deliberately leaving her to her own devices.

Now, however, he was free to spend time with her. After coming to her room at ten o'clock in the morning, he settled down comfortably with the cup of coffee she produced, very willing to listen to her.

For the first time, she was able to tell him in detail of her meetings with Helen and of all she had learned about Unicorn from Helen and Paul, which was confirmed largely by what he had, surprisingly, told her about himself.

Having told Jan all this, she then went on to describe her last meeting with Unicorn and of the surprising invitation he had brought to her from Lord Harry Fairword, who seemed to have decided that she and Unicorn were now in a relationship, and one that he, amazingly, blessed.

'What did you say?'

'I couldn't see any sense in it. I felt it must be another attempt on Unicorn's part to manipulate me. The only argument against this was that he himself seemed almost shocked and very excited about it. I told him finally that I would consult with you and then give him my decision.'

'That was a good decision. I'm glad that you didn't refuse outright.' Startled, she looked at him as he sat opposite her. Even on this cheerlessly cold and wet November morning there was a kind of radiance about him. He was wearing the same dark clothes he always wore, but his deep blue eyes shone like sapphires in his pale, perfectly-sculpted face with its amazing aureole of golden hair. His eyes were fixed on her; she could conceal nothing from him, even if she had wanted to.

'Do you mean that you want me to go and meet the man? Do you know who and what he is?'

'Of course. I know that he is a powerful and dangerous man.' He continued to look steadily at her with those brilliant eyes.

'I still don't see why he should want to meet me. But what puzzles me most of all is all that he knows about me. How does he know it? And why does it matter to him?'

'We can only guess how,' Jan replied calmly, 'but I should imagine that he has an efficient spy system as far as his important employees are concerned. Unicorn is important, and that partially answers your second question.'

'So you want me to meet him?' She stared nervously at him, her hands tightly clasped and her dark eyes dilated with a fear she did not understand. She felt bereft. She had not expected this reply from Jan.

'It is important that you do meet him. Something like this is what we have been waiting for. The enemy has come out of hiding. We can't run away. We must engage with him. I'm only deeply sorry that it cannot be me, but I shall always be there to support you.'

Suddenly, a new fear struck her. 'You think that this has something to do with Emmanuel, don't you?'

'It may very well have.'

His calm irritated her. She felt rebellious, as she had done in her dream. 'Then why haven't you told me? Surely, you should tell me now, if you want me to meet the man?'

After a pause, Jan replied, slowly and decisively, 'I don't know it all myself. Not everything is revealed, even to me. As for you, it won't help you to know more at this moment. What you don't know, you can't be persuaded or deceived into telling. Your honesty and your innocence will be your best weapons in this interview. You must not allow yourself to appear suspicious. Remember that Lord Fairword's interest in you may be solely due to his curiosity about you and Unicorn. He may simply be wondering what has attracted Unicorn to you and whether Unicorn is still to be trusted.'

'And you think that I should assume that this is the truth when I meet him?'

'That is my advice. Simply remember that you are dealing with someone who is extremely clever and unscrupulous. He will, most probably, try to tempt you in some way.'

'Tempt me?' She frowned. 'Why should he?'

'Because he loves demonstrating his power over people.'

'How will he tempt me?'

'I don't know, Chastity. You are intelligent; you must also be wary. Remember that you have powerful support. What is your answer?'

After a moment's thought, she said, 'I will meet him. I'll ring Unicorn and tell him. Do you think,' she asked suddenly, 'that I need a special dress for this great occasion?'

Jan laughed. 'I'm no fashion expert, Chastity, but it seems to me that you should be yourself. Or perhaps you should ask your admirer what would please him. After all, it's his boss you're meeting.'

'Somehow, I don't think he'll care. In any case, I shan't ask him.'

It was about nine o'clock when she arrived with Unicorn at the mansion where Lord Fairword's reception was being held. Unicorn was immaculate in a dinner jacket, but she was wearing her usual plain dress, only relieved dramatically by an elaborately designed jade and amethyst necklace and pendant. Her shining hair fell smoothly to below her shoulders. Unicorn proudly told her that she was the most beautiful woman in the room. The foyer was thronged with richly-dressed people, but as soon as they were announced an attendant came up to her.

'Dr Brown,' he said, 'his Lordship is expecting you in his study. Please follow me.' She had half expected Unicorn to follow her, but, when he made no attempt to do so, she realised that she was on her own.

The study into which she was shown was a surprisingly small and quiet room, dimly lit except for a bright lamp on the antique walnut desk behind which Lord Harry was sitting. As she hesitated on the threshold, the door was closed behind her. At the same moment, Lord Harry stood up, walked around the desk and came to meet her with hand outstretched. The thick carpet deadened the sound of his footsteps, but he moved with surprisingly speed and lightness for such a tall, heavily-built man.

'I'm very pleased you have been able to come, Dr Chastity. I may call you that, may I not?' He smiled at her; a broad, welcoming, fatherly smile. After taking her offered hand firmly in his, he led her to a chair in front of the desk. 'Please sit down.' He spoke in a deep, slightly hoarse, but not unpleasant voice. 'May I offer you a drink? What would you like?' He moved over to a trolley loaded with bottles and glasses that stood near the desk.

'I prefer a brandy, if that is possible.'

He smiled again. 'An excellent choice, if perhaps a little unexpected. I'll join you.'

As he moved behind the trolley to prepare the drinks, she had a few moments in which to study him. His hair was completely white, cut very short but still obviously thick. Beneath the broad forehead, the eyebrows were surprisingly black and bushy. His cheeks had an almost youthful fullness, but his mouth and chin were set in determined lines. There was an aura of power about him that she clearly felt. He was not a man to cross lightly.

As he handed her the glass of brandy, he smiled at her again. His full cheeks creased naturally into genial smile lines, but, as she took the glass from him, she looked into his eyes for the first time. The smile did not reach those grey, cold eyes. They were expressionless. A cold shiver ran through her. *If the eyes are the mirror of the soul*, she thought, *then Lord Harry never had a soul, or he has sold it*. Remembering Jan's warning, she smiled, at the same time lowering her own eyes.

As soon as they had both had their drinks, he sat down, looking at her with apparent admiration. 'The reports on you have not erred, as I feared they might. You are certainly exceptionally attractive, my dear. And there is obviously no doubt about your intelligence. I am pleased to see that my young friend has made such an admirable choice. I drink to you both and to your future happiness.' He sipped his brandy while smiling at her.

Chastity sipped her brandy, too. Although she shrank from his smile, she managed to return it, but she could find nothing suitable to say.

'I hope Unicorn told you,' he persisted, 'that you both have my blessing?'

She forced herself to reply. 'He did, but I'm afraid it may be premature. I think I may be here on false pretences. I have not committed myself to any relationship, nor am I yet ready to do so.' Whilst speaking as coolly and decisively as she could, she managed to avoid looking into those lifeless eyes, which seemed to be fixed on her.

To her surprise, he only smiled even more widely and more genially. 'I would have been surprised, even disappointed, had you said anything different. From what I know about you already, you are an unusually independent young woman.'

'What is it that you do know about me?' she challenged him.

'I believe that you have been working for about seven years in sub-Saharan Africa as a doctor, caring for the wretchedly poor and the dying. You belong to a small group headed by Dr Jan. You have acquired an enviable reputation, both for your skill and for your compassion. Your group has some Christian funding, I believe. Am I right so far?'

'Substantially.'

His smile was fatherly. 'Good. About six weeks ago, you and Dr Jan left Africa, leaving the rest of your group behind. On arriving in London, you rented a room in Alex Woodward's flat, which is still partially owned by Unicorn.'

'I didn't know that.' She was surprised, but she thought it explained many things.

Lord Harry chuckled. 'I wondered if you did. He lent Alex the money to buy it and she's still paying him back. Once you moved in there it was inevitable that you would meet my susceptible reporter.'

'But surely…' She stopped and began again. 'What actually drew your attention to me? You don't bother about all the girls he meets, do you?'

This clearly pleased him. Draining his brandy, he stood up. 'It was a great stroke of luck. I'll explain. But first, will you have another drink?' Although she declined, he still poured himself a second brandy and then returned to his seat.

'It was an incident that occurred one night when you were doing the soup run with Dr Jan for the nuns you had agreed to help. You and Dr Jan were taken to a child who was giving birth in a doorway. Do you remember?'

'I can hardly forget that. It was shocking to find such things happening in London, especially as the baby died.' She shuddered as she so clearly remembered holding the dead baby in her arms. 'It was not a success.'

'No blame can be attached to you or Dr Jan. You both acted promptly and skilfully, or so I was told.'

'How do you know about it?'

'A young and inexperienced reporter of ours joined the small crowd that had gathered, just as the ambulance was pulling away. The story came to me eventually.'

'I'm amazed that you didn't make a headline story about it! Don't tell me that your compassion held you back?' She spoke coldly but without anger.

Rubbing his hands together with satisfaction, he smiled broadly. 'I like it! You are a girl after my own heart. No, it wasn't compassion! You're right there! It was simply that our reporter was an idiot and let everyone go without getting the necessary facts. When it came to my ears I set out to investigate and discovered you. Potential for a much bigger story. Especially when I also came to know that you are my chief investigative journalist's true love. I imagine you can see the potential in that yourself?'

Without answering at once, she forced herself to lift her head and to look into those lifeless, grey eyes. He waited. He was still smiling a warm, friendly smile, but she was only aware of the coldness of those empty eyes. 'I'm not sure,' she replied finally. 'I can see more than one possibility but it's hard to know which you might favour.'

'I favour,' – his voice seemed harsher than ever – 'the one that brings most profit and influence to me and my media empire. Surely you don't need me to tell you that? You're intelligent enough to know it yourself.'

She continued to stare at him. 'I'm not entirely sure that is the whole truth.'

Laughing abruptly, he stood up and moved towards the trolley so that she could no longer see into his eyes. 'The truth! Do you expect truth from me?' He poured himself another brandy.

Without looking at him, Chastity answered him indirectly. 'What is your proposal?'

'One that can bring enormous profit for both of us! The story has all the elements we need! My investigative journalist meets this beautiful young doctor who has come to England after years of helping the starving in Africa and who is shocked to discover such suffering on the streets of one of the world's richest cities. Deciding to help her – a hint of romance here – he brings the story to me and I decide that the *Daily News* will bring all its resources to expose the shocking poverty in our streets after seven years of so-called left-wing government. It gives us a wonderful chance to attack the government and its policies. With the unpopular war with Iraq still going on, this will greatly please the public. Our superior morality will once again make clear their weaknesses. They talk about poverty, but we will show the reality and how little has been actually done.' Lord Harry leaned back in his chair, beaming at her.

'It seems that your aims are political. I thought that you supported the Government, that you are the Prime Minister's friend, so why do you want to do this?'

He smiled even more benignly at her. 'Let us just say that our point of view has changed. It is time to reveal our idol's feet of clay.'

'Why should I help you? Or is the truth that it doesn't really matter whether or not I help you? You could make a story without my assistance, I imagine.'

'We could, but it wouldn't be as good a story. With you, the story will be heart-warming. You can convince the public that there are still good and selfless people in this world, which often seems cruel and pointless to them. Surely, that is not a bad thing, is it?' His hoarse voice was tenderly persuasive, his smile almost paternal, but she still looked into his unchanging eyes. 'If good comes out of it, does it matter if I also profit?'

'What do I gain?'

He leaned across the table and patted her hand gently.

'Admiration, fame, but, if these don't matter much to you, as I suspect they may not, then money for your cause, for the wretched people you are trying to help, you and Dr Jan.'

'Money? How much money? How will you get it?'

He was pleased with her interest. 'We'll set up the *Daily News* fund. We'll make it seem fun to help this beautiful young doctor and our reporter who loves her. We'll make it competitive, too. A competition always encourages people, especially if we throw a few celebrity names in.'

'And this will help you in your political campaign? That, I don't understand.'

'Leave that to me. I can take care of my own interests.'

'I imagine so.' She removed her hand. 'Does Unicorn know all this?'

'He may have guessed some of it, but he's not in my confidence, if that is what you mean. You may tell him what you wish. He won't be shocked, I assure you.'

'I don't imagine that he will be, but it's Dr Jan I must speak to, not Unicorn. He is my superior. He may not agree.'

'You must convince him that it's in his best interests to do so.' His voice had suddenly hardened. Sipping his brandy, he waited for her reaction, but there was none.

After a few moments, she stood up. 'If you have said everything you want to, I'll go. We don't want Unicorn to get worried. I'll discuss your suggestion with Dr Jan and give you our decision.' She moved towards the door.

'Wait a minute. There is one more question I would like to ask. Why did you and Dr Jan come to England? Surely your work in Africa wasn't finished? Or had you begun to run out of funds?'

'Only Jan can answer that question. I simply follow the instructions I am given.'

'How beautifully naïve you seem! But if that is true, why have you been asking questions about Emmanuel? Surely your return had something to do with him?' His voice was hard and rough now. The smile had gone.

For the first time, she felt afraid. 'Emmanuel? I don't know Emmanuel. I have never known Emmanuel. Who is he?'

'He was a young Arab who has disappeared. You have been asking questions about him. Why?'

'An old lady I met asked about him. She had talked to him and liked him, and she wondered what had happened to him. I think that she was afraid that he might have been arrested as a terrorist.'

'He might well have been. In which case it might be wiser not to ask questions about him, especially as he is thought, or so I believe, to have been in Kenya. No one is safe in this perilous time, not even the most innocent.' He smiled again. 'That is just a friendly warning, you understand.'

'I understand.'

Standing up, he moved towards her and held out his hand, which she took. 'It would be helpful if you would send your answer through Unicorn in a few days' time.'

'Certainly, I will do that.'

After shaking her hand, he released it and pressed a bell. 'My secretary will take you back to Unicorn.'

As she re-entered the reception room, she found Unicorn standing with a small group of people. As soon as he saw her, he detached himself and came quickly towards her. 'You've been such a long time I was beginning to think that Lord Harry had been overwhelmed by your charms.' He was smiling cheerfully.

'He had a lot to say to me; more than you had led me to expect. Did he say anything to you beforehand?'

As he became aware of a coldness in her manner, his smile faded. 'Of course not. He only said that he would like to meet you. I was amazed when you were whisked off to his private study. Such an honour is usually reserved for cabinet ministers and above.'

'He has a plan, which involves us. He wanted to make it clear.'

'Am I to know about this?'

'Since it involves you and since you are to take my answer to him, I presume I am to tell you all about it. That is, if you don't already know it all?'

Looking closely at her, he saw that she was unusually pale and that her dark eyes were clouded, as if she were hiding herself from him. 'You are angry and suspicious. Why?'

'I thought we were at least friends. Now I don't know what

we are – friends or bitter enemies? I would be grateful, however, if you would take me away from here.'

'Certainly, but wouldn't you like a drink first?'

'No, thank you. I've already had a brandy with Lord Harry. A very good one, incidentally.'

'It would be, but surely there's something else you would like?'

'Nothing here.' Unexpectedly, she smiled at him. 'But there is something I would really like.'

He was relieved. 'Whatever it is, tell me and I'll get it for you.'

'You're being very rash, but fortunately my needs are simple. I would like food and lots of it. I've scarcely had time to eat all day and suddenly I've realised that I'm very hungry.'

'So am I, for the same reason. Let's go.' He took her arm.

'I don't want an expensive restaurant. I want simple, plain food – home cooked. Something like a steak and kidney pie. There's a challenge for you.'

As soon as he had steered her through the doors, he paused for a moment to think. 'Not too big a challenge. I know just the place. It's some way off, but we can easily get a taxi from here. We can eat our fill and talk. Are you willing?'

'I'm very willing to eat, but I'm not sure about talking... yet.'

Chapter Nineteen

During the days following Chastity's meeting with Lord Harry, Unicorn became steadily angrier and more frustrated. It began when, at the end of the simple meal that they had both enjoyed, Chastity said that she was definitely not ready to talk to him.

Furthermore, as soon as they arrived back at the flat, Chastity had leapt out of the taxi, refusing even to let him come up to her room but insisting on saying their farewells in the street. 'But when can we talk?' he asked, holding on to her hand so that she had to stay for a moment.

'I'm not sure. I have to speak to Jan first.' She pulled her hand away quite fiercely. 'I'll be in touch, I promise.' Before he could say any more she had gone.

Disappointed, he went back to his flat and tried to console himself with several stiff brandies. Surely, he asked himself, she owed him some explanation for the change in her behaviour?

On his return, he remembered, she had seemed to welcome him and even to believe that his protestations of love might be genuine. But, after her meeting with Lord Harry, her manner had changed radically. It was not just that she was cool and distant, but that underlying this there was suspicion and even hostility to him. What had that bloody man said? he wondered.

He could not tackle Lord Harry, so, after a restless night, he went to Chastity's flat in search of her. It was Sunday and he remembered that she had once told him that she usually went to the ten o'clock Mass arriving back soon after eleven.

Not so! He found the flat deserted except for a somewhat hung-over Alex, who emerged from the kitchen in her pyjamas, carrying a large mug of black coffee. She had changed, too. Her hair was dishevelled, her face unusually pale and the eyes which she turned to him were dull. Nevertheless, she managed a mocking smile. 'Are you looking for your new lady love?'

'I was hoping to see Chastity.'

'Poor Unicorn! You've found your match there, at last!' She slumped into an armchair.

'What do you mean?'

'She's not here. She went out early, long before I was awake, but she left a note in case any one wanted to know, saying that she wouldn't be back until very late, perhaps not even before tomorrow.'

He struggled to hide his anger and disappointment. 'Did she say where she was going?'

Alex shook her head. 'Afraid she didn't give us a clue. Sorry, darling. Would you like a cup of coffee to console you? If so, feel free.'

'Thank you, no.' As he moved towards the door, he looked at her with some disgust. 'Coffee with you in that state is hardly an attractive proposition.' He left to the sound of a further mocking laugh.

In the entrance hall he almost bumped into Rupert, who was coming in. Wearing his leathers and carrying his helmet, Rupert had obviously been for a trip on his motorbike.

'You've been out early!' Unicorn exclaimed. 'You look as if you've enjoyed it, too!'

'I have.' Rupert was smiling cheerfully. 'It is a surprisingly good morning for the time of the year, and a run out in the country was just the job.'

'The country? That's not like you on a Sunday morning, is it? Did Paul go with you?'

'God, no. He's still in bed, as usual, finishing his breakfast and reading the papers I tossed at him earlier. I wouldn't have missed the trip for the world. It was exhilarating once we got beyond the London traffic; the country roads were almost empty.'

'We?' Unicorn was surprised. 'So you had a companion?'

'Sure. Didn't I mention that? When I went out to get the papers I met Chastity. She told me that she had to make a journey into Kent and wasn't sure about the trains, so I offered her a lift. She didn't hesitate. She loves riding on the bike.'

'Does she? Yes, of course; I remember that you took her from my flat a couple of weeks ago.'

'Sorry.' Rupert grinned even more cheerfully. 'If you're

looking for her now, I'm afraid that I've got in your way again.'

'It's not important.' Unicorn took pains to hide his anger. 'I wanted to have a chat with her, but it can wait. She did say that she needed to speak to Jan, but I didn't understand that she meant today.'

'She did say something about hoping to see Jan, but there wasn't much time for talking.'

'You didn't see him, then?'

'No; on Chastity's instructions we stopped at a hotel in the centre of Tunbridge Wells. While I ordered coffee, she went to phone. When she came back, she said it was fine to leave her there, as she would be picked up soon. So, after coffee, I said my goodbyes and left. As you know, Chastity can be pretty decisive.'

'I can't dispute that. Did she say when she might be back?'

Rupert shook his head. 'It was never mentioned, but I did get the impression that it wouldn't be before late tonight, if then. Sorry.'

Unicorn managed a casual smile. 'Thanks for telling me, anyway. I shan't waste any more time.'

He went quickly through the front door and down the steps. *What the hell is going on?* he thought furiously. *Surely she could have left me some message?*

He worked furiously for the rest of the day, sorting out his material and preparing his first two articles. Lord Harry, or so his editor had made clear to him, wanted quick and dramatic reports of his latest trip. In the evening, after a quick, solitary meal, he resisted the attempt to ring Chastity either at the flat or on her newly-acquired mobile, deciding it would be more sensible to pursue her on the Monday. She would definitely be back by then.

But a ring from his office on the Monday morning produced only a negative result. No one was there, apparently. Twice during the day he rang Chastity's mobile, but there was no response. His frustration and anger were growing hourly.

On the Monday evening, risking the possibility of having to speak to Alex, he rang the flat. Fortunately, it was a friendly Dot who answered. Yes, Chastity had returned, she told him, bringing Eva with her, much to Dot's amazement. Eva had merely come to collect some clothes and, after some time, she and Chastity had gone off together.

'When was that?' Unicorn asked her.

'Not very long ago. You've only just missed her.'

With difficulty, Unicorn kept his anger in check. 'Did she say where she was going? Or how long she would be?'

"Fraid not. I didn't ask, because Eva seemed to be upset and anxious to get away. Can I give Chastity a message?'

'Please tell her that I rang and that I urgently want to get in touch with her.'

'Sure. I'll leave her a note in case she doesn't turn up before I go out.'

It was obvious that Chastity was determined not to speak to him. But why? Was it connected with something Lord Harry had said to her? If so, what the hell could it be? And where was she now? Had she gone back to Kent? The reappearance of Eva was intriguing, too, but he could think of no answers to his many questions. As he considered them all, he realised how little he knew about Chastity. Furthermore, if she had gone back to this mysterious place in Kent, how would he be able to contact her, since she had apparently decided to keep her mobile permanently switched off?

At that moment, however, Chastity was by no means as far away as Unicorn imagined. She was, in fact, sitting in Mrs Allen's living room with Eva, whom she had brought back to London late that afternoon. Finding herself in a dilemma, she had rung Mrs Allen's bell.

It was Sean, just returned from work, who opened the door and welcomed them in, calling out at the same time to Mrs Allen, who came hurrying to meet them. She was delighted to see Chastity and to meet her companion.

As they settled down in the comfortable sitting room by a welcome fire, Chastity explained the situation. 'Eva had a breakdown and has been recovering in a house our group has in the country. When I went down yesterday to meet Jan as I hoped, she thought she was better and decided, therefore, to come back with me today, but when we got back...' She hesitated.

'I realised that I wasn't ready to go back to my room on my own.' Eva completed the sentence. She spoke quietly, but she was obviously repressing strong emotions. 'I've been very stupid, I'm afraid, and caused Chastity a lot of unnecessary bother, particularly as she needs to stay here now. I'm sorry.' She turned towards Chastity.

She was very different from the young woman Chastity had first met a few weeks before. Now, she was wearing little, if any, make-up and her once brilliant golden hair had returned to its natural light brown. Her curvaceous figure was completely concealed by loose-fitting jeans and a generously-cut, dark red woollen jersey.

'That doesn't matter in the least,' Chastity replied quickly. 'We've just got to decide what to do next, and we don't want to hang about upstairs in case Alex comes home or Unicorn decides to call, so I hope you don't mind, Elizabeth, our calling on you. Perhaps you can advise us.'

'You're very welcome at any time,' Elizabeth replied. 'As for advice, I'll do my best.'

'My advice,' Sean chipped in, suddenly, 'is that we all have something to eat. Speaking for myself, I always think better when I'm not starving.'

Elizabeth stood up. 'That seems a good idea. That is, if you haven't eaten?'

'We haven't eaten, but we can't impose on you like that,' Chastity answered immediately.

'Don't talk nonsense. I have a large joint of beef left from yesterday's lunch. All I have to do is to cook a few extra vegetables. That won't take long.'

As Chastity tried to protest, Sean silenced her. 'It's no use trying to stop Elizabeth when she's made up her mind, but we don't have to let her do any extra work. Come into the kitchen with me, Chastity. I'll make a pot of tea for these two, then we can deal with the vegetables.'

After pushing Elizabeth gently down into her seat again, he moved towards the kitchen, followed by Chastity. 'Your friend, Eva,' he remarked to Chastity, as they started to work in the kitchen, 'looks as if she's had a pretty bad time.'

'I haven't known her for long, but I think you're right.' As simply as she could, Chastity told him all that she had discovered about Eva.

'Poor bugger! She's certainly been through the wringer! And you think she tried to top herself?'

'She first tried some time ago, I think, and she was certainly very close to it when Jan and I took over.'

'It was lucky you turned up. I can only too easily imagine what she felt like. I've been through it myself, you may remember?'

In the living room, Elizabeth poured out the tea that Sean had brought in. As she handed a cup to the sad-looking young woman sitting almost motionless opposite her, she smiled gently.

As she took the cup, Eva gave her a ghost of a smile in return. 'You're being very kind. I've no right to impose on you like this. I've already made things difficult for Chastity. I should have waited until Dr Jan came back. Do you know him?'

'Oh, yes. He and Chastity have both been very kind to Sean and me, so we're pleased to have a chance of repaying. Did you say Dr Jan was away? I didn't know that.'

'Yes; he went suddenly on Saturday, I think. I'm not even sure he told Chastity, because she came down on Sunday, hoping to discuss something with him, I imagine. Instead, I persuaded her to bring me back. I told her I was ready to face everything, but I was wrong. I think she knew, but she didn't stop me.' Eva took several sips of her tea and seemed to find it comforting.

'Is it the place or the people you don't like?' Elizabeth ventured to ask after a minute or two.

'Both, I think,' Eva replied, after a moment's pause. 'It's difficult to separate the two sometimes, isn't it?'

'I suppose it might be, particularly if some of the people in the place have contributed to your unhappiness. Perhaps you should find somewhere else to live?'

'I shall have to, but, at present, I can't even think about that or anything sensibly. I simply am not ready yet to face up to things. Perhaps I never shall be.'

Before Elizabeth could think of a suitable reply, the door from the kitchen was pushed open and Sean came in, laden with the joint of beef, a carving knife and plates. He was followed almost immediately by Chastity, carrying two large bowls of steaming vegetables. There was no time now for serious conversation as Sean took charge of the situation, obviously determined that they should have a pleasant and cheerful meal.

It was not until the dishes had been cleared away and they were sitting over cups of coffee that Sean, suddenly putting his hands flat on the table, looked directly at Eva and asked unemotionally, 'What made you want to top it? I don't just mean recently, but in the past?'

'Sean don't,' Elizabeth protested.

'It's all right,' he replied, unperturbed. 'As both you and Chastity know I've been one of that club myself, so I thought that Eva and I might have helpful discussion. What do you think?' He was still looking at Eva, but now he was smiling at her.

Elizabeth continued to protest. 'I'm sure Eva isn't ready to talk about things like that in front of us all.' She looked towards Chastity for support, but Chastity said nothing.

'It's all right,' Eva said softly. 'I know you're all friends. I'm not sure, however, that I do belong to that club any more; at least, I hope not.'

'That's exactly how I feel,' Sean replied, 'but we can't be sure, can we? I think we might help each other if we tried to bring everything out into the open and talked it through. What do you think?'

There was a brief silence, then Eva spoke more firmly. 'That's what Dr Jan told me I should do. I didn't like the idea, so I pretended I was cured and insisted on Chastity bringing me back.' She turned towards Chastity, 'Did you think I was ready?'

'No, but I thought it might help you in some way. And perhaps Sean has suggested the way. I'm quite ready to remove myself, however, if you'd rather not have me here.'

'Of course I want you to stay. You were the first person to help me. Don't go now, please.'

'I don't see how I can be of any use,' Elizabeth remarked. 'I can easily go to my bedroom.'

'Please don't go.' Eva turned towards her. 'I'm sure I can trust you.'

'Of course you can,' Sean exclaimed. 'She's helped me a lot. She's a born mother.'

'It is agreed, then, that we should stay,' Chastity said. 'But Sean and Eva must do the talking. We will help if and when we can. In the meantime,' she continued, turning towards Elizabeth, 'you must sit in your armchair and relax.' After helping Elizabeth to settle comfortably in her chair and handing her coffee to her, Chastity returned to the table, where Sean was still looking intently at Eva.

For a moment there was silence, until Eva said, with unusual firmness, 'You must begin, Sean, since you started all this. Tell us about yourself.'

'Yeah, you're right, I guess. It all goes back to the beginning, I suppose.'

'Things usually do,' Chastity remarked, with a touch of irony.

He grinned at her. 'It all seems a bit corny; in fact, it is, but it's still true. I was definitely an unwanted kid. My mum was stupid enough to marry this Irish guy and to believe his blarney. He disappeared for good when I was about two. A year or so later, she met this decent English bloke and she could really have started life afresh if it hadn't been for me.

'Looking back, I think that my stepfather tried, but I didn't help him and neither did she. He saw that I was clever and tried to encourage me to do my best at school, but I couldn't see any point in that because my mum never noticed me, except when I got into trouble, which was when I really did get her attention. It was better to be screamed and shouted at than to be ignored. In spite of myself, I did get a few exam passes and got a job in the local factory. It was bloody boring, so I took to drinking and, later, to high-powered bikes.'

'Not a good combination,' Chastity murmured.

'Too right. That's when I first began to think about death and to flatter myself that I was brave enough to risk it. My mates were impressed and I liked that.'

'I'm amazed you're still alive. How come?' Eva asked.

'I was given a shock. The Devil looks after his own, my mum said, but maybe she was wrong and it wasn't the Devil. Whatever, it worked. I was driving round a sharp bend on a foggy night like a bat out of hell. I'd had several pints and felt untouchable. How wrong can you be? I crashed into this wall and ruined my precious bike, on which I still owed a lot of money. Didn't improve my girlfriend or myself. She was flung across the road.

She wasn't seriously injured, but she'd had more than enough of me.'

'You can't blame her, can you?' Eva exclaimed.

'No; I never did. When I came out of hospital, my job had gone. My stepfather had paid off the money I owed on my bike, but my mum had packed my clothes. It was time for me to start life on my own.

'Well, I'd actually done a bit of thinking in hospital and I'd come up with an idea. One thing I liked doing was driving, and I was good at it. So why not earn my living that way? There was one problem: I also liked drinking! That led to another positive thought: I'd have to cut down drinking. Big deal, two positive thoughts! The truly amazing thing was that I actually stuck to it for a few years. During that time, I somehow acquired an HGV licence, a fairly well-paid job, a permanent girlfriend, a house and everything that goes with it and, finally, a kid. I thought I'd really cracked it, until, one evening, I came back early and found her with another guy. I'd been working such long hours to give her all she wanted that she'd got lonely.'

'That's horrible! Whatever did you do?' Eva asked.

Sean shrugged with a laugh. 'I won't go into boring detail. I'll only say that, although it had taken me years to acquire it all, it only took me a few months to lose it. I ended up, finally, homeless, penniless, living on the streets.'

'I suppose that was when you thought of killing yourself?' Eva asked.

'Funnily enough, it wasn't. That was an idea that seemed to have been in my mind for much of my life. I suppose you might say it was a philosophical idea.'

'I'm afraid you'll have to explain that a bit more,' Chastity intervened.

'I'll do my best, but I don't know if I can. It was in my early teens, I think, when I first became obsessed with this idea of the insecurity of life. I tried to put together all the ideas about God I got from my Catholic school with all the scientific bits and pieces I'd picked up. I came up with this idea that we were all walking on a tightrope across an abyss. We talked confidently about time and space and tried to pretend that it was all secure and solid, but it wasn't. And at any time, when God happened to think about it, we could be knocked off. We are all like a man on death row, but we daren't admit it. So I decided that I could kind of spit in God's eye and throw myself off when it suited me. I thought that was the only way I had of asserting my freedom. I expect you think that's pretty bad and stupid, don't you?' Turning away from Eva, he looked directly at Chastity.

'But you do believe in God?' was her only reply.

'Oh, yes, I believe in him all right. I just don't like the way he behaves. He's a bit of a tyrant, I think. And, if I do get a chance one day, I'll tell Him and ask Him to explain himself. I could just about understand Him punishing the real sinners, but why do so many good and innocent people have to suffer? I'm not the first person to ask that, I know, but it doesn't make it any less important, does it?'

'Do you still feel like that?' Chastity asked.

'I'm not sure. I think perhaps I need to get more data.'

'What's changed your mind?' Eva asked.

'Mostly the people I've met after I got into the hostel. Dr Jan, of course, and Chastity. I feel I can trust you both, and I've never felt that about anyone before. And you, Elizabeth, you've given me my first real home. I don't want to let you lot down, and you've made me feel that I've missed something somewhere. And, funnily enough, there was a guy called Emmanuel. I didn't really get to know him, but he made a big impression on me. I was sure that he was good and brave and that he knew something I didn't.'

'You actually met Emmanuel?' Eva asked eagerly. 'How strange! I knew him quite well for a time.'

Elizabeth unexpectedly entered the conversation. 'I met him too.'

'I never met him.' Chastity remembered Lord Harry's question.

'How did you get to know him?' Sean asked Eva.

'He was a friend of Unicorn's, I believe. At least, that's how Alex met him. He came to the flat quite often and he actually stayed there for a few days when Louie was away. I liked him a lot. He was the first man who treated me as an equal human being, instead of just as an object for his amusement.

'I suppose it was partly my own fault that men treated me like that,' Eva continued. 'I wanted to be loved, but I also craved money. I soon realised, helped by my mother, that I was pretty and had lots of sex appeal. I was vain and I liked all the glamorous things. I trained as a model and quite soon I was more successful than I had ever expected, especially when Max took me over. Mine's a corny story, like yours, Sean. And, like yours, it's true. I earned a lot of money, wasted it all, trusted several unsuitable men who used me and left me, consoled myself with drink and drugs. Tried to kill myself a couple of times, but not too hard. I only wanted someone to notice me and to love me. After I'd lost most of my money, I ended up with a room in Alex's flat. I thought she was a friend, but she didn't like it when she found me talking with Emmanuel. I thought it was jealousy, but it wasn't that.

'He wanted to help me to sort myself out, and he warned me not to trust Alex too much and Unicorn not at all. He pointed out that Alex encouraged me to drink, which was true, but I'd never noticed it. Then, suddenly, he was gone. I thought there might have been a quarrel. I asked Alex, and she said that she had no idea what had happened and couldn't care less. I even asked Unicorn. At first he seemed to want to deny that he knew anything about him, but finally he admitted that he was an Arab who might have thought it wiser to disappear after 9/11. He even suggested that the Government might have taken him out of circulation and that it would be more sensible not to inquire about him.' She stopped for a moment, twisting her hands together as her eyes filled with tears. 'I missed him a lot, but I was afraid to say any more, especially to Unicorn. I don't know why. I was frightened.'

'Max told Jan and me how upset you had been by Emmanuel's disappearance,' Chastity said gently.

'Max did? When? Why?'

'It was when he met me recently to ask me if I had any idea of what had happened to you. I hadn't, but Jan, of course, had. He was relieved. He paid your rent because Alex was fussing about it. I'm sure he cares about you.'

'Alex told me that he did, and I believed her. That was why I agreed to go away with him. It seemed like my last chance. Well, I blew that. You saw the end of it. He obviously despises me now, but he's sorry for me. I can do without that. I've got to change, to find my real self again. That's what you and Jan believe, isn't it, Chastity? It'll be tough, but I'm going to do it.'

'You'll do it.' Leaning forward, Sean put one of his hands comfortingly on hers. 'You think so, too, don't you?' he asked Chastity.

'I'm sure you will, Eva, now that you have friends to help,' Chastity agreed. 'But now, I think, I must return you to Kent, since you certainly aren't ready yet to come back to your room.'

'Don't you think it's a bit late at night to do that, Chastity?' Elizabeth objected.

'Of course it is,' Sean interrupted quickly, 'but no sweat. It's simple. Eva can have my bed and I'll doss down on the couch here. You don't mind, do you, Elizabeth?'

'Certainly not. It's obviously the best solution.'

'I really can't put you to all that trouble,' Eva protested.

'Nonsense. It's settled,' Elizabeth said decidedly. 'I'll make sure that Sean does all the extra work.'

'That's settled then,' Sean replied cheerfully. 'You'll be safe with us tonight.'

'In that case,' Chastity said, standing up. 'I'll go back to my room and arrange for you to return to Kent tomorrow, if that's what you want.'

As soon as Chastity had said her goodbyes, Sean took her to the front door. 'I'll look after them both,' he promised. 'You managed that well. Dr Jan would be proud of you.'

'Whatever do you mean?' She was smiling in spite of herself.

'You know what I mean. Don't act coy with me.' He laughed.

'You're right. I thought it would be good for you two to meet.' Suddenly, she leaned forward and kissed him lightly on the cheek. 'Stay with God, Sean dear. There's a lot more for you to learn.' Before he could recover from his surprise, she had gone.

Chapter Twenty

Unicorn's annoyance was not lessened by his receiving, late on Tuesday morning, a curt reminder from Lord Harry that he was still awaiting a reply from Dr Chastity to the proposal he had made to her. It was obvious from the wording of the memo that Unicorn was held responsible for obtaining this. Unicorn could not remember ever feeling so frustrated as he did at this moment.

Picking up his jacket, he rushed furiously out of the office. While he waited for the lift, he studied the memo again, tore it into small pieces and thrust them into the nearest waste receptacle. As he walked out of the building, he decided that he needed a stiff drink, followed by an early lunch. First, however, he must make one more attempt to reach Chastity, now that he was free from any possible spy.

As he had expected, a call to the flat produced no result. There was no alternative left but to try Chastity's mobile once more. To his surprise it not only rang but also was answered quickly.

'I must speak to you,' he told her.

'I can't possibly talk now,' she replied. 'I'm very busy at the clinic.'

'Can you meet me later today? It's urgent. I've just had a demand from Lord Harry to obtain your answer to his proposal, about which I know nothing. He won't leave it at that. I don't think that you understand the kind of man you're dealing with.'

'I have some idea. But are you my friend or my enemy?'

Both the words and tone infuriated him. 'Why do you continue to doubt me? I simply want to help.'

'I see. It seems that I have no alternative but to risk it. If you're willing, I'll come to your flat tonight at 7 p.m.; but only to talk, please note.'

'That's fine by me. I'll provide some kind of meal, shall I?'

'A takeaway will be fine. Chinese, preferably.' Before he could say another word she had gone.

Now, at 7 p.m., he was awaiting her with considerable anxiety and frustration. It was one minute past seven when the bell rang. Hurrying to the door, he opened it. With the beginning of December, the weather had become colder and frostier. The wind had brought a rosy glow to her usually pale cheeks.

Entering quickly and without waiting for his help, she slipped off her long, dark cloak. Underneath this, she was wearing what seemed to be a kind of uniform, consisting of tailored black trousers, a crisp, white blouse and a close-fitting black waistcoat. Her beautiful dark hair was fastened severely back into a tight knot. She still seemed extremely desirable, but he made no attempt to touch her.

'Shall we eat first? It's Chinese. I hope that I've chosen the dishes you like.'

'I'm sure you have,' she replied, following him into the living room. 'I'm hungry and cold. I thought I was managing the English winter well, but the wind tonight has chilled me completely.' She shivered a little as she spoke.

'We could eat by the fire,' he suggested. 'We can fill our plates from the dishes on the table and then bring them to the armchairs. If I bring these small tables over, it will be easy.'

'Lovely.' She was already warming her hands by the fire. 'I know you have central heating, but this fire is much more comforting.'

As soon as he had laid out the food, he called her to make her choice. While she did so, he arranged two armchairs and a couple of small tables in front of the fire. Within a few minutes they were both eating cheerfully.

He waited for her to speak, but finally decided he would have to break the silence himself. 'Don't you think you ought to tell me about Lord Harry's proposition?'

'Why?'

'I don't see how I can answer him if you don't.'

She stopped eating and looked seriously at him. 'I could just ask you to tell him that I'm sorry but the answer has to be no.'

'He's not the sort of man to be satisfied with that. Nor am I.'

'The trouble is you're close to him.'

Unicorn laughed mockingly. 'No one is close to Lord Harry.

I'm just one of his more superior minions. He would destroy me without a pang, believe me.'

'I do believe you and I wouldn't want to be the cause of that.'

'And the other difficulty?'

'In spite of my better judgment, I like you, but I'm not sure how far I can trust you, if at all.'

'I'd hoped that your agreeing to see me meant that you had decided that you could.' He spoke lightly, and it was difficult to tell if her words had hurt him.

'Do you think I can trust you?'

'Most women would tell you that you'd be a fool to do so.'

'I'm not asking them; I'm asking you.'

He helped himself to more food before answering. 'I think you might, even if no one else could. But why haven't you consulted Jan? I thought you intended to do that first.'

'I did intend to. I went down to Kent on Sunday to see him, but he had gone away suddenly the night before. He had left a note promising to get in touch with me as soon as he returned.'

'Very mysterious.'

'Not really. He is often needed elsewhere.'

'I see; so now you have only me to turn to. Poor Chastity! Lord Harry seems determined to force us together. If you find that puzzling, so do I.'

'You had no idea why he wanted to see me?'

'None at all.'

She seemed to take a sudden resolution. 'Then I'll tell you the outline of his proposal.' As quickly and succinctly as she could, she outlined Lord Harry's publicity proposals for her.

'I see,' Unicorn said as she finished; 'he wants to make you and your work the focus of one of his *Daily News* campaigns. He also wants to attack the Government, although the Prime Minister is supposed to be his friend, and, at the same time, present himself as the Saviour of the Poor. There's nothing new in that. It's one of his typical tricks and it's bound to be successful. But why does it upset you? You'll be a heroine and he'll probably raise millions for you. What's so wrong with that? His motives may not actually be altruistic, but the money will still be there and you can put it to good use. So why not?'

'You can't honestly believe that it's all as simple as that. If so, I don't agree with you. You have suggested more than once that I'm naïve, but, if you believe what you say, you are even more naïve than I am. And that I find difficult to accept.'

'So you don't believe that I mean what I say?'

'Perhaps it's more correct to say that you know it's not the whole truth.'

'Can anyone know the whole truth? Even you?' His tone was cynical.

'Perhaps not. But I know this truth. We don't want his money on those terms, nor do we need it. We have to be free to do the work required of us in our own way. Nor do I believe it would be right to publicise that poor child and her pitiful story for money. And it wouldn't end with her.'

'I suppose you think that is what I do all the time?' His sudden anger surprised her.

'I don't understand why you are so angry. When we first met, you admitted that your motives for exposing evils were pretty cynical. Your work, if successful, increased both the newspaper's circulation and your pay. Your readers, so you said, felt better because your reports roused their righteous indignation, but that was usually all that happened. Little else was done or required. And you passed on to the next revelation. Isn't that the truth?'

He slowly finished his glass of wine before answering her. 'That seems to be a pretty fair account of what I said then, but—' He stopped suddenly. 'Forget that. Let's return to the main point. Are you sure that you want me to tell Lord Harry that your answer is "no"? He won't be pleased. Since even he can't shoot the messenger, he will probably just send me to Outer Mongolia. But he won't be pleased with you, and he'll be determined to make you aware of that in some way. Is that what you want?'

She hesitated, wondering whether she should mention Emmanuel and the implied threat that had been made to her. But how far could she trust Unicorn? If only she could consult Jan. Aware that Unicorn was looking closely at her, she finally replied, 'I'm not sure. I really need to speak to Jan first.'

'Why? I should have thought that you were capable of making up your own mind.'

'Jan is my superior. He also knows more than I do.'

This reply seemed to irritate Unicorn excessively; standing up suddenly, he walked across the room to the window. At last, he turned to face her. 'It's a pity, isn't it, if he is so important, that he isn't here? Why the hell does he have to go away now? Tell me that. He doesn't seem to be as loyal a friend as you believe, does he?'

'You have no right to say that. I've known him for years and I'm quite sure that he wouldn't have gone away without some important reason.'

'And so, in spite of his not being here when you need him, you trust him. And you don't trust me, even though you obviously need someone to advise you and I am willing to be your friend. The truth is, you don't trust me because of what others have told you. That surprises me, but that's the real trouble, isn't it?'

'It's hard to trust you when I know so little about you.'

'What the devil do you want to know? Before I went away, I told you more about myself than I've ever told anyone. But, I suppose, you've since decided that was just a sob story, invented to make you another victim of my so-called charm? Did Jan tell you not to believe me?'

'No.' She stood up and faced him. 'It has nothing to do with Jan. Actually, I now know that what you told me then was true.'

'How?' He was obviously surprised. 'I haven't said anything more. I decided it would be useless.'

'I met your son this afternoon.' She looked straight at him. She had not intended to say any of this, but suddenly it seemed to be something that should be done.

'What the hell are you talking about? I haven't got a son.' As he moved towards her, there was a dangerously angry glint in his tawny eyes. She stood her ground.

'I met him this afternoon. He's ten years old and his name's Stevie. He looks so much like you that it's easy to see that he's your son.'

'And his mother, of course, is Helen Wallace?'

'And his father is Gervase Langland.'

His anger was gone as quickly as it had come. 'And what do

you suggest I should do, Chastity? Acknowledge him? Take him in my fatherly embrace? Ask his forgiveness?' He smiled mockingly at her.

She continued to look steadily at him. 'Not unless you want to.' Her voice was gentle.

'Why should I want to? I'm no more his father than any casual sperm donor would be. Helen, in fact, used me as a sperm donor, without my permission. That is all. And then she tried to put the blame on me. Unfortunately for her, I was not the sort to accept that. But there's no point in my saying anything, is there? You've had Paul's version and Helen's version, so clearly mine is wrong. It was no more than an attempt, you think, to deceive you so as to persuade you into my bed. Well, perhaps you're right. I have sinned: *mea culpa*. Is that what you want me to say?'

Suddenly, he noticed that she was smiling. Enraged still further by this, he shouted at her. 'What the fuck do you find so funny?'

'Nothing.' Moving closer to him, she looked up at him. 'I thought you might have learned by now that, although I'm a Christian, I'm not a fool.'

'And what does that mean?'

'That I've taken the trouble to discover that your version is the true one. Helen finally admitted it to me.'

'However did you manage that? No, don't tell me, I know. It was either your devilish devices or your angelic arts. I'm not sure which.' Putting an arm around her, he drew her closer to him. 'Whichever, you're very tempting and I want to kiss you.' Bending his head towards her, he drew her closer, then stopped. 'But I'm not going to. It's too dangerous.' Releasing her, he moved away. 'Have I disappointed you?'

'Not really. You're right. I'm not sure about it being dangerous, but it would be stupid at this moment and we're not stupid.'

Smiling cheerfully at her, he moved towards their chairs. 'Will you join me in a coffee and a brandy, O wise Chastity?'

'Certainly.' She sat down in her chair and, without arguing, accepted the somewhat large brandy he handed to her. 'What about the coffee?' she asked, as he sat down with his own drink.

'You don't need coffee. I haven't forgotten that first evening when I took you to the local pub.'

'And I began to destroy your illusions.' She smiled mischievously at him.

'And you've been doing it ever since.'

'But you don't dislike the truth?'

'Strange for me to say, but I don't; on the contrary, I find I like it.' There was a friendly silence for a few moments, until he asked, 'If you believed my story, why didn't you just say so, instead of telling me about this kid of Helen's? What was the point of that?'

'I had two reasons.' Putting down her glass, she looked seriously at him. 'Firstly, I wanted to convince you that I knew all the story but didn't condemn you. Secondly, the child needs some help.'

'I don't like "secondly". Surely you're not suggesting that I should give this help? If you are, after what I've just said, you must be either very foolish or very brave.'

'I'm not foolish, so I must be a brave woman, because that is exactly what I am suggesting.'

'Christian forgiveness is your line of business. You're the ministering angel; I'm the cynical journalist. Remember?' When she didn't answer, he continued, 'In any case, I can't see any reason why I should help him even if I wanted to, which I don't. He has an intelligent, highly-educated mother and a doting "uncle" in Paul.'

'Nevertheless, he does need help,' she replied, ignoring his protestations. 'Although he's intelligent, he's severely autistic and he needs to go to a special school.'

He was angry again. After gulping down the last of his brandy, he answered savagely, 'I don't want to hear any more, not even from you. I do not want to have anything to do with that devious woman who almost ruined my life, nor do I want to see that wretched child she tried to foist on me. I haven't forgiven her, nor do I want to.'

'It's not Stevie's fault,' she protested gently. 'The truth seems to be that Helen, although she desperately wanted to be a mother, doesn't seem to be a very good one.'

'Why doesn't that surprise me?'

Ignoring his forbidding tone, Chastity continued, 'It's partly due to lack of money. Stevie has always needed so much attention that she can only work as a part-time teacher of English to foreigners. She would be much happier working full-time in a suitable post; instead, she's suffering from poverty, boredom and an inability to deal on her own with her son, who needs far more attention than the local school can give him. Worst of all, she feels guilty that she is unable to love him enough.'

'And how have you come to know all this?'

'By spending this afternoon with them. Helen asked me to visit her because Stevie, as so often happens, had refused to go to school and was being very difficult. She thought that I might be able to advise her.'

'I see.' His tawny eyes had the glint of anger in their depths. 'So we have the doctor's diagnosis. And what, dear doctor, is the remedy?'

Although obviously aware of his scorn, she replied quietly, 'They need help urgently.'

Unicorn laughed. 'And what, then, do you propose? Even you can't be so trusting as to propose that I offer my services as a devoted helpmate and father. I have no love for her or for her offspring. The devious bitch has obviously got round you, hasn't she? You said you understood, but suddenly I'm the villain again. I was foolish enough to think that perhaps—' He stopped abruptly. He was finding this more painful than he had imagined, but he was determined not to show it.

'No,' Chastity said vehemently. 'You're quite wrong. I think Helen is a selfish woman who used you shamefully. Unfortunately, although she loves her son, she is also a selfish mother with only a limited amount of love to give. She is finding the situation too much, and Stevie is suffering. I only hoped that you might feel generous enough to help him.'

He was incredulous. 'No one except you would have said that. And, most surprising of all, I think you mean it!'

'Of course I do.' She was smiling now and her eyes were shining.

'What do you expect me to do? Be careful now. Even a saint can't expect to work a major miracle with a sinner like me.'

'I only hope that you will be willing to make a sufficient sum of money available to send Stevie to a suitable school for the next few years. I think he may be a musical genius, but he needs skilled help.'

'And that is all?' There was a sardonic note in his voice. 'Have you any idea how much would be needed?'

'No, but I can find out.'

'And you think I can afford it, even if I am willing?'

'Not out of your salary, perhaps, but from the family money that is at your disposal.'

'I have never used any of that since I parted from my family.' His tone was forbidding.

'But you could use some for this, couldn't you?'

'Why should I? If I'm not prepared to use it for myself, why should I waste it on that brat?' He waited for her response, but, as she only continued to look at him with those beautiful eyes and say nothing more, he finally broke the silence. 'Very well, I will do it. Not because I forgive Helen, not even for the boy, but for you. It must be an anonymous gift and you must see that it is administered properly. Will that satisfy you?'

'Thank you.' She smiled brilliantly at him.

'I'm only doing it because I care for you and because you are the first woman who has ever treated me honestly and asked nothing for herself.' He stood up. 'Now, before I get maudlin, can I tempt you to another brandy?'

'How can I refuse?' She held out her glass. 'But I would be grateful for the coffee you promised.'

'No difficulty. I'll take these plates out and bring it in.'

In a few minutes, they were comfortably sipping both coffee and brandy.

'Now that you are, I hope, satisfied, can we relax together or is it planned for Rupert to come hammering at the door in a few minutes?'

'No Rupert. But I'm afraid I mustn't be late, as I have an early start tomorrow.

'In that case, we should perhaps get back to the matter we

were originally discussing. Are you sure that you want me to tell Lord Harry tomorrow that your answer is a definite "no"?'

'I don't think I can give any other answer.'

'Why not?' He was puzzled. 'The money will be genuine and you will receive it. Surely you can put it to good use? He's a bit of a scoundrel, I admit, but it wouldn't be worth his while to cheat in a matter like this. Is it the publicity you don't like? I can understand that you might shrink from that, but shouldn't you be prepared to put up with it if by doing so you could help thousands of people? Are you being a little too fastidious?'

'Are you really saying that I'm being selfish, that I prefer to keep myself free from criticism rather than help the people I say I want to help? Is that how you think of me?'

'Definitely not. But I'm puzzled. Why do you shrink from any contact with Lord Harry? After all, you might convert him.'

'You can't really believe that!'

'Probably not. But surely you're not afraid that he will influence you?'

He was even more puzzled by her reply.

'That is exactly what I think he wants to do. You don't understand, Unicorn. He is my enemy.'

'You're exaggerating, Chastity! I have to admit, however, that he won't like being turned down. I expect he'll be furious.'

'I don't see why. If he just wanted to help, he could easily give us a cheque without any publicity.'

'You think he has a hidden agenda, then?'

'Don't you think he has?'

'He always has, but, as usual, it's a pretty obvious one. He wants power even more than money.'

'And he intends to use me and this child to attack the government and to exalt himself. It's wrong. Surely you can see that?'

'I sense that you're going to tell me,' – there was a hint of mockery in his voice – 'that the end does not justify the means. If so, I'm by no means sure that I can agree with you. Perhaps you can convince me?' As he waited for her reply, he had an unexpected feeling that she was no longer listening to him. She was very still and her eyes were wide open, as if she were staring at something he couldn't see. 'Chastity?' he asked. 'What is it?'

She shivered as she turned towards him. 'It's nothing,' she said, almost stammering; 'at least, nothing that you can understand. I simply wish that Jan were here. I need to talk to him.'

'You mean that you can talk to him but not to me? I thought you had agreed that we are now friends?'

'We are friends, but—' She stopped, aware of how near she had come to telling him about Emmanuel and about Lord Harry's threat without knowing the true nature of his involvement.

'But you don't trust me. That's what you mean, isn't it? What kind of friendship is that?'

'I'm sorry, but there are some matters where I'm not free to trust anyone.'

'Except Jan. That's what you mean, isn't it?' Standing up, he spoke with cold anger. 'That's the end, then. I can't pretend to understand the reason for it, but I accept your vote of no confidence.'

'That's not fair! Please don't say it.' She also stood up and put her hand on his arm.

'I think it's perfectly fair. I confide in you, tell you that I love you. You might be reluctant to believe me, but, as a proof of my goodwill, I offer to help Helen's brat, simply because you ask me. But still you don't trust me. You must talk to Jan. I won't do. There is nothing more I can say.'

'You have to understand that this matter concerns Jan as much as it concerns me, perhaps more, and he is better able to decide it.'

'Then why isn't he here to support you?'

'I don't know.'

'Then, perhaps, you will tell me what I am to do? What answer am I to give to Lord Harry?'

'Perhaps you can ask him to wait?'

'I doubt if that will be acceptable. So, then what?'

'It has to be "no".'

'And I'm not to know the reason?' He waited, hoping for some reply. When it did not come, he spoke coldly. 'Very well. I'll ring for a taxi now. It's quite late and we obviously have no more to say to each other.'

For a moment, they stood looking at each other. 'I'm sorry,' she murmured across the chasm that now divided them.

Without bothering even to answer, he took out his phone. Both of them were anxious now for this meeting to be ended as quickly as possible.

Chapter Twenty-one

When Chastity entered the living room of the flat, she discovered Alex on her own, listening to the television. Turning the volume down, Alex greeted her with unexpected news. 'You have a visitor waiting in your room. He's been there almost an hour.'

'Who can that be?' Chastity wondered.

'None other than your colleague, Dr Jan. I told him that I didn't know where you were or when you'd be back, but he decided he would wait for you. I did invite him to have a drink with me, but he obviously preferred his own company.' Alex had clearly been disappointed by his decision.

'I expect he's tired. He's been travelling. I didn't expect him.' Chastity began to move quickly towards her room.

'You're amazingly fortunate, you know? How do you do it?'

'What do you mean?' Chastity paused briefly.

'How do you manage to get the most eligible men as your devoted slaves? I'm surprised, though, you bother with Unicorn when you have Jan. I'm really envious. He's the most handsome man I've ever met.'

'Jan's an old friend and colleague, nothing more,' Chastity answered as she approached her door.

Coming into the room, which was partially lit, she saw Jan, dressed in his usual dark clothes, sitting in the armchair. The light behind him turned his golden hair into a gleaming halo. His expression was composed, his hands loosely clasped in his lap. He showed no sign of impatience but appeared to be meditating.

'Alex told me you were here.' She hurried across the room towards him. 'I wasn't expecting you.'

He smiled. 'I hope that doesn't mean that I'm unwelcome?' Standing up, he took her hands firmly in his.

'You know you're not. I'm so very glad to see you. I really need your advice and help.'

'I thought that might be so. That's why I've come more

quickly than I originally intended.' His brilliant blue eyes looked deeply into her dark, unusually troubled ones. 'You don't seem to have your usual calm. Sit down and tell me what has happened. Is it Lord Harry?'

'Yes, it all began with him. But I've just spent two hours with Unicorn and that has made it harder. He sounded as if he honestly wanted to help, and I wanted to trust him but in the end I didn't, although I think, perhaps, that I was unjust. I certainly hurt him and that wasn't right, was it?'

'I think you'd better start from the beginning,' he suggested. 'Tell me first about your interview with Lord Harry. What did he have to say?'

As quickly and as clearly as possible, she told him all that had been said by Lord Harry. 'I never really thought that I could accept his proposal, but it didn't seem to be frightening until he spoke about Emmanuel. Then I felt he was definitely threatening me in some way. Was I right?'

'It was meant to be a threat, I'm afraid,' Jan replied calmly. 'What answer did you give?'

'I didn't. He gave me a few days to consider before I answered him. Unicorn, naturally, wanted to know what Lord Harry had said, but I refused to talk about it. I said I wanted to talk to you first. I went down to Kent, but you weren't there. When I was there I became involved with Eva, who insisted on coming back with me.' She paused, obviously waiting for him to comment.

'That must have made matters more complicated.'

'It did, but I think I found a temporary solution,' She was unsure of how much to say at this point.

'I think perhaps it would be better to leave Eva for the moment and concentrate on your main problem,' Jan suggested gently.

'Unicorn made several attempts to get in touch with me, but I remained elusive until this morning, when he rang me to tell me that Lord Harry was demanding that he, Unicorn, should give him my answer. So I agreed to go to his flat this evening.'

'And that is where you have been for the past two hours or so? Why did your discussion take so long?'

'That was my fault. I wanted to make clear to him that I completely believed all that he had told me about his earlier life. That I knew now that he had not lied at all and that Alex and Paul had both been very unpleasant about him.' She stopped suddenly, wondering how much more she should say.

'Do you think,' Jan asked, 'that you can explain this a little more without revealing anything that Unicorn would not want revealed?'

'I'll try.' As quickly as she could, she told Jan about Helen and Stevie. 'At first,' she continued, 'Unicorn was not prepared to accept that Stevie was his son in any real sense. He told me that, without his consent, Helen had used him as a sperm donor. I understood him. Do you?'

'Undoubtedly, he was much wronged and greatly affected.'

'Nevertheless, I told him that Stevie was his son and was suffering, most seriously, from Asperger's and that Helen was unable to cope with his behaviour on his own and, of course, that I thought he should help.'

'And how did he react to that "outrageous" suggestion?' Jan smiled at her.

'Not very well at first, but finally he agreed to make a sum of money available for Stevie's special education and training.'

'Family money, I imagine, which he has never touched since he changed his name and broke away from his family.'

Incredulous, she stared at him. 'You know all about that? You know who he really is?'

'It is very much my concern to know,' Jan replied calmly. 'He is Gervase Langland. The Langland family is one of the few ancient families who have continued to hold on to their wealth and power, often by disreputable means. When he became Unicorn, Gervase cut himself off from them and their attempts to control his life.'

'Is he right to use this money?'

'It is his to use if he chooses to do so. But I'm surprised that he should do so.'

'He was reluctant to do it, but he said that he did it for me since I am the first woman he has cared for who has been honest with him and who has not asked anything for herself.'

'I'm sure he meant that. And so you became better friends, closer to each other?'

'Yes, we did.'

235

'And you were tempted to trust him completely, especially since I was missing?' If he was anxious about her reply, Jan's calm voice did not reveal it.

'I couldn't. I was afraid. I said that there were some things I could not discuss with him and that I had to talk to you. He was hurt and angry. Was I wrong?'

Jan turned his brilliant eyes on her. 'Do you think you were wrong?'

'No, but I didn't want to hurt him after he had trusted me.'

'I'm afraid that was your only safe course of action.'

'It's a great relief to hear you say that.'

'What message did you give him finally?'

'I told him that, unless Lord Harry would give me more time, the answer must be a definite "no".'

'And he accepted that?'

'Yes. We had nothing more to say to each other. He ordered a taxi and we waited in silence until it came.'

'You are sad, aren't you? Is it because you have come to like him?'

'Yes, more than I did, but...'

'You wonder how close his relationship is to Lord Harry?'

'Exactly. Do you know, Jan, how close it is?'

As he often did, he did not answer her directly but left her to make deductions from the information he gave her. 'He has been one of Lord Harry's top journalists for years, first on television, now, for several years, working on the *Daily News* as well. He has produced some very successful and sensational stories. He has investigated many so-called scandals. He is highly paid and valuable to Lord Harry, but no one, however talented, is indispensable to such a man, and therefore he must tread carefully and, perhaps, not always truthfully.'

'Are you suggesting that if I trusted Unicorn as a friend and gave him information that Lord Harry might want he would betray me? He would do that after all he has said?'

'I'm not saying that he would want to do it but that he might be persuaded to do so. Lord Harry is very powerful. But I think that you instinctively realised this.'

'I suppose I did. I don't like this situation at all. I'm bewildered. I'm not sure what I'm supposed to be doing any more. I was puzzled when you said we were to come to England, but, for a while, it seemed pretty straightforward. There are many poor people who need medical and spiritual help. And there are others, like Eva and Mrs Allen. Unicorn was just a practised seducer who happened to be around. He thought I was a simple girl, and it was amusing to disillusion him for a time but now it's not. That's not what I was called to do.' Stopping abruptly, she gazed sadly at Jan.

Noticing that there were tears in her eyes, he stood, moved across the room and sat down on the arm of her chair. Speaking gently, he put his arm around her shoulders. 'This is not the first difficult and upsetting circumstance that we have shared, is it? You know that you have my support.'

'I do know that.' She leaned against him. 'But never before have I felt frightened and even rebellious. Why did you go away?'

'It was not my choice. I was summoned by the Lord we both serve. I won't have to go again. You haven't lost faith in me, have you?'

'No.' she moved away a little. 'It's not that. Several nights ago, Tim visited me in a dream. Rosie was not with him. We only had a short, happy time together before he told me that I must be very careful because I was in danger. I woke up not only frightened but, for the first time, rebellious. I needed your help, but you weren't there.'

'It's not the first time you've been frightened, is it?'

'No, but I've always known why before. Now, I don't, but I do understand fairly clearly that the danger has something to do with this mysterious Emmanuel. So many people seem to have met him but I, who am threatened by Lord Harry because I asked about him, not only have never met him but know nothing about him. You must tell me something. Who is he or was he? Is he dead, as most people seem to think? Or, if he isn't, where is he?'

Jan sat very still for a few moments without answering, then, after gently removing his arm, he stood up and walked back to his own chair. 'I can't tell the whole story, because I'm not sure that I know it myself. Even I am not always told everything, but I can tell you that one of the reasons we were sent here was to find Emmanuel or to discover his fate.' He paused, as if there were no more to say.

237

'But surely you can tell me more than that?' She was indignant. 'What connection, if any, does he have with Unicorn?'

'Unicorn apparently met him in the course of his work, and that was probably the way he came to the notice of Lord Harry.'

'Is he an Arab? Could he have been arrested secretly as a terrorist? Could it be that Lord Harry arranged this for his own reasons? Perhaps he is worried that I know something about it? What do you think?'

Jan smiled. 'Such a lot of questions! If they could all be answered we would not be here. But I'll tell you what I know. Emmanuel is partly Arab, but his father was an Armenian Christian whose family fled from the Turkish massacres. After many difficulties, the family ended up in a small Montenegrin town near the Albanian border. The parents died and Emmanuel and his younger sister were left together. Emmanuel tried to look after her, but she was a lively, lovely young girl who, apparently, became rather tired of their poverty-stricken life. One day she disappeared. She was abducted, or so Emmanuel believed, by those men who traffic in young women. You have heard about them?'

Chastity nodded. 'Yes. They're very wicked. But they are the sort of people Unicorn has been investigating, aren't they?'

'You're right. That is probably how Emmanuel met Unicorn when he set out to find and rescue his sister.'

'Did Unicorn bring Emmanuel to London, do you think?'

'He may have done, but all I know for certain is that Emmanuel was in London in the company of Unicorn, where he also met Alex and other people in this area, just before he disappeared.'

'But surely he wasn't killed simply because he was looking for his sister?'

'Don't you think that might depend on how much he discovered during his search and on whether these discoveries threatened some powerful person?'

Horrified, she stared at him. 'You mean Lord Harry, don't you?'

Jan nodded.

'But that is monstrous. Lord Harry is a public figure. Surely, he wouldn't behave like that? He wouldn't need to, would he?'

'It would depend, I think, on how much is at stake and on what Lord Harry's real aims are. What was your impression of him?'

Chastity shuddered. 'I can believe that he is evil. At first, he seemed a powerful but rather genial person, until I looked into his eyes. They are grey, cold and implacable. His look reveals no emotion, but it freezes one.'

'You wouldn't trust him, then?'

'Not in anything good. That was why I couldn't accept his offer. I knew instinctively that it was not what it seemed, although I didn't analyse it closely.'

'His publicity could be used, in the end, to destroy you, if he so chose. Do you find that difficult to believe?'

'I'm afraid not.'

'And when you consider Unicorn you must remember that this is the man for whom he has worked successfully for years. Surely, this, if nothing else, must make you feel that you must be cautious in your dealings with Unicorn himself?'

'I understand what you're saying, but I still can't accept that Unicorn is a truly evil person.'

Jan smiled. 'You don't need to be so defensive, Chastity. I agree with you. He has shown that, when approached honestly and lovingly, as you have done, he is capable of considerable generosity. He seems to have the capacity to be either a sinner or a saint. He is a valuable person, therefore, but you must be careful. Remember Emmanuel. He, apparently, trusted Unicorn, and he has disappeared.'

'I have thought of that.' For a few moments she sat silent, while Jan waited. At last she lifted her head, looking straight into his amazing blue eyes. 'There is one thing you still haven't told me. Why is Emmanuel so important to you, to us? And not only to us but to Lord Harry?'

'Haven't you realised, Chastity, that Emmanuel was not just a poor Balkan boy looking for his lost sister, but one of our company?'

Chastity did not stir but continued to gaze at him as if waiting for more. Finally, she let out her breath in a soft sigh. 'Lord

Harry, then, is truly our enemy, and Unicorn might also be our enemy, even though, perhaps, he isn't so clearly aware of it?'

'That is the situation. Does it frighten you?'

'I'm not afraid now that I know the truth, but I'm not sure yet what I should do. Was I right to give Unicorn the message that I did? Is Lord Harry likely to give me more time, do you think?'

'He may, but he may try to make you suffer for it in some way.'

'Do you think that I may disappear too?'

'No, you're too valuable for that. He may try to intimidate you, but, with me close beside you, he will find that very difficult. We must make some plans, but not tonight. I must have time to think. Perhaps now you will tell me more about Eva?'

'She is staying temporarily with Mrs Allen and Sean. She appears to be comfortable with them. She got in touch with Max today and she is meeting him tomorrow.'

'Are you sure that is the right thing for her to do?'

'I wasn't, but, when she heard that he had paid her rent and been very concerned about her, she felt that she ought to speak to him. I agreed, therefore. Do you think that I was wrong?'

'No. I trust your judgment; you know that.' Looking at the clock on the shelf above her bed, he continued, 'It's almost midnight. I think we've said enough for now and must leave further planning until tomorrow. I'll go now and we can talk further in the morning at the clinic. Or is there anything more you need to say tonight?'

'No.' Chastity stood up. 'You've given me a lot to think about. I feel safer with you beside me and I no longer feel guilty about Unicorn, although I do hope that he's not Lord Harry's willing accomplice.'

Standing up to face her, Jan took her hands in his.

At this moment they were startled by a loud ringing of the front doorbell. 'Whoever can that be at this hour?' Chastity exclaimed. Even as she spoke the bell was rung again even more insistently. 'Perhaps I should answer it?' She moved towards the door, but, as she spoke, they heard Alex hurrying to answer it.

Curious, Chastity opened her door a crack in time to hear Alex say furiously, 'What the hell are you doing here? I've told you already that I don't want you near me any more, and I meant it.'

A man's voice answered. 'For God's sake, Alex, let me in.'

'Why should I?'

'Because I shan't go away if you don't. I'll keep on ringing. I don't care who hears me.'

'It's James, Alex's ex-lover,' Chastity whispered to Jan. 'He sounds a bit drunk. We may have to intervene.'

'Very well,' Alex replied furiously. 'Come in, but you're not staying.' As soon as they reached the living room, Alex continued, 'Tell me quickly why you're here and then go. You look disgusting and you've obviously been drinking. I don't want you here.'

'Don't turn me away, Alex darling. I love you. You know I do.' James sounded almost tearful and definitely not sober.

'Balls! You never loved me. So why are you here now? And why, in God's name, are you wearing your pyjamas under your overcoat?'

'She turned me out.'

'Who is "she"?'

'My dear wife, of course. The bloody bitch! She came in from the bathroom just as I was about to get into bed. Someone had told her about us and she'd been thinking about it all evening while I was out.'

'I shouldn't think you improved matters by coming back pissed.' Alex sounded almost amused.

Ignoring her remark, James continued, 'She wouldn't believe me when I told her we'd finished and that I'd always loved her. We had the devil of a row, and in the end she threatened to call the police and then she threw me out with nothing but my overcoat and slippers.'

'She's a better woman than I am.' Alex laughed bitterly. 'But I don't see why I shouldn't follow her example.'

'You won't turn me out, please, Alex, darling.' James sounded almost near to tears. 'It's freezing out there.'

'How did you get here?' she demanded.

'She gave me enough money to pay for a taxi.'

'I'll follow her good example, then. I think that's pretty generous of me, don't you?'

241

'You can't do that, Alex. It's cruel. You know I love you. I've missed you so much. That's why I've taken to drinking. Just give me a kiss.'

'Let go of me!' Alex suddenly shouted furiously.

'Alex, darling, you know you love me, really.'

'If I ever loved you, which I doubt, I certainly don't now. Go away. I don't want you to touch me. You're loathsome.' She was obviously struggling with him. Suddenly, there was the sound of something hitting the floor heavily, followed by a groan. Then silence.

Suddenly, Alex called out frantically, 'James, don't just lie there! Say something! Oh, God, I think I've killed him! Chastity! Come here, quickly.' She was crying now.

Chastity, followed by Jan, hurried into the living room, where Alex, in her dressing gown, was bending over the now-recumbent James, who was lying on his back near the settee. Alex, almost hysterical, tears running down her cheeks, clutched at Chastity. 'I hated him, I pushed him away hard but I didn't mean to kill him.'

'You haven't,' Jan's calm voice banished hysteria. He was bending over James and feeling his pulse. 'He's still very much alive. He's pretty drunk, I think. That's why he fell so easily. I'll sort him out and he'll sleep it off. He needs a bed, I'm afraid.'

'Why not put him in Eva's?' Chastity suggested.

'Excellent idea.' Jan lifted the now semi-conscious James and half carried him into Eva's room, shutting the door behind them.

Alex, still sobbing, had collapsed onto the settee. 'Thank God you were both here! Oh, Chastity, I've messed up so much! I don't know what to do. Please help me.'

'Of course I will if I can,' Chastity said gently, 'but first you must calm down.' Firmly, she led the shivering and sobbing Alex back to the settee.

'You don't know what horrible things I've done,' Alex sobbed. 'You wouldn't want to know me if you did. I can't bear to tell you, but I ought to.'

'You're suffering from shock.' Chastity soothed her. 'I'll get you a warm, sweet drink. In the meantime, mop up with these.' She handed Alex a handful of tissues.

When she came back, a much calmer Alex gratefully accepted

the drink. 'There are things I ought to tell you.' she began, after she had taken a sip.

'Only if you're sure that you want to.' Chastity waited quietly, but just as Alex seemed ready to speak, Jan returned.

'You have no need to worry,' he reassured Alex. 'I've examined him carefully. He'll have nothing more than a sore head in the morning. All of which leaves you with one problem: how do you get rid of him?'

Alex's mood suddenly changed. 'That's his wife's problem,' she replied briskly. 'I shall ring her now and warn her. I'm sure she won't want him left on the doorstep in the morning.' The normal, ruthless Alex had returned.

'Then I'll take my leave,' Jan replied. 'And you, Chastity, had better go to bed. Remember, we have an early start.' After kissing Chastity gently on the cheek, he smiled at Alex, brushing aside her thanks.

'Do you need me any more?' Chastity asked as the door closed behind Jan.

'No thank you. You've both been marvellous, but I can cope now.'

'I'll follow Jan's advice, then, and go to bed.' It was clear to Chastity that she was not going to hear now any of the revelations that Alex had been about to make.

Alex's Fourth Dream

It was late when Alex finally went to bed after speaking to James's wife, who, after a little protest, agreed to take her husband back in the morning. 'You have to believe,' Alex told her coldly, 'that I certainly never loved him and he only lusted after me. It was nothing more than a stupid game. It's you who are carrying his child, not me. Surely that counts for more?'

It had not been an entirely easy conversation, but Alex had finally convinced James's wife of her complete indifference to him and to his fate. The truth was that she felt no concern for any of the people she had involved in her plans and only relief that she was now free of them all.

After falling asleep with surprising suddenness, she found herself in a strange room, which, although it was large and beautifully proportioned, was unusually bare and empty. The few pieces of furniture seemed to be constructed of steel and glass. The polished wooden floor was bare, the walls were painted white and there were no pictures or ornaments. It was illuminated by a harsh, bright light from some invisible source.

Deeply affected by the silence and cold, Alex opened the one door, only to find herself in a bare hall that led to the kitchen, an unwelcoming place of white wood and stainless steel. It was a showroom of a kitchen. No one had ever cooked or eaten here. No friends would ever exchange confidences or recipes in this dead place.

Hastily, Alex went back to the first room. Her first impression had been correct. There were no personal possessions anywhere in the room, but now she became aware of a screen which had appeared on the one table. By it was a mobile phone. Even as she picked it up, the phone began to ring.

'Welcome, Alex, to your new abode. Here, no one will trouble you or make demands on you.' The voice seemed familiar and, as she continued to listen, she thought she recognised Dr Jan's calm, musical tones. 'Food and drink will be delivered to you at regular intervals and, by pressing buttons on the screen, you can watch humans living without participating yourself. This is not just a games provider; this is a virtual reality machine. You can watch people living their daily lives; see them happy and sad, living and, finally, dying, sometimes most cruelly. If the emotions should get too much for you however, or if you should find yourself getting a little too involved, you can always press the switch and free yourself completely.'

'But I can't spend my entire life watching films,' Alex cried, suddenly terrified. 'Surely you don't think I want to do that?'

'You should find it easy. The chair is surprisingly comfortable; you can change the programme whenever you want. There is so much available: unlimited music to suit every mood; travel to any part of the world, however remote. You can breakfast in the Amazon jungle and have dinner the same day in New York's finest restaurant. All this by merely pressing a button. Your physical wants are all supplied. If you wish to sleep, there is a bedroom with sleep-inducing music and any necessary pills. You can live like a millionaire without any effort and with complete detachment.'

'Stop!' Alex shouted. 'This is ridiculous. I can't stay in here for ever. I won't.' She rushed towards another door, which she had not noticed before. As she tried to release the handle, she realised that it was immovable. The door was firmly locked. 'Give me the key,' she demanded. 'You can't force me to stay here.'

'I'm afraid that there is no key, Alex. The door is permanently sealed. Once you have entered through it, you are here for ever.'

Alex sank down into the chair in front of the table. In spite of her almost overwhelming terror, she noticed that it was unexpectedly comfortable. 'Please,' she begged. 'Surely you can't expect me to live like this?'

'I do not see why you are complaining. Many people would envy you your possession of this machine. By next year, many will be paying a lot of money to try to buy a similar but less comprehensive one when it is launched on the unsuspecting public. These people will not be as fortunate as you will, since they have to earn the money to fund their escape from reality. To you, everything is freely given.'

'But you're forcing me. I'm a prisoner. Those other people are not.'

'Unfortunately, they will easily be persuaded to surrender their freedom by those who seek wealth and power.'

'But why – please tell me, why have you chosen me?'

'It is not I who has chosen for you; you have chosen it for yourself. For years now you have tried to get money and power by detaching yourself from all human obligations and responsibilities. It started ten years ago. You've not forgotten completely, have you?'

'No,' Alex whispered. 'Not if you mean…?'

'Yes, I do. I mean that and many events which have happened since. Your betrayals of your friends to further your own interests and, tonight, your indifferent dismissal of James, your ex-lover.'

'I don't see how you can fairly blame me for that. It was he who let me down. Surely, you remember?'

'Your vanity was hurt, but nothing more. You never loved him, and once you had achieved your promotion he mattered nothing to you. Can you honestly deny that?'

'Does it matter what I say, if I'm already condemned?' She was angry but still very frightened.

'Sit down now and make yourself comfortable. Press your buttons. You will soon forget. It should be easy for you.'

'I don't want to. I never before realised the significance of what I was doing. Is there any hope? Please say there is. I can't stay here, living but not living. I shall go mad.'

'You are very fortunate. There is still a chance, won for you by someone who still loves you. But this is your last warning. There can be no more. Do you understand?'

'Yes, yes. Thank you. What are you going to do?'

'Goodbye, Alex, for now,' was the only reply. Even as she watched, the scene faded; the room began to vanish. Suddenly, she was in bed in her own room. She could see familiar shapes in the semi-darkness. To make sure, she switched on the light. Yes, she was not mistaken. There were all her possessions: her books, pictures and expensive ornaments and also, although she shuddered at the sight of it, her own television set.

She tried to shrug it off. It was simply a stupid nightmare after all, she told herself. But however hard she tried she could not entirely free herself from the memory of the cold and silent isolation of that room. She did not believe that she would ever forget it. This dream was her last chance, she had been told, and only won for her by someone who still managed to love her. Who could that be?

Chapter Twenty-two

There was much activity in the flats at Number 48 early the following morning. On the second floor, Paul and Rupert had one of their more spectacular quarrels. It was made obvious to everyone by Paul pursuing Rupert down the stairs to the front door, hurling hysterical but, fortunately, almost unintelligible abuse at his partner; Rupert, making no reply and moving as swiftly as he could, was determined to get away as quickly as possible.

Alex, opening her front door to discover the cause of the noise, found herself confronting a furious Paul, magnificent in a quilted purple satin dressing gown complete with gold satin cuffs and collar.

'Why the hell don't you keep your lovers' tiffs to yourselves?' she demanded scornfully. 'It's far too early for so much emotion!'

Pausing, Paul drew himself up to his full height and replied with as much dignity as he could muster. 'I do apologise, Alex, for disturbing you. Unfortunately, it is no "lovers' tiff", as you call it, but a serious difference of principle.'

'Principle?' Alex raised her eyebrows. 'It didn't sound like principle. What principle can it possibly be, I wonder?'

'I wouldn't expect you to understand, Alex darling, but some of us do have principles. If you want to know more, however, I suggest you ask Chastity. She is the snake in the grass who has pretended to be my friend.' Without another word, he swept upstairs, leaving Alex somewhat bewildered.

'Oh, dear! Oh, dear!' she exclaimed to Chastity, who was just coming out of her room. 'Whatever have you been doing?'

'Getting dressed. Why?'

'You can't get away with that. I went out to investigate the uproar. You must have heard it.'

'It was impossible not to. But what does it have to do with me?'

'I'm not quite sure, except that, according to Paul, you are the cause of it.'

Chastity frowned. 'That sounds like nonsense to me.'

'It sounded weird to me but you, apparently, are the "snake in the grass", I quote, whom Paul till now considered to be his friend.'

'Is that all he said?'

'Yes; he then swept off with great dignity in his purple and gold dressing gown. What have you been doing? Not seducing Rupert, surely?'

'Don't be ridiculous! I have no idea. I think it would be more useful, however, if I made some coffee, don't you? I imagine that your unwelcome visitor may be in serious need of some. What do you think?'

'Oh, God! James! You may find it difficult to believe, but I'd temporarily forgotten about him. You're right. I'd better go and wake him up, especially as I promised his loving wife last night to deliver him by taxi before breakfast. I can't imagine why she wants him, but she apparently does.'

'You actually rang her?'

'Of course. What else could I do? She was not delighted, but she finally accepted the inevitable. After all, he is the father of her child, as I reminded her.'

'That sounds a little unkind.'

'True, nevertheless. He never cared about me. He simply wanted a little excitement before settling down finally. I suffered too, you know.'

'But not, I think, from unrequited love.' Chastity's cool tone reminded Alex of her dream and of the fear she had felt. What did Chastity really think of her? she wondered. There was no time now, however, for that.

'You may be right,' she agreed, 'but it still felt bad. I'll go and try to wake him up. That will be my penance.'

It certainly proved to be a penance. James seemed to be determined to resist all attempts to rouse him. First she called him quietly, then more and more loudly, but his only response was an unintelligible grunt. Despairing, she shook him quite violently. 'Wake up!' she shouted. 'You've got to go!'

For a moment, he opened his eyes. 'Don't wanna wake up. Don't wanna to go. Like it here with you.' After making an ineffectual grab at her, he sank back on the pillows, his eyes firmly shut.

He is revolting, she thought, as she looked at him lying there, smelling of whisky, unshaven, hair tousled. She almost hated him. Perhaps a life without people wouldn't be so bad after all. 'Stop pretending,' she shouted. 'You can't possibly be as drunk as you're making out. I want you out now.'

'I think, perhaps, he's suffering from the effects of the fall as well as the whisky.' Chastity's quiet voice startled her.

Turning around quickly, she saw Chastity standing in the doorway, holding a small glass of some liquid.

'I think you'd better let me deal with him, unless you'd rather not.'

'God, no. I've no patience with the fool. What's that you've got there?'

'A dose which should clear his head and settle his stomach.'

'You don't think he's got concussion or something, do you?' For a moment, Alex was worried.

'Jan didn't think so. But this will help him in any case. It's one of Jan's special remedies.'

'In that case, I'll leave you to it.' Alex could not hide her relief. 'Although I can't imagine how you're going to get him to take it. He's impossible.'

'Just leave him to me. I'll manage. You go and make some black coffee and plain toast. Bring it in about ten minutes, not before.'

'Thanks. I will.' Alex left quickly, before Chastity could change her mind.

Chastity approached the once more recumbent James. After putting the glass down on the bedside table, she spoke, firmly but kindly. 'It's morning. You have to wake up, James. First of all, I'll help you to sit up. Then you can have this drink. It'll make you feel much better.' Carefully, but very firmly, she raised him up a little, then offered him the glass.

'What is it?' he muttered suspiciously. 'Who are you?'

'I'm Chastity and I'm a doctor. Believe me, this should make you feel a lot better.' He tried for a moment to slip back again, but her firm arm prevented him. 'Drink it, please.' She smiled encouragingly at him.

'I bet it's horrible.'

She shook her head. 'Not at all. Just try it. Don't think about it. Knock it back.'

'If you say so.' Realising that further protest would be useless, he drank it, then leaned back against her supporting arm. In an amazingly short time, his head began to stop pounding and his stomach churning.

'Better already, isn't it?'

'Yes, much. Thanks. I don't know why you waste your time on me, but I'm glad you do. I wasn't all that drunk, you know. Alex pushed me over. She hates me now, I think. I'm no use to her any more. I really did think she would help me when I'd been slung out because of her. But Alex isn't like that, is she?'

Before answering, Chastity produced a comb and a small mirror from her pocket. 'Sit up and I'll straighten out your hair.' Skilfully, she combed through his tangled hair. 'Now part it how you like it. Good. That's a lot better.' She smiled at him. 'Now wipe your face with this eau de cologne.' From another pocket, she brought out a small bottle and some tissues. 'It'll freshen you up and take away the smell of whisky.'

Without protest, he followed her directions.

Standing back from him, she commented, 'That's much better. You look almost human.'

'I certainly feel a lot better. But what am I supposed to do now?'

'Alex is bringing you some dry toast and coffee. After that, she'll order a taxi to take you home.'

'What's the use of that? I'll only be slung out again.'

'I don't think so. If you're honest with your wife, she'll take you back because she still cares for you and because your children need you. You don't want to lose them, do you?'

'No, of course not. You think I've been a bloody fool, don't you?'

'I'm afraid you have, but I'm pretty sure that your wife will understand, especially now, since Alex has spoken to her.'

'You mean that she has some idea now what a bitch Alex is?'

'You have no right to speak like that,' Chastity answered him firmly. 'You must realise that you are also very much in the wrong. You have to be honest enough to admit it and be very grateful if you are given the chance to start afresh.'

He was silent for a moment, then he muttered, 'You're right, of course, but not all women are angels like you, you know. But I promise I'll give it a try. Thanks for everything.' There was no time for more conversation, as Alex came in with the coffee and toast, which she handed to him silently. Both she and Chastity then went out, leaving him to himself until the taxi arrived.

'However did you achieve that?' Alex asked. 'You really are a miracle worker.'

'He responded to kindness and firmness, as most people do.' Without giving Alex a chance to respond, she added, 'I'm going to get ready for my day's work. When the taxi comes, tell me and I'll go with him and see him safely delivered. Unless you would prefer to go?'

'Thank you, no. The ministering angel is much more your scene than mine. I wouldn't like to deprive you of your halo.' She could not suppress the irritation she felt, although she was reluctant to explain, even to herself, why she felt it.

If Chastity perceived it, she made no comment. Soon afterwards, the taxi arrived and the ill-assorted couple departed before dawn had quite arrived.

Some time later, when Alex was finishing her breakfast, the telephone rang. It was Unicorn wanting to speak to Chastity. Again, Alex was irritated. 'She left some time ago,' she replied. 'I have no idea where she is now or when she'll be back. Why don't you try her mobile?'

'I have, but it seems to be switched off. Please leave her a message to let her know I rang and ask her to get in touch with me. It's urgent.'

'I'll leave a message prominently displayed,' she promised. When she was on her way to work, however, she realised that she had made no attempt to leave a message, just as she had not told Unicorn that Chastity could soon be reached at her clinic. She had, in fact, given the opposite impression. Why? She did not want to answer her own question.

It was much later in the morning when Chastity finally received a text message from Unicorn. *Since you didn't get in touch as I asked, I had to give your negative answer to L H. He was furious. Be careful. U.*

It was later that same morning that Eva set out to visit Max. Before he set out for work, Sean had tried to dissuade her from going on the grounds that she was not yet ready for this meeting and might, therefore, find herself being persuaded to go back to her old life.

Mrs Allen, when asked her opinion, suggested that Eva should have another talk with Chastity first, but this would obviously be delayed, since Sean had earlier seen Chastity departing in a taxi with a man who seemed to be ill.

On hearing this, Eva decided to delay no more. Max had been kind to her on many occasions and she now wanted to be honest with him. After quickly tracking him down to his West End flat, she made an appointment to see him later that same morning.

It was just after 11 a.m. when Max received Eva affectionately and led her into his study, where coffee and biscuits were already laid on a table between two armchairs. As he took her jacket from her, he was shocked at the change in her. It was not simply that her brilliant golden hair was now a natural soft brown, nor that she was pale and wore little or no make-up; it was not even her loose jumper and baggy jeans, which completely concealed her once voluptuous curves. No, it was certainly something more fundamental than all that, which was obvious but nevertheless difficult to analyse. He decided to say nothing until he had talked with her.

'I sure am glad to see you, honey!' He kissed her enthusiastically on both cheeks. 'I sure have missed you. Now make yourself at home and have a coffee. It's just the sort you like.'

His first shock came when she said, 'Not black, please. I'd like cream and sugar with it.'

'But you always take it black; you like it that way.'

She laughed. 'The truth is, Max, that I loathed it that way. It was just part of the beauty routine I kept to because I was so terrified of putting on a pound. There was always something to worry about. Now I've come to realise how stupid it is to live like that.'

253

'Well, I guess there's no harm in relaxing while you're having a break.' He passed the cream and sugar to her. 'But don't let it go too far, kid. There's still a contract waiting for you when you feel better.'

After adding cream and sugar to her coffee, she took a sip before answering him. 'It's honesty time, Max. Don't soft-soap me. You made your opinion only too clear. "Beyond my sell-by date", wasn't it?'

'Oh, Christ, Eva! You know I didn't mean that. I was upset and trying to bring you back to your senses. We go back a long way, you and I!'

'We do, and I'm grateful for everything you've done for me, but, as I said, it's time now for honesty. You have to admit that, although what you said was put cruelly, it was pretty true.'

'Isn't a guy ever allowed to say sorry for things he said when he felt pushed?'

She took another sip of coffee, then carefully put the cup down. She could not hold it any more if she didn't want Max to see that she was trembling. Sean had warned her how easy it was to go over the edge again, although she was determined not to. Perhaps she should have waited longer, but, if she didn't make a break, she would never be able to start afresh. 'You're forgiven, Max darling,' she replied, forcing herself to look at him. 'I know why you said those things and I don't blame you. I'd been paranoid for months, but especially when we went away. I couldn't bear you to look at another woman.'

'Well, you know, I'm always looking at women, hon, but it doesn't mean a thing. It's just my job.'

'Yes, I understand that, but when we went to the Caribbean I thought…' She hesitated for a moment and then remembered she had said that it was truth time. 'I thought that it meant something special – that you might ask me to marry you or something like that.'

'I'm sorry, Eva honey,' he said slowly, 'I thought you knew that marriage and me no longer mix. Two disasters are enough for any guy, I reckon. Sure, I like you, but marriage…' He shook his head.

She forced herself to laugh. 'Don't worry. It was just a case of self-deception. The truth is, I wanted out and that seemed the easiest and most attractive way out, but you're right: it would never do.'

'But,' he persisted, 'we can still be friends and you can have a new contract; not, perhaps, the same as the old one, but more suitable for you now.'

She shuddered. She knew what that meant. 'Thanks, but no way. I've had to rethink my life and I've been lucky to find some good friends to help me. Years ago, in my teens, people flattered me and I was persuaded to sell my face and figure. After a few years I hated it and I drifted into drink and drugs, as you know. I wasted everything and ended up living in a room in Alex's flat – she was a devil's advocate if ever there was one. In the end it was lucky, because I met Chastity and Dr Jan and they've helped me tremendously.'

'Have you decided what you're going to do next?' Max was obviously worried. Leaning forward, he took her hands in his. 'We've had some good times together, honey, and we could have some more. I'll look after you better and make sure you have less pressure put on you.' For a moment it seemed tempting to yield, but then he continued, 'I could still fit you into my next schedule and you could be a great help, especially with the youngsters who don't know the rules. What do you say?'

She pulled her hands away. 'I could tell them how to tread the primrose path to ruin more successfully. Is that what you mean? Don't you understand, Max? I've finished. I'm not waiting for you to put in the full stop one day. I'm putting it in myself, here and now. I want to live as a proper human being instead of being a painted doll.' Suddenly it was easy. 'When I was a kid I wanted to be a nurse like my mum, but I wanted money more. Now I know I don't. I want to care for people and have people care for me. It's possible to live happily without loads of money and goods. I can always scrub floors or something.' Picking up her coffee, she drained her cup.

'You're not made for a hard life; you're not used to it.'

Laughing, she stood up. 'There are different kinds of hardship. Max. I've decided to try the simpler ones. Dr Jan has offered to get me a simple job helping in a children's hospice. If I like it, I might decide to take the nursing degree I was preparing to go for twelve years ago, before I met you. If I don't like it, I'll find something else.' She moved towards the door. 'I only wanted to thank you and to make it clear that this is the end of my old life and a new beginning. Wish me luck.'

Standing up, he moved towards her. 'I do, with all my heart. I'll miss you a lot.' He wanted to be able to say much more, but she had said this was truth time and he knew his golden words would sound like dross. He kissed her. 'I wish I was a better man.'

'I understand. I'll be in touch.' With a last smile she was gone. Whether they would ever meet again had been left to him, he realised. Eva no longer needed him as she had always done. The need might now be his.

The explanation for Rupert's stormy exit and for Paul's fury did not come until much later in the day, when Chastity was accosted by Rupert on her way home. Her impression that he might have been lying in wait for her was strengthened by his first words. 'I'm glad I haven't missed you. Can you spare a few moments to talk?'

'Certainly.' She smiled at him. 'Do you want to come up to my room?'

'It would be more discreet to go somewhere else. How about a drink in the pub? It'll be pretty empty at this hour.'

Once they were settled, however, with their drinks, he seemed to find it difficult to begin.

Chastity tried to help him. 'You and Paul seemed to have a spectacular row this morning. Alex said that Paul told her I was the cause. I hope that's not true?'

'Only in his twisted mind. Paul loves to hate. He's hated Unicorn for years and now he's added you to the list.'

'Why? What have I done? We had quite a friendly last meeting.'

'Ah, but since then he's had a talk with Helen and he's now sure that you've only been pretending to be his friend. You're really a secret supporter of Unicorn.'

'What utter rubbish! I only persuaded Helen to give a more

truthful version of her story, which does make Unicorn far less of a villain. I hope you don't believe Paul?'

'Of course not! I think I know you better. And I'm beginning to know Paul better. I've been a bit of a fool.' He sounded angry and bitter.

'Oh, dear; what has happened?'

'I've begun to believe that he's a twisted, devious egomaniac, not simply a harmless eccentric, as I thought.'

Chastity looked at him thoughtfully. 'You're being tempted to exaggerate because you're angry.'

'Perhaps, but there's still far too much truth in what I say for me to be happy with him any longer. I owe him a lot, I suppose. He helped me to liberate myself and to admit openly that I was gay. He was the first close friend I had. I loved him and I thought he loved me.'

'And so he does, in his way.'

'Maybe he does, but it's not the way I want. He's possessive and absurdly jealous. He sees everything only in relation to himself. He wants to keep me in his narrow world. He knows I hate scenes, so that's his last weapon. He's always acting, you see.'

'I understand what you're saying, but what has caused this last trouble? Not me, surely?'

'No; you're incidental, but you're still involved. The real trouble is that Mother Mark rang me up and asked if I would be willing to be a voluntary driver for two evenings a week, and, without consulting him, I agreed.'

'And that's upset him so much? Why?'

Rupert shrugged. 'I'm not sure. Perhaps it's because I want a bit of life separate from him or, worse, that I want to do something that he considers stupid.'

'Stupid? I would hardly call it that.'

'Paul disagrees. He believes that it's stupid to waste time and energy trying to help the losers; they deserve all they get and they'll never change. He is also convinced that I'm being influenced by you, and that makes him very jealous. It's all rather childish, isn't it? I'm sorry for inflicting it on you. But since he made so free with your name today, I thought I ought to explain and warn you.'

'Warn me?' Chastity questioned.

'Paul is a very determined hater and a very narrow minded one. That's why I've decided to leave him.'

'I hope that I'm not the cause of this happening? I have no desire to injure Paul.'

'Of course you're not. It's simply that I can't live in this claustrophobic world any longer, with so much mockery and hatred. Meeting you has helped me to see it more clearly. I want a normal life, as far as a gay man can have a normal life in this world.'

'What are you going to do?'

'Don't look so worried. Nothing drastic. I can afford my own flat, so I'll find one and move in. The voluntary work will give me a chance to care for other people, which I need. It's difficult to say what I feel, but I hope you understand.'

'I do understand. But be kind, if you can. I'm sure that Paul really cares for you, in spite of everything.'

'I'll try to remember it.'

'Jan and I may be able to help you.'

'I was hoping I could still count on your friendship.'

Smiling, she raised her glass. 'Let's drink to our continuing friendship.'

Chapter Twenty-three

As soon as he entered Lord Harry's office, after being summoned there by a curt message, Unicorn was aware of a subtle difference in the atmosphere.

It was not simply anger. Unicorn had faced an angry Lord Harry many times before and was not intimidated by him. It was not, however, anger that faced him on this occasion. In the first place, Lord Harry was not standing to meet him, as he did when he was angry, shouting out some command or insult. Instead, he was sitting at his desk with his back to the room, looking out through the wide windows, which gave him a panoramic view of the City of London.

Unicorn advanced towards the desk with his usual confidence, but, when Lord Harry did not speak, he stopped and waited. After at least a minute, Lord Harry swivelled his chair slowly around until he was facing Unicorn. In his hand was a piece of paper, which resembled the memo about Chastity that Unicorn had sent him earlier. Still he did not speak.

'You sent for me, sir,' Unicorn ventured with a slight smile.

There was no answering smile. Those slate-grey eyes were fixed on him with terrifying coldness. At last, he spoke. 'Is this, then, to be considered as Dr Chastity's final and considered answer to my proposal?' Slowly, he put the paper down on his desk. His voice was as chilling as his glance.

It was then that Unicorn realised that Lord Harry was far beyond anger. A feeling of terrifyingly cold fury and hatred emanated from him. There was no time to consider why, but it was immediately clear to Unicorn that he must attempt to mollify his boss, who, for some reason, seemed to threaten Chastity.

'I think it would be unfair to say that it definitely is that,' he answered as calmly as he could. 'Late last night, Chastity asked for more time to consider your offer and perhaps to consult her partner, Dr Jan.'

'Then why did you send me this?'

'I failed to contact her again; you demanded an answer, so I gave you what I thought you wanted.' He was far from sure that this would be sufficient, but he waited before saying more.

'It was a dangerous course you took,' the chill voice answered. 'If you want to save your woman from my anger, you must get the right answer without delay. You have till midnight.'

Recklessly, Unicorn decided not to accept this dismissal. 'I can't honestly see why this matters so much, sir. Chastity is simply a doctor who loves her work but shrinks from publicity. That's disappointing, I agree, but I don't see why it should make you so angry.'

'You don't?' For the first time, Lord Harry smiled slightly, then he continued speaking in a more normal manner. 'Dr Chastity is a very beautiful and intelligent young woman. She has bewitched even you, I'm afraid – experienced as you are.'

'I don't understand you.' Suddenly, Unicorn felt uncertain.

'Of course you don't. Sit down, my boy, and I'll try to make it clearer to you.' Without further question, Unicorn sat down. This sudden avuncular tone adopted by Lord Harry only succeeded in making him feel even more uneasy. 'Tell me, how long have you known Dr Chastity?'

Unicorn shrugged. 'Only a few weeks, but I've got to know her pretty well, I think.'

'That's what you think. But what do you really know about her?'

'I know she's an excellent doctor – a genuine Christian, who cares for the poor and has worked with them for years in Africa.'

Lord Harry nodded. 'Then why,' he asked sharply, 'is she here in London? Do you know that?'

'I'm not completely certain. She told me that she and Dr Jan had been sent on a mission here. They certainly have a clinic in a poor area, close to the Convent of Divine Mercy. They frequently work with the nuns.'

'All that is easily verified. Has she told you anything else?'

'She has been married, I believe. Her husband is dead and she no longer uses his name.'

'And how is it that such an unlikely person became one of Alex Woodward's lodgers?'

'She saw Alex's advertisement and recognised the name because her cousin had been at the same school as Alex.'

'And Alex has verified this?'

'I imagine so. It didn't really concern me much.' He broke off. 'Where is all this getting us?' he asked irritably.

'Just be patient a little longer and you'll see. Do you know where Dr Chastity trained as a doctor?'

'In London, definitely. She told me so.'

'Then it might surprise you to be told that Julian, who has been doing some investigations for me, has been unable to discover any Chastity Brown at any London medical school during the appropriate period.' Before Unicorn could protest, he raised his hand and said firmly, 'Before you try to dispute this, you should know that he has covered a wider period and a wider area and has discovered no trace of a Chastity Brown. Chastity is an unusual name, you must admit. Have you any explanation?'

'I don't understand it.'

'It is a mystery, I agree. And when one looks further into it, as Julian always does, the mystery becomes greater. He has been unable to find any trace of a Dr Chastity Brown until just over seven years ago, when she suddenly appeared in Kenya, working as an assistant to Dr Jan for an association called Doctors Against Poverty, which does not seem to be sponsored by any church or similar organisation but which, apparently, has unlimited funds, since they never ask for help. It is Julian's belief that some eccentric Middle Eastern millionaire is behind them, but he can't find any trace of him.'

'Surely that must be the real explanation for Chastity's reluctance to accept publicity? She is probably afraid that it might annoy their sponsor.'

'It may be. Perhaps the mysterious Dr Jan himself is the real sponsor?' It was difficult to tell what Lord Harry was thinking.

'Whatever else he is, I believe he's an excellent doctor; an unusually dedicated one, in fact,' Unicorn commented.

'The trouble is,' Lord Harry replied, after a long pause, 'that we can't afford to leave it at that.'

'Why not?'

'They've come too close to some of our activities – Emmanuel. You must remember Emmanuel?' The grey eyes looked coldly at him. 'Julian believes now that Emmanuel was somehow connected with their organisation.'

'That's hard to believe, surely?' Unicorn was surprised. 'I understood that he was seriously suspected of terrorist activities. You told me so yourself, sir.'

'Such was the generally accepted view in government circles. It is irrelevant, however, for us to discuss its merits now. We have to face the facts. The organisation to which Dr Chastity and Dr Jan belong is hostile to us, and they are, therefore, dangerous.'

'But is there any proof?' Although he knew that he was being threatened, Unicorn could not avoid asking this question.

'Proof? Why do you need more proof? I have told you, and that has always been enough for you before. Here is another subject, ready for investigation. You are my chief investigative reporter. Do I have to ask someone else to do this job?' The menace of cold fury was again obvious, although neither Lord Harry's expression nor his tone of voice had changed. Something had changed fearfully.

Unicorn tried to avoid the insistence of those lifeless, grey eyes boring into his, so that he might have a chance to think. But it was useless. No chance was to be given him.

'Are you willing to take on the job or not?' the icy voice asked him. 'It is in your interests as well as mine.'

'I'm not quite sure of the nature of the assignment,' Unicorn found the resolution to say. 'Originally, I thought it was to persuade Chastity to accept your plan for a great publicity campaign. Is that now abandoned?'

Lord Harry laughed, but there was no mirth in his laughter. 'I do believe that the beautiful Chastity has truly affected your wits, Unicorn! Don't deny it. There's no shame in that. She is exceptional in many ways. You can still have a try at that, although I have little confidence that you'll succeed. But, if you do, that will be fine. We will still have our emotional publicity campaign, followed by the shocking revelation that the saintly Chastity is nothing more than a sham. The public will love that, too. Nothing satisfies their envy more than to discover that their former idol has feet of clay. You know that, for you've often worked on that assumption. It is our duty to expose the ugly truth beneath the attractive exterior. Goodness is often nothing but an outward show. Self-interest is the only real driving force. You're not going to tell me, I hope, that Dr Chastity has caused you to change your beliefs?'

Ignoring this rhetoric, Unicorn asked, 'If I can't persuade her to agree to this campaign, what, then, is my job?'

'I'm amazed that you should ask that again. Find out the truth, of course. There are mysteries here. You must unravel them, to their disadvantage. If there were such a being as a truly good person, he or she would have nothing to hide. There is something hidden here. It will be a pleasure to make it known.' He rubbed his hands in anticipation and smiled.

'And if we're wrong?'

'Nonsense, we're never wrong. It is your duty to make sure of that. Now, go and do it and don't waste any more time.' Abruptly, he turned his chair around until his back was towards the room. Dismissed, Unicorn left without another word.

It was immediately after this interview that Unicorn sent his text to Chastity. After having had no response to any of his communications, he decided that he must see her. The best way would be, he thought, to go to the flat and to await her return.

As he travelled across London, he admitted to himself that he had no clear idea as to his intentions. It seemed clear that Lord Harry was determined to discredit Chastity, either by persuading her to accept his offer of publicity or in some other way, which Unicorn had to discover by probing into the guilty secrets of her past, if, indeed, there were any.

It seemed to him that Lord Harry had become obsessed with an irrational hatred of Chastity and of the organisation to which she belonged. This was not a new side to Lord Harry's character, but this particular obsession was more sudden and more violent than any others he had experienced. Did he, Unicorn asked himself, want to continue serving this man? He had done unpleasant jobs before without many qualms, but now he was required to attack someone whom he had come to admire greatly.

Perhaps he should allow Chastity herself to choose her own way, for, after all, she had Dr Jan to advise and support her. But could he ever respect himself if, knowing what he did, he allowed her to walk into this trap?

It was only as he walked towards the flat that he remembered Lord Harry's reference to Emmanuel. This was a disturbing thought. Surely, it wasn't true? Certainly, Chastity had inquired about Emmanuel. Alex had told him that, but that could have been quite an innocent question based on something she had heard. With these questions still unresolved, he let himself into the flat. It was empty. Restlessly, he wandered round the room, pausing occasionally to stare out of the window, until, at last, he heard the sound of the front door being opened.

As the living room door opened, he swung round hopefully, but it was Alex's mocking tones that greeted him. 'What a delightful surprise! Why am I so honoured, I wonder?'

'Don't be absurd,' he answered her irritably.

She laughed as she threw her briefcase and handbag onto the floor and settled herself into an armchair. 'Don't tell me that it's the enchanting Chastity you want and not me?'

'I've been trying to get in touch with her all day. You know that. Not that you've helped much.'

'I admit I didn't try, but I don't think it would have helped much if I had. She's often very elusive.' She looked at him. 'Oh, for God's sake, stop wandering around and sit down. She's sure to come back soon. Whatever's the matter? I don't believe I've ever seen you look so upset before. In fact, I didn't think it was possible. I begin to believe you really are in love.'

'I need to speak to her. It's pretty urgent. Lord Harry wants an answer to a suggestion he's put to her. Her refusal to answer is making him suspicious, and that is making unnecessary difficulties for me.'

Alex stared at him. 'You know, I really thought you were

in serious danger of becoming human. But, no, it's business as usual. Poor Chastity! Nobody loves her, apparently!'

'What the hell are you talking about?'

'Well, only this morning, Paul told me that she was "a snake in the grass" for some reason. And now you, her supposed lover, only want to see her because Lord Harry, that old devil, is making a fuss. It's a good thing that she still has Dr Jan.'

'Has she been talking to him?' Unicorn asked quickly.

'Do I detect a little jealousy after all? Yes, he was here yesterday evening, for a couple of hours, until they both kindly helped me deal with a difficult situation with a pretty drunk James. Chastity took him off early this morning. That's why she wasn't here when you rang. She really shines as a ministering angel, doesn't she? Her halo's kept well polished.'

'You really are a bitch, aren't you? She helped you and all you can do is mock her.'

To his surprise, Alex seemed suddenly struck by what he had said. 'You're probably right.' She spoke slowly, staring at him. 'But, even so, I'm not as bad as you!'

'What is that supposed to mean?'

'Well, I admit I'm a pretty jealous type, and bitchy with it, too, but I'm at least capable of appreciating Chastity's real worth. You, on the other hand, only care about your paranoid Lord Harry and his suspicions. You're so worried about your precious job that you immediately come chasing Chastity, hoping to bring her to heel. So much for your love. You might not believe it – you almost deceived me – but you're simply making use of her, I guess, as you've always done with people.'

'Who are you to talk?' he asked furiously. 'What about James?'

She shrugged. 'True, but James was just as bad as I was. The difference is that you're trying to exploit someone much better than either of us.'

'And you're sure of that?'

'Sure of what?'

'Chastity's impeccable virtue.'

'Yes. She has her weaknesses, I'm sure, but she's basically good while we may have some good points but we're basically pretty bad. That's not politically correct, I know, but it happens to be true.'

'You sound pretty sure.'

'And you're not?'

'I'm beginning to wonder. Lord Harry has serious doubts.'

'Lord Harry! Christ! Since when has he been a judge of morals? You make me puke.' She looked contemptuously at him.

'It's not morals, exactly. It's more serious.' Ignoring Alex's mocking laugh, he continued, 'What do we really know about Chastity? Where has she really come from?'

'Perhaps you'd better ask me?' Chastity's calm voice interrupted their heated discussion. She had come in without either of them hearing her.

Unicorn leapt to his feet to face her. 'I've been waiting for you. I must talk to you.'

'I'm here now.' Chastity sounded completely unconcerned. 'You would probably get more information, you know, by talking to me rather than about me.'

Alex laughed, a friendly laugh this time. 'You deserved that,' she said to Unicorn. 'But before you say any more, Chastity, please let me answer him as I was going to, since he asked me.' She too stood up, looking straight into Unicorn's tawny eyes with their angry glint. 'I know all that I need to know about Chastity. Since she is the cousin of my school friend, I know that she comes from an excellent background. Although I hate her guts sometimes, I know from experience that she is a good doctor and a caring, honest person, far too good for you.'

'Thank you for your testimonial, Alex.' Chastity turned towards Unicorn. 'If you want to know any more, don't hesitate to ask. Or is it Lord Harry who really wants to know?'

'Of course it is!' Alex intervened. 'Lord Harry is furious, so Unicorn, as usual, does his dirty work for him.'

Suddenly furious, Unicorn turned towards Chastity, his eyes flashing dangerously. 'Stop trying to fool me! Alex is amazingly impressed by your honesty, but the fact is that you haven't told the truth and you know it. I suggest that we go to your room and talk about it privately. This has nothing to do with Alex.'

'I don't agree,' Alex interrupted. 'If I've been lied to, I want to know, but then, I don't believe that I have been.'

'I would rather Alex stayed,' Chastity said firmly, 'since you have accused me of lying to her.'

'Very well, if that is what you want.' His eyes flashed fire at her. His voice was almost a snarl. 'You are not the person you say you are. Julian, Lord Harry's chief investigator, can find no early trace of Chastity Brown. No Chastity Brown ever studied medicine at any London college or hospital at the time when you must have been training, as you say you were. The first mention of Chastity Brown is just over seven years ago, when she appeared as a fully-trained doctor assisting Dr Jan. You have no reputable past. And that's why, I imagine, you don't want Lord Harry's publicity. You're afraid that he might discover the truth: that you're nothing but a fake.'

Chastity stood pale and still. 'I'm not a fake,' was all she managed to say.

It was Alex who replied with unexpected violence. 'Of course she isn't! What utter rubbish! It's fantastic that you, of all people, should say that!'

Turning swiftly towards her, Unicorn exclaimed, 'Why do you say that?'

'Because the same could be said of you. Who is Unicorn Jones? His history is only about ten years old, I believe, although you have never told me. Why shouldn't other people change their names, probably for a better reason than you did?'

Silently, Unicorn considered this. 'Is that the truth,' he asked at last; 'that you changed your name?'

'Yes.' She looked directly at him with her dark, luminous eyes. 'I did change my name, seven years ago. I told my true story to Alex, although she didn't realise it at the time.'

'A very clever confession. But we still don't know who you really are, and it does actually confirm that you did lie to Alex. So, you see,' he said, turning triumphantly towards Alex, 'you are wrong. She's trying to deceive us again. She lied, but she didn't. She told you the truth, but you didn't know it and you still don't know it. What do you say to that? What can you say to that? Obviously, there's something she's afraid to make known.' Every word he spoke with such bitterness was like a dagger piercing his heart. He didn't want to believe what he was saying. He loved her, but some devilish fear seemed to drive him on.

To his surprise, Alex ignored him. She continued to stare at Chastity with a puzzled frown, as if trying to make sense of something.

'I did tell most of my story,' Chastity said slowly, 'but not quite straightforwardly.'

'You lied, you mean.' Unicorn was triumphant. 'And you're still lying. We don't know anything even now, do we?'

'But I do,' Alex interrupted him. 'I've had some little suspicions all along, but now I'm sure.' Looking straight into Chastity's eyes, she smiled. 'You're really Caroline Brown, aren't you? My old school friend herself. Now I can't think why I didn't recognise you before. You're older, of course, and even more good-looking; your hair's different, you dress differently but I can see the old Caroline now clearly. But why did you tell me that you had died? That wasn't true.'

'In an important sense, it was. I died of fever in a remote village. At least, everyone thought I had died, but Dr Jan brought me back to life. He told me there was a job for me to do, so I started life afresh as Chastity.'

'You wanted to forget all that had happened?' Alex tried to express the sympathy she felt.

'As far as possible, yes.' She turned towards Unicorn. 'You have your story now. You know who I am. If you'll excuse me, I'd like to go to my room and rest. I've had a long and difficult day.'

'You certainly started early enough,' Alex commented, 'by taking care of James for me. Have you eaten yet?'

'No, nothing since a quick sandwich for lunch.'

'I thought as much. Go and relax and I'll get a quick meal for us both.' Glancing swiftly at Unicorn, she added, 'You can go now. You've got the story for your boss.'

Ignoring Alex, Unicorn moved towards Chastity who was just about to go into her own room. 'Please, Chastity, I must speak to you alone.'

'Very well.' Leaving the door open for him to follow her, she switched on a lamp and sat down in the armchair beside it.

He stopped in front of her. 'You must believe me: I didn't

simply come to get the story Lord Harry wanted. I came to warn you.'

'Why should I need to be warned?'

'Because he's furious and he can be vicious when he's in that mood.'

'And that is the man you work for? It hasn't worried you before, has it?'

He couldn't deny that. 'Not particularly. I didn't really think about it.'

'Then why should it worry you now?'

'You know why. I love you. I don't want you to be hurt. I don't suppose you can believe that, but it's true.'

Unexpectedly, she stood up and came close to him. 'I do believe you. That is what is so sad.' She looked up at him, smiling slightly. There were tears in her eyes, he was sure.

He was lost. His arms went around her and he pulled her close to him. They kissed with a passion he had never experienced with her before.

After a moment, he drew back a little, framing her face with his hands. 'Damn Lord Harry. I'll throw up my job. I don't need his lousy money, anyway. We'll go far away and be free together.'

Gently, she drew herself away. 'I can't throw up my work, nor do I want to. And you're bound to Lord Harry.'

'No,' he replied vehemently. 'You matter far more to me.'

'It can't be done like that. You can't run away or sit on the fence. This isn't just about you and me. It's about truth and lies, about love and hate. Or, to put it more simply, it's about Emmanuel and other simple people like him. I stand with them. If you don't repudiate him, you are with Lord Harry. This is war. And you are my enemy.'

For a moment he stood as if frozen, and then, as he realised the full meaning of her words, his eyes flashed with fury and he almost threw her from him. 'It seems Lord Harry is right. If that's what you think, there's no point in my staying. You've chosen. May your God help you, though I doubt if He will.' The door slammed behind him and he was gone.

Chapter Twenty-four

The world into which Unicorn angrily hurled himself was cold and unwelcoming. The street, with its tall, once splendid Victorian terraced houses, was dark and forbidding. If the inhabitants were within, most of them had drawn their curtains tightly against the night, for scarcely a glimmer of light shone out.

The wind came in fierce gusts, bringing with it icy rain, but Unicorn scarcely noticed it, so great was the tumult in his mind. He had intended to hail a taxi from the nearby rank, but he had passed that without noticing it. Pushing his hands deep into his pockets, he strode of with the vague intention on going to the next Tube station on the Piccadilly Line. But even that he missed.

Furiously, he recalled how Chastity had calmly said that he was her enemy. And yet, only a few moments before, they had been closer than they had ever been. He had held her firmly in his arms and she had returned his kiss for the first time, with a passion that had brought him a joy he had never before known. Almost immediately afterwards, however, she had rejected him without explanation, apology or any apparent indecision.

'You are my enemy,' she had said. There could be no neutrality, she had implied. And he had suddenly been furious, so furious that he had pushed her away and left her.

Why? Why? Why had he not stayed to argue with her or even to plead with her? Yet what was there to plead? He had told her that he would give up his job with Lord Harry, that he would sacrifice his career. He had said that he would take her away and they would be free.

She had cared nothing for any of that. She could not or would not give up her work. What a fool he had been to imagine that she loved him. The truth was that he mattered nothing to her. The bitterness of that rejection was terrible. He had never been rejected before, but neither had he allowed himself to love before. What a fool he had been!

As he turned a corner, a sudden gust of wind hit him, bringing with it stinging icy drops of rain. He pulled up sharply, realising as he did so that he had already passed the Tube station. He either had to retrace his steps or walk to the next station. As that would bring him nearer to the centre and nearer to his present home, just south of the river, that seemed the more sensible alternative. In any case, he realised that he could not possibly sit passively on a Tube train while his mind and heart raged so passionately. He had been deceived and rejected and he had, therefore, every right to be angry, or so he told himself repeatedly.

It was not until after he had reached the shelter and warmth of his flat that he allowed other thoughts to surface. He had put his wet jacket to dry and had poured himself a whisky, which he was now sipping in front of the fire.

You're lying, and you know you are, a quiet, little voice within seemed to say. *She didn't reject you. She simply put the truth before you and you ran away.* Although he tried to tell himself it was nonsense, the voice persisted. *Why did you really run away? It was because she put the truth before you, wasn't it? She didn't reject you. She showed you the true situation and you couldn't face it. Remember?*

Taking another gulp of whisky, he tried to forget. He couldn't escape, however. It was like a film running before his eyes. He saw a pale and resolute Chastity telling him that neither of them could run away. Again, he heard her quiet voice saying, 'This isn't just about you and me. It's about Emmanuel and other people like him. It's about good and evil; love and hate. You can't pretend to be neutral. You have to decide.'

It was then that not only anger but also fear, a wild, irrational fear, had overcome him. He could not do what she suggested. She didn't know the things that he knew. At that moment, he had pushed her away and had told her that he hoped that the God she believed in would protect her but he doubted if he would.

He could see her standing there, with her dark, unfathomable eyes fixed on him. Why hadn't she protested? Why hadn't she called him back? Why hadn't she been afraid? He hated that silent courage of hers. He buried his face in his hands. What could he do? It was then that his phone rang and he remembered what he had to do.

Slowly, he took his phone out. Obviously, Lord Harry was impatient. He could switch it off, but it would only postpone what was inevitable. Reluctantly, he answered it. It was, as he had suspected, Lord Harry demanding his answer.

'I have quite a lot of information,' Unicorn told him. He decided quickly that he would tell what he had learned about Chastity's early life and true name, but he would not mention the final scene alone with her.

To his surprise, Lord Harry listened without interrupting. Only when Unicorn had finished did he ask, in a dangerously mild tone, 'And Alex Woodward corroborated all this? Is that what you're saying? She suddenly recognised her dearest and oldest friend?'

'Yes.'

'Didn't that seem strange to you?'

'Not entirely. It is twelve years since they last met and Chastity has changed a lot. Alex admitted that, although she also admitted that once or twice she'd had her suspicions because Chastity seemed to know so much about her.'

'Did she really?' It was obvious that Lord Harry was amused. 'How convenient for both of them!' Suddenly changing his voice, he asked briskly, 'Is this what you are telling me: that Chastity Brown was originally Caroline Brown, who can be traced?'

'That's right.'

'And that she changed her name because she wanted to forget some unpleasant experiences of her life?' There was no doubting the ironical undertones.

'They were extremely unpleasant experiences. Her baby died suddenly and, soon afterwards, her husband was murdered. Soon after that, she nearly died of fever. When she came back to life, she decided to start afresh.'

'And this satisfies you?'

'Yes; why not?'

'Why not, indeed?' Lord Harry's tone was worryingly suave.

'Naturally, you want to believe in your beautiful friend, but for me there are still too many gaps. I'm an old cynic, as you know. I'll call in Julian again. He will easily be able to corroborate when you've been told, for sure. There is obviously more to discover. But you have given us a good start.'

'I doubt whether there is much more that I can do at present.' Unicorn was ill at ease.

'You're not required to. There are others who can take over now. I have a much more interesting assignment for you, taking in Israel, Egypt and Turkey, perhaps even further afield. Take a week's break now and prepare yourself for two or three months' travelling. Report to me in a week, if you're willing.'

'Of course I'm willing. Whatever do you mean?'

'I mean,' – the voice had suddenly become hard and steely – 'two things: firstly, are you ready to leave your new love for such a long time and secondly and more importantly, are you prepared to give me your total support?'

'I always have. Surely, you don't doubt that?'

There was a moment's pause before Lord Harry continued, in the same cold, hard voice. 'Perhaps you haven't yet realised, Unicorn, that Dr Chastity and her friends belong to a powerful organisation that is a threat to all we support?'

'I'm afraid I don't quite understand. Surely a few charitable doctors can't in any way injure you?'

Lord Harry laughed, if that cold, spine-chilling sound could be called a laugh. 'Your naivety is entertaining, even if utterly unbelievable in one so experienced in the ways of the world. I'm afraid you can't stand aside any longer. This is the moment for decision.'

'Decision? What do you mean?' Chilled and afraid, he was again desperately seeking a way out, although he knew that there could be none. This was only another version of what Chastity had said to him.

'It is perfectly simple. Are you with them or with us? Neutrality is impossible here.' When Unicorn did not immediately answer, he continued, 'Perhaps I should remind you that you are deeply involved in some matters.' He paused.

'There is no need,' Unicorn replied. 'Of course, I'm with you. But can I ask you not to be too hard on Chastity? She may be mistaken, but she is a good person.'

Lord Harry's laugh, which was his first answer, chilled him

utterly. His words, which came next, were just as chilling. 'Leave the dear doctor to me. We'll soon have an understanding, I'm sure.'

Just as you did with Emmanuel were the words that came unwanted into Unicorn's mind. He knew that he dared not utter them. 'Very well,' he said instead. 'I'll leave Chastity to you and prepare myself for my next assignment.'

Lord Harry's triumphant chuckle was horrible to his ears. 'Good. You've made the sensible choice as I expected.'

'I'll await your instructions.'

Lord Harry was still laughing even as he rang off.

Unicorn poured himself a double whisky. 'She rejected me first,' he told himself, 'and now I've made my choice.'

You've betrayed her, the quiet inner voice said. *You're a coward.*

'What nonsense! It's nothing to do with cowardice.'

No? The old devil bared his teeth a little and you immediately toed the line. Let Chastity take her chances. Why should you put yourself at risk?

'And why should I? She rejected me, didn't she?'

You might at least be honest, the little voice answered with some contempt. *She didn't actually reject you, did she? She gave you a choice. She told you this was a war and you couldn't run away. She refused to run away, even when you tempted her. But you! My God, what a worm! You couldn't get away fast enough! And you even pretended that you love her!*

'I do love her. She's the first person I've ever loved.'

You make me laugh! When you love someone, don't you feel some responsibility for that person? Don't you want to help her, care for her and stand by her? A poor sort of love yours is. She's better off without it, if you ask me.

'I don't believe she loves me,' Unicorn muttered.

Then why do you think she kissed you as she did? You knew what that meant.

'Then why did she say that I was her enemy? How can she love me, if she thinks I'm an enemy?'

Chastity could easily answer that, I'm sure. She simply wanted you to understand the situation clearly.

'She gave me no time to make up my mind.'

You're lying again! You threw her off straight away. You were terrified. You didn't need any time, did you, when Lord Harry offered you the same choice? You couldn't sacrifice your love quickly enough, could you?

'I didn't want to. I didn't know what to do. No matter what you say, I do love her. She's the first person who's ever come close to me.'

The trouble with you is that you're too weak and selfish to love anyone. Only the strong can truly love. You actually had a chance, and now you've thrown it away.

'What can I do now?'

Pray that you get another chance to redeem yourself before it's too late. But that doesn't seem very likely.

'I'll go back to her tomorrow.'

And what about Lord Harry? You've already made him suspicious.

'Damn Lord Harry!'

He'll do that for himself, I imagine. The question is: what are you going to do, my bold lover?

Unicorn poured himself another drink.

I see you've already decided. Drink enough, then you'll forget love, Chastity and her fate.

Unicorn put down the half-drunk whisky. It seemed to him, as he continued to argue with himself, that he would never be able to rest again; but, at some point during the long, early hours, he fell asleep.

He was walking swiftly through city streets that were strangely deserted. It was a kind of twilight, but it might have been a winter's dawn. The tall buildings were dark shadows against the colourless sky. One or two people were lurking in doorways. One, a beggar, he presumed, tried to stop him, but he brushed him aside without a word.

He was filled with a terrible anxiety, a pressing need to get to his destination before it was too late. Abruptly, he stopped. He was there. This was the house where Alex had her flat. Chastity would be in her room. She was expecting him, he thought; but, if that was so, why was he so anxious?

He opened the front door with his key and ran up the stairs. The door to Alex's flat was slightly open. Without hesitating, he hurried along the hall, towards the living room door, which was also ajar. Everything was in darkness, except for a faint glimmer of light coming from beneath Chastity s door.

He halted, frightened by the darkness and the strange stillness. After a few moments, he walked as silently as possible towards Chastity's door. He could not give up now. She must be in there if her light was on. He was horribly afraid, although he seemed unable to remember why. The door opened easily to his touch and he took one step inside the room. Then, he froze.

By the light of the one reading lamp, he saw that there were two people already there. One, the old lady who lived in the ground floor flat, was sitting beside Chastity's divan. The other, a young man in jeans and a checked shirt, was standing next to the old lady. They were both looking at Chastity, who was lying on the divan. He moved a little closer. No one seemed to be aware of him. He realised that he must be invisible to them.

Now, however, he could see Chastity lying on the divan. Her head was resting on the pillow, her shining dark hair spread around. Her eyes were closed and her face was completely colourless. The old lady was holding the one hand that lay on top of the coverlet.

She's dead, he thought, *and it's my fault. I betrayed her.*

Even as he thought that, however, the old lady gently pressed the hand she was holding and murmured something. For a second Chastity's eyelids flickered open in response and then almost immediately closed again.

'She's still alive,' the young man said, 'but for how long? What in God's name has happened to her?'

'Only someone truly evil would want to hurt her,' his companion replied, still holding Chastity's hand. 'We must pray hard until Dr Jan comes. He won't desert her.'

At that moment, Unicorn became aware that someone else had entered the room behind him. Moving aside, he was able to see Dr Jan standing in the doorway, wearing his usual long, dark coat. His amazing golden hair gleamed like a halo and his startlingly blue eyes shone like sapphires. Apparently quite unaware of Unicorn, he advanced towards the bed. Stopping at the end of the bed, he called, in his deep, musical voice, 'Chastity, my dear one, you must wake up.'

Slowly, very slowly, she opened her dark eyes. 'I am very sad and weary. I need to rest. Tim and Rosie are gone from me. Unicorn has betrayed me. It has all hurt too much.'

Dr Jan's voice was very gentle. 'I know, my dear Chastity, that it is very hard. Suffering and evil are woven into the fabric of this world, but we have to continue with our work.' As he moved towards the head of the bed, the other two moved aside. 'See, you still have two faithful friends,' Dr Jan said. Bending down, he laid his hand gently on her head as if blessing her. 'The Lord of the Universe, my Father and your Father, needs you to continue your work in this world in support of his Beloved Son. You won't fail him, will you?'

Again he laid his hand on her head in blessing while he murmured a prayer. Suddenly, Chastity opened her eyes wide and spoke firmly. 'I won't fail my Lord. I forgive Unicorn and pity him.'

'Good. Now you must rest for a few hours and I will stay with you.' As he sat down on the chair beside the bed, Dr Jan turned towards the other two. 'You, too, must now go and rest. Chastity will be safe with me. We will meet later.'

Feeling like a ghost, Unicorn left the room with the other two, just in time to hear the young man say savagely, 'That fucking bastard, Unicorn! If I could find him, I'd break his fucking neck.'

The old lady smiled at him. 'I understand how you feel, Sean, but neither Chastity nor Dr Jan would want you to do that, would they?'

As they walked away, Unicorn turned back towards the door, determined to return to Chastity. He must explain to her.

He lifted his hand, but suddenly he was no longer in the flat; instead, he was standing outside another familiar door: the door to Lord Harry's office. No one was in the outer office, so, without hesitating or knocking, he walked straight in.

Lord Harry was sitting at his desk but did not appear to see or hear Unicorn. He was apparently concluding a conversation on the phone. 'Good; very good. You have done well. Unicorn didn't let us down, after all. There is nothing to fear now.' His face creased into a broad grin of immense satisfaction. Suddenly, all was changed as he turned to look in surprise at the monitor on his desk, which had unexpectedly lit up.

It was as if someone had torn a mask off his face. Instead of the ruthless but genial tycoon he usually saw, Unicorn found himself looking at the face of a defeated, old man, with sunken cheeks and sagging chin. Even the cold, grey eyes now seemed only like empty sockets. What had caused the change?

Unicorn moved swiftly across the room so that he could look into the monitor. To his amazement, he found himself looking into the unforgettable countenance of Dr Jan. Serenely and clearly he spoke: 'I'm afraid your subordinate misinformed you, Lord Harry, or perhaps he lied because he was afraid to tell you the truth. We, who serve the Lord of the Universe, are not so easily defeated. Chastity's love and courage were greater than you thought. The Dark Angel you serve has retreated once more from the Splendour of the Lord.'

'There will be many more battles,' Lord Harry managed to mutter.

'Perhaps.' Dr Jan smiled. 'But the last one may be nearer than you think and the final victory is assured. You will find that you have sold your soul for nothing, as many before have done.'

The picture faded; the voice was silent; the room was empty except for the travesty of Lord Harry, sitting alone at his desk. Darkness came slowly...

Unicorn was staring at the illuminated clock which always stood at the table by his bed. 4.45 a.m. Dawn was about two hours away. It had been a dream. Sitting up, he tried to make sense of his dreams but all he could feel was loneliness, emptiness and the pain of his loss.

One thing was, however, now clear to him. The old Unicorn was now dead and the new Unicorn could not live without Chastity. He had to take back his words of betrayal before terrible things happened. Nothing was more frightening than the emptiness and futility of life without love. He had to speak to her or to Dr Jan. But how?

Chapter Twenty-five

It was not long after Unicorn's violent departure when Alex produced the promised supper. Chastity came as soon as she was called. Alex searched her face for some trace of anger or distress, but she appeared to be as calm and composed as usual.

'Unicorn made a somewhat dramatic exit,' Alex remarked, dishing out the pasta. 'I presume he didn't exactly get what he wanted.'

Chastity looked steadily at her. 'I don't think he really knew what he wanted, so it was difficult for me to give it to him.'

Deciding that it would be unwise to ask any more direct questions, Alex diplomatically moved to another topic. 'He seemed to have lost his usual self-assurance. He was certainly taken aback by my acknowledgment of you. Perhaps you were, too?'

'I was, rather. Have you been suspicious for long?'

'I was never really suspicious. Occasionally, I was puzzled when you appeared to know things that seemed too trivial for Caroline to have mentioned to you. Tonight, the truth seemed to strike me like a revelation from heaven or something. When you said you had told the truth, I believed you. I looked at you and suddenly I saw Caroline. I can't think why I never have before. Perhaps it was because Unicorn made me so angry. I knew you would never be a liar, so you had to be Caroline. By the way, you don't have to tell me more if you don't want to.'

'Caroline's story was my story, so there isn't much to tell, really.'

'Perhaps not.' Whether or not Alex was convinced by this, she made no further comment; instead, she continued excitedly, 'All the same, it leaves a lot of things to talk about, doesn't it? It should be fun!'

The sound of Dot's return prevented her from saying more, particularly as Chastity said quickly, 'I'd rather you didn't say

279

anything about this to Dot at the moment, if you don't mind.'

'I understand. Of course I won't.'

Dot did not seem to be her usual cheerful self; in fact, she seemed to be quite depressed. She refused food, declaring that she had already eaten, but gladly accepted an offer of coffee.

'What's happened?' Alex asked, as she handed her a cup of coffee. 'You look pretty grim.'

'I've just had a stinking row with Richard.' She joined them gloomily at the table.

'Well, we're all in the same boat, then,' Alex said, comfortingly, smiling at her.

'What do you mean?'

'I've just completely finished with James, since he turned up here drunk last night. Unicorn has been dismissed by Chastity rather forcibly, I think. So, I think we should drink to the independence of women.' Pouring out another glass of wine, she handed it to Dot.

Dot drank the wine, but, as she still looked unhappy, Chastity asked sympathetically, 'I do hope that your quarrel wasn't serious?'

'It wasn't meant to be, but it escalated. You know how things do? It all started with this bloody farewell party of his.'

'I thought that was sorted out some time ago?' Alex was surprised.

'So did I, but in the last week or so it all seems to have changed. Richard seems to have gone completely bonkers.'

'Whatever do you mean?' Alex asked.

'He's invited several more people. I've scarcely met them and, from what I've heard, I don't want to know them. He's picked them up in some pub, I think.'

'Are these the chavs you were talking about?' Chastity enquired.

'I don't know what you'd call them. I think they're some kind of press people; freelancers, probably. Richard seems to think they're exciting to know and that they're fun to be with, but I think they're vicious and crude. My feeling is that they'll get very drunk and ruin the party because that's their idea of having a good time. I told Richard this and he didn't like it. He asked what was wrong with him having a final fling before he settled down as a respectable registrar with a wife. When I wondered if he really was going to settle down, he reminded me that the announcement of our engagement was to be the climax of the party. I said I'd rather that took place among friends.'

'I hope you didn't end by breaking up?' Alex asked her.

'No, but we nearly did. He's promised, however, to keep things under control. He particularly wants you, Chastity, to come. These new friends have apparently heard of you. You're becoming famous. You won't let me down, will you?'

'Of course she won't,' Alex said quickly, before Chastity could speak; 'neither of us would want to miss it.'

'I'm not sure.' Chastity was very hesitant. 'I don't go to parties any more. I doubt if I'll add much to the fun.'

'Oh, please, do come,' Dot begged. 'I particularly want you to be there. It means a lot to me. And your being there will probably make these horrors behave decently.'

'How can you resist such a plea?' Alex asked. 'Furthermore, I need your support, as I haven't got a partner. Come on, Chastity, we can always leave early if it gets too much. Remember those dreadful mixed parties arranged at school? It couldn't be worse than they were, could it? We always managed to have a good laugh, didn't we? I promise you I'll come away if it gets too heavy.'

'Please do come,' Dot begged again.

As it seemed impossible for Chastity to refuse, she agreed as graciously as she could, but she was not pleased by Alex's mention of their joint school days, nor could she remember any of these parties they were said to have enjoyed together. But, then, it was often surprising how different people's memories often seemed to be.

After a few minutes, Dot, obviously cheered by her friends' promise of support, went to bed. As they cleared up the supper, Chastity again asked Alex not to mention her real identity to Dot or anyone else at present. 'There are episodes in my past life which I would find painful to have to discuss,' she explained.

'I'm sorry,' Alex apologised. 'It was thoughtless of me, but it won't happen again. But can't we have a little chat now? There's so much I'd like to talk to you about.'

'Not now, I'm afraid. I must go to bed, especially as I have to be up extra early in the morning.'

'Never mind. We can talk tomorrow. Leave all this now. After all, it was all my fault that you were up so early this morning. I'll see you tomorrow.'

Chastity was embarrassed. 'I'm afraid not. Jan has a special job for me and I probably shan't be back before Friday evening or even Saturday morning.'

'That sounds exciting. What are you doing? Where are you going?'

'I don't know. He simply asked me to be ready early and to have my emergency bag packed for two days.'

'Ah! A mystery assignment! That sounds fun. And you really haven't any idea about it?'

'Not the slightest.'

'But you will be back for the party, won't you? You won't let us down?'

Since Alex seemed to be so eager, Chastity finally promised.

The following morning, Alex heard Chastity leave the flat soon after seven o'clock. Hurriedly getting out of bed, she ran to the window and looked out. There was a large white van parked outside. It was impossible to see the driver. In a few moments, Chastity emerged and hurried towards the van. The driver then dismounted and came to meet Chastity. To Alex's surprise it was not Dr Jan, whom she had expected, but the young man who lodged in the ground floor.

He spoke at some length to Chastity and handed her an envelope. They then both got into the van and drove off, leaving Alex very mystified.

After travelling a short distance, Sean, at Chastity's request, drew up in a quiet side street so that she could study the letter and the instructions which Dr Jan had given to Sean earlier. 'He told me he had hoped to come with you himself but he was now not free to do so, so he had appointed me not only your driver but also your protector. I'm to take that seriously; he emphasised that.'

'However did you manage to get the day off?'

'Dr Jan fixed that. Apparently, he knows my boss.'

'He seems to be sure that I can rely on you.' Chastity returned to her letter. Sean waited patiently until she had finished reading and had stuffed the papers into her pocket.

'What are my instructions, boss?'

'We are to drive to Hackney. Once there, we go to a particular group of council flats, park in front of one; and then ascend to a room on the twelfth floor. I'll direct you as soon as we get to Hackney. In that flat, we'll find someone who urgently needs my medical assistance.'

'I see.' Sean, concentrating on driving through the morning rush hour traffic, made no further comment and asked no questions, for which she was grateful. Although she was outwardly calm, she had an inner feeling of crisis. This was not the way Jan usually acted, nor was this a normal assignment.

In the flat, Jan had written, *you will find a young African Muslim known as Hassim. His sister, Hannah, is looking after him. She is expecting you. He has a bullet wound in his right arm, which urgently needs attention, so I'm told, if septicaemia is to be prevented. It is very possible that the bullet is still in the wound. In the van you will find all the equipment you need. With your previous experience, I'm sure you'll know what to do. Don't approach the local hospital. He has dangerous enemies, so the utmost secrecy is essential. Hassim is not a terrorist. I have chosen Sean to go with you because he is loyal, tough and has army experience.*

Looking at Sean, she wondered how much she should tell him but decided not to decide this until later.

The main street of Hackney was crowded with traffic and people of all kinds. As they crawled along, looking for the right turning, Sean looked out with disgust. 'I feel more of a foreigner here than I did in Iraq! Fucking Pakis everywhere! Except when they're blacks. God, there's a white face. Can you believe it?'

She looked sharply at him. 'I didn't know you'd been in the Middle East.'

'Yeah, First Gulf War – the last bit. The army sent me there. I was driving tanks. It was more interesting than on Salisbury Plain, at least. That war didn't make a lot of sense but this one's fucking stupid, don't you think?'

Without answering, she asked, 'Do you hate all coloured people?'

He laughed. 'Of course not! It's just a way of speaking. I've met one or two decent Iraqis and one of my best friends came from Jamaica – he saved my life in the desert but not his own. Why do you ask?'

'No reason, except that our patient is a Muslim, by name Hassim. I'm not sure exactly where he comes from – possibly Somalia.'

'Poor devil. He's probably had a rough life. Is he an illegal?'

'I don't know. Does it worry you?' Before he could answer, she said quickly, 'Turn right at the next turning, then take the first left.'

In a few moments they found themselves in the open area before several large, grimy blocks of towering flats. 'We want Bevan House,' she told him. They soon found the right block and parked in front of it. Having turned off the engine, Sean waited for further instructions, while Chastity took Jan's letter out of her pocket and studied certain paragraphs again.

'How much did Jan tell you?'

'Very little, except that he trusted me to be your driver and protector. Looking round this place, I can understand the protector bit.'

'I see. He didn't tell you that it might be dangerous, not only because of the neighbourhood?'

'No. Should he?'

'It might have been fairer to you. Hassim, our patient, has been shot, and the same people who shot him might not care much for our intervention, if they become aware of it.'

'Fucking hell, Chastity! Jan knows better than to think that would bother me. I know you guys are on the right side and I want to be there with you, especially you.'

She flashed him a sudden smile. 'Thanks for that! Now you can help me collect the stuff that I'll need.'

'We'd better lock up as securely as possible,' he warned. 'Some of the guys round here would sell their grandmothers for a fix.' To their surprise, however, they discovered that everything had been prepared for them in two large stout bags in the back of the van. Chastity insisted on taking one, reminding Sean that he might need a free arm.

It was a grim, grey place. All available walls were decorated with graffiti: some striking and obscene, much simply obscene. The cold wind brought eddies of biting rain and scattered debris everywhere. No one was visible, but they had the unpleasant feeling that they were being watched by hostile eyes. It was a relief to enter the evil-smelling foyer of Bevan House.

'Pray that one of the lifts works,' Sean muttered. The second one did. It smelt overwhelmingly of urine and vomit, but at least it moved when they pressed the button. Miraculously, it stopped on the twelfth floor. When they had looked at the numbers on the door nearest to them, they realised that the one they were seeking must be near the end of the corridor. Chastity paused for a moment to look down at the ant-like city far below. The wind was colder and stronger on the twelfth floor. The corridor was deserted; no sound of life anywhere.

'Who would choose to live here,' Sean asked himself, 'in this monument to twentieth-century inhumanity?'

Turning towards him, Chastity said quietly, 'I think I ought to warn you that our patient is very ill, possibly near to death. He's too afraid to go to the hospital or to the police; that's why his friends have called on us. Jan believes that the bullet may still be in his arm, and, if so, I shall have to operate to remove it.'

'Operate here?' Sean was incredulous.

'I'm afraid so. It'll be difficult, possibly dangerous and certainly very messy, but I may have no alternative. Can you face it?'

'Why not? Are you sure he isn't a terrorist?'

'No, just a victim.'

'Would you treat him if he was a terrorist?'

'Naturally. I'm a doctor. After I'd treated him, however, I'd hand him over to the authorities. We must respect the law. But there is no possibility that Hassim is a terrorist; I can assure you of that.'

'Good, then you can count on me.' Suddenly, he realised that they had reached the right door. 'We're here!' he exclaimed.

Chastity knocked gently on the door facing them, then more

loudly when nothing happened. Again, they had the feeling of invisible watchers. 'This isn't a nice place,' Sean muttered. Chastity nodded agreement as they waited.

To their relief, they heard footsteps coming towards the door. There was a pause, then the door was cautiously opened a few inches on a chain. 'Who is it?' an unseen woman asked fearfully.

'I'm Dr Chastity, and this is my assistant. We've been sent by Dr Jan to help Hassim. Please let us in.'

After a slight hesitation, the door was opened sufficiently for them to step through into a dim hall. The woman who shut the door behind them was young and obviously frightened. She was wearing Muslim dress, with a scarf that covered her head and shoulders. She stared at them with dark, scared eyes.

'Will you please take us to Hassim?' Chastity asked her gently. 'He needs our help urgently, I think.'

'Allah be praised,' the girl said in a soft voice with only the slightest of accents. 'You have arrived in time. Please follow me.' Leading them down the corridor, she stopped at the first door. 'He is in here.' She opened the door for them.

The room into which they entered was small and dark. The heavy curtains were almost completely drawn over the one window. Moving swiftly across the room, Sean drew the curtains open so that they could see more clearly. The room was scarcely furnished at all. Before the window, there was a bare table with two chairs. Nearby was a shabby armchair with broken springs. Along the wall farthest from the door was a bed, on which Hassim was lying. Although it was cold, he was bare to the waist, the blankets having been thrown back. With his dark skin, long black hair and beard, he would easily have been identified as a typical terrorist.

Without hesitating, Chastity hurried across to her flushed and restless patient, while Sean put their bags on the table and opened them. After laying her hand on his forehead, Chastity produced a thermometer from her pocket. While waiting to discover his temperature, she felt his pulse.

She turned towards Sean. 'His temperature is high, his pulse fast and irregular. We must not waste any more time.'

'Tell me what to do and I'll do it.' Nervous though he was, Chastity gave him confidence.

At this moment, the young woman opened the door and looked in timidly. 'Is he very ill? Is he going to die?'

Chastity looked at her briefly. 'He is very ill but, please God, we have come in time, I hope.' Looking at the girl again, she asked, 'Who are you? What is your name?'

'My name is Hannah. I am his sister and I love him very much.'

'Then you must pray for him and for me.'

Hannah bowed her head reverently. 'I will pray and I will wait outside the door. Let me know if there is anything I can do.'

Even before she had withdrawn, Chastity had turned again to her patient and was beginning to unwind the large, clumsy bandage on his upper left arm. When he flinched, she said gently, 'I must do this to help you. Do you understand? You must be very brave.'

It was obviously an effort for him to speak, but he managed to whisper, 'Yes. May Allah reward you.'

Chastity had soon unwound the whole of the bloody bandage and placed it in a metal bowl, which Sean had found in one of their bags. She surveyed the wound. It certainly did not look good. It was oozing still and the flesh around it was red and swollen. For a few seconds, Chastity appeared to consider the situation.

It's hopeless, Sean thought. *What can Chastity possibly do in this place?* The only sensible course of action it seemed to him, was to get Hassim to hospital as quickly as possible. Surely she must realise that. Dr Jan must have been wrongly informed. He could not have known how sick the man obviously was.

Before he could say anything, however, Chastity began to issue her orders quickly and crisply and, to his surprise, he found himself meekly obeying her. This was a Chastity he had never met before. The table was moved closer to the bed; with Hannah's help, a lamp was set up to shine on Hassim's arm. Chastity injected him with a powerful tranquilliser and painkiller and, while this took effect, they prepared themselves for the operation. All instruments that might be needed were set out;

they were gowned, masked and gloved. With horror, Sean suddenly realised that it was actually going to happen. He was about to take part in a dangerous and, for all he knew, illegal operation.

And for what? For a pathetic, probably illegal immigrant who had stupidly got himself shot. Suddenly, he was angry. Why didn't people like this stay in their own country, instead of causing trouble here? *Chastity's too soft hearted*, he told himself. *He probably is a terrorist or a friend of terrorists.* And for a guy like this he was expected to risk losing his chance of a new life.

'Don't you think—' he began, but Chastity interrupted him sharply.

'There's no time to think; pass the scalpel I asked for.'

He was still resentful, but found himself obeying her and her cool skill.

The next forty-five minutes passed like a nightmare from which he wanted to awake but couldn't. Half his mind was engaged in a fierce argument with Chastity and Dr Jan, but the other half was fully occupied in carrying out her crisp orders as quickly and efficiently as possible.

He dared not look at Hassim, but he was aware that there was a lot of blood and that Chastity was anxious. *What the fucking hell do we do if he dies?* he asked himself. *Has she thought of that?* He wanted to ask her, but that was now a totally futile question. He would almost have welcomed a loud knock on the door and the shout of 'Open up! Police!' At least it would take away his responsibility.

Suddenly, he heard Chastity say, quietly and triumphantly, 'Got it!' He looked up to see her holding a bloody bullet in a pair of tweezers. Dropping it into a glass dish, she said urgently, 'Now I must get him sewn up as quickly as possible. He can't afford to lose any more blood.'

Without a word, he began to hand her all she asked for, while fervently praying that Hassim would live and that they could soon get safely back to normal life. After what seemed an eternity, Chastity said with quiet satisfaction, 'That's it. We've finished. Start clearing up, Sean, while I give him a strong injection of antibiotics.'

'Is he all right? Is he going to live?'

'He should do.'

At least let him live until we've gone, Sean thought, as he helped to settle Hassim more comfortably.

As soon as the room was tidy again, Sean called Hannah in to see her brother. He was lying quite still with his eyes shut, but, when his sister spoke to him, he opened them briefly, managing to smile at her.

'He'll sleep now for a little while,' Chastity told her, 'but, as he's very weak, he needs nourishment when he wakes – a little soup, perhaps. Can you manage that?'

'Of course.' Hannah looked up at Chastity, the tears running down her cheeks. 'You are the first person who has cared for him. You're an angel from heaven! How can I ever thank you enough?' Seizing Chastity's hand, she kissed it.

Smiling, Chastity replied gently, 'A little coffee would be good. I'm sure Sean would appreciate that, too. I couldn't have managed without his help.'

'I thank you too, Sean,' Hannah said gravely. 'The coffee will be ready in minutes. Will you come to the living room?'

'We'd better stay here now,' Chastity decided. 'We still need to do some more tidying up.'

Thank God! thought Sean, as he looked around the now-tidy bedroom and sipped his coffee. *The nightmare's over and we can make our escape*. This, however, was not to happen immediately, for, as soon as Chastity had persuaded Hassim to drink a little soup, they were warmly invited to lunch by Hannah. Suddenly realising that he was very hungry, Sean did not object to this slight delay. He readily followed Hannah to the living room, while Chastity lingered for a few minutes to check Hassim's temperature and pulse.

'He's doing pretty well,' she told them as she joined them. 'Sleep is what he mostly needs now – sleep and regular nourishment.'

'Well, that shouldn't be difficult. It's certainly quiet here,' Sean remarked, as Hannah went into the kitchen to get the meal. He looked around the barely-furnished living room with pity as he drew his chair closer to the one-bar electric fire, which seemed to be the only source of heat. Apart from the table and four chairs, the only furniture consisted of two shabby armchairs and an ancient cupboard. The curtains were faded and tattered and the only covering for the floor was a grimy rug in front of the fire. 'Poor devils, they don't exactly live well, do they?'

'They have no permanent home. This is only a temporary refuge.'

The arrival of Hannah with the food prevented him from asking further questions. The food, although it consisted mainly of rice and vegetables, was hot, spicy and plentiful, and Sean appreciated it. As he and Chastity drank a second cup of coffee, Hannah slipped out to see if her brother was still asleep.

Looking at his watch, Sean realised that it was later than he had thought. If they were to miss the worst of the rush hour, they ought to set off soon. He looked out of the window. The van was still safe. 'When are you thinking of leaving?' he asked Chastity.

'Possibly late on Friday or, more likely, early on Saturday morning,' was her astounding reply.

'Whatever do you mean?' He stared at her.

'But surely Jan told you?'

'Dr Jan was in a hurry and told me very little, except that he asked me to be your driver and bodyguard on a difficult assignment. Knowing something about this area, I was only too willing to help.'

'And is that all he said?'

'He told me that you would give me the necessary information, but there's never been a chance for that.'

'Then, I'm afraid, you've got a lot to learn.' She looked worried.

Suddenly, he grinned. 'No sweat. I'm with you all the way, whatever. You know that.'

'I'll tell you everything,' she promised, still serious. 'And then you are free to make up your own mind.'

He sat down, suddenly relaxed. 'Shoot.' He put his hand reassuringly on hers.

Before she could begin, however, Hannah hurried in. 'Please,' she begged Chastity, 'Hassim seems to be very restless. I think there is something wrong. Will you look at him?'

Chastity stood up immediately. 'Later,' she promised Sean, as she left the room.

Chapter Twenty-six

It was certainly much later before Sean was able to talk freely to Chastity. In fact, it was not much before midnight on the Friday evening, some thirty hours later that he at last found himself alone with her. He was lying, fully clothed, on one of the twin beds in the spare bedroom of the flat, while she sat, fully clothed, on the other, brushing her hair.

Since she had hurried off on the late Thursday afternoon to attend once more to the restless Hassim there had been no time for talking. Chastity had spent most of that night with Hassim, whose wound was still giving trouble. At first, Sean had assisted her, as he had done before, but as soon as Hassim was stable again she had ordered him to bed in spite of his protests.

On the Friday morning she had spoken to Jan and it had then been decided that they must stay until early Saturday, when Hassim would be fit to move. As there was scarcely any food in the flat, Chastity had provided money and Sean had taken the frightened Hannah to the nearby shops. No one seemed to notice them, but Hannah was obviously ill at ease and he felt it necessary to be steadily watchful.

During all this time he had found himself in another world, one in which, although the menace was unknown, he was more frightened than he had ever been in the army or anywhere else. It was Chastity who kept them united and calm. If she had fears, she had not revealed them. As she sat brushing her long, dark hair, she told him quickly, 'I have spoken to Jan again and he says that since Hassim is much fitter he will arrange for him and Hannah to be picked up early tomorrow morning and we can then leave.'

'Where will they go?'

'To a safe place,' was all she said.

'And that's it, is it?' He raised himself up on one elbow and grinned somewhat sardonically at her as she turned to look at him.

'What is that supposed to mean?' She smiled at him.

'Nothing, except that I was remembering that some thirty hours ago you were about to explain the situation to me and give me a chance to leave if I wanted to. I don't imagine I would have left, but I didn't fucking well have the chance, did I?' He lay down again, still grinning.

'You're right. I'm afraid I cheated you by taking advantage of your good will. I'm sorry.'

'Forget it.' He turned to look at her. 'I couldn't have left you here on your own. Besides, I'd promised Dr Jan and I owe him plenty, so that's it, but…'

'But what?'

'I'd still like to know a bit more.'

'Such as?' She was very cool.

'Why do you do things like this? How the hell did you come to be doing them, anyway? We have some time now. Hassim's asleep and recovering. Couldn't you trust me a bit, now that you've got the chance? It would be good to know that you were willing to trust a dropout like me.'

'I do trust you. Jan obviously trusted you and so do I.'

'Then talk to me.' He sat up, looking unusually serious. 'I've been thinking about it on and off during the last few hours, and it seems to me that this has been one of the most significant experiences of my life. It seemed mad, crazy. Sometimes like a horrible nightmare but it was *real* – fucking real, as a mate of mine used to say. I'll admit that I was mad with you at times for putting me in this position, helping with a dangerous and probably illegal operation. I was scared, too, although I didn't know why, but I had to carry on. But I'm glad I did. Life will never be the same again.' He stopped, waiting for her to speak.

'Thank you, Sean. I couldn't have had a better companion. I was frightened, too, at times. But I'm used to it. I do it for love.'

'Love?' He raised an eyebrow. 'What does that mean? Nobody pays you? Nobody thanks you? Is that what you mean?'

'That may be true, in some part, but it isn't exactly what I mean. What I'm saying is that, years ago, I met the Lord of the Universe, or God as he is more often called. I met Him and I was changed. That is what has happened to you, and you, too, are changed. Isn't that right?'

'I met you. Guys like me don't meet God, do they?'

She smiled. 'Perhaps God uses intermediaries for guys like you.'

'Why should he?'

'To lessen the shock, I imagine.'

He was silent for a moment. 'OK,' he said at last. 'You may be right, but can we leave God out of it for a while?'

'Why not? If that's what you want. But, I warn you, he'll be back.'

Ignoring her last remark, he went on. 'God or no God, the last few days have been a life-changing experience for me. At first, I hated the whole situation and I almost hated you for getting me into it. Then, suddenly, a few hours ago, when I realised you'd succeeded and I'd helped you, I felt good. It was like a light was switched on. I, who had always been a no-good bum, had actually helped to save someone's life and had helped him to escape from some pretty nasty people. Free, *gratis* and for nothing. Am I right?'

'You certainly are. The people who tried to kill Hassim are evil.'

'They have to be, because I soon realised that he was a nice guy: not complaining, much braver than I am and grateful for the slightest bit of help. Then I asked myself, why was I doing this when I wasn't going to get anything out of it – no money and certainly not a better job or anything like that? After that, I considered you. With all your skills and experience, you could easily earn a fabulous salary; instead you were here, doing this for peanuts. Yet we were both happy. When we realised that everything had gone right, we were like a couple of kids having a birthday treat. I don't believe I've ever felt so good. Everything was changed. And it still is. I'm living in the same world, but everything seems different. Can you explain that?'

'You have entered the Kingdom of God. It exists already in this world, but most people don't recognise it. And sometimes – what is worse – if they have a glimpse of it, they run away. But you haven't.'

He shook his head. 'Get real, Chastity. I'm not a saint like you.

I've been pretty bloody awful. I guess there isn't a sin I haven't committed, except murder, and I've come pretty close to that sometimes and it wasn't conscience but cowardice that stopped me. All this God stuff's not for me!'

'Surely, you must have heard it said that Christ came into the world to save sinners and not the righteous? You've got another thing badly wrong, too. For years I was a pretty good sinner myself, until I was taught a lesson.'

'I don't believe it! How?'

'I was a beautiful girl and I enjoyed playing with men. Being also very intelligent, I did brilliantly at college. I thought I had it all worked out. I would earn a lot of money and be a really independent woman. Of course I intended to do a good job, but patients really represented cash and success.'

'You! I don't believe it!'

'I'm afraid it's true, but, just after I qualified, I met Tim. He was about twelve years older than I was. A brilliant lawyer who'd gone into the diplomatic service. We fell deeply in love; so much so that, just before his leave ended, I'd agreed to throw away my brilliant future and marry him instead. That also meant going to Kenya.'

'That doesn't seem to be exactly sinful! It seems to me you made an improvement.'

'I had, and I should have been satisfied, but I wasn't. There were several men attached to the embassy, married, most of them, but to boring wives. I was much younger, exotic and exciting. Because Tim was quiet and serious, they thought he was dull and that it would be fun to tempt his ridiculously young and unsuitable wife.'

'You're not going to say that you encouraged them?'

'I'm afraid I did. I really loved Tim, but I couldn't resist the excitement. I persuaded him to come to parties he loathed where he had to watch me flirting with other men. I must have hurt him a lot, but he rarely complained. Horrible, wasn't it? I told myself it was all right because I never actually committed adultery. I knew, however, that it was wrong. I was always promising myself that I would stop it, but I didn't.'

'I know what you mean,' Sean agreed. 'I was always going to

stop drinking, but I didn't until I'd lost everything. What happened to you?'

'I was more fortunate than I deserved. I discovered I was pregnant. Suddenly, Tim and I were both so happy that nothing else mattered. We stayed at home in the evenings, played music and talked. For the first time, I learned how much Tim cared about the Africans and wanted to improve conditions for them. With his encouragement, I set up a clinic for African mothers and babies. It was successful; the women trusted me and I liked them. I was happier than I'd ever been, especially when our daughter, Rosie, was born. She was perfect and Tim adored her.' Suddenly she was silent, staring ahead, seeing things he could not imagine.

He was almost afraid to speak. 'What happened?' There was no Tim or Rosie in her life now.

'When she was just a month old, Rosie died. We thought it was just some childish ailment, but she had a severe brain haemorrhage and she died in my arms, while Tim stood helplessly by us.'

Sean held her hand tightly; he couldn't think of any suitable words.

'That was very bad,' she continued quickly; 'but then, three months later, Tim was shot dead by a terrorist. It was a mistake; he thought Tim was someone else. I was now completely alone.'

He still had no adequate words, but he tightened his grip on her hand. At last he forced himself to say, 'What did you do?'

'I went to work full-time in the African hospital. I had money, but I needed so much more, or else I wanted to die. I couldn't make decisions, but they seemed to be made for me. A few months later, there was an outbreak of some strange kind of fever in one or two villages. It was like malaria but different. They needed a doctor and so I volunteered. We struggled to cope with it and finally seemed to find the right treatment. Then, just as the worst was over, I went down with it. I was dangerously ill.' Unexpectedly, she stopped talking and turned to look searchingly at him. He returned her look without turning away.

'I'm going to tell you,' she said at last, 'something I have never told anyone, except, of course, for Jan, who knows it all.'

Feeling suddenly humble, Sean protested, 'Are you sure that

you should, Chastity? I'm not much of a guy. People don't trust blokes like me.'

'Jan trusted you, or he wouldn't have sent you here with me. He understands people. He sees into their hearts. You must have realised that.'

'Jan's a tremendous guy! I understood that as soon as I met him that night in the hostel. Everything seemed to change when he came in. He had a sort of magnetism. I don't know why he came, but I'm glad he did. My life has never been the same since.'

'He was looking for you.'

Sean stared at her in complete disbelief. 'No way! How could he have been?'

'For the moment, you must take my word for it. For the moment, I can only tell you my story, which may suggest an answer. Are you willing to hear it?'

He hardly knew what to say. 'Of course I am! You know that.'

'You may not believe what I say,' she warned him. 'I won't blame you if you're sceptical. I only want you to understand that I'm speaking the truth as I know it. You are free to believe or not to believe.'

He nodded. Whatever could she be intending to tell him? he wondered.

'As I told you, I was desperately ill. The remedies we had discovered had no effect perhaps because I had lost the will to live. As I was lying there, I heard the other doctor say to the nurse, "She's sinking fast. We can't save her." The nurse replied, "I will pray for her. May God's will be done."

'Suddenly, everything changed. I seemed to looking down on myself lying on the bed. I could see the doctor was worried and the nurse was praying. I began to move away, along a wide, bright corridor. I was happy because I felt sure that I was going to Tim and Rosie. Even as I thought this, everything changed again. A brilliant light shone in front of me and I knew that I could go no further.

'An indescribable feeling of peace and joy flooded over me. It was like going into a beautiful garden on a sunny spring morning, when fluffy white clouds are floating across a deep blue sky and the daffodils are dancing in the breeze. Everything was perfect. As

I stood there, I heard the sound of music, and the music seemed to speak to me in deep crystal tones. Overwhelmed by the glory of the light and the beauty of the music, I knelt down, feeling that I was in the presence of a great and wonderful being.

'He spoke to me without words, but I understood. I realised that this was a great moment of decision for me. I could go on, where I would eventually be reunited with Tim and Rosie, or I could return, if I had the courage to continue the healing work which I had been born to do. I had been given much, and much could therefore be required of me, but I was free to choose.

'I knew almost immediately that I had to go back and that that was what Tim would expect me to do. I had already wasted my talents and this was my last chance to put this right. "I will go back," I said, "but I'm afraid. I'm so very weak."

'"Do not be afraid," I was told. "My messenger is awaiting you. He will always teach and guide you. You will not be alone."

'The music ceased, the light faded and I found myself back in my bed in the ward. The first person I saw was Jan. He was sitting on the side of my bed, leaning over me, with his hand resting lightly on my head. His compassionate, deep blue eyes were fixed on me; his hair shone like a halo in that dim ward. I thought he must be a saintly vision. But then I felt the wonderful, reviving warmth in his hand spreading through my entire being. I knew it was the healing power of love.

'I heard the doctor say with amazement, "She's opened her eyes! She's not dead!"

'"She is very much alive," Jan said, "but she needs nourishment as quickly as possible."

'The doctor hurried away and a few minutes later, when he came back, I was able, with Jan's help, to drink a bowl of soup, after which I fell into a deep sleep and awoke fully recovered, ready to become Dr Jan's assistant.' Chastity was silent. Sean had no idea what to say. Suddenly, she laughed. 'That's how my new life began. I took a new name and deliberately cut myself off from my previous life. Don't look so astonished and upset, Sean. I'm still the same person.'

'I don't know what to say,' he finally managed to stammer. 'Are you telling me the truth? Or are you having me on?'

'That's my truth. It's the only truth I know. You are free to believe it or not. You must try to understand, Sean, that this world is not the only one and even in this world we are not the only inhabitants. There are good and bad spirits also dwelling here, and we are involved in the great spiritual struggle between Good and Evil. Most people are unaware, but those to whom it is made known have then to choose whether to take part or to turn away and to pretend to be neutral in a situation where neutrality is impossible.'

'Are you telling me,' Sean demanded, 'that I have been chosen?'

'What else? Jan chose you and I have revealed myself to you. You have definitely been chosen.'

'But why me? I'm a useless waster. I've been a pretty bad lot most of my life. I never go to church or anything like that. No priest would want to have anything to do with me, anyway. Be real, Chastity. I'm not the right sort. You know that.'

Chastity was still smiling. 'Don't worry. You're not my choice, nor even Jan's, but the choice of the Almighty, from whom nothing is hidden. My advice is to give in. You can't win.'

'Great! And what am I supposed to do?'

'Nothing immediately, except go to sleep. Tomorrow morning, early, a special car will arrive to take Hassim and Hannah to a safe refuge. You will then drive me back – if you're still willing?'

'Bugger that. You know I am. Oh, fuck, I suppose I have to apologise for my bad language now?'

She laughed. 'I'll leave you to decide about that. Jan will meet us at Mrs Allen's in the morning and talk to you.'

'Do you know,' he said suddenly, 'I expect I've gone mad, but I do believe you. Even if I didn't believe you, I'd have to when I thought of Jan. He's such a fantastic guy! He doesn't care what people think about him. He knows what to do and what is right. And you're my friend, which is unbelievable. I won't let you down!'

'Thank you. I especially need a friend at this moment, as I'm in a rather dangerous situation. You must be very careful not to tell anyone any of the facts I have shared with you or anything about the last two days. Jan doesn't want anyone to know where we are or what we have been doing.'

'You can rely on me.' Standing up, Sean walked across to her bed and sat down on it. 'My life has been transformed since I met Jan, but never more than in the last two days here with you. I would never do anything to hurt you, but, I must admit, I'm a bit scared of the future.'

They were silent until Chastity, standing and taking his hand, led him towards the window. After drawing back the thick curtains, she said quietly, 'Look out there!' The full moon was sailing majestically among the dark clouds. The sordid buildings around were suddenly touched with magic by its silvery light. 'Never forget the true glory of the heavens. You are setting out on a precarious and sometimes dangerous path, but you need not be afraid, for your Guide is a Friend who will never fail you. There is good work for you to do in His Name. You must always remember that.'

'I will,' he promised. Suddenly, he realised that he was happier than he had ever been before.

Chapter Twenty-seven

It was on the same Friday evening that Alex began to feel both extremely frustrated and irritated. She had come home to find several messages on the phone from Unicorn to Chastity but nothing for her. She had hardly finished reading these when the phone rang. It was Unicorn once more, sounding unusually desperate.

'Chastity is not here,' she told him crossly, 'and I don't know where she is. According to the limited information she gave me, she will definitely be back tomorrow, because she has reluctantly promised Dot to go to Richard's party. There's no use, therefore, in ringing again before tomorrow. It seems to me that you've got to realise that you've blown it. Which doesn't worry me.' With a quick press of the button, she cut him off.

Half an hour later, the front door rang. To her amazement, she found Paul standing outside. Elegant, as always, in dark red corduroy trousers and jacket with a tastefully toning cravat, he was smiling ingratiatingly at her.

'I hope you've come to apologise for your behaviour the other morning?' she asked him tartly.

'Of course, darling. I know it was outrageous, but I hope you'll forgive me, as I was exceedingly distressed.'

She shrugged. 'It was amusing, actually, but I'm not sure that Chastity really enjoyed being called "a snake in the grass", particularly by a "friend".'

Paul flinched. 'That was in shockingly bad taste, I agree, and quite undeserved, as I have now discovered. That's why I've come to apologise most humbly to her and to invite her to have coffee with me tomorrow. Is she at home?'

'I'm afraid not,' Alex was delighted to say. 'She's away and won't be back before tomorrow morning. You should be able to see her at Richard's party, if you're going?'

'We are planning to go, I think, but I very much hoped to see

Chastity before then. Do you think that I could leave her an apologetic note?'

'Why not?' She invited him into the hall and watched while he wrote a short note on a page taken from an elegant little notebook that he carried in his pocket. Having written the note, he folded it carefully into a triangle, addressed it and handed it to her with a flourish and profuse thanks.

After seeing him out, Alex returned to her interrupted supper. Before she had finished, Dot arrived home. Her first enquiry, too, was about Chastity, and she was unhappy to be told that she had not yet returned. 'I promised Richard that she would be at the party. He's very anxious to meet her, and so are his new press friends. Is there any way of getting in touch with her?'

'Not that I know of,' Alex replied irritably. 'But she promised to be at the party, and she always keeps her promises. You know that, surely?'

'Yes, I suppose so, but I particularly wanted to talk to her.' When Alex gave no further reply, she disappeared into her own room, muttering that she had 'a lot of things to see to'.

As she poured herself a second glass of wine, Alex's irritation seemed to boil over. Nobody, it seemed to her, could think of anyone except Chastity. She wished that they had never met again. Why had that wretched girl come back into her life to disturb her? But, then, she hadn't even come back; she'd done it secretly as someone else, but the result had been the same. Chastity was just as annoying to her as Caroline had been. *Why do I think like that*? she asked herself immediately. *What do I mean*?

As she looked back, it became clearer to her than ever before that she had never thought of Caroline Brown as a friend but as a rival, a rival whom she'd never quite been able to defeat. At the same time, she had to admit that Caroline had never appeared to have anything but grateful and friendly feelings towards her.

She remembered how she had befriended the desperately lonely and unhappy thirteen year old, who had been thrust, unwanted and unwelcome, into a dormitory of girls who, during the previous two years, had become close friends. Caroline had been truly grateful for her kindness, but even then Alex had known in her secret heart that kindness had not been her only motive. She had wanted to please their housemistress and to be recommended as the best dormitory prefect, so Caroline had to be made happy. She had been successful, and Caroline had never forgotten.

How do I know that? she asked herself. Then she remembered that it was one of the things that had been told her in one of the strange vivid dreams she had had recently. Caroline's prayers had saved her, the voice in her dream had said. Surely, that was just a dream, so why should she imagine that it was true? Could it be that these dreams were really important? Perhaps, instead of trying to forget them, she should consider them seriously?

'But,' she told herself angrily, 'if Caroline really cared about me, she would have been ready to talk to me once I had proved to Unicorn who she really was. I was ready to be friendly and talk about the past, but she couldn't get away fast enough. It was just as she was in the last term at school. When the last day came, we scarcely had time to say goodbye, she was so anxious to get away.'

She finished her glass of wine thoughtfully. Someone, she decided, must have said something unpleasant about her and persuaded Caroline to believe it. There must have been proof, or Caroline would never have listened. What could it have been? It seemed ridiculous that, after all these years, it should matter, but suddenly it did. She picked up the bottle of wine, but, deciding that it would be more sensible not to have any more, she put it down again. As she did so, the front door bell rang again.

Who on earth could that be? she wondered, as she hurried to the door? To her complete surprise, it was Unicorn. She was not pleased and, as soon as they reached the sitting room, she turned on him. 'I'm amazed you didn't let yourself in with your own key. What do you want, anyway? I told you earlier that Chastity wasn't here, and she still isn't.'

Without answering her immediately, he took off his coat, flung it on the floor and sank down into one of her armchairs. 'I needed to talk to someone, even you,' he answered, running his fingers through his already-dishevelled tawny hair.

She stared at him. Not only was his hair dishevelled, but he was unusually pale and unshaven. Furthermore, his usually-elegant clothes looked as if he had slept in them. 'Whatever is the matter?' Pouring out a glass of wine, she handed it to him. 'You'd better have this.'

Taking it without a word, he drank it straight off. 'Thanks,' he muttered, then, looking at the table, he asked, 'have you got any food? I don't remember when I last ate.' His yellow eyes were strangely dark and dull.

This was all so unlike him that, for a moment, she was speechless. Without a word, she handed him a couple of rolls and a piece of cheese on a plate. 'That's all. I wasn't expecting a visitor, so I only cooked enough for one.'

'This is fine.'

She watched him as he ate hungrily. 'Whatever's the matter?' she asked again. 'I've never seen you like this before.'

'I've never felt like this before.'

After offering him a cup of coffee, she poured herself one. 'It's Chastity, isn't it?'

'Yes.' His eyes flashed with something of their usual fire. 'It's Chastity. You apparently knew her far better than I thought. Surely, you must have some idea where's she's gone now or of how I can get in touch with her?'

'I knew her at school. That's true. But, until she turned up here, I hadn't seen or heard from her for twelve years.'

'But, after I'd left the other night, surely you talked?'

'Dot came back, so there wasn't much time. I think that's how Chastity preferred it. All she told me was that Jan had a special assignment for her and that she wouldn't be back until late tonight or, most probably, early tomorrow.'

'Ah, Jan; then it was work that took her away.'

'I suppose so. But she didn't go with Jan. Apparently, she's already got a new boyfriend!'

'What the hell do you mean?' His eyes flashed with some of their normal fire.

'She was driven off by Mrs Allen's good-looking, young lodger. I don't know his name.'

'Sean, I believe. But why?'

'I don't know why. But it was definitely he who went off with her, and not Dr Jan. It's interesting to know that she hasn't changed much in some ways, after all.'

'What do you mean?'

'It's just that she never lacked a partner at the school ball, nor at any of the parties we sometimes had with the boys from the nearby public school. I used to think that it was strange, because she was fearfully moral and all that, but she loved flirting and was good at it.'

'"Flirting?" What an old-fashioned word.'

'It is, I know, but I can't think of a modern word that describes it better.'

'I don't imagine that her popularity pleased you.'

'There were a lot of things about her that annoyed me.'

'I thought you said you were friends? Was that not true?'

'You really want to know about her, don't you?' She looked directly at him, but his glance did not waver. 'Well, why not, even if it means telling you about myself? Perhaps people are right when they say that confession is good for the soul, although I rather doubt it. Nevertheless, I'll try it. Most people thought that we were friends, even Caroline, but, as far as I was concerned, she soon became more of a rival than a friend. She was better-looking and more intelligent than I was, and, worst of all, she enjoyed working.'

'I can't see how you would ever be friendly with someone like that. You're not the generous type.'

'Thanks for the testimonial! Whatever you may think, the truth is that I befriended her at first, because she was unhappy. Her mother had just died and her father had sent her off to boarding school at thirteen, so she ended up in my dorm, among girls who had been together for two years and didn't want an intruder. You know what that's like?'

'Of course: pretty foul. But I still don't see why you had to do something. It's not really your style, is it?'

'You don't know everything about me. Perhaps I was nicer then? If you insist on an ulterior motive, I'll give it to you. I was dorm prefect and wanted to make a good impression on my housemistress – which I did!'

'That sounds more like the Alex I know!'

'All the same, I was rather fond of her at first, but my feelings changed when she not only began to catch up with me but to overtake me.'

'You found her competitive. I'm surprised.'

'She wasn't a bit competitive. I was the one who was, and I simply couldn't show it! I still managed to become Head of House, much to Caroline's genuine pleasure, but, a few months later, she was made Head of School and I was only her deputy. I tried to hide my feelings, but I felt sometimes that I hated her and myself for being so mean. Nothing was ever said, but I think she must have realised something because, in our last term, she became rather aloof and at the end of the year we parted without any promises to meet. I was rather preoccupied with my first serious boyfriend, but it wasn't just that.

'I never heard from her or saw her again until she turned up here. And I truly didn't recognise her! She resembled Caroline, but she seemed, in many ways, completely different. A lot of tragic things had happened to her: both her husband and her baby had died within a few months. She didn't, however, tell me this as her own story, but as Caroline's. It is very strange. She had, apparently, put it all behind her and, for seven years, had been doing "good works" with Dr Jan. Caroline was dead. That's all I can tell you. She should be back tomorrow morning. I don't know where she is or what she is doing.'

'Are you sure she will be back?'

'Why ever not? She promised Dot she would be here for the party, and Chastity keeps her promises. Why are you so interested, anyway?'

'I have to speak to her. It's extremely important. I've already told you that.'

'I got the impression that she dismissed you the other night. Can't you believe that anyone would really do that to the fascinating Unicorn?'

'You don't understand. It's hardly likely you would.'

'What don't I understand?'

'I actually love her. For the first time in my entire life, I love someone, and I've ruined it.'

He looked and sounded both weary and defeated. She had never seen him like this before. Once, she thought, she would have been pleased to know that he had been treated as he had treated so many other people, including herself. She might even have rejoiced to think that he was suffering, but now she only felt curious and even a little sorry for him. 'I believe you're serious. Am I right?'

He laughed bitterly. 'It's ironic, isn't it? You actually warned Chastity against getting involved with me. Perhaps you should have warned me against her?'

'If I'd known who she actually was, I might have done so.'

'What do you mean?'

'In the sixth form she was the "Ice Maiden" who attracted all the eligible males and discarded them all. I sometimes suspected that Martin, my boyfriend, had been passed on by her. But, in the end, it didn't matter.'

'What happened?' For a moment, he was interested. 'Did he leave you for her?'

'Oh, no. It ended, as such things do, but it was about a year after Caroline had gone out of our lives. But I don't want to talk about it. It's past and long forgotten.' She smiled to hide the pain she felt whenever she mentioned it. 'Let's come back to you. Why did Chastity send you away? Was she angry because you didn't believe her without my testimony?'

'Not exactly. I thought she loved me, then she told me I was her enemy.'

'Her enemy? What did she mean?'

'It's all to do with Lord Harry. He is furious because she has refused to accept all his offers of publicity. I tried to persuade her not to antagonise him further. When she refused, I offered to give up my job so that we could go away together and be happy. I wanted her to understand that I loved her, but she rejected all my suggestions and accused me of trying to be neutral in a situation where neutrality was impossible. Furthermore, she said that, by asking her to go away, I was her enemy.'

'Surely, you couldn't be so mad as to expect Chastity to say anything different? You say you love her, but you don't seem to understand her.'

'Whatever do you mean?'

'You are only asking her to give up her entire life. For the last seven years, she has devoted herself to her work with Dr Jan. You are only giving up a job. Of course, you've been successful at it and it's earned you a lot of money, but that's all it is – a job. She has given up everything for her work. She has scarcely any clothes or possessions. We noticed that when she arrived, but she doesn't mind. She's happy because she loves the work she does and the people she works for.'

He was amazed at her vehemence. 'I thought you disliked her, even laughed at her.'

'I do, at times, because she challenges me. But that doesn't mean that I'm incapable of appreciating her. God, what do you take me for? Think about it, Unicorn; you are asking her to give up all that, and for what?'

'My love and a happy life.'

'What crap! Listen to yourself! Anyway, how can you be sure of doing that when you don't love her enough to have the guts to stand by her?'

Before replying, he stood up, walked over to the drinks cabinet and helped himself to a whisky, while Alex waited impatiently for him to speak. Without hurrying, he strolled back to his chair and sipped his whisky thoughtfully.

'Do enjoy my whisky,' she said at last, with heavy irony. 'But perhaps you'll enlighten me at the same time? Does your silence mean that our conversation is over? If it is, I'd like to go to bed.'

'I'm not sure. I'm afraid that you don't understand the true situation.'

'In that case, I'm obviously no use to you.' She yawned. 'It seems that I might as well go to bed. I'm convinced that Chastity can take care of herself.'

'Normally, I would accept that, but now I'm doubtful. Lord Harry is a powerful and dangerous antagonist. I've told him that she's finally refused to meet him. I've given her no loophole. I wouldn't have done that if she hadn't made me so angry with her.'

'Spare me your pitiful confession.' Her tone was scornful. 'What's the difference? You always let your women down eventually, one way or another. The only difference that I can see is that Chastity is very strong, unlike many of the others, including me. I really don't care.'

He laughed. 'You will care when you realise that you're involved.'

'Me? Don't be ridiculous. It's got nothing to do with me.'

'I'm afraid it has, my darling.' His tawny eyes were flashing. For a moment, he was almost enjoying the situation. 'Because you see, Alex, it concerns Emmanuel.'

'Emmanuel! He went away months ago. I've never thought about him since.'

'Not until Chastity asked you about him. You thought about him then. You were sufficiently worried to tell me.'

'And you told me not to worry. You said that Chastity had no purpose in her questions, that it was just something that Mrs Allen had said which made her curious. I believed you.'

'Not entirely. Why don't you try to be honest for once, Alex? It's Unicorn you're talking to. Remember?'

'I don't know what you mean.'

'I mean that, in order to safeguard yourself completely, you let Lord Harry know through the usual channels. I'm right, aren't I?'

When she didn't answer, he continued, 'It's no use denying it. You are the only person who could have done it, since I didn't.'

'I didn't think it was really important.'

'No? Well, Lord Harry differed. He put Julian on to it and he questioned me in a friendly way about my new girlfriend. I suppose it was jealousy that prompted you, as it so often does. You admire Chastity as you admired Caroline, but you hate her, too.'

'It's nothing to do with that,' she almost shouted at him. 'I passed on the information because...' She hesitated.

'Because,' he finished for her, 'you were afraid that it might just be important and you didn't want to be blamed if it was.'

'You should know. I'm just like you: a self-seeking coward. You're worse than me.'

'You're right. I wish you weren't, but you are.'

'It was you,' she reminded him, 'who got me involved in this in the beginning. You persuaded me to befriend Emmanuel and even to offer him a room for a while. Like a fool, I did it, all because I wanted to please you. You can't deny that.'

'I don't, but it was you who negotiated with Julian and gave Lord Harry the information.'

'I understood that Lord Harry was going to help him to get back to his own country.'

'If he did, it was in a coffin.'

'Oh, no, you can't mean that!' Alex exclaimed.

'I'm ninety per cent sure. And I suspect that Dr Jan knows even more.'

'Dr Jan! So that's why Lord Harry wants Chastity?'

'It looks like it. I didn't understand at first, but now I'm pretty sure.'

'So that's why you wanted to go away? You think Lord Harry's too powerful to oppose?'

'I know he is.'

'If all this comes out, we're both finished. Both our careers will be ended.'

'I fancy that it will be worse for Chastity, if he gets hold of her. That's why I want to warn her.'

Alex was calm again. 'Chastity has Jan to protect her. She doesn't need either of us. As long as he keeps her hidden, she'll be safe. She always finds some man to look after her. She was just like that at school.'

Ignoring her spiteful tone, Unicorn replied firmly, 'I believe that, if she returns tomorrow, she is in great danger. You must particularly warn her not to go to that party. That could be just the opportunity he wants.'

'She won't listen to me. She's promised Dot she'll go, and good girls always keep their promises.'

'You must make her listen.' His eyes glinted savagely. 'You'll regret it if you don't.'

'And what about you? Are you going to take the easy way out and let me rescue your lady love?'

'I intend to try another way.' After finishing his whisky, he stood up, put on his coat and moved towards the door. 'Remember what you have to do, if she does turn up. You'll regret it if you don't, my darling. Believe me.' Before she could answer, he had gone.

It was not until he arrived back at his own flat that Unicorn admitted to himself that the time had come for him to speak to Dr Jan, however humiliating that might be. In fact, it was now imperative. But how? He did not know where Jan was. He had no phone number, no address. How could it be done? Yet it had to be done. With a humility unknown to him before, he admitted that he needed Dr Jan, not to save himself but to help Chastity.

Even as he reached this conclusion, someone rang his bell. He expected no one, but, as he opened the door, he was not surprised to recognise the unexpected visitor – the tall figure in the dark coat, with his aureole of golden hair glinting in the light from the hall. Eyes as blue as summer skies looked searchingly at him.

'Come in, please. I've been hoping to find you,' he said, as Dr Jan followed him into the living room. As they faced each other, Unicorn felt small and humble, but, at the same time, he felt the peace that he had never known before, except with Chastity.

'If you are now willing,' Dr Jan said quietly, 'as I believe you are, the time has come when we should talk.'

'I'm willing and grateful that you have come.' They sat down.

Chapter Twenty-eight

Richard's party had been going for about an hour when Chastity entered the big room where it was being held. Richard, the much-indulged only child of wealthy middle-class parents, had spent lavishly on his farewell fling. He had hired the hall of a nearby church; persuaded his friends to decorate it colourfully with balloons, streamers and lights; provided food and an abundance of mostly alcoholic drinks; and, most importantly, had secured the services of a local group guaranteed to produce a suitable sound.

When Chastity entered, the lights were dim and the four-man band was pounding and throbbing the latest hit. No one had seen her during the day, but, at one point, she had left a note to say that she would be at the party, although a little late.

Alex had said nothing and had certainly made no attempt to warn Chastity, as Unicorn had asked her to do, that it might be dangerous to appear in such a place. She told herself that it was all nonsense. Nevertheless, she shivered at the thought of Emmanuel and of the possibility that her own involvement might be made known.

Why should she risk her entire career, she asked herself, because Chastity had been so foolish as to antagonise Lord Harry? The only question was whether she should remain neutral or take a more positive line. She had tried to reach Unicorn, but she had failed, so the decision must be her own entirely.

Because she was looking out for Chastity, Dot was the first person to see her, as she hesitated just inside the doorway. Rushing up to her, she greeted her enthusiastically. 'I'm so glad that you've come. Richard is dying to meet you and to introduce you to his friends. After that, he's going to announce our engagement. He really is! You know, I wasn't entirely sure until tonight that he would actually do it. He says he wants to do it now, while people are still sober.' She laughed happily.

'He's almost left it too late, then, don't you think?' Chastity remarked, looking around a little sardonically.

Dot laughed even more. 'I'm afraid it'll get a lot worse later.' She seemed to be too happy to care. Suddenly looking more closely at Chastity, she exclaimed, 'You look fabulous! Absolutely beautiful! And your dress! I didn't know you owned anything like that! You look like a queen or a high priestess!'

'It's my "Very Special Occasion Outfit". The gold necklace and bracelet and the material for this dress were given to me years ago by a grateful African chief, whose son I had cured.'

Dot was full of admiration as she examined the silky, velvety folds of the long, deep violet dress. Chastity's outfit was severely elegant and unadorned except for the heavy gold necklace and bracelet. Her shining, dark hair flowed over her shoulders and her luminous eyes shone out in the half-gloom. It seemed to Dot as if there were a strange otherworldliness in Chastity's beauty. No one who saw her that night would ever forget her.

Being unable to think of any suitable words, Dot was almost relieved to see Richard coming towards them. Beckoning to him, she called out, 'Richard, Chastity's come at last. Do come and meet her.'

Whatever he had expected, it had obviously not been this beautiful, graceful woman with her haunting dark eyes. He had been somewhat amused by Dot's apparent fascination with the missionary doctor who had taken a room in her flat. He had dismissed it as one of Dot's earnest enthusiasms and would not have troubled to meet her had he not heard rumours that she was unusually gifted and likely to become one of Lord Harry's celebrities. Now he understood why and was pleased that he could produce her as promised.

While they exchanged a few obvious pleasantries, Chastity examined Richard. He was much as she had expected. Slim and a little above average height, he was dressed casually but expensively. His features were unremarkable; his light brown hair was fashionably cut and layered; his eyes were of that undetermined colour between grey and blue. It was his smile, however, which distinguished him. His full mouth, when he was not smiling, hinted at the selfish, small boy who still lingered within, as did the watchful eyes; but when he smiled all was changed. His warm smile embraced you with its ready friendliness, its eagerness to please you above all people. His voice, too, had the same warm, caressing quality.

As she smiled back, it seemed to Chastity that she could already see the highly successful consultant he would be in a few years' time. But why then, Dot? she wondered. Honest, strong Dot? As she looked at him again, she saw the answer in the vanity and weakness also revealed in his face. He needed Dot's strength. But Chastity realised it was that same weakness and vanity that made him especially dangerous to her at this moment.

'There are four guys, I know, who are really keen to meet you,' he said, still smiling at her.

'Fellow doctors?' Chastity raised her eyebrows slightly.

'No, they're pressmen I met recently when they were doing a feature on my department. They'd already heard about you. You may not be aware of it, but you're already a bit of a celebrity. And when they heard that Dot knew you, well, that was it. I had to promise to introduce you.'

Chastity's smile remained unchanged, but she said nothing.

'If you don't mind waiting here with Dot, I'll go and find them.' Before either Dot or Chastity could answer, he had already vanished into the semi-darkness.

'I'm sorry about that,' Dot began to apologise, but before she could get any further Chastity was cheerfully greeted by Sean, who had apparently just arrived.

'Sorry, Chastity,' he said. 'I didn't mean to keep you waiting, but I was held up by an urgent message.'

'That's all right. I've only just arrived.' The smile Chastity gave Sean was quite different.

'In that case, sit down here,' – he had miraculously discovered a couple of unoccupied seats – 'and I'll get you both some drinks and food.' He, too, vanished as Chastity and Dot sat down.

Two girls, obviously rather drunk, were giggling nearby, while a third staggered up with more bottles. It seemed to Chastity as she looked around that there were several people in a similar condition. She was also aware that Dot was not happy.

Suddenly, the lights were dimmed a little more as the music

became soft and seductive. Dot spoke. 'It's pretty awful, isn't it?' She looked at Chastity. 'Not really what I wanted at all.'

'But I thought you were planning it?'

'So did I.' Dot sounded bitter. 'But, somehow, it's come out quite different. Other people have taken over. I don't know half the people here. And I'm not sure that I want to know them. I rather hoped that Richard and I had outgrown these antics.'

'I'm not sure that I understand.'

'You remember, don't you, soon after you arrived I told you that I had worries about Richard? You told me that I should stop playacting and be myself and that, if Richard really loved me, it would be the right thing to do. Well, I did it, as you know, and it seemed to succeed. Richard seemed to think that the real Dot would make a far more suitable wife for an ambitious doctor.'

'So I understood. You seemed to be happy. Was I wrong?' Chastity looked around, hoping to see Sean returning, but it wasn't possible to see anyone clearly.

'No, I was happy for a time, but it's all changed recently, ever since Richard met these new people.'

'Do you mean the ones he's going to bring to meet me?'

'Yes, mainly those, but there seem to be lots of hangers-on as well.'

'Do you know these four?'

'Not really; I've hardly spoken to them. I know that one's a journalist and another one's a photographer. I'm not sure what the other two are. They behave like thugs, but Richard seems to think that they're funny. He says I'm just old-fashioned.'

'Do they, by any chance, work for the *Daily News* or for Lord Harry Fairword in some way?' Dot could not miss the sudden change in Chastity's voice.

'I believe they're mostly freelancers, though they may do some work for him. They're not in the same class as Unicorn, of course.'

'No, of course not.' Unexpectedly, Chastity stood up and looked around the room. As she stood proudly erect in her splendid violet gown, she looked, Dot thought, not just regal but somehow otherworldly. There had always been something strange about her, but that now seemed to be intensified. But all she said was, 'I wish that Sean would come back.'

'If you're thirsty,' Dot volunteered, 'I'm sure I can get you a drink.'

'I don't need a drink, I need to speak to Sean. Can you see him?'

Dot looked around, but it was difficult to distinguish anyone. 'I'm afraid not.' She was aware of a growing tension, which she couldn't understand. It was almost a relief, when she sat down again, to hear Paul greeting Chastity in his familiar artificial tones as he and Rupert emerged from the semi-darkness, coming towards them.

'Darling Chastity,' Paul exclaimed, as he gracefully took her hand and kissed it. 'I'm too delighted to see you at last! I had begun to think that you had vanished for ever and that I would never have a chance to apologise. I would have been desolated.' He was outstanding as always in black velvet and white lace ruffles.

'You have no need to apologise.' Chastity removed her hand gently.

'Not even for the terrible things I said to Alex about you the other morning, when, I admit, I was unreasonably angry?'

'Certainly not. I'm sure that you believed that you had good reason at the time when you spoke.'

'How truly noble!' Paul murmured. 'You not only look like a queen but you behave like one, darling. I apologise humbly for my past rudeness.'

'And you are forgiven, Paul.' Chastity smiled at him.

Why ever doesn't she get rid of him? Dot wondered. *Surely she doesn't like him or think that he can be trusted?*

'I'm sure that Chastity has better things to talk about,' Rupert interrupted, almost rudely.

Ignoring him, Paul continued, 'There is only one thing I have left to do, and that is to beg you, dear Chastity, to accept an invitation to tea with me. Would next Tuesday be possible?'

For a moment Chastity hesitated, then she answered, gently, 'Although I would be pleased to accept your invitation, Paul, I'm afraid I'm unable to agree to a date at the moment.

My future plans are uncertain. I'm awaiting my instructions.'

'I hope that doesn't mean that you're going to leave us?' Paul sounded regretful.

'I'm afraid I can't say,' was Chastity's disturbing reply.

Paul bowed slightly. 'We'll all be sorry if it does. But, at least, I'm gratified to know that if we have to part, we shall part as friends.' Abruptly, he straightened up. 'Now I've seen you, Chastity darling, I'm happy to go back to our quiet retreat. We're grateful for your invitation, Dot, but I'm afraid that this isn't really our kind of party. I think we should go now, Rupert, don't you?'

'You may do what you please, Paul, but I intend to stay for a while to look after Chastity.'

'Very well,' Paul's tone was icy and his eyes flashed. 'If that is what you prefer. I may be out when you return.' With considerable dignity, he went towards the exit.

'Oh, dear.' Dot laughed nervously. 'I'm afraid that you've seriously annoyed him.'

'It hardly matters, since our relationship is practically over anyway.'

There was an embarrassed silence, broken finally by the welcome return of Sean with a tray. 'Sorry I've been so long. There was a fucking scrum at the bar, but I've managed to get us something.' Noticing Rupert, he added, 'You're in luck, mate. I got myself two beers but I'll spare one for you. You need a beer to face this mob!'

'Thanks.' Rupert gave him a grateful grin.

Dot was obviously getting anxious. 'I can't think what has happened to Richard. It's ages since he went to fetch his friends to introduce them to Chastity.'

'Could that be them?' Sean asked, pointing into the crowd. 'They look like a lot of clowns or something.'

Turning to where he was pointing, they all stared in amazement at Richard and the four men making their way towards them. 'Perhaps they thought it was a fancy-dress party?' Rupert suggested to Dot. The appearance of the strangers seemed to her so grotesque that she couldn't think of any reply.

The music seemed to have faded away, while people moved

away from the strange company as if afraid to be touched by them. Apart from a few drunken giggles, there was an eerie silence. Richard looked anxious, Dot noticed, and she suddenly felt afraid.

The four men, led by a very nervous Richard, seemed to glide in a weird dance across the intervening space. They were dressed in a mockery of Tudor costumes, with brilliant yellow hose topped by slashed breeches in vivid green and red. Their jerkins were a deep, harsh blue. Most surprising of all, they all wore black masks.

Dot was terribly afraid, without knowing why. Instinctively, Sean and Rupert placed themselves on either side of Chastity. Standing like a queen, erect and fearless in her beautiful gown, Chastity faced the approaching strangers. Everyone seemed to be waiting as the four men came to a halt a few yards in front of her.

Richard tried to move forward, as if to make the introductions, but one of the men neatly stepped forward and obscured him. One of the men, who was distinguished from the others by the soft crimson velvet cap he was wearing, moved a little nearer to Chastity, doffed his cap and bowed low.

'Oh, illustrious Dr Chastity,' he announced. 'Zig and his companions greet you with great pleasure.' His deep voice was harsh, with almost a metallic ring to it.

'What the fuck?' Sean muttered, and he would have moved forward had Chastity not checked him with an imperious hand. Dot looked to Richard for enlightenment, but he seemed as astonished as she was. Rupert grimly prepared himself for all eventualities.

Only Chastity seemed to be unmoved. It almost seemed as if she had been expecting something like this. Perhaps, thought Rupert, that was the explanation for her own unusual and dramatic dress, which gave her an imperial air.

'I thank you, Zig,' she replied in a clear, cool voice. 'What do you want of me?'

'We have come to invite you to the mansion of our mutual friend, who, as you know, much desires to speak to you.'

'I presume it is Lord Harry to whom you refer?' She looked fearlessly and proudly at Zig and his companions.

He bowed and, without answering directly, merely said, 'First, we would invite you to dance with us.'

There was a strange silence while Chastity considered her reply. Someone giggled tipsily and was immediately hushed.

A woman's voice rang out. 'Oh, no, don't have anything to do with them, Chastity! I never expected this to happen.' Looking across the room, Rupert saw Alex trying to push to the front.

'Whatever's going on?' Dot asked Sean urgently, but he didn't answer her; his eyes were fixed on Zig.

'But it has happened,' Chastity answered Alex in the same cool voice, 'and the challenge must be met.' She turned towards Zig. 'I will dance with you, but first I must have a moment to speak to my friends.' She indicated Rupert and Sean. Zig bowed without speaking.

'You must not go near them,' Sean muttered fiercely. 'Rupert and I can hold the buggers off while you get away. You're willing, aren't you,' he asked Rupert.

'Of course.' There was no doubting Rupert's determination.

'Why isn't Unicorn here?' Dot asked desperately. 'He could stop them. He knows Lord Harry.'

Ignoring all they had said, Chastity spoke firmly to Sean and Rupert. 'You must get out while you can and ring Jan straight away on this number. Don't hesitate.' She thrust a piece of paper into Rupert's hand. Turning swiftly towards Zig, she addressed him. 'I am ready.' Just as she moved forward to take the hand Zig offered her with a bow, she whispered fiercely to Sean and Rupert, 'Go now!'

Suddenly, the little band started to play a strange, slow, highly rhythmic music, quite unlike anything that had been played before. Dot shivered at the eerie sound. Taking Zig's hand, Chastity moved with him and the others into a strange, slow dance. The guests, as if mesmerised, began to clap rhythmically.

'Quick, now!' Catching hold of the reluctant Sean, Rupert pushed him towards the exit.

'I can't leave her!' Sean protested.

'We must do as she told us and call Jan. These are not ordinary people.'

As they pushed their way out of the door and ran down the

stairs, they became aware that the beat of the music was quickening with a strange, wild note. As soon as they were in the street, Rupert rang Jan on his mobile phone.

'God, I hope he's there,' Sean muttered.

Even as Sean spoke, Rupert heard Jan's voice. Quickly and concisely, he told Jan what had happened. 'Can't we help her?' he asked finally.

'Not immediately,' Jan replied calmly. 'Run to the road outside your flat, where you'll be picked up by our van. My plans are made.'

Inside the hall, the dance became wilder and faster and the clapping louder. Suddenly, it became obvious that Zig and his companions had closed around Chastity and were moving her inexorably towards the door. 'We must stop them,' Alex cried out hysterically. 'They're kidnapping her.' Nobody moved, but the music and the clapping began to stop. Before it had, however, Chastity and her companions were gone from the room.

There was a stunned silence. One or two women screamed. Clutching Richard, Dot struggled with him towards the door to avoid the confusion. They were just in time to see a large, black van moving out of the deserted street.

'What have you done?' Dot demanded. 'Who are those men?'

'I don't really know,' was all he could say, helplessly.

She stared incredulously at him. 'Well, you'd better do something about your precious party,' she snapped at him, 'and then try to ring the police. You'll find me in my room, but I'm not sure if I ever want to see you again. If you hadn't been so vain and stupid, this terrible thing would never have happened.' Without another word, she was gone.

Chapter Twenty-nine

When Chastity, escorted by Zig, came into Lord Harry's office, the vast room was in darkness except for two standard lamps, one of which was standing behind his desk, slightly to his left, while the other was nearer to the middle of room so that, as she advanced towards him, she was clearly seen. The rest of the room was shadowy, except for the vast window behind him, through which the myriad lights of the city could be seen sparkling like precious jewels scattered in the dark heavens.

As Chastity came into the circle of light, Lord Harry stood up to receive her. Wearing full evening dress, he looked at his most powerful and impressive. Unexpectedly, he seemed to be impressed, if involuntarily, by her. 'You are magnificent, my dear Chastity; beautiful and courageous. I offer you my sincere admiration. Please sit down.'

Coming around the desk, he pulled forward a chair and offered it to her. Accepting with a slight inclination of her head, Chastity sat down gracefully, folding her hands in her lap.

With a casual gesture, Lord Harry dismissed Zig. 'You've done well. Wait nearby. If I want you, I'll call for you.' Zig went silently and Chastity was left alone with her enemy.

Lord Harry sat down opposite her. 'May I offer you a drink?' He smiled his most benign smile.

'No, thank you.' She did not move or smile but remained steadily looking at him.

After pouring himself a brandy, he leaned back comfortably and sipped it slowly. The silence seemed to envelop them completely. The brightly-lit city was too far away for them to be able to hear any of its noise. There was no sound or movement in the room, nor from outside it. It was as if they were suspended alone in the vast space of the universe.

He looked at her, but she still did not speak or move. He was forced to speak first. 'Are you surprised to find yourself here? Alone with me?'

For a moment she did not answer, then, smiling slightly, she replied. 'I wasn't sure where it would be, but I was sure that it would happen somewhere.'

'Aren't you afraid? All your protectors, even Dr Jan, have apparently deserted you.'

'I'm not afraid.'

'But surely you must resent the fact that they have abandoned you? You can't have expected that? Even I find that outrageous.' He was determined to get some emotional reaction from her. She was too still, too controlled.

'So you have me at your mercy.' It seemed impossible to touch her.

'I have no mercy. You should know that.' The tone of his voice had changed. It was now hard and cold. 'Unless, of course, you can tempt me by offering me something that I really want?'

'I haven't yet asked you for mercy. Why should I? You have had me brought here. Surely it is for you to say why? Or perhaps you should tell me why you were so sure that I would be at that party?'

He laughed. 'You're too trusting. One of your friends told me that it was certain. Someone you trusted, who knew how much I wanted to get hold of you. Perhaps you can guess who it was?'

'I don't need to guess.' She was still apparently calm, still looking directly at him. 'It wasn't Unicorn. It was Alex. It could only have been her.'

'Why not Unicorn? Surely you don't still believe in his undying love?'

'It's not a question of my belief or otherwise in him. He did not have the information. It has to be Dot or Alex. Obviously it was Alex, although I'm not sure why.'

'You think, because you were at school together, that she is your friend, as she seemed to be then? Surely you must have realised that there were times when she hated you for being better than she was in so many ways? It is quite common to hate those who make us feel inferior. The more so, perhaps, if they do it unintentionally, as I imagine, you did.'

'I understand that. I understood it just before I left school, and so I separated myself from her.'

'A wise move! Why, then, did you seek her out when you returned to England?'

'There were several reasons. One was that I wanted to be sure that she was happy. She had been kind to me.'

'I'll accept that for the moment, unconvincing though it is. But now you find her betraying you to me. What do you think of that?'

'I'm sorry, but, most of all, I can't understand what connection she has with you. Why should she now want to do something like that?' She looked closely at him, surprised to find that they should be talking like this.

He appeared to understand her look. 'You and I are enemies, but we can talk with one another. That surprises you, perhaps?'

'I've talked to enemies before. I know it to be possible. Unfortunately, it doesn't always change the situation.'

'And you don't think that it will in our case. You are right. Nevertheless, I will explain Alex to you. She wanted to free herself from Unicorn, who lent her the deposit on her flat. It was simple. I offered her money in return for information about Emmanuel. She hesitated, but in the end she gave it to me.'

'Emmanuel!' She was startled.

'You thought that was entirely due to Unicorn, didn't you? He was involved, but he was not the original betrayer of the man who thought they were both his friends. Alex has been afraid ever since you first mentioned Emmanuel to her. Because she was guilty, she thought that you knew more than you did. It was easy, therefore, for her to betray you. I persuaded her that it was a trifling matter, and it was simple, then, for her to tell herself that it was.'

'She repented, I think, when she saw Zig and his friends.'

'And that comforted you, perhaps?' He appeared to find this amusing.

Unexpectedly, she smiled. 'It was too late. I told her that. The challenge had been given and must be accepted.'

'And you were not going to avoid it?'

'No. I invited it. That was why I was there.'

He admired her apparent courage but wondered how much of the truth she knew. 'And what of Unicorn? Didn't you hope that he would be there, willing to support you?'

'I sent him away when I last met him. He could not understand the true situation. He thought he could be neutral and be my lover. That is impossible. Surely you know that?'

'I know that and much more. Unicorn may have told you much, but he has not told you everything. He's afraid.'

'Afraid?' She looked thoughtfully at him. 'I suppose you may be right.'

There was a pause. And then, as if changing the subject, he asked, 'You do believe that Emmanuel was murdered, don't you?'

'Yes. Do you deny it?'

'No. Who do you blame for his murder?'

She was surprised for a moment. 'Surely it is obvious that it was you? Of course, I don't imagine that you actually killed him yourself, but you wanted him removed and you arranged for it to be done. You don't deny that, do you?'

'No. You can't prove it, but I won't deny it to you.' He smiled sardonically. 'You have no witnesses. You have no case in law.'

She looked almost scornfully at him. 'I'm aware of that. I'm not interested in taking you before a court of law. It is the truth that interests me.'

'Then surely you must want to know who actually killed him?'

'Perhaps you can tell me?'

'I think not. You must ask Unicorn for that. He has told you much; he has laid bare his heart to you, but he has not told you everything.' His look challenged her.

She met the challenge without flinching. 'Are you suggesting that Unicorn killed him?' She waited for his answer.

'I am saying that you should ask him. He alone knows the full truth. I do suggest that it is his feeling of guilt that stops him from supporting you fully. That is why he is not beside you tonight. Why are you left to face me alone?'

'I'm not afraid to do that.' She seemed unmoved.

He admired her as she sat erect, looking steadily at him, but that only encouraged him to continue his attack. 'But then, you are very much alone, aren't you? Where are your stalwart supporters? Where, in particular, is the great Dr Jan? Does he not care that you are in my power? Or does he, perhaps, not know? Have you been over confident, my gallant Chastity?'

'Jan knows, I believe. I sent him a message. But I know no more than that.'

'Then you are truly deserted, it seems? And in my power?'

'That seems to be the case.' She looked around the room as if she expected to see someone advancing from the shadows.

'There is no one out there,' he mocked her. 'Neither foe nor friend.'

'What do you intend to do with me? Am I to share Emmanuel's fate?'

'I hope not. You are a creature of too fine a quality to be so lightly thrown away. He was an irritating nobody. You are capable of greatness.'

'He was a human being. I am no more.'

'Your modesty is charming, but that is not the truth. You are superior. You must be aware of that?'

'What do you intend to do with me?' Ignoring his flattery, she repeated her question.

'That rather depends on you, my dear. We must talk more. Are you sure that you won't have a brandy?' She shook her head. 'Very well; I will, and then we can talk in a civilised way.' After pouring out his brandy, he began to sip it slowly. After a few moments, he put down his glass and began to talk to her again.

'When I first invited you to visit me here, I had two main reasons. Firstly, you had been asking questions about Emmanuel which had upset several people, and I desired to know why. More important, however, I wanted to meet the woman who had attracted Unicorn's genuine admiration. He said that you were remarkable, and, as soon as I met you, I realised that he was correct. I was sure that we could make an agreement that would be profitable to both of us. I was disappointed when you were not even prepared to consider that. I had expected better of you.' His voice was persuasive, his smile benign. He had an almost hypnotic force, which, she knew, she had to resist, if she were to survive.

'I had no wish to disappoint you; I merely tried to speak the truth about myself. I do not desire publicity. It's hateful to me. I must be free to serve the one to whom I have pledged my loyalty. I cannot honestly serve two masters.'

'Then perhaps you should consider changing your allegiance?' He waited for her to answer, but, when she continued to look steadfastly at him without a word, he continued, 'As you know, I am very wealthy and very powerful. My newspapers are read all over the world; my radio stations and television centres circle the globe. I don't go to seek leaders of state; they come to me. Many people are influenced by my organisation, although they don't always realise that.'

'I'm aware of all this.' She sounded impatient. 'I also know that much of your wealth comes from different sources. Or are you going to deny that?'

He laughed. 'Can you prove it? Be careful. Your answer may be dangerous for you.'

'I can prove nothing, although there may be others who can.'

'In that case, I have no need to worry; neither have you. If some people who I employ are also engaged in nefarious activities without my instructions, then, if they are discovered, they must pay the penalty.'

'And that does not worry you?'

'Did you think it would?'

'You are not concerned about the suffering of the poor girls who are abducted and forced into prostitution or about the young who are ensnared by drugs brought into the country?'

'When I was unaware of these sufferings, they obviously did not concern me. Since I did not know, I could not be said to have any responsibility, but, now that I have been made aware of the true situation, my opinion has changed somewhat. That is why I wanted to talk to you. And, in spite of your refusal, I have insisted on that, even to the extent of abducting you.'

'I don't think that I understand you.'

'If you are patient, I will explain. These people need help. I'm sure that you will agree with that. It seems clear to me that you and I together could organise this. I have the money and the power needed, while you have the charisma and the healing abilities, which are also needed.'

'I can't possibly heal thousands of people. I'm only one doctor.' She was puzzled by what he was saying.

'Alone, yes, but you need not be alone. We are both exceptional people, you and I. We should not be enemies. We can help each other.' Standing up, he offered her his hand, then led her behind his desk to stand in front of the window. 'Look!'

As she looked out, she saw below her the sparkling lights of the city, stretching out for miles. 'There,' he said, holding her arm firmly, 'is a vision of the world which needs you – a vast city with many lonely, suffering people in it. This, of course, is only a microcosm. There are cities like this all over the globe: Paris, New York, Calcutta, Rio de Janeiro. Cities full of people needing compassion and healing.'

Without answering, she gazed out at the myriads of lights, seemingly overcome by the vision he had presented to her.

'If you accept my help, my power and my money, I can make you the saviour these people long for. I can make you known to them as the saintly woman who, in spite of the tragedy of her own life, only wishes to heal the poor and the rejected. Of course, you can't do it alone, but, once I have made you known, people will flock to help you. Surely that is an inspiring vision? If you will work with me, we can make this vision a reality – you and I.'

'Why should you want to do this?' Her luminous dark eyes gazed into his cold, grey ones. They were still cold and empty of all expression, although his voice was warm and persuasive and his smile benign.

'Perhaps I want to make amends? Surely you, a Christian, believe in the repentance of the sinner? Is it not, therefore, your duty to embrace me and my offer? You will be the second Mother Teresa, for whom the world is longing.'

'And you. What will you be?'

'I will be your support and guide.'

Without saying more, she gazed out over the city. It was true what he said. Many were suffering out there, in thousands of such cities. This was a way to reach thousands, eventually, perhaps, millions, instead of a pitiful few. It was tempting.

She seemed to linger on the idea. He was encouraged.

'What,' she asked suddenly, 'will happen to Dr Jan? He has been my friend and mentor for seven years. He is a greater healer than I can ever be. What of him?'

'He will obviously find plenty of work to do, but not with

you. I'm afraid you have to abandon Dr Jan. He is not included. He does not have your appeal.' He felt sure that she was about to accept. 'Surely, you can understand that? Yours is the appeal of the eternal mother figure, reaching out to offer love and care to the suffering. I shall make sure that your face and your name will be known worldwide. You will be enabled to do the good you may, perhaps, have already imagined in your dreams.' He was exultant. What woman could resist such an opportunity?

'And your master will be pleased?' she asked, turning towards him. This unexpected question, so quietly asked, struck him like a whiplash.

'My master?' For a moment, he seemed to be confused. 'Who do you mean?'

'Surely it is obvious. The Dark Angel whom you serve. The one who provided Zig and his companions.'

He tried to laugh. 'You're being ridiculous. Zig and the others are just a joke.'

Ignoring his words, she continued: 'Where will the money come from to sell me as the saintly world mother?'

'I have my resources. You know that.'

'I understand. Setting aside your legal income, which is subject to scrutiny, you have the money from your drug trafficking and the sale of women, for both of which you are atoning. Isn't that so?'

'You know that. But the money is now going to be used for a good end. Surely, you don't disagree with that?'

'Unfortunately, my master has always taught that the end, however good it may seem, does not justify the evil means. Jesus refused his tempter three times. I have only to refuse mine once.'

He refused to believe that she could mean what she was saying. Tightening his grip on her arm, he challenged her. 'You are not considering what you are saying.'

'You are wrong. I am considering it very carefully. If I agree, your evil ways will continue and that will nullify and corrupt any good I may do. I, too, will be corrupted. I was tempted for a moment, but my considered answer has to be "no". I cannot agree.'

'You do understand the consequences, I hope? You know too

much to go free. I told you that I have no mercy, and that is true.'
His face and voice were horribly changed.

She was very afraid, but she could give no other answer. 'I can only refuse.'

'I suppose you're going to say,' he sneered, 'that you're not afraid to die, that you're ready to be a martyr.'

'It wouldn't be true. Everyone is afraid to die, even you, but perhaps I'm less afraid than many.'

Again, he mocked her. 'You're not the first person to say that. I imagine that you are still expecting to be rescued. But how? Dr Jan appears to be indifferent to your fate, in spite of your touching devotion to him. Your lover, Unicorn, is preparing to go on another overseas assignment for me. He has chosen safety. Perhaps your prayers will help? Or maybe you would welcome a little longer to consider. Look out there again and think of what could lie before you. Death is very final.'

'I don't see it quite like that.' She was trying to delay him, convinced that Jan would never desert her.

Puzzled by her reaction, he questioned her. 'What are you talking about?'

'Death. I don't see it as final. In fact, I know it isn't.'

'You speak with great confidence.' He still mocked her.

'Yes, because I have already died and come back.'

He was still amused. 'You mean, of course, that you seemed to die. This has happened to many people.'

'No,' she replied firmly. 'I died seven years ago. I was on my way to another world, but the Lord of the Universe stopped me and sent me back here to do his work of love and healing with Dr Jan and others.'

'I'm offering you a bigger chance to do it, so why refuse?'

'Because you are asking me to do it in your way and not in His. If that is all you have to offer, you'll have to kill me or be defeated yourself. But perhaps you should consider more. You are growing old. Death is close to you, too. Why not truly repent, while there is still time? The Lord will forgive you.'

Taking her arm in an even more painful grip, he swung her around to look at him. It was as if a mask had dropped from his face. There was no benignity now, scarcely any trace of humanity.

The cold, grey eyes shone with a burning hatred. 'I'll make you long for a lasting death,' he hissed. 'I'll hand you over to Zig and his companions to be their sex slave. You shall indeed share the sufferings of the women you pity. I shall destroy you.'

Although she was very frightened, she managed to keep her eyes fixed on his. He seemed totally changed. 'Who are you?'

'I'm the Dark Angel who rules this planet. Lord Harry is one of my creatures.'

'This planet belongs to the Lord of the Universe, as does everything,' she managed to say. 'He will—'

She felt a blinding pain as he hit her across the face. She could feel the blood running from her lip. She could no longer speak.

He laughed. 'Where are He and His friends now?'

As she struggled to answer him, he pushed her away so hard that she fell, hitting her head against the corner of the desk. As she tried desperately to retain consciousness, it seemed to her that the room was filled with a brilliant light, seeming to emanate from the monitor.

She seemed to hear a voice like Jan's speaking from the monitor. 'It is all over for you, Lord Harry, and for many others.' While he spoke, his face appeared on the monitor. To Chastity, still struggling against oblivion, he appeared like Jan as she had never seen him before. His hair shone like gold; his face had an unearthly beauty and radiance. 'I am Xaniel, the Healer, sent by the Lord of the Universe to this planet as his special representative to announce the coming of the End Time.' The light vanished as darkness overwhelmed her.

There was a furious knocking at the door. As Lord Harry slumped in his chair, Sean and Rupert rushed in to find an unconscious Chastity and a speechless Lord Harry.

Chapter Thirty

It was several hours later when Chastity again opened her eyes. She had a confused memory of being brought to her own room and laid on her bed. There had been much noise and confusion and her head had ached intolerably. 'Just leave me alone,' she remembered shouting. 'I need quiet.' Suddenly, she had heard Jan's calm voice. *If he is taking charge, then everything will be all right*, she had thought. Darkness had then descended again.

Moving as little as possible, she now looked around the room and saw Jan sitting in the armchair, the golden halo of his hair shining clearly in the single light. Memories came rushing back into her mind: the intense and frightening temptation by Lord Harry; her refusal; his cruel anger, followed by a terrible blow across her face; his threat to hand her over to Zig. He had pushed her, she thought, and she had hit her head. After that, everything was confused. She remembered the fierce pain and trying to struggle against unconsciousness, then, suddenly, seeing a blinding light and hearing Jan's voice. What had happened? She could no longer be sure, but clearly he had rescued her, as he had promised.

'I should have realised,' she said aloud.

'What should you have realised, my dear?' Standing up, Jan moved close to her and sat down on the edge of her bed. Smiling, he took her hand in his.

'That you would rescue me. I was so afraid that I no longer felt sure.'

'It was Sean and Rupert who actually rescued you.'

'But you were there, I know, although I can't remember exactly.' She put her hand to her head, feeling the dressing.

'I was there. You are right. Don't worry about it now. As you know, people often forget the things that happened immediately before they became unconscious.'

'I suppose that's true.'

'More importantly, how do you feel now?'

Sitting up very carefully, she told him, 'Amazingly good. That must be as a result of one of your cures.'

'It was no miracle; just medical common sense. I turned everyone out and, with just Dot's help, I treated you. I sewed up your scalp wound, the source of all the blood which upset everyone. Dot put on the dressing and I prepared a soothing drink, which enabled you to get the sleep and rest that you needed. I'm afraid, however, that your cheek is still bruised.'

She felt it gently. 'It doesn't feel too bad.'

'I am very sorry that you had to suffer so much. We had intended to get there sooner.'

'It doesn't matter as long as our mission was successful. It was, wasn't it?'

'Completely successful.'

'Lord Harry admitted everything to me in order to persuade me to join him. He promised to make me a second Mother Teresa with his evil money.' She shuddered.

'But you refused in spite of his threats.'

'I did, but for one shameful moment I was tempted.'

'There is no shame or sin in being tempted,' he told her gently, 'but only in yielding. And you did not do that.'

'You say we were completely successful, but I still don't quite see how.'

'The police have been given valuable information about his trafficking in drugs and women, and by tomorrow his whole organisation will be under investigation for fraud. All this will be widely reported. He has no future.'

'I didn't think that he had anyway, because he seemed to collapse completely before my eyes. He understood, I think, that the victory was entirely yours and that his trust in the Dark Angel was utterly misplaced. No one else was needed.'

Sensing a hurt that she did not express, Jan hurried to explain. 'That would never have been sufficient by itself. Your courageous opposition, which caused him to understand not only how unexpectedly strong you were but also how close you and I were, caused him to realise that his position was far weaker than he thought. He must also have thought of

Unicorn, your professed admirer. How much could he rely on him now?'

'I'm sorry about Unicorn. This must be terrible for him. How much will he be implicated?'

'You have no need to worry about Unicorn, for he has, in fact, been a great help to us in this.'

'I don't understand how that can be. When he left me, he was determined not to risk opposing Lord Harry. He was very angry, indeed, when I told him that he could not be neutral in this matter.'

Jan smiled. 'Poor man; he was in a turmoil. His whole way of life had been attacked. He wanted to take his usual cynical attitude and walk away, but, in the end, he couldn't – chiefly because of you.'

'But he did walk away.'

'True, but late on Friday night I went to talk to him. I was sure he needed me. He didn't disappoint me. We talked for hours. He felt guilty and ashamed that he had betrayed you and very afraid of what you might have to face. He had been trying all day to get in touch with you, but, of course, you weren't there and nobody knew where you were. In the end, he spoke to me because there was nowhere else for him to go. He had had a dream about the evil and hollowness of Lord Harry. Finally, he told me all we needed to know about Lord Harry's illegal activities. It was only when he began to see the situation clearly that he realised how much he actually did know. It was enough to inform the police and to put Lord Harry under investigation for fraud. Lord Harry, however, had to be confronted spiritually, and you courageously undertook that. That was what mattered most.'

'I understood that. It was why I went to the party, although I knew it was dangerous. But surely you could have done it without me?'

'No! He had to be defeated first by a fellow human being: a weak woman, as he thought, who showed what strength the Lord of the Universe gives to those who love him and put their trust in him. That was tremendously important, Chastity; you must understand that. That was why I had to leave you alone until the end. I didn't want to expose you, but it had to be done and I was sure of you. I'm very proud of you. You have helped to save many from misery and death. Others have also been given the opportunity to see the power of good and to repent.' Holding her hand firmly, he looked steadily into her eyes. 'You have done all that the Lord wanted you to do and more.'

'I couldn't have done it without you. You know that.' For a few moments they were both silent, until she asked sadly, 'And that means that our mission here is over?'

'That was, indeed, our main reason for coming to London, but the other things we have done have all had their value. We have touched the lives of many. You know that.'

'I'd always hoped to help Alex, because she was kind to me when I was most desolate, but I've failed. She told Lord Harry that I would definitely be at the party. He boasted of it. That makes me sad.'

'I'm sure that it does, but I think you'll discover that even now you can help Alex. There is still time.'

'Then we're not going away immediately?'

'You are not going away immediately, but I must go soon, for a time.'

'Oh, no!' She clutched at his hand. 'You can't leave me now, Jan. I need your support.'

'You know that you will always have that, but I have to continue the work in Eastern Europe to save others. Unicorn not only gave me the knowledge he had but he put me in possession of Emmanuel's briefcase that contains all the evidence which he discovered when looking for his sister.'

'Does that mean that Unicorn is implicated in Emmanuel's death?'

'I'm not sure about that. He says not. But, for the time being, I must leave not only Alex but also Unicorn to you.'

'Do you think I can do it without you?'

Jan smiled gently at her. 'You're feeling weak at the moment, Chastity, but, before I go, you'll be your old self again. Remember, you are never truly alone. You have immortal help, and not just mine.'

'I know.' She sat up suddenly. 'I think I can tackle Alex. There is something in the past she needs to talk about. But Unicorn – that's different.'

'I believe that he genuinely loves you.'

'Perhaps, but what does that mean?'

'That, you must discover. You'll have to be careful.'

'You realise, don't you, that I find him attractive?'

Jan smiled at her. 'I'm afraid that is obvious. That is why I'm cautioning you.'

'Do you believe that you can trust me?'

'Yes.' Bending down, he kissed her on the cheek.

Holding on to him, she looked directly into his eyes. 'I love you dearly. You must also realise that.'

His brilliant look did not waver. 'I love you. Although we come from different worlds, we have been chosen by the Lord to work together. It is right for us to be united in love.'

'Then why must I have to deal with Unicorn?'

'He is your responsibility because you have changed him. He needs help.'

'You're not suggesting, are you, that I might marry him?'

'That is for you to decide.'

'But—' she began to protest.

Sitting up, he silenced her. 'It need never affect our relationship. That is different. But you may find that you now want a human sexual relationship with the possibility of children.'

'I have never considered that since Tim died.'

'It may be that now is the time for you to do that.'

'You're not suggesting, are you, that our love is wrong? That it isn't what the Lord wants?'

'True love is never wrong,' he reassured her. 'Ours is certainly a unusual partnership, perhaps a unique one, but it was the Lord himself who decided that we should work together. He expects us to work together harmoniously, loving one another. There is no other way. Love is the force that holds the universe together and, if that holds firm, evil must eventually be defeated. You understand that, don't you, Chastity?'

'Yes, I do, but I still love you in a special way, Jan. I couldn't have done some of the things I have done without you. The companionship we have is very precious. Surely you think that, don't you?' She looked appealingly at him.

'I do.' Bending down, he kissed her gently on the forehead.

'But now you must have the time to make a fully-informed decision about your future. While I am absent, you must try to do that.'

'I don't think that I understand. What must I do?'

'It is not my will, but our Lord's will. You have served him faithfully for seven years, since you agreed to return to this world. You have helped to make this last mission a great success. The truth about Emmanuel's death has been established; the Dark Angel has been deprived of one of his closest allies, and much evil has been prevented. Your help was needed for all of this.'

'But the struggle still goes on.'

'And will do until the end of time, when our Lord will reveal himself and his faithful servants will be made known. Many of them will not be the people the world would expect. Many priests and Princes of the Church will be absent, while sinners will shine out.'

'People like Unicorn; is that what you mean?'

'Yes, people like Unicorn. He has undergone a conversion and he needs help and encouragement. We don't yet know how far he is prepared to go.'

'Are you telling me that it is my new job?'

'For about three weeks, yes, but after that you have a choice. I shall return at Christmas and you must then decide whether to go away again with me or to stay here. There is work for you to do here and you may wish to stay with Unicorn.'

'It sounds rather trivial when it is compared with what we have been doing.'

'You know, Chastity, that no work for our Lord is trivial. The consequences of some apparently unimportant action may be awesome. That is in our Lord's hands and we cannot know.'

'I'll try to do as you say. When will you be going?'

'Tomorrow.'

'Oh, no, not so soon! I'm not prepared. Please give me a little more time.'

'I'm afraid that's not in my power. But you know I'll always be with you in spirit. I must leave you now, for a time, since Lord Harry will probably not recover. There is much, therefore, which must be done swiftly. You do understand, don't you? What we have achieved so far must not be wasted.'

'Of course I understand.'

'Good.' Standing up, he put on his long, dark coat. 'You need to spend this day quietly in your room. Dot, who has been waiting anxiously, will bring you a meal soon. Do you think you can eat?'

'Actually, I'm very hungry.' She sounded surprised.

'That's a good sign.' Bending over her, he kissed her gently. 'Unicorn is very anxious to see you and will, I'm sure, get in touch with you soon.'

'I'll see him, if you think that's the right thing to do.'

'He needs your help, as do several other people.'

'Will I see you again?' She was almost afraid to ask.

'Yes; I'll come again this evening, when there'll be time to talk. Now I'll tell Dot you're fully awake and will soon be ready to eat.' With a final smile he was gone, closing the door quietly behind him. Chastity felt very much alone.

She was not, however, allowed much time to feel sorry for herself, for, after a few minutes, Dot popped her head around the door. 'Hi!' she greeted Chastity cheerfully. 'Great news! Dr Jan says that you're recovering well and are ready to eat. Would a really big breakfast suit you? Bacon, eggs and sausage, perhaps?'

'That sounds marvellous. Thanks. It's amazing, but I'm actually ravenous.'

'That's encouraging! Do you need help to get to the bathroom?'

'I'm not sure.' Very carefully, Chastity got out of bed and stood up. She did not feel as good as she had expected.

'Don't worry.' Dot was bright and encouraging. 'I'll help you. You need to take it easy for a bit. Lean on me. When you're ready, we can have breakfast together in your room. How does that sound?'

'Lovely, thanks.' Gratefully, Chastity took the arm offered to her.

Later, when they were starting to eat breakfast, Dot exclaimed, 'I'm so glad to see that you're all in one piece and getting better! I was terrified when those weird men swept you off. And furious with Richard!'

'Why were you furious with Richard? He hadn't kidnapped me.'

'Because, if it hadn't been for his ridiculous vanity, they would never have been invited to the party. I was so angry that I told him that I wasn't sure if I ever wanted to see him again.'

'That was a bit harsh, Dot.' Chastity smiled at her. 'Richard didn't arrange the kidnapping. Other people planned that.'

'Perhaps, but, if he hadn't been so easily flattered by them, it might not have happened. You can't deny that.'

'No, but that doesn't make him the villain; he's just another victim. They used him.'

'He should have had more sense.'

'Do you love him, Dot? Do you still want to marry him? Does he still want to marry you?'

'Yes, to the last question. At least, he said so even after my outburst. In fact, he insisted on giving me the ring he'd bought.' Holding out her left hand, she displayed the pretty diamond ring she was wearing.

'So, there's only one question to answer: do you love him?'

'I suppose so, but he's so terribly weak and conceited. You have no idea.'

'I think I do. I saw it in his face, but I'm also sure that he loves you and that he needs you a lot. You can help him to become a better and more conscientious doctor. But, before you get conceited, remember that you have faults, too.'

Dot considered this, then laughed. 'I have a quick temper and I make hasty judgments. Will that do for a start?'

'It's not a bad beginning. Do you now think you can forgive him?'

'I'll try. You're good at sorting me out. I shall miss you when I go north.'

'I shall probably be going away again myself, soon.'

'Dr Jan mentioned that he would be going away for two or three weeks. Are you going with him?'

'Not this time. He thinks I need a rest. But he's coming back by Christmas, and then we shall decide.'

'He's a wonderful person. I almost wish—'

'No, you don't,' Chastity interrupted her. 'You would much

rather be safely married to Richard and have a couple of children to bring up. That is a very good life, if you're prepared to do it properly.'

'You're right,' Dot agreed. 'I'm just being an idiot. I could never do what you do.'

'You haven't been called to do it.' For a moment, Chastity continued to eat silently, until she asked suddenly, 'Have you seen Alex since the party?'

'Not really. She was very upset and rushed back here and shut herself in her room. When I tried to talk to her, she shouted, "Shut up, Dot! You don't understand. It's all my fault." I didn't know what she meant, but I didn't dare to ask her any more questions. Should I have done?'

'I don't think so. I think I'm the only person who can help, if she'll let me.'

'Do you want me to ask her to come to see you?'

'It will be better if I go to talk to her, I think.'

It was over an hour later, however, before Chastity felt strong enough to walk to Alex's room. Her first knock having produced no result, she knocked again, more loudly.

'Go away!' Alex sounded tearful. 'I don't want to speak to anyone. Don't bother me.'

'I think I'm the one person who has the right to bother you. Surely you have something to say to me?' She had hardly finished speaking before the door was wrenched open. Alex stood in front of her, pale and dishevelled, wearing a crumpled negligee.

'Good God! It really is you! I thought you were dying or worse.'

'On the contrary, I'm almost completely better.' Chastity smiled cheerfully.

Retreating before her, Alex almost fell onto her bed. 'You looked terrible when they brought you back – pale and covered with blood. There was nothing I could do, so I shut myself in here. To be honest, I didn't really want to know. I'm a coward about blood. Still, I'm glad to see you so much better. I suppose Dr Jan is responsible for that?' Alex had begun to pull herself together now and was obviously trying to speak normally. 'I'm hardly fit to be seen. The truth is I drank too much last night—'

'Do stop it, Alex,' Chastity interrupted her, sitting down on the nearest chair as she did so. 'I know why you're upset. I know what you did.'

'What the hell do you mean?' Reaching for her brush, Alex began to tackle her disordered hair vigorously.

'I know that it was you who told Lord Harry that I would definitely be at the party.'

'How can you possibly know that?'

'Because he told me himself during our talk last night. He told me the story about you, Unicorn and Emmanuel. Obviously, you were in a difficult situation.'

'And you have now come, I suppose, to offer me your Christian forgiveness. You needn't bother. I don't want it. It would revolt me.' For the first time, she looked fully at Chastity, noticing as she did so the livid bruise on her cheek. 'Oh, Christ! Your face is terribly bruised. I didn't expect anything like that. I'm sorry. How did it happen?'

'Lord Harry is not a gentleman. He hit me across the face rather hard; I stumbled and cut my scalp on the corner of his desk, I think. Hence all the blood.'

'He told me that he simply wanted to talk to you.'

Chastity laughed. 'Perhaps I wasn't a very satisfactory listener. Or he has a strange idea of talking. Help came, however, at that moment, which was lucky.'

'As I said, I'm very sorry. It was kind of you to come, but don't you think you ought to rest now?'

'Am I to take it that my Christian forgiveness has now been accepted?' Chastity looked steadily at Alex for a moment, waiting for her reply. When this did not come, she continued, 'I do find it difficult to believe that you were unaware of the violent side of Lord Harry's nature.'

'I had no reason to suspect it.' Alex's reply came with suspicious quickness.

'Not even when you remembered Emmanuel?'

'Why should I? The last time I saw Emmanuel, I took him to meet Unicorn and I left him with Unicorn.'

'And it didn't worry you that you never saw him again?'

'No. Why should it? Unicorn told me that some stranger

turned up and Emmanuel went off with him. I imagined that it must have been some friend of his.'

'Instead, it was probably his killer.'

'Don't be so melodramatic, Chastity! Why should it have been his killer?'

'Because he was killed. Probably by Zig, from whom I narrowly escaped. It's no use, Alex. You can't run away from the truth any longer. Jan and I know what happened.'

'Then Unicorn must have told you.'

'He told Jan, not me.'

'The bastard! Oh, what a bloody fool I've been! I've managed to mess up my whole life! First Unicorn, then James, now this! Go away, for God's sake! There's nothing you can usefully say! I'll grovel if that'll satisfy you, but, for Christ's sake, go! I've just messed up. I'll admit it, if that pleases you.'

'It doesn't. But, Alex, you know it didn't start with Unicorn. It started long before that.'

'What the hell do you mean? Are you referring to the fact that we didn't part as the best of friends? Do grow up, Chastity! I admit that I was pretty furious when they made you Head of School instead of me, but that's years ago! Even then, I soon had lots of compensations, such as the right place at a first-class university.'

'To say nothing of my first boyfriend as your devoted admirer. You haven't quite forgotten that, surely?'

'Surely you don't mean Martin?'

'Who else was there?'

Standing up, Alex straightened out her wrap and walked across the room to switch on the coffee maker. 'You must be joking! I knew you were a bit upset, but I didn't think it really mattered much to you. And surely not now, after twelve years?'

'It didn't as soon as I realised that you were both deeply in love. I left you to it. But what happened?'

Apparently preoccupied with the coffee maker, Alex replied casually, 'It ended as things like that usually do.'

'And you weren't much upset?'

'No. Why should I have been? I'd just finished my first year very successfully. Future prospects looked good.'

'Martin didn't see it like that. He was heart-broken.'

Alex swung round. 'How do you know that?'

'We'd kept in touch occasionally and he wrote me a note to say that it was finished and that he was devastated. He couldn't understand you.'

'And that was all he told you?'

'Yes.'

'And what did you do? Did you rush to console your friend?'

'No. Did you think I would?'

'Why not? It would have been a real act of Christian forgiveness, surely? It's what I would have expected of you.' Without waiting for Chastity to answer, she poured out a cup of coffee and offered it to her.

'No, thanks.' Slowly, Chastity stood up. 'I think it's time I went back to bed.' She had hoped that they might speak truthfully, that Alex might at last be ready to do so, but apparently she had been wrong.

As she moved slowly towards the door, Alex said quickly, 'Oh, dear, you look terribly pale and ill! You shouldn't be out of bed.' Ignoring Chastity's protests, she took control, helping her back to her room and making sure that she was comfortably settled in bed, with a cup of coffee and a biscuit, before she made to leave.

'You don't have to earn Brownie points with our housemistress now,' Chastity exclaimed, her smile taking out any sting in the words.

'Did I actually say that?'

'Yes, once. But I didn't believe you.'

Pausing in her tidying activities, Alex said thoughtfully, 'I think you were right. That may have come into it, but it certainly wasn't the only reason.'

'I knew that. You were simply determined to hide your good qualities and you still are.'

'Stop it!' Alex almost shouted. 'You don't know everything. I'm not a school kid any more; I'm a woman who has messed up her life thoroughly and who knows she can't blame anyone except herself. Don't waste your time on me. It can be dangerous.' She was almost through the door when she paused. 'But, if you promise not to ask questions, I'll cook a meal for us later.'

'I promise,' Chastity replied cheerfully. As the door shut, she added quickly to herself, 'I'll go on praying for you all the same.'

Chastity was alone again. As she sipped her coffee, she admitted to herself how tired and weak she still felt. She was dreading Unicorn's call and she longed to talk to Jan, but, for the moment, she needed to sleep.

Chapter Thirty-one

Chastity was left undisturbed until Dot came to tell her that Unicorn was on the phone. 'He wants to know if you will speak to him.'

'No,' Chastity replied without hesitation. 'I'm not ready to do that.'

'What shall I say? He's very determined.'

'Just tell him I'm feeling better but I need to rest today.'

'OK.' Dot departed, only to come back with a further message. 'He sends you his love and hopes very much that he will be able to see you tomorrow. I suggested that he phone first. Was that all right?'

'That was fine.' Chastity lay back and closed her eyes again. She was determined to have the time she needed.

It was nearly six o'clock when Alex, after tapping on the door, came in to announce that the evening meal would be ready in about a quarter of an hour. 'I'm afraid that it will only be the two of us. After several texts from Richard, Dot has finally gone off to meet him. Rupert has sent you a card with his love. Mrs Allen sent her lodger up with a bunch of roses. She hopes she'll be able to see you tomorrow. I've put the roses in a vase.'

'Thanks. That was kind of her. Did Sean say anything?'

'He sent you his love and said that he'd see you soon. Perhaps you'll introduce me. I rather fancy him.'

'Don't be wicked! He's not your type.'

'Perhaps not, but you can't be sure. Shall I bring the food in here or shall we eat in the living room?'

'I'll just put my gown on and come into the living room. It's time I got up again.'

The tasteful order of the living room was surprising to Chastity. The heavy, dark green velvet curtains were closely drawn to cut out the chilly darkness of the early winter evening. The false flames of the gas fire not only warmed the room but also helped to create a friendly, cosy atmosphere. Everywhere had been tidied; no disorder was visible.

Alex, too, was at her most elegant in expensively-tailored dark grey trousers and a flatteringly close-fitting, rose pink cashmere jumper with a low neckline. Her hair, which had been so disordered in the morning, had been brushed into a smooth, shining cap. Fashionable long faux pink pearl and crystal earrings dangled from her ears and were matched by the elaborate necklace she wore. Her make-up was faultless. The mask had been resumed.

The table, brought close to the fire, was laid with the bold, modern china Alex preferred, the best cutlery and two large wine glasses. The roses in the vase had been placed to one side. Chastity, wearing only a very plain, dark gown and her dark hair falling loosely, felt that this was in some way a re-enactment of their first meeting, when she had been made to feel the outsider. Now she only felt the falsity of the situation.

'I've experimented with a new chicken dish with orange, tarragon, fromage frais and a dash of brandy. I hope you'll like it.'

'It looks and smells delicious,' Chastity replied politely as Alex spooned out her helping.

'Would you like some wine with it? It's Australian; very good, or so I'm told.'

'Thank you, but I think I'll be wiser to keep to water.'

It was all too polite and too civilised. All that had recently passed was to be ignored. Chastity couldn't even hear the prowling wind that she had been aware of in her own room. It was not what she wanted, but she was prepared to be patient, sensing that something wild was waiting to pounce.

'Are you planning to go out?' she inquired. 'You're looking very elegant.'

'Not until later. I've agreed to have drinks with a man I met at a party recently. He's quite pleasant; he has a good job in a City bank. One of the lucky ones who didn't get the push when disaster struck.' She poured herself a glass of wine. 'You won't mind being on your own, will you?'

'Of course not. Jan is coming later, in any case. He has to go away for two or three weeks, so he's coming to say goodbye.'

'I'd have thought he would have waited until you were well enough to go with him.'

'That was never a possibility. I may stay in London permanently.'

'I see.' Alex seemed to consider the statement as she sipped her wine. Putting down her glass, she finally asked, 'Does that mean that you have decided to settle down with Unicorn? Of course,' she added hastily, 'that hasn't anything to do with me, but it's obviously what he wants.'

'Would it upset you if I did?' Laying down her fork, Chastity looked directly at Alex.

'For Christ's sake! Why should it?' Alex tried to laugh.

'I can think of many reasons why it might. You were very much against it when I first met him. You were prepared to hint that he had ruined your life. That wasn't true, was it?'

'Not exactly, perhaps, but he certainly didn't improve my life. Surely that's clear, even now?'

'To a certain extent, yes, but it's also true that you'd already changed by the time you met him. He recognised a kindred spirit.'

'So what? I was always selfish and ambitious. You knew that. You're making a fuss about nothing.'

'I don't think so. The change is great. When I knew you last, you may have been selfish and ambitious, as I was then, but you were also deeply in love with Martin. I don't know why you broke with him, but it seems to me that that is when you changed – changed into a person who could betray Emmanuel, who could be amused at poor Eva's misery and who could even betray me. The Alex I knew at school would never have done those things.'

Alex slammed down her glass so violently that some of the wine spilled. 'Why the hell don't you leave me alone?' Her voice was unsteady and she was trembling. 'It's no business of yours.'

'It is my business, because I owe you a lot and because I love you.'

Jumping to her feet, Alex moved furiously across the room. 'You don't expect me to believe that hypocritical crap, do you? I suppose you think you have to talk like that now? The truth is, you've never forgiven me for snatching your first boyfriend.'

'He was never my boyfriend; you know that. And, even if he had been, I wouldn't have cared after I met Tim.'

'God, how I hate you and your smug ways. I could kill you, if I weren't a coward.' She moved towards Chastity, then abruptly checked herself. Instead she sat down suddenly, all her anger apparently gone. 'The truth is that I'm trying to make you my scapegoat. When I say horrid things to you, I avoid admitting that it's all my own fault, which it is. Seeing you again has just made everything worse. Twelve years ago we were pretty similar, but now there's a great gulf between us.'

'My husband was killed and my child is dead, so I'm as much alone as you are.'

'But none of that was your fault. That's the difference. You have no guilt, as I have.'

'How are you guilty? Why don't you tell me? It might help.' Chastity put her hand gently on Alex's. 'I'm still your friend.'

The words poured out of Alex. 'Your husband was killed. Martin left me, broken-hearted, as you told me.' She stopped abruptly.

'Why was that?' Chastity was very gentle. She knew this was a decisive moment.

Alex did not answer directly. 'You said that your baby died in your arms. That must have been terrible. I've thought about it often since you told me. But there are worse things. No one could blame you and Tim, and you were able to comfort each other. Do you know, I actually envy you.' She stopped, dry-eyed but obviously agonised. 'You must think that is a terrible thing to say.' She tried to laugh. 'But that's the truth, isn't it? I've always envied you. You know that. I still do. That's why I didn't try to stop you from going to the party. The funny thing is that I've never really asked myself why until now. And the answer I have to give myself isn't very pleasant.' She stopped suddenly. There was a pause.

'What is it?' Chastity asked finally. 'Can you tell me?'

Alex looked directly at her. 'It's simple, really. I always knew that you were a much better person than I was. You were never competitive. The trouble is that you won every competition between us without even realising that there was one, and I hated you sometimes for that. You must have got some idea of that towards the end of our school career?'

'I suspected it. That was why I withdrew myself. But what has this to do with Martin?'

'Haven't you even now realised that I wanted him at first because he was yours? But then we did actually fall in love. I've never loved anyone else.'

'That was what I believed.'

'You were right. But what you didn't understand was that I felt triumphant because I'd taken him from you. Horrible, isn't it? But it's true.'

'It's not the whole truth. I'm sure that you really did love him.'

'That's true. But, since you've asked for the whole truth, you'd better have it all. It seemed, in the end, that I didn't love him as much as I envied you.'

'I don't understand! What do you mean? What had I got to do with it?'

'At first, everything was fine. I felt on top of the world. We had both started the courses we wanted at top universities. We were both doing well and, in addition, I had Martin. I was really pleased with life. Then it was all ruined.'

'How? Surely Martin didn't do anything?'

'It wasn't Martin; it was me. I did it all on my own. I couldn't bear to think of failing when you were doing so well. I thought you would pity me and I couldn't bear that. I didn't understand how differently you might view things.'

'What do you mean? Please explain, Alex. What happened?'

'It's quite simple, almost laughably ordinary. I killed our baby. We were very much in love, as you said. We were also inexperienced and, just before the end of my first year, I discovered I was pregnant. I wrote and told Martin. He wanted us to get married. We would be poor until he got his law qualification but we could manage, he said. I would have to postpone my career for a time, but nothing mattered as long as we were together.' Alex's voice was choked suddenly with the sobs she could no longer hold back.

Standing up, Chastity put her arms around her. 'What did you do, Alex?'

'I couldn't face it. I was doing brilliantly and I was so ambitious. I thought he just didn't understand but that eventually he would accept it, so I had an abortion.'

'Do you mean that you had it without consulting Martin again or even telling him?'

'Yes. I had it before I went home and then I told him. Naturally, he didn't understand how I could do such a thing. We had a terrible row, which ended with my telling him that he was right, my personal career did matter to me more than anything else, even more than he or our baby did. I never saw him again.'

Chastity could think of nothing to say or do except to hold her close.

'I was pretty successful. I achieved what I'd hoped to achieve. I was determined to push all regrets out of my mind. I thought I'd been successful, but it had changed me. And when you came back and told me about Caroline, it hit me really hard. I even had a vivid dream about aborted babies being looked after in some heavenly place. All the hurt came back and, when James told me about his wife's pregnancy, I couldn't bear it. It seemed as if everything was reminding me of what I had wilfully thrown away and what I could now never have.'

'Are you sorry now for what you did? Do you now think that what you did then was wrong?'

'I suppose I am, but what does it matter? You can't kill someone, even an unborn baby, without being brutalised. I've wondered recently if that is one of the things that has changed our society. So many women are guilty of murder. Perhaps it helps to destroy our compassion?' She was quiet now, but her tears were still falling.

Releasing her, Chastity sat down. 'There are no sins that cannot be forgiven,' she said at last.

'You may say that and believe it, but I don't find it easy to believe and I know that there are some things that can't be put right and this is one of those. It changed me. Unicorn understood this and used me, but I did what he wanted for money. I betrayed Emmanuel. But then I went further than Unicorn would. Because I was angry and jealous, I betrayed you, my oldest friend, to Lord Harry. I was a real Judas.'

'Good came out of that, and I have forgiven you, if there is anything to forgive.'

'I know that you mean that. You've proved it by the way you've behaved. But do you think that Martin can ever forgive me for what I did to us? Have you forgiven the man who murdered Tim?'

Chastity looked at her steadily. 'I forgave him, but not straight away. I was heartbroken and very angry, and then he came weeping at my feet. I wanted to kick him away, but something made me listen to him. And then I understood.'

'Understood what?'

'That he was a victim, too. He was desperately poor, his wife was ill and his child had died. It was not Tim he wanted to kill, but any white man. Then someone told him that Tim's wife was the white doctor who had started a clinic for poor African women and that Tim had always supported my work. He realised how wrong he had been.'

'And what did he do?'

'He offered me his gun and asked me to kill him and have my revenge.'

'Christ! What did you do?'

'I took it. For a moment, I almost wanted to do what he asked. But then it seemed as if Tim touched my arm and said, "Don't, Caro! You know that's not what I want. Love will put things right; anger will only make them worse." So I returned his gun. As a sign that I forgave him.'

'Didn't you hand him over to the police?'

'No; that wouldn't have done any good. It wouldn't have resulted in justice. I told him to look after his sick wife and to send her to my clinic, which he did.'

Alex sat down suddenly opposite Chastity. 'Why have you told me this now? I haven't got anyone to forgive, so why?'

'For two reasons, chiefly. Firstly, I want you to understand that forgiveness is possible, and, secondly, to make it clear to you that, if you want to receive forgiveness, you not only have to be sincerely sorry for what you have done but you also have to ask the person you have hurt to forgive you.'

'I see.' Alex pondered over this for several moments, until she finally said, 'What you're really telling me is that I should seek out Martin, tell him how bitterly I regret what I did and ask him to forgive me. I can't imagine that he'll be pleased to see me. Even if he isn't still angry, he might be very embarrassed, because his life's moved on since then. I might seem ridiculous.'

'Perhaps. Asking for forgiveness always means taking a risk, just as giving it does. I can understand, however, that it might be difficult for you to find Martin now.'

'Actually, it isn't,' was Alex's unexpected reply. 'He hasn't moved far. He practises as a solicitor in Bradford, helping the poor, mostly, and he isn't married. My parents like him and have always kept tabs on him.'

'Then you know what to do, but you must be sincere and without any romantic expectations, please.'

Alex smiled sadly. 'It may surprise you, but I haven't any. I would just like to think that we could be friends again, as I hope you and I may be.'

'We are, so let that encourage you.'

'It does, but I feel I can't go on, Chastity. The days are bad enough but sometimes I have frightening dreams that show me how empty and futile my life really is. I don't know what to do.'

'You don't have to go on like that.' Chastity was firm but kind. 'With my help, you can start life afresh. You just need a bit of courage.'

After a moment's pause, Alex responded warmly. 'I'll try to. I really will. I'll go home at Christmas and arrange to meet him if I can. Having you as a friend again makes such a difference. I can't thank you enough!' Impulsively, she hugged Chastity.

'I will help you,' Chastity said firmly, 'just as you helped me years ago. Sometimes, dreams are meant as an instruction and a warning. I think you should speak to Jan. He understands these matters and can help to heal you.'

'I can't possibly talk to him. I scarcely know him.'

'You won't need to tell him much. He will understand and help you. He is an exceptional being. He helped me when I was in despair. Don't think about it; just do it.'

'When can I see him?'

'If you can manage tonight, it would be a good opportunity.

351

He is coming to see me before he goes away. But – I'd forgotten – you're going out.'

Alex shrugged her shoulders. 'A few drinks with a man I scarcely know; what does that matter compared with the opportunity to talk with someone who can help me? When do you expect him?'

'About nine o'clock. I'll have a few words with him first, then you can talk to him. Is that all right?'

'I don't know how to thank you enough!' Alex kissed and hugged her new-found friend. 'You've given me hope. You must be my good angel!'

Chapter Thirty-two

Chastity, wearing her loose, dark robe, was sitting in an armchair by the window, awaiting Unicorn's arrival. She had given much thought to this meeting, which she had agreed to the evening before when he had again telephoned her. She had invited him to come at eleven thirty. Dot, who was on the afternoon shift, would still be there to answer the door and to bring him to her room. Dot's presence also gave her an added sense of security.

She was aware that this was an important meeting. Jan had given entirely into her hands the responsibility for Unicorn. This worried her, for she felt that this was not only a test of Unicorn but also of her. Why had Jan done this? She had prayed and meditated about this for many hours, but no clear answer had come to her, except that she was more convinced than before that she must be very cautious; a conviction that Alex had reinforced that morning when her parting words had been a warning. 'Be careful, Chastity! Remember that, although he's very charming, he's also very, very devious!'

Was she wrong to listen to that, Chastity asked herself, when he seemed so much to have changed?

A ring of the front door bell told her that he had come promptly. The door to her room was opened by Dot and Unicorn came in, carrying an elegant sheaf of red rosebuds.

For a moment he hesitated, and then he moved swiftly towards her. 'I'm very surprised but very pleased to see you are getting better.' He offered her the rosebuds. 'Please accept these as an expression of my love and repentance.' Such formality on his part was unusual but effective.

As she took them, she noticed that, unlike most out-of-season roses, they had a delightful perfume. 'These are lovely. Thank you.' As she smelt them and then put them gently on the table beside her, she studied him. She had expected him to be changed, but, outwardly at least, he wasn't. He was wearing the same expensive, casual clothes. His hair was slightly disordered, as always. Those strange, yellow eyes were looking sympathetically at her, but the odd little glint still lurked there and warned her.

'How can I ask you to forgive me?' He took one of her hands in his as he sat down close to her. 'I treated you shamefully and you suffered so much. I can only tell you that I'm truly sorry and that I love you more than ever.'

'There is nothing to forgive,' she replied quietly. 'You did so much to help when you talked to Jan.' Leaving her hand in his, she lifted up her head and looked straight into his eyes, realising that, as she did so, her dark gaze discomfited him for a moment.

It was only for a moment, however. Leaning forward, he softly touched the livid bruise on her cheek. 'Oh, my darling, you have suffered so much! You should have been rescued sooner. That was what I hoped. Why didn't it happen?'

'It was necessary for me to confront Lord Harry. I knew that from the beginning. I had to prove to him that not every human being has a price. What you told Jan, however, helped a lot.'

'You're being too kind to me. I don't deserve it. I'm afraid you can't stop me from feeling so bloody guilty!'

'Guilty?'

'Yes. Guilty as hell because I was prepared to let you suffer instead of me. I wouldn't admit that it wasn't possible for you to run away. I rejected the chance you gave me. How can you possibly forgive me?'

Ignoring his emotional questions, she replied quietly, 'Jan has told me how much you helped. You talked freely and told him all you knew. As a result Lord Harry was completely overthrown.'

'That's true, I suppose. I've already been approached by the police. It appears he's had a severe stroke and so no one can talk to him. Which puts me in a funny position.'

'How do you mean?'

'I've betrayed my boss, but I haven't been sacked. In fact, there doesn't seem to be anybody with the power to sack me. I suppose I'd better dismiss myself.'

'Does all that worry you?'

'Not much; there are several alternatives. I might freelance for a time.'

'Haven't you any plans for the future?'

'That rather depends on you.'

'I still don't understand.'

'Because you have changed my whole life. I suppose that, in my small way, I feel a bit like St Paul must have felt after his encounter on the road to Damascus. I feel lost. My whole past life seems like a waste of time and my future seems utterly dark. You have brought me to this strange place. Now, what do I do?'

'It seems as if you need someone to help you.'

'I need you, Chastity.' He looked deeply into those dark eyes, pleading with her wordlessly. 'Please don't reject me. I love you, woman! Don't you understand? I betrayed my boss for you. I chucked away my job for you. Haven't I the right to expect something in return?' Taking both her hands, he moved closer to her. 'Marry me, Chastity, my darling, and we can start a new, good life together.'

Before she could answer, he bent and kissed her. First, he tenderly brushed the bruise on her cheek with his lips, and then he kissed her on the mouth with growing passion. For a brief moment, she seemed unwilling to resist him, and then suddenly and almost fiercely she pulled herself away from him.

'Don't! I – we are not ready for that!'

Amazed by the firmness of her tone and her resolute look, he released her and moved away. 'I didn't mean to annoy you! I'm sorry, my dearest. I should have realised that you're still far from well. Please forgive me.'

It was hard to resist the new humble Unicorn who pleaded with her, but something within her did. Perhaps it was the memory of Alex's words, *'Remember, he's very, very devious'*? She looked carefully at him. It was hard, but she must be firm. Jan had trusted her to deal with Unicorn and to make a proper decision.

'You're quite right. I'm not as well as I thought I was.' Leaning back, she closed her eyes.

'Would you rather I left?'

Smiling, she opened her eyes again. 'Actually, I would really like it if you made some coffee.'

He was both relieved and pleased. 'Your words are my command.' A few minutes later, he was smiling cheerfully as he handed her a cup of coffee. 'This reminds me of the first day we met.'

'How?'

'Instead of arousing your interest in me, I found myself then taking you to a pub and buying you a double brandy, which you promptly knocked back without any effect.'

'And now?'

'Now, having set out to make passionate love to you, I find myself instead persuaded into offering you a cup of coffee.'

'And a biscuit, I hope.' She looked mischievously at him.

'Very well.' Putting down his coffee, he stood up again. 'Where are they?'

'In the tin in the cupboard.'

'I don't know how you do it.' He offered her a biscuit.

'Chocolate, please. Do what?'

'Resist all my wiles and still keep me interested.'

'That's what I'm trying to tell you. We're not ready yet to talk of a permanent relationship. We don't know each other well enough. If we were teenage kids, I suppose we might stupidly plunge into action and have sex, as they say now. But we're not. We know the difference, I hope, between lust and love.'

'Don't underestimate me.' He smiled wickedly at her. 'Just believe that I'm sure that I love you. If I didn't, events might have been very different.'

'You mean that you would have had me in bed before now?'

'Exactly.'

'I can assure you, that would never have happened.' She took a sip of coffee, then bit her biscuit with satisfaction.

'Where is Jan?' he asked unexpectedly. 'I thought he would be keeping an eye on you.'

'He went away last night.'

'He went away? When you most needed him?' He was incredulous.

'He knew that I was mending,' she answered serenely. 'Beside that, he had no choice.'

'What do you mean? How could he have no choice?'

'The Lord called him, and therefore he had to go.'

Unicorn stared at her. 'What the hell do you mean? You

sound like a pious old woman, but I know you're not. Who is this Lord?'

He found himself looking unexpectedly into her dark, unfathomable eyes as she explained clearly to him: 'The Lord is the Lord of the Universe. He who creates all things and holds all things in being. Without Him, there would be chaos. We, who know Him, seek to obey Him.'

'Do you mean God?'

'That is what many people call Him, yes.'

'And He speaks to you?' He was looking at her as if she had suddenly gone mad.

'To me only once directly. It was overwhelming and changed my whole life. It is different for Jan, of course.'

'What do you mean? Why is it different for Jan?'

For a moment she hesitated, unsure of her right course of action. How much could safely be said? Jan had left it to her; she must decide.

'Well, are you going to tell me?' He was impatient. 'Or is this all a joke?'

'You'll find it hard to believe.'

'I doubt it after what you've already told me.' His tone was slightly mocking.

'Jan is not the same as us. He belongs to a different order of being, a more spiritual order, and therefore he is much closer to the Lord.' She paused.

'Go on. You can't leave it at that.'

'Jan is a messenger and a healer, who has been sent by the Lord to work on this planet. There are others, I believe, but he is the only one I have met. There are also evil beings, who work for the Dark Angel. They supported Lord Harry – Zig and his companions.'

He stared at her, apparently at a loss for words. Her gaze did not waver. Suddenly, she smiled. 'I imagine that you think that I'm completely mad?'

'I'm not sure. Either that or you're not serious.'

'I'm serious. Just consider what I'm saying without preconceptions.'

'I think you're trying to tell me that there is some kind of war going on. Am I right?'

'That is exactly right, and that is why I told you last Thursday evening that you could not be neutral. I think that perhaps you realised the truth of that and that is why you welcomed Jan when he came to you.'

'I welcomed Jan because I was desperate to save you and for no other reason. I couldn't bear to think of life without you. But I don't have any of these spiritual ideas you talk about. Do you understand that?'

'Of course.' She seemed surprisingly unconcerned.

'Does that actually mean that you won't want to see me any more?'

'No; why should it? I said that we needed to get to know one another better. It's more likely, isn't it, that you don't want to see me any more after what I have just told you?' Smiling, she handed him her coffee cup. 'You may think it might be dangerous?' She waited for him to challenge that, but he didn't.

After putting down her coffee cup, he took her hand, raised it to his lips and kissed it. 'I'm sure it is dangerous,' he replied a moment later, 'but I rather enjoy danger.' He kissed her hand again. She did not resist, but he decided to attempt no more. He was determined to overcome her. He knew it would take time and patience. The thought pleased him. He was confident that he would eventually succeed.

She studied him as he tenderly caressed her hand. This was pleasant, but there was something wrong, something missing. What was it?

Before she could pursue the thought, he spoke. 'I'm afraid you're not well enough to come out tonight, but perhaps you'll be ready for a celebration meal tomorrow?'

'A celebration meal?'

'Yes; we must celebrate your miraculous escape and the renewal of our relationship. Don't you agree? Knowing your bizarre taste for genuine English dishes, I'll allow you to choose the menu and then I'll find a restaurant to supply it. What do you say?'

'That sounds splendid!' She was relieved that he had not suggested a meal in his flat. 'But won't it take some time?'

'That hardly matters, does it? Now I'm unemployed, I have plenty of time.'

'Oh, dear, what are you going to do next? Have you thought about it?'

'Not much. As I've already said, that very much depends on you.'

'On me?' She frowned slightly.

'Yes, on you, as I've already said. You can't deny that you have changed me and my life. You have made me love you. Because of you, I've settled money on Stevie, I've betrayed my boss and lost my job. Obviously I need help and guidance and you're the one to give it. It's your responsibility.' Although his tone was humorous, he was clearly serious.

'What do you want me to do?'

'You know what I want. I've already told you. I want you to agree to marry me.'

'And you have my answer.'

'Yes; I must wait. All right, I will, but I'll keep trying. You won't blame me for that, surely? You're the first woman I've ever waited for. I've always taken what I've wanted before and they've always been willing. Now I am prepared to wait, but you must give me my chance. Do you agree?'

She smiled but said nothing.

Apparently taking her smile for agreement, he stood up. 'Good.' He kissed her lightly on the cheek. 'I'm going now, because you look tired. I'll ring you later. Don't worry; I'll make everything easy for you tomorrow. You're very precious to me.' With a final wave, he was gone.

Chastity leaned back and closed her eyes. She knew that she needed to think, but she felt too weary to do so. Nevertheless, doubts worried her. Why had he taken the strange information she had given him so calmly? Why had he not asked any questions? Did he disbelieve her or was he in some way mocking her? It was useless to try to decide; she was too tired.

Some hours later, she was startled to hear someone opening the front door. It was certainly too soon for Dot. Alex must have decided to come home early. She relaxed, only to be startled again by a sharp knock on her own door. 'Come in,' she called out.

To her surprise, it was Sean who entered. Hurrying over to her, he offered her a brilliant red-and-gold gift pack. 'A present for a good girl!' Grinning cheerfully, he kissed her, giving her a friendly hug at the same time. It was comforting.

She smiled happily back at him, holding the unopened bag on her lap.

'Aren't you going to look at what you've got?' After pushing aside a couple of books, he perched on the edge of the table next to her. 'They cost me a bloody arm and a leg, but I thought, she's worth it and she'd never spend the money on herself.'

Intrigued, she opened the bag. Inside was a large, tempting box of luxury chocolates.

'I know you wouldn't eat them normally, but this is a time for a celebration and since I've bought them you've got no excuse for refusing!'

'I certainly won't refuse! They are too tempting and too comforting!' Her eyes were shining as she looked at him. He was the same old Sean in his shabby jeans, open-necked checked shirt and scuffed leather jacket – the same old charmer, too, with his curly black hair and dark eyes, but at the same time refreshingly honest and trustworthy. 'They're marvellous! Thank you!'

'Aren't you going to open them and give me one? We humble truck drivers don't usually come within a mile of goods like these. They only sold them to me in this posh Bond Street shop because I tempted them with the cash! But they made their opinion of such low life quite clear!'

'Rubbish!' Laughing, she opened the box and offered it to him.

'No, the first choice is yours. It would be bloody disgusting if I took your favourite, and I know you'd let me have it without a word.'

'All right. I like hard centres.'

'I guessed you would! That's why they are all hard centres. They're like you, you see: soft and pretty on the outside and tough in the centre!'

She laughed. 'Whatever's happened to you, Sean? Talking like that. It must be the Irish in you coming out.'

'Probably.' He chose his own carefully. 'Fuck it, woman, can't you understand that we're all so happy that you're alive and not too much damaged? It's really something to celebrate!'

'All? Who is that?'

'Me, Ma Elizabeth' – Mrs Allen, Chastity guessed – 'and Rupert. In fact, I've got orders from Ma to bring you down for a celebratory meal, even if I have to carry you!'

'It sounds lovely.' She realised that she didn't want to be on her own any more. She wanted to be with people who loved her. 'But I can't have Elizabeth cooking a special meal for four people. I know that her arthritis has been worse lately.'

'Don't worry. I've refused to allow her to even think about it! It's my treat and I'm in charge. I rang Rupert at his work and he's coming. He's been bloody frustrated not being able to see you since the early hours of Sunday. Stop fussing, girl. Leave it all to me. I've decided we shall have a traditional meal loved by all right-thinking Brits!'

'What's that?'

'Have a guess. What do Brits always eat in Spain, Greece, and so on?'

'I haven't an idea, unless it's a vindaloo?'

Sean grinned derisively. 'Balls! That's only for drunks who've lost all sense of taste! Since you can't do better than that, I'll tell you. It's fish and chips, well cooked, of course, from the best fish and potatoes and served with all the trimmings. You can't beat it! It might be fattening, I suppose, but we don't need to worry about that, do we?'

'No, of course not.'

'Well, then, what do you think of the idea?'

'It's perfect!'

He grinned back at her. 'I bet you're too posh to have eaten fish and chips before! Now's your chance to start living! We'll have salt, vinegar, pickled onions and tins of Coke with them.' Without waiting for her answer, he continued, 'Stand up and I'll wrap you in that fantastic African blanket of yours. We're going now.'

Before she could think of an answer, she found herself warmly wrapped in her blanket, being carried downstairs. Relaxing, she let him take charge of her. Elizabeth received her lovingly and she was quickly installed in a comfortable chair by the fire.

'I'll leave you two while I go to the best fish and chip shop in the area. Remember, you're not to do anything, either of you, except to let Rupert in if he arrives before I get back.' He was gone.

'He's a good lad and means well.' Elizabeth seemed a little worried. 'I wasn't sure about giving you fish and chips, but he said you'd enjoy it and it would do you good.'

'He was right.' As she looked up at Elizabeth, standing close to her, Chastity's eyes filled with tears that turned to sobs as Elizabeth put her arm around her. The tears needed to be shed, but gradually she found herself comforted.

Chapter Thirty-three

Rupert arrived some time before Sean returned. Chastity was surprised by the warmth of his greeting as he hugged her and kissed her on the cheek. 'I can't say how glad I am to see you looking so fit! When we picked you up you looked ghastly! I was scared.'

'Fortunately for me, it looked much worse that it was. Scalp wounds often bleed a lot, even when they're quite superficial.' Drawing back a little, she inspected him. 'You look fine!' She had forgotten how handsome he was.

Sitting down, he answered her seriously. 'I feel a different person. You and Jan and even dear old Mother Mark have made me realise for the first time what's important in life.'

'And what is that?'

'Love, caring for others.' There was no hesitation about his reply. 'I never really gave much thought to that before I met you. There's why I find it hard to stay with Paul. He doesn't want to know.'

'It's all happened pretty suddenly. Perhaps he needs more time.'

'Maybe, but he's used me and I find that hard to forgive.'

'Don't you think that you should perhaps think about the Being who is the source of this love?'

'You mean Christ? Mother Mark is always talking about him.'

'Then you must remember that he told us that we must forgive if we want to be forgiven.

'That's very important,' Elizabeth added, as she stood up and moved towards the kitchen.

'What are you doing?' Chastity asked her. 'You're supposed to rest.'

'I'm only going to put some plates to warm in the oven. Sean won't be long now. You carry on talking.'

'Have you forgiven Lord Harry?' Rupert asked Chastity.

'He has suffered far more than I have. And he may die before he can repent.'

'But he's caused a lot of people great suffering, not only you.'

'I don't condone what he has done, but he may well pay a terrible price. The Dark Angel exerts a powerful influence over those who stupidly support him.'

'What do you mean by the Dark Angel? I don't understand you.'

'It is the name given by some people to the evil force who is trying always to raise a rebellion on the planet against the Lord of the Universe.'

Rupert was still bewildered. 'Do you mean Satan? That's only a story, isn't it? Surely no rational being believes any more in that?' He stared at Chastity as if he thought she had suddenly gone insane.

'That is where he has been so clever: in persuading millions of people to believe that he does not exist. How can you look at the evil in this planet, particularly during the last century, and accept that lie? I'm afraid that you need to look at our situation more clearly. Whether we like it or not, we human beings are involved in a spiritual struggle.'

'You really believe that?'

'I know that it is the truth.'

The sounds of Sean's ebullient return prevented Rupert from asking any more questions. As Elizabeth emerged from the kitchen carrying the warmed plates, Sean entered the living room carrying two large plastic bags, which he rapidly emptied. There were several bulky packets, several tins of Coke and an unexpected bottle of wine. 'Here we are, Ma Elizabeth!' he exclaimed. 'Everything we need.'

While Rupert placed the plates round the table, Chastity laid the knives and forks and tumblers. 'Since you've bought a bottle of wine, we need more glasses,' she remarked.

'I decided that we couldn't drink a proper toast in Coke,' Sean explained, as Elizabeth took more glasses out of the cupboard.

As soon as Elizabeth began to lay out the food, it was discovered that Sean had, strangely, bought an extra portion of everything. 'I'm afraid you can't count to four,' she remarked.

'Don't worry,' Chastity interposed quickly; 'the extra food is obviously for the unexpected guest. We'll keep it warm in the oven until he or she arrives.'

'You're expecting another guest? I didn't know that I was.' Sean was obviously puzzled by what he had done.

'Perhaps.' Without giving any further explanation, Chastity took the extra food into the kitchen.

When she returned, Sean had opened the bottle of wine. 'Before we sit down to this special meal,' he announced, 'we're going to drink a toast in celebration of Chastity's courage and the amazing overthrow of Lord Harry!'

'If this is to be a thanksgiving and a celebration, let us make it a proper one.' Chastity held up her glass. 'Let us give thanks to the Lord of the Universe for my delivery from danger and for the overcoming of Lord Harry's evil. I also thank you, Lord, for the courage and loyalty of the friends who came to my rescue, and for Jan, who is always there when he is needed. For all these blessings we give thanks to you through Jesus Christ, your son.'

After a moment's surprised silence the others joined her in saying, 'Amen.'

As he refilled the glasses, Sean said, 'Jan should have been with us. I must have been thinking of him when I bought the extra food.'

Chastity smiled. 'Jan is always with us in spirit and he'll soon be back again.'

As soon as he had refilled the glasses, Sean raised his and said, 'Let us drink to Our Lord Jesus Christ.' After raising their glasses, they all drank, then sat down to eat.

'This is certainly excellent,' Rupert remarked, 'but why fish and chips, Sean? It's not exactly the usual food for a celebration.'

'Two reasons: I can afford it and, secondly, I know that Chastity prefers simple food, and it occurred to me that she might not have eaten the Brits' favourite dish either when she was a posh lady in the embassy or as a doctor in Africa.'

As they all laughed, Chastity confirmed this. 'You're right on both counts, Sean. I think this is delicious!'

They had only been happily eating for a few minutes when the front doorbell was rung loudly and imperiously several times.

'Who on earth can that be?' Elizabeth started to her feet, but Sean gently pushed her back.

'Whoever it is, he seems to be pretty mad,' he remarked, as the bell rang again.

'I think it may be Paul.' Rupert stood up. 'I said I'd be home tonight, but I came here instead.'

'And you didn't get permission?' Sean looked at Rupert with mock horror. 'That was very naughty.'

Although he flushed, Rupert did not answer him but continued his walk towards the door. 'I'll deal with him,' were his parting words. 'He has no right to interfere. I thought I'd made that clear.'

As Rupert opened the front door, Paul's voice could be clearly heard, loud and shrill, as it always was when he was angry and upset. 'So, you are here. I might have known. When you didn't turn up as you promised, I rang your boss and he said you'd gone home some time ago. Your promise to me meant nothing, as usual. You do this sort of thing just to humiliate me, don't you?' There was real distress behind his anger.

'Poor man!' Elizabeth murmured.

'I've thrown the casserole away,' Paul continued, 'although I don't suppose you care for all the effort I made.'

Before Rupert could make an inflammatory reply, Chastity had already reached the door.

'Paul, dear, I'm so glad you've come.' Her voice was gentle. 'I was hoping you would. Your portion is being kept warm in the oven, so come straight in.'

There was a pause. Rupert did not make his intended reply, while Paul obviously struggled to regain his self-control. When he did speak, it was in his normal voice but without any of his usual affectations. 'Chastity, my darling, you are kind as always.' Sean, who was now standing in the doorway of the living room, saw that Paul had taken Chastity's hand. 'I'm very pleased, in fact, to have the chance of telling you how delighted I am to see that you were not severely hurt the other evening. I only heard later what had happened.'

'In that case,' Chastity said, smiling at him, 'you must join my celebration party.'

'I'm afraid, darling, that I may not be welcome.' Paul drew himself up proudly with a flashing look at Rupert, who made no response.

'Nonsense.' Chastity took Paul's hand firmly. 'It's my party, and I'm inviting you because you are my friend. Sean,' – she turned towards him – 'will you please go and put out Paul's portion for him?'

With a broad grin, Sean turned to obey her as she led Paul towards the living room. Rupert followed silently. As Sean came back, he whispered to Elizabeth, 'I'm putting out the extra portion for the "unexpected" guest. How the hell did she achieve that?'

Elizabeth only smiled as she turned to greet Paul.

'Please, Rupert,' Chastity ordered him gently, 'bring that extra chair over here. Paul can sit next to me.' Without a word, Rupert did as she requested.

In a few minutes, Paul was settled before a large plate of fish and chips. If the plebeian nature of the food offended his gastronomic sensibilities, he made no comment except to thank everyone and even, graciously, to accept a tin of Coke from Sean.

'As you can see,' Chastity told Paul, 'we've only just started. I wasn't sure exactly when you would come.' Her smile was most beguiling.

Paul looked bemused. 'I'm not sure I quite understand, Chastity darling,' he managed to say at last, with something of his usual manner.

Sean came to the rescue. 'Don't worry, mate. Chastity has that effect on all of us at times. That's right, isn't it, Ma?' He turned to Elizabeth, who smiled but wisely said nothing.

Conversation languished as they attacked their food. Chastity remained enigmatic; Elizabeth seemed totally preoccupied with her duties as a hostess; Paul was obviously still puzzled; Rupert seemed to have taken a vow of silence. Sean was content to wait to see what would happen.

It was, surprisingly, Paul who broke the silence. 'Isn't Jan coming?' he asked Chastity.

'Oh, no; he went away late last night and won't be back for two or three weeks.'

'Oh, dear, that is a great pity. I very much wanted to speak to him.' Before continuing, Paul, irritatingly, carved up a chip with his usual precision. 'I'm so sorry that I've missed him.' He delicately lifted a portion of the chip towards his mouth.

'Why? Why does it matter so much to you?' Chastity obviously thought he was exaggerating.

'Why?' Paul raised his eyebrows and put down the wretched piece of chip. 'Because I wanted to thank him properly. One should always try to show recognition for a generous favour. Surely you agree?'

'Of course I agree in principle, but I don't know what you're actually referring to.'

'Chastity dear, please forgive me. I should have realised that Jan would not have bothered you with my small problem when you were so desperately unwell. Nor should I do so. The trouble is, one is so desperately self-centred. Don't you agree?' He looked round to meet Rupert's scowl. 'I see you do agree.'

'Paul,' Chastity interrupted him, firmly and clearly. 'Will you please tell me what you are talking about? You're making me quite anxious.'

'Chastity, darling, there's nothing for you to be anxious about – really, quite the contrary. I bumped into Jan yesterday. I think he was leaving you. After he had given me news of you, I told him how concerned I was about Helen and Stevie.'

'But I thought Unicorn had helped them. He told me he had.'

'Yes, of course. Thanks to your kind intervention, he has at least done what he should have done from the beginning. His money settlement has been quite generous.'

'Then why are you still so worried?'

'Well, one knows, doesn't one, darling, that money is not the answer to all life's problems?' He paused and looked around, while they waited for him to continue.

'Well, surely it helps?' Rupert sounded extremely irritated. 'She can send the kid to a special school, which is what she needs to do, can't she?'

'She could theoretically do that, but the truth is that, in recent days, Stevie has become so unmanageable that she can't persuade him to do anything. I thought Jan might know what to do, since he is a doctor. He very kindly offered to see them. He talked briefly and kindly to Helen and then spent more than an hour alone with Stevie. I don't know what he said or did, but the change, Helen tells me, is miraculous. I only wanted to thank him properly.'

'It was a miracle.' Chastity said. 'A miracle of love. Unicorn doesn't have that ability. He can't even love his own son, while Jan sees everyone as a child of God and reaches out to them. The poorer and the weaker they are, the more he cherishes them.'

Elizabeth turned towards Chastity. 'You're right, and you, too, have learned from him to do the same.'

'While I,' Paul said, with unaccustomed humility, 'could do nothing, although I genuinely believed I cared about them both. How easy it is to deceive oneself.'

'You're not being fair to yourself,' Rupert answered him suddenly. 'At least you cared enough to find the right person to help them.'

Paul was moved by his unexpected support. 'Thank you, Rupert.'

'I can't say anything,' Rupert continued. 'It's obvious that I've been deceiving myself a lot lately. I expect that's what Chastity is thinking, isn't it?'

'I'm only thinking two things,' she answered brightly. 'That I shall have to carry on Jan's good work while he is away…' She paused.

'And what's the second?' Sean asked.

'Oh, that's very mundane. I'm thinking that I've enjoyed the first course but we haven't got a pudding and I'm still hungry!'

'Women!' Sean groaned. 'They're never satisfied.'

'This is where I can do my bit.' Paul suddenly sounded cheerful. 'I made a simply delicious lemon meringue pie for Rupert and me. I know he likes it, and, if you do Chastity, your problem is solved.'

'I haven't had one for years, but I loved them when I was a child.'

'Then I'll go and fetch it at once.' Paul stood up. 'It'll only take a couple of minutes.' Before anyone could speak, he had gone.

369

'Don't dare to move, Ma,' Sean warned Elizabeth. 'I'll clear away the plates and get clean ones. Come on, Rupert, it's time for you to do your bit and prepare some coffee.'

They had hardly gone to the kitchen when the doorbell rang loudly for the second time that evening.

'I think I know who that is.' Chastity stood up. As she hurried towards the door, the bell was rung again, even more loudly. The visitor was obviously impatient. As Chastity quickly opened the door, Alex almost fell in, obviously very agitated.

'I suppose it didn't occur to you,' she almost shouted at Chastity, 'that I might be upset, even worried, when I found that you were missing?'

'Oh, dear. I'm very sorry, Alex.'

'I should think so! When I returned, I thought you must be asleep, so I quietly prepared a meal and even sat down to eat it. Then I thought something might be wrong. When I had no reply to my knock, I went into your room. Behold, there was no Chastity. No note of explanation, either. That's not like you!'

'It was my fault.' Sean's voice came from behind Chastity. 'I practically kidnapped her. I wrapped her in her blanket and carried her downstairs for a celebration. She hadn't a chance.' He gave Alex the benefit of his most beguiling grin. Susceptible as always, she melted.

'OK, I'll forgive you both, but only on condition that I'm no longer excluded from the party.'

'Come right in,' Sean invited her. 'You're just in time for coffee and Paul's home-made pie.'

'And that will be delicious,' Chastity assured her. 'Paul is a brilliant cook.'

'I was so worried,' Alex told Chastity, 'that I actually rang Unicorn.'

'Oh, no.' Chastity was dismayed.

'Oh, yes! He was really put out to discover that his beloved had apparently vanished without a word. He suggested that he should come round, but I said I would ring him again when I had more news. It suddenly occurred to me that you might be here. I suppose I'd better ring him now or he'll be arriving. What shall I say?'

'Tell him I've only gone to visit Mrs Allen. I do not want to see him.' Chastity was very decided.

'Oh, dear!' Alex raised her eyebrows. 'Trouble in paradise?' She was obviously enjoying the thought of Unicorn's possible discomfiture. 'He'll want to speak to you.'

'No, he won't!' Sean interrupted suddenly. 'Not if you manage it properly, as I'm sure you can do. Take yourself and your mobile into the kitchen, and I'll come with you to see fair play.' He was exerting considerable charm, and Alex was enjoying it, apparently.

He was interrupted by another ring of the doorbell.

'That will be Paul.' Rupert hurried to answer the door as Sean and Alex vanished into the kitchen.

Elizabeth put her arm around Chastity. 'Don't worry, my dear. You need to rest here with us a little longer. Sean will take care of it. He will do anything for you!'

It was an unusually subdued Alex who returned to the living room later with Sean. To Chastity's relief, she made no mention of Unicorn, except to say that he was satisfied with her message, and seemed content to enjoy her coffee and pie without any provocative comments. Paul basked in everyone's approval and it was clear that he and Rupert were coming to a better understanding.

Soon after the end of the meal, Sean insisted on carrying Chastity back, sending Alex on ahead.

'Whatever did you say to Alex?' Chastity asked him.

Grinning widely, he said, 'Just the truth. I told her to stop being a bitch and to stop wasting her efforts on me. Even if she wasn't, I said, some of us are mature enough to know the difference between love and lust. I suggested she find some kid if she needed to practise.'

'Was that necessary?'

'Yes, and I enjoyed it too. She was making her intentions quite clear. But she took it well, I must admit. Said she deserved it.' Wrapping the blanket firmly around Chastity, he picked her up. 'She said she wanted to be better but that old habits died hard.'

'I'm sure that's true,' Chastity agreed. At that moment,

however, she was thinking not only of Alex but also of Unicorn. Was that the reason why she felt uneasy about him, or was there something even more important?

Chapter Thirty-four

The party had its origins in the moment when Chastity and Sean, strolling up the street from the shops, saw Rupert in the side lane where he often parked his motorbike. Rupert, who had just returned from work, was talking to an earnest-looking schoolboy, who was obviously admiring the powerful and magnificent bike. It was a Friday evening, nearly three weeks after Sean's celebration party for Chastity.

Seeing them approaching, Rupert called out to them and they went up to him. Putting his hand on the boy's shoulder, Rupert said, 'Ryan, meet Sean, another biker.'

'Ex-biker, you mean. I can't afford to be a biker any more.' He patted the bike appreciatively. 'But it's still a joy to see one like this.'

'I think it's fantastic!' Ryan looked curiously at Chastity.

Seeing the look, Rupert introduced her. 'And this is Chastity. She's a doctor, but, more importantly, she's brave enough to ride pillion with me a couple of times a week.'

'Cool!' Ryan looked at Chastity with some respect.

'We're going to have tea,' Sean announced; 'or, to be more truthful, I've bullied Chastity into providing me with some, as Ma's spending a couple of days with her daughter. Why don't you join us? You, too,' he added seeing Ryan's hopeful look. 'That's all right with you, isn't it?' he belatedly asked Chastity.

'Of course.' She included them all in her cheerful smile. 'I like a party. But I haven't got a lot of time. I'm going out to dinner with Unicorn, as I told you. It's supposed to be a very special evening!'

'Well, we'd better get started, then,' Sean retorted. 'Come on, Ryan. There's bound to be chocolate cake, as Chastity loves it!'

'Won't your mother be worried?' Chastity asked Ryan, as they moved towards the entrance of Number 48.

'It'll be all right. She won't be home till eight. I get my own tea on Fridays.'

'That's fine, then. How about you?' she asked Rupert.

'Paul is expecting me soon, I imagine.' He sounded very reluctant.

'I'll ask him to join our party.' Chastity was oblivious, as she often was, to any possible difficulties. 'Go on ahead.' She handed her key to Sean. 'I'll run upstairs and persuade Paul to bring some of the delicious food he always has.'

'He's probably got masses,' Rupert told her. 'Today was going to be a baking day.'

'Good. Put the kettle on, Sean. I owe him a tea anyway.' Ignoring their comments, she turned to run up the stairs.

'Who is Paul?' Ryan asked, as Sean unlocked the door of the flat.

'He's the guy I live with,' Rupert explained.

'Is he a biker, too?'

'No, but he's all right. He's a television actor.'

'Cool!' Ryan was clearly affected by this information, although he asked no further questions.

Sean had only just put the kettle on when Chastity reappeared. 'We're in luck!' She smiled triumphantly. 'Paul's not only coming, but he's also bringing scones and two mouth-watering cakes. You and I will make some sandwiches, Rupert, and, Sean, you can get Ryan to help you to lay the table.'

Once they were in the kitchen, she wasted no time before asking Rupert about Ryan. 'His family won't think we've kidnapped him, will they?'

'I don't know much about him. This is only the third time we've met. But, from what he has told me, I think this will be a great treat for him. He's a carer.'

'A carer? What do you mean?'

'He looks after his mother and younger sister.' Rupert paused for a moment to lay out the rolls, while Chastity rummaged in the refrigerator for ham, cheese and salad.

'Why does he do that?'

'His mother has MS badly and his father left them about three years ago when the going got tough, and so Ryan took over. He does most of the shopping and the cooking; takes his six-year-old sister, Emily, into school and brings her home. He takes charge of the three of them.'

'What an amazing boy! He must like you to tell you so much.'

'It's the bike that did it. He's mad about bikes and mine's just the sort he'd like to buy when he's older, so he couldn't resist talking to me. Today was the first time I'd seen him on his own. On the other occasions he's had Emily with him and couldn't stay long.'

'Why is he free tonight? Do you know?'

'I'm not exactly sure. I think his mother and Emily are taken to a friend's house every Friday for a few hours.'

'And poor little Ryan's left out?' Chastity stopped her tomato chopping for a moment to consider this.

Rupert paused in his roll buttering to answer her. 'I believe that it's his choice. He values his freedom for a few hours. I imagine he's given money and usually buys himself a beef burger and chips or something like that.'

'I can imagine that he might.' Taking a couple of rolls from him, she began to fill them.

'Chastity,' Rupert said after a moment, 'do you ever wish—' He broke off suddenly. 'Gosh, how thoughtless of me! I'm sorry.'

'Do you mean,' Chastity answered him calmly, 'do I ever wish that I had a child?' Before he could answer, she went on, quickly. 'The honest answer is that sometimes I do. My daughter would have been eight. I've never forgotten her. How could I?' She took two more buttered rolls from him.

'I'm sorry.' Distressed, he put his hand on hers. 'I'm a thoughtless idiot – self-centred, as Paul would say.'

'Tell me.' She turned towards him. 'Do you wish that you had a child? Is that why you asked me? I remember that, when we first talked, you said that you sometimes wished you could have an ordinary life. Or have you changed?'

'No. I still do wish sometimes that I could be a father, although helping with the destitute has helped.'

'Paul really loves you,' she reminded him.

'I know. I understand that better now than I did, and I think I appreciate him more. But…'

'You could adopt a child, perhaps.'

'I don't think so. I don't quite see Paul and me as mum and dad.' Picking up the last two rolls, he sliced and buttered them.

'Do you mind if I ask you an impertinent question? You don't have to answer if you don't want to.'

'I don't mind. I shan't answer if I don't want to.'

'Is that one of the principal attractions of Unicorn: that you might marry him and have a family?' When she didn't answer immediately, he said quickly, 'I'm sorry, I had no right to ask.'

'I'm not offended; I'm just thinking about it. I haven't clearly admitted it to myself before, but perhaps you're right. Do you think that's wrong?'

'Of course not, as long as that's not your only reason.'

'There are other reasons, but there may still be stronger reasons for me not to do it.' As she took the last rolls from him, the front door bell rang.

'That'll be Paul.' Rupert pulled off his apron. 'This meeting of minds I must see.' Nevertheless, on Chastity's insistence, it was a few minutes before they entered the living room, where an amazing tableau met their eyes.

Paul, eccentrically perfect as always, wearing a magnificent brocade waistcoat and frilly white cravat with black velvet jacket and trousers, was leaning forward slightly towards Ryan and delicately offering him a thin sliver of cake. 'You really must taste this, Ryan,' he was saying in his most persuasive voice and dulcet tones. 'It's made from a recipe I discovered recently in an old book. I think it may be the perfect orange and chocolate cake. You are exactly the right person to tell me. Please do try it.'

Ryan, in his school uniform with loosened tie askew, shirt hanging over his trousers, jacket unbuttoned, was staring almost wildly at Rupert. His normally-tousled hair was even more unruly than usual; his too-pale face was flushed with excitement; his brown eyes were wide open. 'I know you,' he almost shouted, ignoring the fragment of cake. 'You're not Paul; you're Ferdy. I've seen you on TV a few months ago. I'm right, aren't I?'

'If you insist,' Paul replied, more calmly than Chastity expected. Then, almost pushing the fragment into Ryan's open mouth, his patience exhausted, he suddenly shrieked, 'But please taste this cake, you idiotic boy!'

Shocked into obedience, Ryan took the cake, chewed it carefully and finally swallowed it. A sudden smile transformed his normally anxious expression. 'It's fabulous!' he decreed.

'You're clearly a boy of excellent taste! Would you—'

But, before he could complete his sentence, Ryan interrupted him. 'You are Ferdy though, aren't you? I can't wait to tell everyone at school that I've met you. It's the coolest thing that's ever happened to me.' Suddenly anxious, he added, 'I'm right, aren't I? You really are Ferdy. But these others, they're not Maggy, Tom and Andy.'

Looking at him with horror, Paul replied in his most didactic tones, 'My dear boy, you seem to be living in a world of illusion. You're suffering from the common TV syndrome. This, I must tell you, is the real world, not the one you see on the screen. In this real world I'm Paul and these people are my friends. I actually loathe Maggy and Tom.' He shuddered. 'And Andy's frightfully uncouth but just about bearable. Now,' he continued, in a kinder tone, 'pull yourself together and have a real piece of cake.'

'No, definitely not,' Chastity said firmly, stepping forward. 'You'll spoil his appetite, Paul! Surely you remember we had to eat the bread and butter first; in this case, the sandwiches?' In the excitement, her magnificent dark hair had fallen loose over her shoulders, framing her face. Her unusual beauty shone out.

Ryan stared at her. 'You're beautiful! Much better-looking than Maggy! Couldn't you get her a part in the show?' He turned towards Paul.

Amazed, Paul stared at him. 'My poor boy, Chastity wouldn't want to be in that silly show! She is a famous doctor!' Ignoring any further protests from Ryan, he turned to Chastity. 'Of course you're quite right, darling! You always are. Bring in the real food.'

Emerging from the corner, where he had been hugely enjoying the scene, Sean handed Ryan a Coke and pushed him into the nearest chair. Meanwhile, Rupert brought in plates of appetising rolls. Paul transferred his cakes and scones onto plates. Chastity brought in a pot of tea for those who preferred it.

Staring at her, Ryan asked, 'If you're a doctor, why haven't

I seen you at our local practice? I'd remember you if I had.'

'I don't work there. I'm working temporarily at a clinic in the East End. Before that, I've been in Africa and other places.'

'Cool!' He looked at her with increased respect. Before he could ask any more questions, Rupert handed him a roll. For nearly twenty minutes there was little opportunity for talk. Ryan, who was obviously hungry, quickly ate three rolls, two scones with jam and cream and two large slices of cake, washing them down with quick slurps of Coke. He was closely followed by Sean, who was almost as hungry.

When he had finished his second slice and drunk the last of his Coke, Ryan turned towards Chastity. 'What part of Africa did you work in?'

'Mostly Kenya and places nearby. Why?'

'I was wondering if you knew anything about this "Global Warming" they're all talking about? Isn't there a terrible drought there?'

'There is, and people are starving – thousands of them.'

'Then it is true?' He looked at her with earnest, brown eyes.

'Did you think it wasn't?'

'Don't know. I suppose I just hoped it wasn't. I thought it might be another media stunt or something.'

'I'm afraid it's not. It is actually happening. And not only in Africa. A few months ago, I spent two weeks in New Orleans, where I was sent with three other medics to help to rescue a group of elderly, disabled and sick people who had been abandoned by the hospital staff.'

Ryan stared at her with growing respect. 'But,' he protested, 'that wasn't because of a drought. It was just the opposite. I don't understand.'

'Briefly, it's because these powerful winds are passing over the Gulf of Mexico, which is now much warmer, and this increases their strength. Why don't you ask your science teacher? Why don't you get him or her to think about it? You might get the whole class involved.'

'They'd probably laugh at me. They do when you get serious about something. They already think that I'm a nerd.'

'Does that matter?' Paul asked.

'I suppose not.' He turned towards Paul. 'People laugh at Ferdy all the time, don't they? But my mum likes him 'cos she says he's got perfect manners. I shall tell her that you really are like that, although I'm not sure that you really do mad things like climbing out of windows and all that.'

As everyone laughed, Paul replied graciously, 'I'm afraid, dear boy, it's not unknown. Please give my profoundest good wishes to your mum.'

'I will. She'll be thrilled, especially when I tell her how cool you are.' He turned towards Chastity. 'About that global warming? If it is happening so much, why don't people know about it?'

'Because they don't want to know. It's too frightening.'

'Then the Prime Minister and people like that ought to make us know about it. Why don't they?'

It was Rupert who answered. 'I think perhaps it's because they might have to tell people to give up things they like, and that would make them unpopular.'

'So nobody does anything,' Sean added. 'It's the same as usual – the "haves" saying "F— you, Jack, I'm all right".'

'Expect you're right,' Ryan agreed. His life had already taught him this lesson.' I suppose TV's the same, too.'

'You could try the Internet,' Rupert suggested.

'I've got a much more exciting idea,' Chastity exclaimed. 'It's old-fashioned, but it could be fun and might have quite an impact.' As she stopped, the others all stared at her.

'Aren't you going to explain?' Sean asked finally.

'Yes; I was just working out the details.'

'Well, go on. Perhaps we can help.'

'Here it is, then. If I had the money and knew how to organise it, I'd hire a hundred men or more to walk round the centres of London, Birmingham and Manchester with billboards!'

'Do you mean the sort of thing they used to have years ago saying "Repent Ye" on one side and, on the other, "The End is Nigh"? Or something like that?' Rupert asked.

'Yes, that's the idea.'

'My dear, what a simply fascinating thought!' Paul was

suddenly enthusiastic. 'I can just imagine it. But the message is the important thing.'

'Just think of the traffic jams and the police trying to sort it out!' Sean added. 'You'd have them in all three cities at once, I suppose?'

'Of course!' Chastity agreed cheerfully.

'Cool!' Ryan was obviously in favour. 'That would be really fantastic! Perhaps I could be one of the men?'

'I'm afraid not,' Rupert answered him firmly. 'You need men about the size of Sean and me.'

'Men who don't mind a punch-up,' Sean added. 'There'd probably be one or two.'

'No,' Chastity interrupted them firmly. 'That was not my idea. Publicity, not punch-ups, was what I intended!'

For a moment there was silence, until Paul intervened. 'You seem to be forgetting, darlings, that the really important thing is the message. Have you any idea as to what that should be?' He looked towards Chastity.

'Not a very clear one. Perhaps "Repent" would still do on one side?'

'What does "repent" mean?' Ryan asked.

'I'm afraid it doesn't look as if "repent" will do,' Rupert remarked.

'In this secular world, probably not.' Chastity leaned back, closing her eyes as if concentrating. 'How about "Wake up Now" on one side and on the other, "The End of our Planet is Near"?'

'That might do for a start, but I'm sure we can improve on it.' Paul seemed ready to start instantly.

'I think we need some awesome pictures,' Ryan suggested. 'People notice pictures more.'

'My dear boy, you are a genius!' Ryan blushed at this praise from 'Ferdy'. 'I think I might draw some, with your help. I used to be a bit of an artist. Still do my own designs. But we need drawing paper and colours.' He looked around.

'We have some,' Rupert said. 'I'll go and get them.'

'In the meantime, we'll clear the table,' Chastity ordered.

In an amazingly short time, the table was cleared and the drawing paper spread out. Ryan and Paul were getting more and more enthusiastic.

'The slogans are fine,' Ryan exclaimed, 'but we must have pictures. We've got to scare people, don't you think?'

'What do you suggest?' Paul asked, crayon poised. 'A skull and crossbones, or Death the Reaper?'

'Why not one on each side?'

'Splendid!' Paul began to sketch quickly.

'Wait a minute!' Chastity, who had been standing nearby, intervened. 'This might go all wrong.' She was obviously troubled.

'What do you mean, darling?' Paul protested. 'This is a magnificent Death's Head, although I say it myself.'

'Awesome,' Ryan agreed.

'That is what worries me.' Chastity was more decided. 'I'm not sure it's a good idea to frighten people too much. It often has a very bad result, quite different from what was intended.'

Ryan was about to protest, but Paul stopped him. 'Explain yourself, Chastity, darling.'

'I think that when people are afraid they either run away or, more often, they get violent and angry and hit out. We might cause riots and violence. Plenty of publicity, but not the right kind. We'd probably be branded as troublemakers, or even terrorists, and the real message could easily be smothered.'

'Possibly deliberately,' Paul agreed thoughtfully, putting down his crayon. 'I think you're right, darling.'

Ryan was rebellious, throwing down his crayon. 'Well, I don't. I think it was a fantastic idea! After all, it was yours.' He looked accusingly at Chastity.

'I know; I thought it might be great fun! But I was wrong. We have to persuade people to do something good and unselfish. It's hard, but that's what has to be done.'

'I don't know what you mean!' Ryan was still cross. 'How can we do that?'

'We can't do it by being bad ourselves, dear boy,' Paul told him. 'As a coward, I know I'd run away.'

'But you're Ferdy; you can't run away.'

'As I told you before, you must try living in the real world, Ryan.'

'What have we got to do, then?' Ryan asked Chastity. 'If you know so much, you'd better tell us.'

'We've got to spread love, not hate and fear. First of all, people need to know that they are loved. Until they know that, they can't even love themselves and they certainly can't love others.' She turned directly to Ryan. 'Would you love your mum as much as you obviously do if you weren't sure that she loved you?'

He couldn't lie as she looked directly at him. 'No, I guess you're right. Lots of parents don't seem to love their kids, and then the kids hurt others. They're quite nasty often. They laugh at me because I look after Mum and Emily, but I don't care.'

It was at this moment that Alex slipped into the room and stood quietly, listening.

'You know what?' Ryan said suddenly. 'You remind me of someone we once knew, called Emmanuel.'

'Emmanuel?' Chastity was startled. 'Did you know him, Ryan?'

'Of course we did. Is he a friend of yours? Because, if he is, you can tell him that Mum still misses him a lot.'

'I'm afraid I can't do that. I don't know where he is now. How did you meet him?'

'I think he lived around here for a time. Anyway, he helped me one day when I was shopping and Emily was kicking up a fuss. He took charge of the shopping so that I could deal with Emily, and then he came home with us. After that, he helped me several times and visited Mum when I was at school. He always said how important it is to love people, but he said we can't really do it until we know that God loves us. Is that what you mean?'

'Yes.' Chastity looked steadily at him.

'But can it work? It doesn't seem very likely to me.' He looked wistful.

'It's a long, hard way, but in the end it's the only hope we have.'

'That's why you've helped people in Africa and all that, isn't it? You must be very brave.'

'Of course she is.' Alex's unexpected intervention startled them all. She moved into the room. 'My God, you seem to have been having quite a party,' she exclaimed, as Rupert and Sean came in from the kitchen.

'It's all my fault,' Rupert said. 'I brought Ryan round to tea, since his mum's out today.'

'That's OK but I'm afraid it will have to end now and quickly.

Surely you can't have forgotten' – she turned towards Chastity – 'that Unicorn is due to arrive in about twenty minutes, expecting to find you ready for a very special evening?'

'In that case,' Paul said, with unusual force, 'I am going. I will not meet Unicorn. I'm sure you understand, darling.' He began to gather together the sheets of paper, while Ryan packed up the crayons.

'Did you say Unicorn?' Ryan asked suddenly. 'I remember now: that was the funny name of the guy who promised to get Emmanuel away from some people who were threatening him. Did he manage it?'

'I don't really know,' Chastity told him.

She and Alex stared at each other silently until Alex asked softly, 'Something you'd forgotten?'

'Not entirely,' Chastity replied.

'Come on, Ryan,' Rupert said firmly; 'it's time for us to go now.'

'Take this bag of food we've put together for you,' Sean said.

'And my second cake,' Paul added.

Before the delighted Ryan was swept through the door, he managed to call out, 'You will come and visit Mum, won't you, Dr Chastity? I'll give Rupert our address.'

'Very sweet,' Alex remarked, 'but now you've got to hurry, Dr Chastity, unless you've changed your mind after what Ryan just said?'

'No, of course not. By the way, did you make the inquiries I asked you to try to make?'

'I did, and the result was much as you expected.'

'Good. Thanks. I'll have a quick shower first, then go to my room. If he calls before I'm ready—'

'Don't worry. I'll be very sweet to him and tell him that you had an unexpected complication today.'

'Thanks.' Chastity hurried to the bathroom, while Alex settled down to a leisurely glass of wine and a study of the evening paper.

'Remember,' she called out, as Chastity hurried past her to her bedroom, 'this is a very special evening. You've only got ten minutes to transform yourself.'

'I'll do my best.'

Almost exactly ten minutes later, the doorbell rang.

'He's here,' Alex called out.

'How do you know? It might be someone else.'

'I know. As Shakespeare said, "By the pricking of my thumbs something wicked this way comes".' Still smiling, she opened the door to Unicorn.

Chapter Thirty-five

Looking across the restaurant table, Unicorn thought once again that he had never seen Chastity look so beautiful. That, indeed, had been his first thought when she entered the living room of the flat a few minutes after his arrival. As she had stood in the doorway in her shimmering violet silk gown, hair piled up in a loose knot, jewels sparkling in it and around her neck, she had had a remote, unattainable aura, like a priestess of some ancient cult. For a moment, he had been unable to move towards her or to speak.

The spell had been broken when he had heard Alex whisper, 'Why this dress?'

With a smile, Chastity had replied, 'It's my "Special Occasion Dress". Surely you recognise it?' She had then advanced towards him, offering her dark, warm cloak, which he had placed over her shoulders. The evening had become normal. She was simply an extraordinarily lovely woman whom he intended to possess and to marry.

Now, in this hushed, expensive restaurant with its dim lights and soft music, she seemed to shine like a star. She was apparently studying the menu with irritating intentness.

'Have you decided?' he asked her.

'Not really. It's difficult to find any of the simple dishes I prefer.'

'Darling, I told you that this is a special occasion. People don't come here for simple dishes. This is probably the most highly-rated restaurant in London at the moment.'

'Then I'll leave the choice to you; I'm out of touch,' she replied firmly, putting down the menu.

'Very well, I'll do my best. I don't think you'll regret it.'

As soon as he had finished talking to the waiter, Chastity said, smiling beguilingly, 'Hadn't you better tell me what the special occasion is?'

'Quite simply, it's the occasion when I ask you to marry me and you agree, or so I hope.'

'Is that all?' was her surprising reply.

'Surely that's enough?'

He was faced with the full gaze of her unreadable, dark eyes. 'I think that a little background information is necessary,' she said finally.

'Background information?' He was puzzled.

'Yes. When, for example, do you suggest that the marriage should take place? Where are we to live? And, even more important, perhaps: how?'

The arrival of the waiter with the first course gave him a few welcome moments in which to collect his thoughts. How best to present his case? As he watched the waiter move across the room, he answered the first question. 'As to when: as soon as possible, of course. Surely you realise by now how much I love you and that I can't bear to wait any longer than is absolutely necessary.'

'Do you require an immediate answer here and now?'

'I do want it tonight, but not necessarily here.'

'In that case, can we agree to postpone the discussion until we have eaten? Food as expensive as this should be given due consideration, don't you think?'

Was there irony in that quiet voice? He couldn't be sure. It was better, he decided, to accept without question. 'Agreed,' he answered quickly, 'but only if you agree to come to my flat afterwards for coffee and cognac, so that we can talk freely. There is so much I want to tell you.'

'That seems an excellent idea.' She smiled mischievously at him. 'We have our "Special Occasion", and then we talk.'

'Champagne?' he suggested.

'Certainly, but remember that I am almost immune to the effects of alcohol.'

'How can I forget?' They both laughed. The meal was going to be a success, he was sure.

Two hours later, when they came back to his flat, Unicorn was still confident. As he helped her out of her cloak, he bent and kissed her throat, while the cloak slipped to the ground. Pulling her closely towards him, he kissed her passionately on the lips several times. When she seemed to be yielding, he murmured, 'Darling Chastity, you must know how much I love you. It's hard to keep aloof. Please don't keep me waiting any longer.'

Without answering, she gently but firmly pulled herself away and walked towards the nearest armchair, where she sat down. 'I thought we were going to have a discussion.' She sat unmoving, waiting for him to begin.

After walking across the room, he sat down opposite to her. 'My main question is: do you love me, and, if you do, will you marry me?'

'That's two questions. But supposing I say that I do love you, when do you plan for us to be married?'

She was provoking, but he tried to appear calm. 'I thought January.'

'Why January? That is very soon.'

'There's no need for us to waste any more time, is there? We are not in our first youth.'

'True, but, therefore, we – or perhaps only I – have commitments.'

'I understood that this might be a convenient time for you to leave your organisation?'

'Nothing has been decided. Jan will be back very soon, and I shall give him my decision then. That was what I promised him.'

'Then you are free to make a decision now for me, or, rather, for us? Surely you can have no objections to January?'

'It's possible that Jan might need me for another two or three months. Since you are now freelancing and have no definite commitments, surely two or three months' delay wouldn't worry you too much?'

He was baffled and convinced that she had some hidden agenda, but he could gain nothing from the clear gaze of her dark eyes, so he answered her simply. 'That was one of the matters I wanted to discuss with you.' He paused, but, as she made no comment, he was forced to continue. 'When I thought of marriage, I realised that I wanted to offer you something stable. Being a freelance journalist can be a somewhat erratic way of life.'

'And you have found something better?'

'Yes. That's why I wanted you to celebrate with me. I've been offered a splendid opportunity. I didn't look for it. I was actually headhunted by Bill V O'Connor himself!' He waited for her reaction.

It was disappointing when it came. 'Who is Bill V O'Connor?'

He laughed. 'You never cease to amaze me, Chastity! Your simplicity is one of your greatest charms! Bill V O'Connor, since you apparently don't know, is the most powerful media boss in the US, possibly in the world. Even George Bush has to listen to him.'

'I see, and he has offered you a job. Have you accepted it?'

'Not completely. I said I would, naturally, like to consult with my future wife first.'

'Didn't that rather annoy him?'

'Not when I told him all about you. He was most impressed and is looking forward to meeting you.'

'When will this job start?' She smiled unexpectedly at him. 'Let me guess. The end of January. Am I right?'

'You know you are. I can't deceive you.'

'And where will it be?'

'I shall be based mostly in New York and Washington. There is, moreover, an added incentive of a luxury apartment in New York, overlooking Central Park. So, you see, I can offer you not only a devoted husband and a stable future but also a home where we can start a family, which, I think, you want now as much as I do. You do want these things, don't you? Or am I mistaken?'

'In her secret heart, every woman, I imagine, wants a loving husband, home and children,' she replied softly, trying in vain to hide the agony she felt. The reminder of what she had lost seemed unexpectedly to be almost more than she could endure, and the longing it aroused took her by surprise. 'You are tempting me, Unicorn,' she whispered. The look she gave him clearly revealed her pain.

Apparently filled with compunction, he moved swiftly towards her. Seating himself on the arm of her chair, he embraced her gently, holding her comfortingly close. 'Oh, my dear, I'm so sorry. What a thoughtless idiot I am.' As she leaned against him, he stroked her hair gently. 'I only hoped to make you happy by reminding you that these joys might be yours again. Forgive me.'

She was surrendering, he was sure. It would be impossible for her to refuse him again, he thought. 'You are so good, my darling. I want to give you the happiness you deserve.'

'You are tempting me,' she murmured again. But she did not move away. For a moment, they remained close. Suddenly, however, a shiver seemed to pass through her body. She sat up, moving away from him. 'You are giving me so much. What is the price I have to pay?'

Outraged, he released her. 'What the hell do you mean by that?'

'You are giving me so much; what must I give you in return?'

'Nothing except yourself. That is all I want.' Fighting his anger, he stood up and prowled around the room. 'Obviously, you don't trust me. That's the truth, isn't it?'

'It's simply that I would like to know more.' She sat straight up. 'Sit down and tell me.'

'What more is there to tell?'

'Lots. For example, what sort of a man is O'Connor? Is he another Lord Harry?'

Laughing at her, he sat down, apparently once more at his ease. 'He couldn't be more different from that old rogue. To begin with, he's highly respected. He's a leading Evangelical Christian, a well-known supporter and friend of George Bush. As I said earlier, he's definitely looking forward to meeting you.'

'Whatever did you tell him about me?'

'Everything, particularly the Christian work you do.'

'I see. Am I right in thinking that, if he's an Evangelical supporter of Bush, he's anti-abortion, anti-homosexuals, et cetera, and pro the war against Iraq? And that those will be, roughly, the views of the media he controls?'

'To some degree, yes.' He was puzzled.

'And will you be required to support them?'

'I shan't be tied down, if that's what you mean. But you support most of these causes, too, don't you?' He tried to hide his irritation.

She smiled slightly. 'True: I am pro-life, but that means all life, and I find it hard to understand how anyone can be against abortion and, at the same time, support a brutal, aggressive war. I believe, you see, that there are sins even greater than abortion, such as injustice, cruelty and exploitation of the poor and vulnerable. I'm not sure, Unicorn, that your Mr O'Connor will like the real me.'

'For Christ's sake,' he burst out, 'what has this got to do with us? You're marrying *me*, not O'Connor! I'm offering you all my love, a secure life and the time to indulge your—' He stopped suddenly, realising what he had almost been betrayed into saying.

'My little hobbies. Is that what you were going to say?' Her voice was gentle. He looked sharply at her, but she was gazing down at her hands.

'Why are you so suspicious? Will nothing convince you of my sincerity? After all, I defied Lord Harry and risked my job to help to save you. What more do you want? Be reasonable, darling!'

'Of course,' she agreed. 'You sacrificed everything for me, and you didn't know that Mr O'Connor would rescue you.'

'How could I? I only heard from him a few days ago.'

Suddenly, she looked directly at him. 'I was more fortunate than Emmanuel, then, or so it seems.'

He was shocked by this unexpected thrust. 'What the hell has Emmanuel got to do with anything? Have you gone mad?'

'No, definitely not. It's just that Emmanuel trusted you and you failed to save him. I was reminded of that this afternoon when I met a boy who had known him. He quite innocently told me that Emmanuel had gone away with a journalist called Unicorn, who was going to save him from his enemies. The boy wanted to know if you had been successful. I couldn't tell him, could I? Although I rather think that you weren't.'

'What's new?' His eyes suddenly had that yellow gleam in them. 'I told you that I handed him over to someone who was going to help him.'

'I rather think that you handed him over to Zig and his companions – Lord Harry's weird executioners. I'm right, aren't I?'

'I know nothing about that.' Furious, he leapt up and began to pace around the room again. 'What are you trying to do?'

'I'm trying to discover the truth. That's all.'

'It may have been Zig. I wasn't aware of his function at the time. But what the hell does it matter? Emmanuel wasn't important. He was just a stupid young fool, who insisted on prying into matters even after he'd been warned. He infuriated Lord Harry.'

'But you didn't realise exactly why?'

'Of course not. He only approached me because he thought that, as an investigative reporter, I might be privy to secrets, which I wasn't. When Lord Harry asked me to take him to Zig, as you now tell me it was, I simply did as instructed.'

'And you had no idea of what was really happening?'

'Of course not. I was simply doing a service to Lord Harry by relieving him of someone who was annoying him.'

'I understand.'

Abruptly, he stopped his furious pacing and turned to face her. 'Does that mean that at last you believe me and are ready to stop this ridiculous interrogation, which has nothing to do with what I'm asking you?'

'And what exactly is that, now?'

Fury and a strange dread nearly overcame him, but he held them back. Instead, he smiled tenderly and asked, in his most persuasive tones, 'Darling, you can't pretend you've forgotten? You must be teasing me. I told you that I loved you with all my heart, and I asked you if you loved me and were willing to start a new life with me. Remember?'

With those yellow eyes and tawny hair, he suddenly seemed to her like a big, purring but dangerous cat. Silently, she called on Jan for help. 'You said I should decide for myself,' she told him. 'But that's not the problem now, is it?'

As she hesitated, Unicorn came closer. 'You told me it was two questions. But, if you answer the first, the second should be easier.'

She seemed to hear Jan telling her to speak the truth. 'I will answer you.' She looked straight into those strange eyes. 'I do love you.'

Taking her in his arms, he triumphantly lifted her from her seat, kissing her passionately. Then, holding her at arm's length, he declared, 'I don't know why you have tormented me so much, but it doesn't matter any more. Now we can make plans for our future. Do remember how impatient I am!'

Gently but firmly freeing herself, she sat down again. 'There are one or two things I would like to be sure of first.'

Although he frowned slightly, he replied lightly, 'Ask away, darling.'

'Are you happy about your contract? Does it offer us a secure future?'

He laughed. 'I never imagined you'd be so prudent, darling. But you don't need to worry. You can trust O'Connor. He's a man of his word. I know that from experience.'

'So, he's not someone you've just met? You actually know him quite well? We can be sure?'

Pitying her unexpected vulnerability, he was quick to reassure her. 'I'd say I know him pretty well. He won't let us down. You don't need to worry.'

'But how can you be so confident when you've only just met him?' His eyes flashed again, but, before he could answer, she continued quietly, 'But that isn't true, is it? You haven't just met him. You met him before you deserted Lord Harry, didn't you?'

He was very angry, all the more so because her question was so completely unexpected. He had at last felt sure in his possession of her. 'What the devil are you getting at?' He almost spat the words at her.

She was afraid again but silently summoned Jan to her aid. 'You know why,' she replied, with apparent calm; 'that's why you are so angry. But I'll put it into words for you. You primarily betrayed Lord Harry to please Mr O'Connor and to secure your own future. You knew, I suspect, that Lord Harry's days were numbered and that you were only hastening the inevitable. That was primarily why I was more fortunate than Emmanuel.'

He was a tiger again, but no longer a purring one. His fiercely-blazing yellow eyes glared into hers. 'It's a fucking lie,' he hissed. 'I betrayed Lord Harry to save you, because I love you.'

Her heart was beating so strongly that she was sure that he could hear it. She managed, nevertheless, to speak calmly. 'Then why have I been told that you were seen lunching with Mr O'Connor on at least two occasions several days before?'

'Who told you that? How could you know?' She hardly recognised his voice.

'Alex confirmed the truth of it today.'
'And you believe her?'
'Yes; she is my friend and she has no reason to lie to me.'
'Except that she hates me, as you know.'
'And I also know why. She has recently told me the full story. I'm sure that you now understand why I cannot marry you, even though I love you?'

For a moment he was silent, then, with an obvious effort, he replied calmly. 'Even if all you say is true, it still doesn't prove that I don't love you. You have to accept that, because you know that I love you and that I would have saved you even without O'Connor. Your whole being tells you that I love you, just as it tells you that you love me. You want me as much as I want you. You can't deny it.'

Meeting the challenge of those tawny eyes was hard, but she did it, though she trembled.

He laughed. 'It's no use pretending, Chastity. It's time we ended this silly sparring, and I intend to end it.'

'How?' she forced herself to ask.

'I intend to take what you really want to give.'

'You mean you intend to rape me?'

He was smiling as he came closer to her. 'Don't be melodramatic! You know that won't be necessary. Simply let yourself do what you really want to do. I promise you it will be a wonderful experience for both of us.'

'And then what?'

'Don't worry, darling. It'll be exactly as I promised you. We will be married in January and we'll live in luxury in New York.'

'And what about my work?' She stood up and moved back, hoping to get away, but he followed her.

'You've given seven years to the poor. Isn't that enough? If your conscience troubles you, however, there are plenty of poor you can visit occasionally in New York when you have the time. You can give me material for articles. We can work together. That'll be good for the O'Connor image.'

'And not too bad for yours.'

'Right. Now, don't let's waste any more time.' He was exultant. Reaching out, he seized her, pulling her body close to his. She was limp and unresisting as he kissed her. He laughed. 'Let yourself enjoy it, my darling.' He was like a wild beast purring over its prey as his hands and lips caressed her. He was sure of her now.

Oh, Jan, help me! she prayed silently. Suddenly coming alive and exerting all her strength, she pushed him away, so unexpectedly that he staggered and almost fell. 'If you take me by force,' – her voice rang out loud and clear – 'I'll endure it, but I'll never, never marry you. You are unworthy of me.'

As she stood there in her shimmering, violet gown, with the jewels gleaming in her hair, she seemed transfigured, like a priestess of some ancient cult. He stared at her, amazed.

'What reason could I have for marrying you? I hate lies, and you have lied all the time. You lied to me about Emmanuel. You didn't kill him, but you knowingly handed him over to be killed. What is the difference? You betrayed Lord Harry in order to gain the favour of O'Connor. But your real master remains the same, and he is directing this farce.'

'What do you mean?'

'I mean the Dark Angel himself, who opposes in this planet the Lord of the Universe, whom I serve. You understand nothing. I don't want to help you to write articles about the poor so as to give myself a celebrity status and to give others the pious satisfaction of having felt a momentary pity. No; I love the poor and the vulnerable and I hate injustice and cruelty. If you want to help the poor, you have to be with them, and that is why I choose to live among them. They are my Lord's people and they are my people. Nothing you can offer tempts me.'

His mouth was a cruel line. His eyes flashed fire as he mocked her. 'Splendid but irrelevant. You are not with the poor now, but with me and at my mercy. Where is your Lord of the Universe now?'

Suddenly, electrifyingly, the front doorbell rang long and loud. 'Who the fucking hell can that be?' As he stood there, the bell rang again, even more insistently.

'It is Jan,' she told him confidently. 'You would be wiser to answer it.' As the bell rang a third time, she picked up her cloak, 'Don't worry. I will answer it.'

'How can it be Jan?' Bewildered, he found himself following her towards the door. 'He's away. You told me so.'

'He was, but I called him and he has come.' As she opened the door, Unicorn saw the tall, familiar figure in the dark coat, with his gleaming aureole of golden hair. Without a word, Jan took Chastity's cloak and wrapped it gently around her. 'Goodbye, Unicorn,' she said softly. 'I do not think that we shall ever meet again in this world. I'm sad, because it could have been so different for us.'

'Goodbye, Chastity,' he answered her, realising painfully that his last chance had gone. Without moving, he watched as she walked away with Jan's protecting arm around her – out of his life for ever.

Printed in the United Kingdom
by Lightning Source UK Ltd.
122256UK00001B/4-12/A